Well's Ferry

By

F. E. Chaps

D1715946

Photography by Bill David
Editing by Jeanne & Carol
ISBN-13:978-1548312398
ISBN-10:1548312398

Introduction

Well's Ferry explores the world of narcissistic personalities, between the wealthy, socialites, and those they try to control, including victims who are often disparaged because of bigotry, status, and the darkness of despair. A battle between good and evil is ignited, as well as the relentless power of extraordinary, everlasting Love.

The author has a master's degree in psychology, specializing in human behavior. Writing has become a sanctuary for expression and release through fiction. The author writes of dysfunctional characters and the constant battle between good and evil by way of creativity, education, and experience.

This is a work of fiction. Any resemblance to persons, living or dead, is purely coincidental.

Blessed are the meek: for they shall inherit the earth.

Contents

New Hope, Pennsylvania (Originally Well's Ferry)
April 14, 1865

To lose control or to have none were thoughts he loathed, and a condition never to concede to. Arising from the soldier or leader within, or perhaps the past he had been dealt. This was his code of ethics, his way of life.

But he knew better. Though he did not want to, he remembered. He had always believed resistance, suppression of the mind, could be the antidote from its dark, painful existence. But if succumbed, even slightly, this madness would give way to an irreversible path. A path to absolute defeat.

His ignorance, which were few for he truly was an intelligent man, had even thought it to be evil. It had always been his greatest enemy. Against a hundred confederate rebels would be greater odds.

As a child, he had felt its wrath. And fought with all that he could muster, and he had won. He had taken control and swore never to submit. The experience left permanency. A strong, ambitious, honorable young soldier. He feared no one. Though he had seen it all, his heart had remained pure.

But again it had returned revealing its hideous, mocking face to now, the man. Representing the devil himself, causing him to doubt his thoughts and worst- his mind. Nothing could ever cause the amplitude of destruction as that of this one condition, this one word. Control.

By proud choice he had been a soldier first, then a man, and now a leader, a husband, a lover, and soon a father. And if it were to be, something decided long ago, he'd rather take death. For he believed his mind could never again regain wholeness. And it was inevitably the mark of one's weakness.

A mind that is robbed leaves a body empty, a useless shell an embarrassing, weak, humiliating excuse for a man. This he could not stand. And he knew he could never live this way.

His mind had all but yielded, unable to continue the fight. It had all finally become too much. Though refusing to accept, he subconsciously knew the outcome of what this day would bring. Unlike other battles, it would become the first to be lost and the last to be fought. This one he would not win.

His body, numb and still, could be compared to the black wrought iron gate that surrounded his estate. And his sad, lost eyes stared at nothing through one of the large windows of his study. His body frozen from fear, afraid to move or continue. He was a man waiting but not anticipating the inevitable. Perhaps his fragile condition imagined he could stop time if he did so.

Nevertheless, the grandfather clock next to the large fireplace began to chime noon. The sound startled him. With nerves nearly shattered, he began to shake uncontrollably. To himself, he whispered in a reprimanding tone, "Stop it! God help me!" Though there was no one in the room to hear or see, he still felt shame. It was as though his emotions had taken over and he could do nothing but follow aimlessly.

Disoriented, he could now barely recognize himself. A voice deep within desperately tried to cry out, "*Be in charge, take control!*" And even with all that pain, he could not shed one tear. He acknowledged the voice but could not make the body or mind respond. "Could that voice be me? All that is left of me?" He contemplated this as he trembled in fear, something uncharacteristic.

Death was certainly no stranger. He had dealt with it often in the past. Since he was a young boy he had longed to join the army. He could think of no other career that carried as much honor as did protecting his country. He had lied about his age in order to be accepted as soon as possible. Jon was an intelligent, courageous man who swiftly moved up the ranks of command.

When only nineteen, he stood strong and bold next to General Taylor. As the U.S. Army pushed the Mexicans back and out of Texas, claiming her as their own. Through many years of hard work he was finally promoted to general. And in the year 1860, elected senator of Pennsylvania.

He had followed Lincoln's policies and beliefs, and at this very time was working on the Thirteenth Amendment to abolish slavery forever. Jon had been responsible for saving thousands of lives and many honors were bestowed upon him during his lifetime.

He recalled the death of his mother and father. They were good people who came from inherited wealth. The Covington family had originated from England. When his parents were young adults, they travelled to America and settled in Philadelphia. Though he could not shed a tear, he had mourned sadly for them. He had never cried before and believed it was impossible for him.

Suddenly he recalled why. He remembered his youth. Those days were not all consumed with pain. When his parents were alive his life was filled with much happiness, but after their death his life changed for the worse.

She, barely of legal age, received custody of him and control of the estate. It was as though he had been sentenced to hell. For a moment he stopped feeling sorry for himself as he painfully remembered her.

His body filled quickly with anger and hate, his face became red and flushed. He hated to become this way, but she always brought out the worst in him. From the time she had legal custody, she began to abuse him both physically and mentally. He had always known, if given the opportunity, she would.

Even before his parents died he witnessed the evil that lie within her. She could never touch him in those days; he knew it as well as her. This made her crazy with frustration.

Mother and Father never knew, or maybe they suspected but

could not bring themselves to face the truth about her. Jon believed they would have sent her away if they had known for sure. But she was too clever, too cunning to ever let her real self be known to those two.

Only him, he was the one who saw. She made it so, it was all intentional, a demented game. It was her revenge for not being able to touch him. He would hold onto mommy's hand as he would smile up at her. This was his revenge because he knew what it did to her.

In those days his parents were his protectors. They made him feel safe and loved. As a child, never in his wildest dreams did he ever imagine they could die. That they would leave him.

He remembered how unfair it all was. Who would protect him now? Being only a child, who would have even believed him? *How could they do that to me? How could they have left me with her,* he questioned bitterly.

To hold on to his sanity, he had convinced himself that she must have been born to the devil. How else could he make reason in his little mind the horrors she did to him.

Of course after each punishment, she would tell him that it was essential as part of his needed, refined tailoring into becoming a well-bred gentleman. Her game was control. And he often fantasied of the day he would be strong enough to fight back. Like a reoccurring nightmare he recalled what would happen when he would defy her.

Since his parent's death, she had forbidden the entire staff from the west wing of the estate in which his parent's bedroom had been. She had the groundskeeper board up the main entrance to the wing. The only other known way in was from a secret panel hidden behind an old grandfather's clock on the second floor.

Though the entire staff was quite aware of her abuse toward Jon, they were all too afraid for their jobs but mostly their lives. Because of her inherited wealth, she soon become a powerful figure in the community.

When she became angry with him it would always be at the appropriate moment, a time in which there never seemed to be any staff about. This he was sure was quite calculated on her part. She would drag him up the circular staircase as he would frantically try to grasp onto the rail, screaming out in horror to anyone who could hear him.

But after years of the same abuse, realizing there would be no one coming to his aid, he began to recognize the punishment and no longer resisted or cried out. She would drag him through the secret panel, closing it tightly behind her. Always remaining calm and subdued, looking straight ahead, and never saying a word.

The punishment would begin by locking him in the old cedar closet located in his parent's sitting room. He would be kept a prisoner for a few days; no water or food would be given. Since the staff was forbidden to enter that part of the estate, he knew there would be no one coming to his defense.

She would torment him by eating meals in the overstuffed Victorian chair that positioned itself next to the closet. The woman was quite void of empathy and decency. She would wait until he had become dehydrated and close to unconsciousness before she would let him out. Never, although she knew he prayed for it, allowing him to come too close to death.

Then she would finally unlock the door to the closet. With a sinister look upon her face she'd stand there glaring down at him, as he would collapse out of the closet from lack of food and water, unable at that moment to stand.

Laying in his own soiled clothes, barely conscious and squinting from the light, he'd be looking up at her when she would calmly command him to clean up the mess before supper as though everything was quite all right. Because she had done this to him so often, he eventually learned to hide food in the closet when he thought she was not about.

Every so often, she would go away on business, "Covington business," she would announce, leaving him alone at the estate with only the servants. Though these times were few, they were about the only pleasurable remembrances he and the servants would ever have of the old estate.

He then remembered how it all ended. One sunny afternoon when all seemed well, she found him in the library sitting on the hearth reading one of father's old English novels.

Unaware of the intrusion, he shuddered, as he looked up to find her staring at him only a few feet away. Her face exhibited a frightening expression that he had been, so often, a witness to. Suddenly, she threw a handful of loosely wrapped food in front of him.

In an instant doom fell, as he immediately recognized the food he had hidden in the old cedar closet. "You've been a naughty boy, haven't you, Jonathan! When will you ever learn?"

It was then, as she reached for the collar of his shirt when he knew he would no longer tolerate her abuse toward him.

She calmly began to drag him through the library as though it was a boring, repetitive, daily task that needed to be done. He noticed his opportunity, as he eyed the silver letter opener that laid upon his father's desk.

Martha, the cook, accidentally walked in to go over the evening's supper menu. "Get out!" she screamed, continuing to drag him. Quite startled and frightened, Martha immediately ran from the room.

Jon had dreamt of this day for years. How stupid he recalled she was at that moment. For years she had been so cold and cunning, but she had forgotten to consider that he would soon grow to be a strong young man driven by bitterness and hatred toward her.

As she began to pass the desk, he reached out his arm and grasped the knife bringing forth all that laid within its path toppling to the floor. This caught her attention, as she quickly turned to see what he had done.

At that very second, he brought the knife up and slashed the arm in which restricted him. Completely unaware and thrown by his actions, she let go of him, falling to the floor in pain.

He lunged upon her like a hungry lion to meat. As Jon straddled her, he positioned the knife to her throat. Past thoughts of killing her became real, as he for the first time in his life felt so near and in control.

"I could kill you in an instant, without any remorse," he swore with much hate pointing the tip of the knife into her flesh. How very little and pathetic she looked laying in her own blood begging for her life. She was indeed afraid; something new.

With much disgust he finally ended, "You're not worth it; you're not worth ruining my life. If you ever touch me again… I will surely kill you without any hesitation!" And with those last words, he took all the money he knew she had hidden inside the desk and fled from the estate never to return.

Although he had never laid eyes upon her ever again, he knew through the years she had made inquiries about him. But she never did come close enough to him, for she knew he would surely carry out his vow.

Alas, when he was only twelve years old he traveled throughout the countryside working odd jobs to survive. When he was fifteen, he convinced the army he was indeed of age. It was at that point his life changed for the better. He'd thank God for all that was good. But he never entirely forgave his parents for leaving him with that woman. He had always felt it was their responsibility as parents to protect him. After all he was only a child, he sadly ended.

Reality quickly crept back as he remembered his current dismay. The pain burned inside him like a knife slowly entering the body but never leaving. He thought how irrelevant reminiscing about his past was while his beloved Mary lay so near to death. It was all so unreal, so unbelievable. He felt his fate too should be as hers. Life without Mary, he imagined, could never be.

In many ways she had saved him. She had helped him become

the man that he was. Mary had witnessed the good and the bad, and never had she lost faith or respect. She truly loved him unconditionally. But most importantly their love for each other had grown deeply. A love so strong neither man, woman, nor past or present, could ever pierce.

He had never loved another as he did her. This he knew was an exceptional life experience. She was his life. She was every breath that he took. The love that they shared was of one that is rare.

Again he began to reminisce, but this time he recalled when he had first met Mary. How soothing the memory was, even if temporary. It was during the Mexican war. He awoke in a hospital bed and his first vision was of her. Jon imagined he had died and gone to heaven. Never had he laid eyes on a woman as beautiful as she.

He could still see the image of her lovely face as she patiently took care of him. Jon remembered Mary tenderly squeezing his hand for reassurance and telling him in a soft, gentle voice that she was his nurse and would take good care of him and not to worry.

Her touch was as soft as a rose pedal, her eyes brown, large, and simply captivating. He noticed how full and red her lips were, as she spoke so compassionately to him. He wished he could have kissed her then and there. But he dare not, he was a gentleman first and most certainly an officer.

He still felt beneath her, unworthy of such a beautiful creature. She was truly enchanting. Little did he know she too, at that very moment, felt the enchantment. From that day forth their love would become eternal.

The sun began to meet the horizon, as he realized how long it had been since he had first stood there. He could now barely make out the large oak trees that lined his cobblestone entryway. Darkness began to enter the sky like a plague. Jon felt an overwhelming sense of doom. It gently began to rain.

He had been shut up in his library since morning, requesting to see no one but the doctor. Or to be notified immediately if there was a change for the better or worse. Jon was a proud man and preferred to be left alone to wallow in his grief. He of all people could not bear for anyone to see him in such a state of mind. Silence filled the room.

Jon began to falsely hope perhaps the silence was a good sign. After all it had been hours since the doctor had handed down his gloomy diagnosis of Mary and the baby to him. *Doctors have known to be wrong, right?* He questioned his mind. *They're only human and what does he know anyway? How many babies has he given birth to?* Jon challenged. Maybe his wife's condition had stabilized, he hopefully imagined.

He slowly let out an exhausting sigh as he realized this could not be. He knew deep down, the longer there was no news the more his Mary would become weaker. She was near death and he knew it. Jon fell to his knees and began to pray. He begged God to spare Mary's life in exchange for his.

After a few minutes he pulled himself back onto his feet. Jon had never felt so desperate in his life. He would have given or done anything to save his beloved.

He imagined, perhaps it was all so devastating because there had been no warning. It was all so ironic. A time that should have been the most wonderful experience of their lives was turning out to be the most tragic.

Everything was going so wonderfully for the two of them. The war was ending, Lee had surrendered and his country would be united. His love would soon give birth to their only child. It had been all a man could ever wish for, he sadly thought.

They had tried for years to have a baby. When Mary told him that she was with child, he thought God had finally answered their prayers. Jon remembered how it was only yesterday that he and Mary laughed and danced with joy, as they thought of the new life they would soon bring. And only a day later their doctor telling him that his Mary would not live pass this day.

He longed to see her now. He had stayed with Mary up until

the doctor had asked him to leave. Jon reluctantly agreed as long as he promised to alert him immediately to any changes in her condition. Or if Mary came to and asked for him.

His mind and body were now depleted. He could no longer think or make reason. With his mind numb from exhaustion he again began to stare out the window at nothing, silence becoming his only companion.

Jon flinched as a sudden knock abruptly startled him. Trying to quickly pull himself together he hesitated, afraid of what fate may have brought him behind the door. "What is it?" he said in a quiet but stern manner, not honestly wanting to know.

The door slowly opened as Miss Abigail cautiously peered in. "Sir… I'm sorry to disturb you, Senator. I know you specifically asked not to be," she said in a nervous tone.

"What is it, Abby?" he demanded, interrupting. "Is it Mary? Is she…"

"Oh no, sir! That is not why I'm here. There has, unfortunately, been no change in Mrs. Covington's condition," she quickly assured him. "And I would surely know, since I've been with her as much as the doctor will allow."

"And I am grateful for that," responded Jon.

"It is you, sir, I am worried about. You have been locked up in this room since," she hesitated, not wanting to refer to his wife's sad prognosis. "Well, since yesterday, sir. You really need to eat something. Or you too may become ill," she blurted carelessly from exhaustion.

"Anyway, I brought you a tray. Please don't be angry with me. I know you said you did not want to be disturbed unless there was word. But I just could not help myself. I'm very worried about you."

"That's quite all right, Abby. You may leave the tray on my desk. Thank you."

Miss Abigail had been with the Covington's for years. They had grown to love her as much as she loved them. He had hired her for Mary, under much protest from his wife, as her personal assistant. Mary had always been quite independent and at times a little stubborn.

Though Jon knew his wife was a strong woman, he worried that she took on more than she could handle at times. He felt Miss Abigail could keep an eye on her when he could not. This would help to put his mind to rest when he had to go away on business.

When Mary realized how sufficient and irreplaceable Miss Abigail had become, she wondered how she ever made on without her. Though she was much younger than Mary, Miss Abigail cared for the Covington's almost like a mother.

Jon knew he could not eat but he did not have the strength to argue with Abby. She slowly walked into the room. He watched from the corner of his eyes as she gently put the tray on his desk. Although she was a beautiful woman, she hid behind her attire. Abby dressed handsome, neat, and was always well organized and proper in every way, he agreed, studying her patiently.

The spectacles she wore always looked as though they were about to fall off her nose. They made her appear older than she really was. Her hair was always kept back in a neat bun. And she never wore anything but dark colors that matched her hair.

She kept her head down not wanting Mr. Covington to see that she had been crying. "Senator… if there is anything else I can do or get for you, please don't hesitate to ask."

"There is something that I must take care of tonight, Abby. Please have Joseph come and see me immediately."

"Certainly, sir," she replied, swiftly leaving the room.

Jon glanced out the window worried as he realized the rain was now turning into a nasty storm. But he knew what he needed Joseph to do for him could not wait until tomorrow.

Soon there was a knock at the library door but this time he was not startled. "Come in, Joseph. Please shut the door behind you." Embarrassed by his grief, Jon continued to stare out the window hoping he would not notice.

Joseph had lived and worked at the estate for Mr. Covington since before the war. He was a tall (over 6 foot), handsome, lean, Negro man who was admired by all of the local, pretty, Negro ladies. They all tried shamelessly to win his affections but for whatever reasons, had no success.

Jon believed that it was probably due to his shyness and left it at that. He needed Joseph more than he needed him so he never pushed the issue. Joseph respected the Senator because of his beliefs and convictions in freeing his people. He knew the Senator truly believed all men were created equal, as he listened to him speak in many rallies before the war, often placing his own life in danger.

Through the years he gained much admiration for Mr. and Mrs. Covington and would do anything for them. He became Jon's right-hand man and most trusted friend. Jon thought reassuringly how he had never let him down in the past and tonight would be no exception.

"Joseph, I realize the weather has worsened," began Jon, "but it is imperative that you go to Philadelphia and deliver important documents for me tonight to my lawyer. I would not ask you if it were not so crucial. Do you understand?"

"Yes sir, I'll leave right away before it does goes and gets worse."

Jon turned from the window to retrieve the large envelope wrapped twice in tweed from his desk top. He slowly walked over and placed his left hand on Joseph's shoulder. Embarrassed, Joseph lowered his head.

"In all these years," he hesitated. "You have never let me down. I want you to know that a day does not go by that I do not realize your devotion to Mary and myself. You have truly been a friend and I have been a better man to have known you."

"Thank ya, sir," he stammered, embarrassed from never hearing the Senator speak in such a way. Joseph raised his head and looked up into Jon's eyes, as they revealed the pain that lingered deep within them. "Are ya OK, sir?"

Trying to lighten the mood, Jon answered, "I'll be fine." He again thought of the storm with much concern. "Remember to weigh down the wagon and check the axles before you leave; the roads ahead may become dangerous."

"Make sure the horses are fed and watered before you leave. Don't forget to dry them down after you arrive. There is an additional note to Mr. Holt asking him to give you shelter and food for the night. There is no need for you to try and make it back in this storm. Good luck and Godspeed, my friend," ended Jon.

He quickly took his eyes from him. As he slowly closed the door, he wondered if Joseph had sensed the agony that was consuming him.

His thoughts were interrupted by another abrupt knock, this time he knew it would be about his Mary. He took a step back and slowly inhaled deeply before opening the door. Behind it stood the doctor. No words were said. No words were necessary. The doctor's sad expression said all that was needed.

Like a death march, his body felt numb as he followed behind. Before entering the room in which Mary lay, Dr. Carlton turned to face him.

"Mary has given birth to a girl… God has at least left you a beautiful daughter," he senselessly remarked. "Congratulations," added the doctor, unable to hide his pity for him.

"Thank you." Jon responded, trying to remain strong and in control.

He went ahead of the doctor, as he opened the door and slowly walked in. The doctor followed. Jon immediately filled with hopelessness. It seemed to engulf the room. Thinking back to his past experiences, death he felt was surely near.

The room felt warm and cozy. It was barely lit by the fireplace and candles positioned about. Nighttime had fallen upon the house, as the windows were filled with blackness. The room was almost silent except for the quiet whimpering of Miss Abigail who sat in the shadow of the bed not wanting to be seen. A nurse stood over Mary placing a cold compress on her forehead.

He swiftly came to Mary's bedside and knelt down beside her. His eyes began to anxiously roam her face and body out of desperation of not knowing what to do. Or how to help her.

Next to her bed, in front of where he knelt, was a small cradle which held his new daughter. He peered in and for the first time all day smiled, for she reminded him of her mother. How beautiful and tiny, he agreed, as he gently caressed the small baby's face.

"Everyone… leave us, please," he begged, wanting to be alone with his wife and child. Miss Abigail began to lift the child from the cradle when Jon interrupted her. "Leave her!" he ordered. "As you wish, sir," she obeyed, gently placing the baby back in her cradle. They left the room closing the door behind them.

He gently placed Mary's hand in his. Slowly, he bowed his head bringing his lips to her hand as he softly began kissing it. "God, if you can hear me. Please help my Mary. Don't let her die; I couldn't bear it… I beg of you," he ended exhausted.

He felt a gentle brush on the top of his head. Jon looked up to find Mary trying to comfort him. He thought then how very blessed he had been to have ever known such selfless, loving woman. Her eyes looked glassy and worn and her face was white and pale.

But as fragile as she had become, Jon still believed she was the most beautiful woman he had ever known. Her voice was soft and frail as she began to try and speak to him. "Jon, my dearest, did you see her? Isn't she beautiful?"

"Yes. She is the image of you, my love," agreed Jon smiling.

"Please, Jon. Name her Sara… Sara Beth. After my mother whom I admired so dearly," she gently pleaded.

"As you wish, my Mary," he replied, gently caressing her hand. She began to cough uncontrollably. Worried, he moved closer to her. "Shall I get the doctor, Mary?"

"No, my love, I need for you to hear these words in private. He offered her a sip of water. Then he moved as close as he could to Mary's face holding on tightly to her hand.

Mary gently stroked his hair trying to comfort him. "Don't be afraid or feel guilty to love again, Jon. Sara will need a mother. I could not bear to see you so sad or lonely."

"You have made me very happy, my love. Thank you. I am not afraid to die. I have lived a good life, Jon..." Frozen, he could hardly bear her words.

They would be the last words Mary would speak. Her gentle smile left her face, as her eyes closed and body became still. Jon began to shake in disbelief. Her hand went limp in his own.

With his body trembling, he tried to calm himself as he gently kissed his beloved's lips for the last time. And for the first time that he could ever recall, Jon wrapped his arms tightly around her body. He bowed his head into her bosom and quietly wept in despair. She was his Achilles' heel. And he knew it.

Jon held Mary in his arms for what seemed like hours. He finally stood and softly kissed both of her hands then laid them gently together. He knelt down beside his child's cradle being careful not to allow any of his tears to fall upon her. Jon patiently began to watch the tiny baby sleep.

How peaceful she looked, he thought. "Mary was right. I would love again," he softly whispered, gazing down at his child. "I remember the war when terror outweighed the cold and hunger in my men. And the hopeless eyes of the Negro man, as he listened with skepticism as I spoke in many rallies... promising that one day he would surely be free. I would speak that a strong man could endure all that was given. I believe now, either I am not such a strong man—or those words are untrue." He paused.

"Alas, I have become a man without use. I am a coward to have loved in depth as I did your mother. And without her, I am truly lost... Forgive me, my child," ended Jon sadly. He gently kissed the sleeping baby.

Then he stood pulling out his handkerchief to wipe his face

trying to regain the last self-respect left in him. As he straightened his attire, he took a slow, deep breath for he knew the staff would be lined up behind the door awaiting the outcome.

He found himself to be correct, as he opened the door to find a filled entryway. Sobbing throughout the estate became evident, as Jon so regretfully handed down the news of his Mary.

Though tears ran gently down her face, he found Miss Abigail to be surprisingly comforting as she tried so hard not to lose control. He was in a numb state, she knew this and became more worried for his sake.

Miss Abigail had never seen Jon like this. She knew he was a proud man, embarrassed easily, but she still wanted him to know that she was there for him if he needed her strength. He asked her to his library for a private meeting that could not wait until day break.

Jon positioned himself behind his desk, only the dim light of the fireplace lit the room. "Come in, Abby."

With her head down, she slowly entered the room gently trembling. "What can I do for you, sir?" she offered, trying to be strong and helpful.

He took a deep breath and began, "Now that Mrs. Covington has left us." He paused, steadying himself. "I feel I must pass on my wishes to someone that we both have held dearly through our lives. I can't think of anyone else best suited than yourself, Abby. And I am certain Mary would have agreed."

"Thank you, sir," she replied exhausted and confused.

"Though my wishes are documented in the envelope Joseph is delivering this evening, I feel I must also express them to you at this time. He paused. In case anything should ever happen to myself. It is my wish that you would stay on and raise Sara Beth as her personal guardian until she reaches the age in which she would inherit the estate and all that is mine."

Jon's voice became suddenly raised and intense. "Under no circumstances shall she leave the estate under anyone's care but your own. Most importantly, my sister! You must swear! I must have your word, Abby. Do you understand?"

Without hesitation she replied, "To my last dying breath, I give you my word. I would love her as if she were my own, sir."

"Thank you, Abby… and may God bless you and everyone in this house. Now I would like to be alone. Goodnight, Abigail."

Jon relaxed, relieved with his decision. He once again found himself alone to wallow in his grief.

The wind and rain now hailed like a force from hell. The reins bled into Joseph's skin, as he wrapped them even tighter around his hands. He could barely see as he tried so desperately to keep control of the wagon.

Most would have probably turned back, but he felt compelled. He wanted so to help Jon in any way he could this night. Making it to Philadelphia was all that he knew. Joseph had become a driven man, possessed by the mission. Nothing would stop him, he swore, as he continued onward through the storm.

He did not see the boulder that had slid into his path from the hillside until he was on top of it. Sudden horror filled his mind, as the wheel of the wagon smashed into it causing the axle to spin off as quickly as the wind itself.

The wagon tossed and turned into the night as though it were as light as a feather throwing Joseph to the ground. He lay there bleeding and unconscious.

And when the occurrence finally ended, all that could be seen was a faint cloud of dust in the mist of the storm, as the quest of the mission slowly drifted down a nearby river bed, never to be seen by Joseph again. The storm immediately ceased.

The sky stood silently still except for the faint, muffled sound of one gun shot that could be heard from afar at the Covington estate. The sound would linger on forever in the minds that witnessed it. A new era had truly begun as the Covington estate would never again be the same. And if the tragedies of the evening seemed more than one could bear, silence filled the remainder of the night as if to give homage to the morning in which again, tragedy would weave its twisted web with the news of Lincoln's death.

Bethie
1873

It was an absolute glorious day! The sky was clear and blue as the oceans abroad. And the meadows and hillsides were as green as the eye could see. Even the trees had finally filled, as the sound of new life among all God's creatures was quite evident. Certainly, no one could deny that spring had surely come.

Especially this day, if one had not known, would have made it difficult to believe adversity had once struck this inheritance in such magnitude. Standing within the wrought iron gates, one would gasp from awe at the beautiful stone architecture and stunning landscape the Covington estate possessed.

The sun was bright and warm, as Bethie danced and twirled about with arms stretched out. Eyes now closed, she stopped for a moment to feel its warmth flood her body. Once again, she began to spin around as fast as she could until her nose tickled and head became dizzy. Giggling out loud, she fell to the ground no longer able to balance herself. With eyes still closed and arms and legs stretched out she lay peacefully in a bed of daisies.

After a moment of thought, she sprang to a standing position. Shading her eyes with her hands, she stood on her tippy-toes struggling to see as far as she could. "I bet they go to the ends of the earth!" she remarked, amazed at how far the daisies seemed to reach. She wondered if they went beyond her father's estate. She soon became annoyed at the hill that now obstructed her view.

Cautiously, she looked back toward the stables to make sure Joseph was not watching. And as quick as a fly, she sat on the ground removing her stockings and boots allowing them to fall in every which way. She struggled as she tried to readjust her dress and walk at the same time, desiring to be out of Joseph's view as quickly as possible.

The daisies tickled her toes as she swiftly ran up the hill. She suddenly remembered the creek at the bottom that ran vertically to the estate and beyond the wrought iron gate. Her pace slowed as she descended down the hill not wanting to tumble into the water. *Aunt Liz would be ever so angry*, she thought, the creek finally coming into view.

Miss Elizabeth, or "Aunt Liz" to Bethie, was Miss Abigail's older sister. She came to live and work at the estate soon after her husband had passed away.

Miss Elizabeth's hair was quickly turning white compared to Miss Abigail's ebony black hair, and she was also quite chubby to Miss Abby's thin and lean body. However, if you would remove Miss Abigail's spectacles, one could see a close family resemblance. Both wore their hair in a tightly braided bun. Miss Abigail was quite fond of her sister; she was a good Quaker woman who over the years had grown quite fond of the child.

Bethie stopped at the very edge of the creek as she peered in. The stream was still and quiet. She could see her image in the reflected water.

The beautiful long, brown, spiral curls that hung loosely on each side were kept neatly back from her face by a red, silk ribbon. She wore a pretty, lightly colored and pleated, dress that fell a few inches passed her knees. A silken sash that matched her headband was tied slightly above her waist.

Staring into the water, she patiently examined herself. From the picture hung above the fireplace in the library, she knew she was a portrait of her mother. Miss Abigail, known to Bethie as "Miss Abby," whispered often to the staff how the likeness was uncanny. Like her mother, she was quite beautiful.

Again, her current adventure popped into mind as she wondered how to get across the stream to follow the daisies. She looked toward both sides of the creek until finally seeing a series of rocks horizontally staggered across the stream. Deciding they were her best option, smiling, she briskly skipped over to them.

Skillfully, she began to examine each stone that would make up the route across the stream. She had more fear of what Aunt Liz would think of this endeavor than the water itself. *Aunt Liz would surely have my hide if she could see me now. I mustn't fall in,* decided Bethie a little worried.

Finally, satisfied with her choices, she carefully began her pursuit across the water. Before placing her entire weight onto a stone, each rock was tested for firmness. One by one, it received a vigorous nudge by the right foot to check for stability; meanwhile, she tried to maintain a steady balance with the left. Cautiously, but quite excited, she continued the expedition across the creek.

Bethie came upon a rock large enough to sit on. She slowly squatted with legs crossed, while examining a group of gold fish swimming directly in front of her.

They did not seem to be frightened by her presence and continued to swim in a circular motion near the large rock. How interesting they seemed to her, as she was able to view them up closely. Their movements with togetherness seemed almost poetic.

She smiled and let out a long, lazy sigh. *How lucky I am to live at such a beautiful place,* she agreed, looking all about. Bethie suddenly felt sad that her parents were not here to enjoy its beauty with her and began to think about them. Sadness not for herself, but for them. She felt as though she was a princess in a palace. God had blessed her with all that there was. She was truly grateful and prayed her parents, too, were in a place such as this.

Through the years, Bethie asked often about her parents. She wanted to know everything there was to know about the two of them. Miss Abigail would always take the time, no matter what she was doing, to sit and talk about Mr. and Mrs. Covington to her. She could tell the way Miss Abby spoke that she must have loved them dearly.

Although Miss Abigail had not gone into detail of her parent's death, feeling Bethie was too young, she had told her that her mother died giving birth to her and her father from a broken heart. She told Bethie, except for the birth of her, that day was one of the saddest she could ever recall.

So she would not think of her father as weak, Miss Abigail spoke often of Jon's heroic efforts during the Mexican War. How he had saved lives and won many honors. Bethie was proud to know her father was liked so, and to have a father who was an elected Senator was more than she could imagine.

She thought often of her parents and longed to known them. She would beg Miss Abby to repeat the stories; there was never any protest from her. It was important to her that Bethie grow to love and understand the two of them as she felt she had.

Bethie believed her mother to be a gentle, giving woman. "Even the last few hours, with all her pain, she never complained!" swore Miss Abby. "My mother must have been very brave!" she would boast proudly.

Miss Abigail often reminded her she was never to blame herself for her mother's death. All the two ever wanted was a child. She told Bethie she was sure her mother and father were now angels one on each side of her to protect and guide Bethie for the rest of her life. And that she must never feel guilty about their deaths, for it would surely make them both sad.

In her own little way, Bethie believed in God and what Miss Abigail had told her. She could easily image her parents as angels by her side. When she would find herself thinking and longing for them, she would go into the library and stare at their portrait hung above the fireplace. Her mother so beautiful and father so handsome. She'd swear that she would be just like them one day, kind and gentle as her mother and honest and courageous like her father. She honestly believed they could see her and longed to make them proud.

Her thoughts were interrupted as she recognized a familiar voice in the distance. "Bethie... Bethie! Miss Sara, where have you wandered off to," shouted Miss Elizabeth becoming a bit worried, unable to see Bethie from where she stood.

"Oh My!" shrieked Bethie, as she quickly stood turning back toward the direction of the estate. "Aunt Liz mustn't catch me on these rocks. It would surely cause her more grey hair," whispered Bethie anxiously. She swiftly continued her departure from the rocks being extra careful not to fall in.

After returning to the bank of the creek, she quickly looked around trying to decide what to do next. There at the bottom of the hill was a tall, large oak tree. She swiftly ran over to it and sat underneath its huge branches.

Bethie noticed a few daisies growing next to where she sat and decided to pick them for Aunt Liz as a peace offering gift. The sound of footsteps moving closer became evident, as Bethie, again, shrieked in horror. She remembered her bare feet now exposed for Aunt Liz to see. She quickly crossed her legs under her dress to hide them from her view.

Miss Elizabeth descended down the hill looking every which way. She began to panic as the stream came into view. With hands mysteriously behind her back, she reached the bottom where worried eyes met Bethie sitting under the tree trying not to look guilty.

"Miss Sara Beth Covington! Whatever are you doing so far from the estate? I've been worried sick trying to find you. You know perfectly well young lady that you are not to wander so far from the estate," rambled Miss Elizabeth trying to remain calm and diplomatic. "Whatever will I do with you, dear," shaking her head, frustrated.

Bethie knew she had to think quick to throw Aunt Liz's angry thoughts in another direction. She swiftly stood and ran over to her. "Oh, Aunt Liz, don't be cross with me. I was only picking daisies… especially for you… when I noticed the prettier ones seemed to be over the hill and in this direction. So you see, I had to find out for myself if that were so." She was so impressed with herself for coming up with such unrehearsed nonsense.

"Sara," started Miss Elizabeth exhausted at Bethie's never ending imagination. "Your Miss Abby and I have known you all of your life, dear. And we know you're as quick as a whip. Don't you think it is about time that you agreed we are not two push overs that fall for tall tales from Miss Sara," reprimanded Miss Elizabeth sternly.

Embarrassed, realizing Aunt Liz was right as usual, Bethie lowered her head in shame while hoping she would take pity on her. "Bethie," she hesitated calmly, "I realize you are eight years old now, but in my eyes you're still quite a young child. We love you with all our hearts. My sister gave her word to your father that she would protect you with her life! And that, my dear, is what we both aim to do."

"I know you, Bethie, like a book. You know better than to play near a stream. Now, run along inside and go up to your room and change for supper. Do not forget to wash up too!"

Bethie slowly peered up to meet Aunt Liz's eyes. She noticed a small grin trying to escape on Miss Elizabeth's mouth. She let out a sigh of relief and smiled up at her, "Yes, ma'am."

She began to skip away as though she no longer had a worry in the world, when Miss Elizabeth's tone again stopped her. "Bethie," she cunningly began, "are you forgetting something, dear?"

Bethie stood frozen for a second or two trying to figure out what she could have possibly done now. She slowly turned around to face Miss Elizabeth when she noticed her boots and stockings that were now dangling in front of Aunt Liz.

"Do these items belong to you by any chance, dear?" she questioned, knowing quite well that they were indeed Bethie's. "Yes ma'am, they are mine," she answered, wondering how angry Aunt Liz was.

"Well don't stand there staring, dear, come and get them." Bethie slowly walked over to her and was handed her belongings. "Thank you, ma'am…"

"Oh Bethie, one more thing," added Aunt Liz, as she bent over and kissed her softly on the cheek. Not expecting the kiss but loving it all the same, she threw her arms around Aunt Liz and hugged her tightly.

"I'm sorry, Aunt Liz, I promise it will never happen again. I love you and Miss Abby so much, oh, and Joseph too!" she added. Miss Elizabeth could no longer refrain from laughing.

Though she had known the child most of her life, Bethie still had the gift of catching her and Miss Abigail off guard with loving words and sentiments. She'd make them forget why they were angry in the first place.

Miss Elizabeth returned the hug then gently patted Bethie on her bottom, "Go on now!" She resumed her skipping while humming a favorite nursery rhyme. Miss Elizabeth watched protectively with loving eyes.

She opened the main door to the servant's entrance, located near the kitchen, to find Joseph waiting for Miss Elizabeth in the foyer. When Bethie spotted him, she ran and jumped into his arms giving him a big hug while yelling, "Josephhh!"

"What's that for? What ya gone and done now, child?" Joseph questioned, suspicious but secretly pleased. He continued to stare at her with a stern face and squinted eyes.

Joseph had grown to love Bethie, as a father would their own child, and watched over her like a hovering hawk. It made him feel pleased when she, without warning, would run and jump into his arms for no apparent reason other than the love she had for him.

She had been kept quite sheltered in the old estate. She knew very little about slavery or the civil war that had only ended when she was born. Abigail, Elizabeth, and Joseph were the only family she knew.

Joseph would tell Bethie of the heroic speeches her father made before and during the war concerning slavery and freedom. He made it a point, to have Bethie know and understand what her parents stood for.

Although Joseph tried to explain slavery and bigotry to her, they were issues hard for Bethie to comprehend. He had tried to explain, though his people were needed tremendously, how long and difficult it was for the Negroes to be accepted as enlisted US soldiers. He would forever recall trying to explain to her, still overly embarrassed.

"Different like that mean old, bull?" blurted Bethie, proud of herself. "Miss Abby says only boys have that—not girls, thank goodness! Is that what you mean, Joseph?" she sighed dramatically, preoccupied with her doll.

He just stood dumbfounded and overwhelmingly embarrassed, looking down at her.

"No, child. That ain't what I meant," he replied, relieved the women had finally returned from their outing. Bethie just shrugged her shoulders, and continued playing with her doll.

Joseph hurriedly passed the women in the foyer. "Ladies," respectfully keeping his eyes down. Both women stopped to stare at his hasty departure, caught off guard.

"What's wrong with Joseph," questioned Abigail confused.

"Was he blushing," Elizabeth added. In sync, both women instinctively turned their attention directly to Bethie who was oblivious to it all, lost in play.

Joseph also remembered that Negro soldiers were often placed in the front lines and usually all massacred. They were given old muskets used in the Mexican War; most did not fire. It had been rare for any of them to be taken as prisoners of war; normally they were just shot. Joseph was the youngest of five brothers. Yellow fever had taken his mother at a young age and his father had raised them as slaves on a South Carolina plantation.

His father fled with him and his siblings north to freedom, only to lose all his brothers to the war. Joseph had told Bethie it was her father that had hired and kept him from the war and was probably the reason he was alive today.

Though Bethie felt sad for his family and people, Joseph was neither white nor black to her, but someone she had grown to love, admire, and feel safe with. He was her friend; he was the only father figure that she had ever known.

"Oh my Joseph! I better go upstairs and change before Aunt Liz comes in. She's already cross with me for wandering so far away," blurted Bethie loudly.

"Go on, child, do as ya told," reprimanded Joseph, not wanting Bethie to get further yelled at. He gently, but swiftly, put her down.

"Git on upstairs now before Miss Liz takes a cattail to ya," he scolded. The thought of Aunt Liz or any of them punishing her with a cattail or anything else struck Bethie's funny side. Running and laughing up the stairs, she paused to peer down at him.

"Awe, Joseph, Aunt Liz has never taken a cattail to me—and neither have you."

"Go on child, ya hear!" he snapped, shaking his head at her, trying not to laugh.

Though he had never been the same after his accident and the tragedies that occurred at the estate, he remained on as the only man of the house. He still felt an obligation to the Senator and Mrs. Covington. His mind had become plagued with guilt, as he continued to relive events before the accident and thereafter.

He had never been able to fulfill his last sworn promise to Jon. Being unable to recover the lost documents, and the tragic deaths of Mr. & Mrs. Covington, haunted him constantly. He had loved and admired Jon and his wife dearly, making his failure even worse.

Joseph had suffered a serious head wound due to the accident; it caused partial blindness in one eye. Because it was difficult for him to see at night, he always made sure his chores were completed before sundown.

As bizarre as one would think, he felt his partial loss of sight was a small owed debt for his inability to forgive himself. His self-made promise of protecting Miss Sara was now his main goal in life.

Entering by the same door, he greeted Miss Elizabeth in the foyer. Both faces turned sober as a very serious conversation began to take place. After hanging her bonnet and cape, she rushed him into the kitchen where they would have more privacy.

The cook had prepared supper and was now setting the table in the main dining room. Miss Elizabeth pulled shut the double pine doors leading to the area. She and Joseph stood closely facing each other, while they tried so desperately to keep their voices low.

Bethie, who had quickly washed and changed, could hear both Joseph and Aunt Liz's voice beginning to rise in volume. She knew she was not to ever eavesdrop, but she became concerned from never hearing the two of them argue before. Bethie knew whatever it was, must be serious.

She slowly and quietly crept down the back stairs and hid behind a cloak rack that stood next to the entrance of the kitchen and began to listen.

"I'm tellin' ya, Miss Elizabeth, those papers are long gone. I search for hours, day after day. They just ain't there no more! The current done gone carried them to that old river. I just know it!"

"Ya know if they was there, I'd surely find them. No one feels more guilty than I do about those papers," pleaded Joseph anxiously. I'd do just about anything to get them back!"

"Hush now, Joseph, before Bethie hears you… Nobody blames you for those missing papers. We know you've done all you can. The only thing we can do now is pray…" Miss Elizabeth sadly hesitated, "Pray Abigail and the Covington's lawyer-will prevail!"

"I'd so much as die before giving up Bethie to that wicked lady! I know it's a sin to talk so harshly of a woman I've never met before, but I know my sister she would never tell such stories about anyone unless they were absolutely true."

"She's an evil woman; I'm sure of it. It's a feeling I get at the pit of my stomach every time Abigail speaks of her. With all that money and power… God help that child!" she ended, exhausted from worry.

Crouching on her knees, Bethie covered her nose and mouth with both hands. Her eyes were as big as saucers, as she silently gasped at the words that were just spoken by her Aunt Liz and Joseph.

Most of the information heard made no sense to her, but one thing she was sure of was that the conversation, indeed, was about her. Bethie knew Aunt Liz mustn't find her behind the rack so she carefully crawled out from underneath it. She quickly walked through the back hallway leading to the main rooms on the first floor and turned to enter her father's library.

Bethie took a moment to glance up at her parent's portrait that hung above the large fireplace. With hands clutched in prayer she began to speak softly while looking up at them.

"Oh, Mother, Father... what were they talking about? Was it about me? Why did Miss Abby lie and tell me she was going to the city to purchase new clothing? I don't understand, Miss Abby has never lied to me before. And who is that evil woman they keep talking about? Is she coming to live with me? Oh help me, please! I need you... I'm scared." Tears began to form in the child's eyes.

Her prayer was interrupted when she heard Miss Elizabeth calling for her. "I'm in Father's library!" she blurted loudly, not wanting her Aunt Liz to know she was upset.

From her sleeve, she hastily pulled out the laced handkerchief hidden away and wiped off the tears from her swollen face. She was able to shove it back into place before Miss Elizabeth entered the room.

"Bethie... you know you're to be in the dining room. It's hard keeping up with you these days, dear. And I'm getting much too old to run after you," she commented frustrated.

"I'm sorry, Aunt Liz. I was thinking of my parents and wanted to see their portrait."

"Apology not necessary," softened Miss Elizabeth, "Are you OK, Bethie? You look a little blue." She walked over to the child and placed her chubby arms around her shoulders and gave a little squeeze.

"Aunt Liz," began Bethie, wondering if she should confess to her that she was eavesdropping. She had no desire to get reprimanded but wanted desperately to understand the disturbing conversation between Joseph and her.

"What is it, dear?" questioned Miss Elizabeth, wanting to comfort her.

After some careful consideration, Bethie decided whatever it was about would come soon enough and to let it be for now. "Oh nothing, Aunt Liz. It wasn't important."

"Are you sure, dear?" she questioned, curious and concerned at what could possibly be bothering her.

"I'm sure," she smiled looking up at her. Hand in hand, the two left the library silently. Bethie was scared and still wondering, while Miss Elizabeth suddenly became horrified by the thought that she had heard their conversation in the kitchen.

Philadelphia, Pennsylvania

The sounds of the bustling city began to compete against the angry and frustrated voices coming from Judge Benjamin Buchanan's chambers. He stood abruptly walking over to shut the windows facing the clatter and racket.

He was hoping to cause a diversion or a short pause, while wondering how long it would take before the room felt like a hothouse making matters even worse. Because of the stress that was making his head ache with pain, he decided the heat would be a better choice over added noise.

Miss Abigail, as far back as she could remember, had been complimented on many occasions as a kind, fair, modest woman hating no one. But this day, deep within her soul, fear lie dormant but intense allowing no one to see but herself.

Abigail was a proud woman and was thankful, at least, for that. She was different this day, and it scared her. The feeling was uncontrollable as she had finally come face to face with her nemesis, kept apart only by the smallness of the width of a table.

Through the years her tormented nightmares of this woman had become a relentless battle that had finally become reality. Miss Abigail had prayed many nights believing that goodness would prevail over evil. But even all those prayers, including the Covington's lawyer Mr. Holt, could not stop her. And by no choice of her own, she now was forced to face the inevitable.

Abigail's eyes stared back into the woman's, with chin and shoulders up, refusing to give in or appear afraid or intimidated. The woman's demeanor displayed anger and dislike toward Abigail. Abigail's refusal to back down sent a clear message that she would be nobody's fool this day.

Although she still believed Abigail was indeed beneath her, nothing more than a servant, she soon realized it was impossible to stare her down.

Mrs. Emma Mae Calhoun annoyed, and somewhat amused, by the fact that Abigail was one of the rare few not afraid or intimidated by her, shrugged her shoulders and continued her argument. After all, she truly believed Abigail to be irrelevant, a mere obstacle in the way of what was rightfully hers.

She had become quite curious in finally meeting the only living being who she had ever known who could not be bought, as was her earlier failed attempt. *Who is this woman?* Emma Mae wondered as she examined Miss Abigail as though she was some kind of strange specie. *And who does she think she is? She's nothing more than a servant. How dare her to refuse my money! Why does she care what happens to the child?* Emma Mae challenged, glaring back at Abigail.

Emma Mae was a whip, she picked up immediately on the fact that Miss Abigail was quite aware of her and Jon's childhood. Her small concern was not that of the embarrassment of someone knowing of her inhumane behavior toward a child, but that of a new potential weapon that could be used against her. She confidently agreed, without the lost documents, if brought to the Judge's attention would remain hearsay.

"This hearing is an absolute atrocity!" blurted Emma Mae loudly and quite dramatically, speaking directly to the judge in a glaring fashion.

"It is unbelievable that I have and still continue to with much despair, I might add, fight for the custody of my own dead brother's child. Who happens to be my legal blood niece! Over..." stammered

Emma Mae, "a mere servant of my late brother's estate! This child belongs with ME! I am her only living relative, not to mention my son who is her only living cousin."

"She needs to grow up with other children, not imprisoned in some stone mansion where her only companions are a few old servants trying to portray the role of her family. Where is the justice? I ask you, Judge Buchanan, where is the justice!"

One could have fallen for Emma Mae's performance, if one did not know of her, as a frustrated, concerned aunt that of genuine. But even her own lawyer, who too was among the fallen driven by greed, by no choice of his own, instinctively rolled his eyes to her performance.

"Now, now, Emma Mae… calm down and listen to reason. We've been at it for hours, accomplishing nothing. It is already late afternoon and I believe Miss Abigail intends to travel back to New Hope tonight."

"If I'd let it, we'd be here all night listening to you two women bickering back and forth. But since, thank the Lord!" His hands shaking and looking up to the ceiling exclaimed Judge Buchanan sarcastically. "I am the judge presiding over this hearing. It is I who have the authority to make the best decision based on Miss Sara Beth's behalf."

"First, Miss Abigail…" begged Judge Buchanan, as he stared deeply into Miss Abigail's eyes trying to convince her of his sincerity and compassion for her and Miss Sara. "I understand your concern for Miss Sara Beth. Well, you've raised her from birth and what a very fine job you've done!"

Abigail, who was not impressed with the Judge's patronizing tone, sneered back at him. She knew though the last will and testament had never been found, the existing will should have been enough to keep Bethie in her care.

Emma Mae was a powerful woman who had a reputation of using her money to buy whatever or whomever she wanted. After years of Emma Mae's failed attempts to claim Miss Sara, finally ending up in a closed hearing that would determine the child's fate was evidence enough to her and Mr. Holt that Judge Buchanan was a bought man.

Mr. Holt, through the past years of battling with Emma Mae, had continuously kept Miss Abigail's sanity intact by trying to convince her that a will was a will and no judge could change one. He had told her the best her lawyer could do was find loopholes. Mr. Holt had reassured Abigail that he would take no chances and would continue to stay ahead of them. So any type of loopholes found would be easily dismissed.

Though Miss Abigail thought of him as a good and honest man, from the first day Emma Mae interfered with their lives, there had not been a day gone by where she did not worry. She couldn't remember the last night in which she slept peacefully.

Realizing there would be no winning over Miss Abigail he continued. "I'm sure it's quite normal, if I were to imagine Miss Abigail, for one to become very attached to a child that one has raised from birth. Not only attached, but on the contrary, one could become quite protective and possessive while in return possibly cloud one's view of reality. Wouldn't you agree Miss Abigail?" remarked Judge Buchanan, accusingly.

"How dare you!" shrieked Miss Abigail, quite offended. "Abigail, don't! Stay calm…" whispered Mr. Holt in her ear, as he began to panic from her facial expressions.

Overwhelmed with anger, Miss Abigail was unable to hear him. She could feel the last straw break as she continued to lose any control left from this exhausting, monstrosity of a day.

No longer able to sit, she stood angry and in disbelief. "How dare you! I have never been so insulted in my life. Atrocity! I'll give you Atrocity! These past couple of years, this hearing, but most of all This Woman!"

"It is absolutely inconceivable to me… Inconceivable that a woman, so malevolent and devoid of empathy, could have the power to buy off anyone she feels fit to."

The Judge now quite angry with Abigail's remarks defensively cut in, "Miss Abigail, you are out of line! Are you accusing Miss Emma of paying me off? If you do not calm down, I'll hold you in contempt. Will you please sit down!"

Still frustrated and angry, she stared down to Emma Mae who at this time was gloating and loving every moment of Abigail's uncontrollable outburst. The cold and pleasing grin displayed upon Emma Mae's face, most definitely expressed no regrets or remorse. It made Abigail sick to her stomach. She began to feel an overwhelming sense of defeat.

Realizing her behavior could do nothing but endanger Miss Sara's future, she took a deep breath and exhaled slowly. For a moment the room was silent, while all eyes remained on Miss Abigail in disbelief.

With both hands she nervously adjusted her bonnet and jacket but continue to stand. Choosing to regain her calmness but refusing to apologize to Judge Buchanan, Miss Abigail continued in a calmer tone of voice. "Please keep in mind, Judge Buchanan, this is neither a court room, nor is this a trial. But please know this for certain, I will do whatever it takes even if I have to go to the Supreme Court to protect Miss Sara Beth."

"I am confident, at least most of us in this room would agree, Mr. Covington was an intelligent man. Yes. It is true his last will and testament has never been retrieved. But there was and is indeed a will filed with Mr. Holt, Mr. and Mrs. Covington's attorney."

"It firmly states that I would be left executor of the estate, and in charge of any living children left by Mr. and Mrs. Covington in case of their joint death. To myself, the Covington's lawyer, and I would hope and pray The Law, this most definitely existing document is plain and simple!"

"Judge Buchanan… it is true that I cannot supply you with written proof from Mr. Covington proclaiming the abuse that he had endured by Emma Mae Calhoun, but I'd swear it on my life it is true. Mrs. Covington was the most honest, kind woman I have ever known and would never lie about such things.

And the stories! They were terrifying. Who could or would invent such horrors? This woman's behavior toward her own brother was simply evil!" remarked Miss Abigail, while staring straight into Emma Mae's hateful, empty eyes.

"If you give custody of Miss Sara Beth to this woman, it will lie fixed on your conscience for the rest of your life. Can you honestly live with yourself knowing that there could be even a slim possibility that these accusations are true?" she ended, slowly sitting, mentally exhausted from the whole ordeal.

A few moments of silence filled the room. Emma Mae secretly glanced over to Judge Buchanan signaling him with a swift nod to quickly end this for good. He was a weak and greedy man and like many times before, found himself in a difficult position.

He now thought how most of those times had been quite easy for him. But it was only when children were involved did it cause his conscience to become a nuisance against his greed.

It wasn't about money this time, but fear. He was a coward and was more afraid for himself than the child Sara Beth. The judge had known Emma Mae for many years and had no doubts that the accusations Miss Abigail brought forth were accurate. Emma Mae was a powerful woman that one never crossed and he knew this.

"Miss Abigail, are you quite finished?" he remarked, trying not to let Abigail's speech get to him. "I must agree with you on one issue and that one you are absolutely right on, Miss Abigail, accusations! That is all they are, accusations!"

"These are serious allegations you are making against Mrs. Calhoun. Do you realize this? Without any living witnesses or substantial evidence of any kind, you do not have a case. And if I were you, Miss Abigail, I would refrain from making these types of accusations for fear you may place yourself in jeopardy of being sued for slander by Mrs. Calhoun."

"I hope that I am making myself understood to you, Miss Abigail," reprimanded Judge Buchanan, unable to continue eye to eye contact with her. Abigail, who was quite aware of what was happening and where Judge Buchanan stood answered sternly but calmly, "Yes, Judge Buchanan. I believe I understand you perfectly well."

"Although I have listened very carefully with empathy and compassion for both sides today, it is not necessary to break or continue another day. I have made my decision."

Judge Buchanan cleared his throat then continued. "Though it has been assumed by Miss Abigail and her attorney that there was a new will apparently being delivered to Mr. Holt's home on the very eve of the Covington's tragic deaths, since it has never been found it becomes irrelevant to this hearing."

"But what becomes quite relevant is the current standing will. This will lists strictly that in the case of their joint deaths, Miss Abigail would be left executor of their estate along with governess of any living children until he/she or they reach the legal age of eighteen. In which all lands, property, businesses, material wealth, and possessions owned by Mr. and Mrs. Covington would be evenly divided among all living children."

"In the case of there not being any living children, the Covington's direct all properties, monies, and possessions to The House of Philadelphia, orphanage for children, located here in Philadelphia. An organization once dear to Mr. Covington's own parents. Executor of funds, Mr. Holt, their attorney and excluding funds set aside for the Covington house staff—which of course includes, Miss Abigail.

Both situations exclaimed would include, but not limited to only, the following: The Covington estate and acreage located on River Road in New Hope, Pennsylvania, with control of the waterways. All mills, businesses, and other properties, etc., along with financial funds and material possessions, etc., etc."

"This I cannot change, it is a standard, written will submitted in a lawful manner and must be upheld by the law!" exclaimed a worried Judge Buchanan, as he looked toward an unhappy Emma Mae. Miss

Abigail began to breathe a sigh of relief and immediately began to thank God.

"However... although Mrs. Calhoun, Miss Sara's only living relative was not mentioned in this will, for whatever differences the two siblings may have had in the past, should not cause punishment upon the child. The child should have the opportunity to know and be loved by her only living relatives." Miss Abigail again began to panic.

"It is my judgement, in behalf of what is best for the child, Miss Sara Beth Covington, she shall immediately transfer to the Calhoun Plantation located in Savannah, Georgia. Accompanied by Miss Abigail, as her governess. She will submit a timely report on behavior and circumstances surrounding the child in her new environment. In which she shall reside until the age of eighteen years old unless otherwise revoked by myself due to unfavorable reports."

"In which time, she shall inherit the Covington estate and all thereof. This hearing is now adjourned. Good luck and good day to you all," ended Judge Buchanan wanting desperately to escape the room before verbally attacked by Miss Abigail.

"No... No! You can't do that! What kind of a man are you? Have you no conscience?" Miss Abigail was outraged as Judge Buchanan ignoring her, quickly exited the room.

"Abigail, stop! Let it go. It's over! Just be thankful to God that this is the worst that happened," begged Mr. Holt desperately trying to convince Abigail. His hand gently gripped her arm, preventing her from physically getting up from the table to pursue the judge.

He had known from the day Miss Abigail began to raise Sara Beth how protective she had become. And could only imagine what she could possibly do, as he continued to refrain her while coaxing Abigail to calm down.

"Good Lord... What could be worse than that poor child being raised by that horrible woman? I've failed Mr. Holt... I've really failed," she whispered, subdued and exhausted trying so hard not to cry.

Mr. Holt turned her around to face him. "That's not true, Abigail, you still remain executor of Sara's estate. And you will still be able to be there to watch over her. All Emma Mae wants is Sara Beth's wealth and control over her, you know that as well as I do. She doesn't love that child and probably isn't capable of it. Because of that will, she receives neither."

"It is you and Sara who have prevailed. You must look at it as a small triumph for Emma, but you and Sara have won the war. As much as he may not have wanted to because of greed, the judge was right when he said that a will cannot be changed. All he and her lawyer were able to do is alter it by a simple loophole. They based it on the fact that the Covington's original will did not express that any child of theirs must remain on the estate."

"Understand this, Abigail, she cannot take her without taking you. And with you there to love, nurture, and protect this child, Emma Mae cannot harm her. You need to be strong now, for you as well as the child's sake. Let's get out of here, Abigail. It's getting late and Sara Beth needs you. It's time to go home." There was a moment of silence as Mr. Holt held Miss Abigail's hand in comfort.

"Not quite yet," began Miss Abigail, as she stood proud while asking the lawyers to leave the room so she could speak to Emma Mae alone. Emma Mae nodded to her lawyer, though Mr. Holt was reluctant, both men left the room closing the door behind them.

The two stood stiff, still, and eye to eye. The dislike between them was quite evident and seemed to fill the room. "It's Mrs. Calhoun to you, Abigail. Don't you think it is about time you learn your place?" She ignored her remark and began to speak.

"Before I leave here today, and while in privacy, I believe it to be important to make myself clear to you. It is true that in reality I may only be a mere servant to you and people around you, but know this—I love that child no less than if she were my own flesh and blood."

"I swore a promise to your brother; I would never let you touch her. And as God is my witness, I will protect that child from you with my life if I have to! Mark my words, Emma, you will never get what you want. I'm here for good, and I'm here to see to it."

"Keep in mind that if anything happens to me, Mr. Holt becomes executor and gains control of Sara Beth's custody. Understand this, he is another who cannot be bought. He's already a very rich man and neither desires your money, nor is he intimidated by you."

"In addition, I have signed a sworn affidavit accusing you of the crimes that I believe you have committed against your only brother and at that time most likely myself. Besides the fact that Mr. Holt would see to it that you would be prosecuted to the fullest."

"Every newspaper from New York to Savannah would receive a copy. Ruining you and your so called reputation. And as far as Miss Sara Beth is concerned, it's quite simple you see… If you harm her in any way… I'll surely kill you myself."

"Are you threatening me, Abigail?" replied Emma Mae in a sarcastic manner, as she stood there grinning back at Miss Abigail not intimidated in any way by her comments.

"No, Emma… They're not threats—only promises." She began to leave the room with her back to Emma Mae.

"Oh, Abigail…" Miss Abigail stopped to listen but refused to turn around and face her. "Make sure Sara Beth is on the train to Savannah Friday morning. That gives you a week. You can handle that can't you? After all, I could only assume being a servant as long as you have must have taught you some discipline. Miss Abigail refused to acknowledge Emma's last remark and continued to leave the room.

Emma Mae discouraged by the fact that she could not see Judge Buchanan immediately, for it would not have looked quite right, began to take it out on her lawyer. He did not desire to return to where Emma Mae waited but was a sufficient enough target for her anger.

"You let him know that he is ruined! I am going to personally see to it. And if he has the audacity to believe that I am actually going to pay him for that monstrosity, he is as crazy as that silly servant what's her name… Abigail."

"You best beware, Emma Mae, I believe Miss Abigail to be a woman to be reckoned with. She could be more trouble than you want to imagine. I would stay on that one's good side if I were you," he warned.

"Hogwash! She's nothing more than a servant. But a crazy one at that!"

"And you, my fine, well-paid attorney, what help were you? I barely heard a peep out of you the whole time."

"That's uncalled for, Emma Mae. I've done the best I can for you today and for many years. You have no right coming down on Judge Buchanan anyway, I agree with the man. There wasn't a thing more that he could have done. Not with a legal will in front of him. What was he supposed to do? Go to jail for you?"

Emma Mae shrugged her shoulders discouraged but intelligent enough to know that there was not much more that could have been done. But nevertheless she was not a woman who took disappointment or defeat well. Someone would surely pay, someone always did.

"Emma Mae, there is a question that has plagued my mind since this hearing. I simply must ask you. When you found out that there was no way you would ever receive controlling interest to your brother's estate, why on earth did you continue to pursue custody of that child? We both know that you're not the least bit interested in her. Why did you do it, Emma? You have your son William, he makes you happy. Why didn't you just leave the child alone, Emma?"

"He owes me!" she snapped with much contempt, pacing about.

"Who owes you?"

"Jon, my brother…"

"Many years ago he almost ruined me. I've never forgotten. I hope to hell he's rolling in his grave from this day. I had taken over Daddy's shipping business here in the city and had made it stronger than it had ever been. Bigger and better than when the two of them were alive."

"I had Durham boats traveling down the river and through the canals from the city and New York, delivering pig iron and coming back with cloth, flour, linseed oil, whatever was being manufactured in those mills along the river at that time. I was making a fortune. Times were very good."

"And then he came along after many years of disappearing and bought out a great deal of land alongside the river and canal. Land that I had tried for years to get my hands on, but to no avail! Anyway, he refused me way of passage through the ferry tracks and nearly ruined me. I stopped delivering west up until the railroad became more accessible. It just wasn't worth it, money wise."

"Shortly afterwards is when I met my husband, Edmund. He had come to the city for a political convention. We met and fell in love with one another. He asked me to marry him and to return back to Georgia with him. There wasn't much keeping me here, so I reestablished my shipping business in Savannah. It took me many years to get back to where I had been. And I swore he'd pay."

"But, Emma Mae, that estate belongs now to Miss Sara Beth. You're never, Never, gonna get your hands on it. Why can't you just let it go?"

"Those mills and land are mine! I earned them. You just make sure you express our concerns to their lawyer about the banks possibly failing. There's a depression comin', I'm sure of it. I didn't become a rich woman for nothin'. You best watch over my interests before there's a run on the banks. It's certainly not over. No my friend, it's only the beginning."

Miss Abigail's return home was a somber and silent one, as it slowly and gently rained which seemed almost fitting. With folded hands placed in her lap, she gazed out of the side window of her carriage worried and exhausted. She would have at least a few hours now of needed silence, as she searched her tormented mind, soul, and heart as to how to tell Bethie. But what being more difficult of all, how much to tell her.

To Abigail, Bethie was a gift from God during a time in which hell seemed to break through entering their world to create havoc. But still, there was good. It was as though God was saying to always remember that good will prevail, as he handed down to them the child Sara Beth.

She need only be about for one to smile and regain remembrances of being a child again. A child of purity and most certainly innocence. And it broke Miss Abigail's heart to know that after this day she would no longer be the little child of naivety and innocence that she had been blessed to raise from an infant.

Abigail felt as though she had failed the Covingtons by her own shortcomings. She had always thought of herself as strong, fair, organized, intelligent, and even well-mannered. *Where was that woman today?* She pondered, devastated. She had no choice but to tear down the walls of innocence created and maintained in the private world of the Covington estate. So that in turn the harsh realities of what was, is, and could be would be disclosed and acknowledged for the child's own sake.

Exiled to Savannah

It was nearly midnight as the wrought iron gate to the Covington estate came into view. The carriage began its approach onto the oak lined, cobblestone entryway. All was jet black except for the dim light that glowed from inside the library window.

The night was still, peaceful, and almost soothing thought Miss Abigail, as she was gently escorted down from the carriage by Abner. He was a round, little, old white haired gentleman who took care of the horses but mainly kept to himself. He lived outside of New Hope with his wife Abilene.

Abner had been hired by Joseph to help with the horses and had been asked the night before to accompany Miss Abigail into the city. Joseph, of course, requested to remain at the estate to continue his desperate, hopeless, and endless search for the lost documents.

Abigail, wanting to crawl into bed placing this horrid day behind her for even one night, was approached by Joseph coming from the barn hollering, "Miss Abigail... Miss Abigail!" Although she immediately recognized his voice, she was still startled by the abrupt sound in the still of this late night.

"Quiet, Joseph! You're gonna wake the entire county up going on like that."

He followed Abigail inside to the foyer, as she began to remove her cape and bonnet. Joseph lit a nearby lamp that hung on the wall and from that flame lit a candle that sat upon a trestle table. Out of exhaustion, she wished desperately not to talk about the day's events until tomorrow. From the look on Joseph's face she knew she had no choice. He was anxious and quite concerned. There would be no sleeping for him this night unless Abigail explained the outcome.

"Glad to see ya home safe and all. How did it go? I been worryin' all day and night, couldn't sleep till ya got home."

Miss Abigail had spent the whole trip back trying to figure out how and what she would tell Bethie that she had forgotten about Joseph and Elizabeth. She knew they were both worried sick. But her mind was empty now and her head ached; she could not think of one comforting word.

"Joseph, sit down please. We need to talk." His face turned somber and serious for he knew what Miss Abigail was about to tell him would not be good news. He slowly sunk onto the entryway bench with Abigail following next to him.

Facing Joseph but unable to keep her head up any longer he gently took her hand in comfort. "Everything's gonna be juss fine. Don't worry now, ya hear!"

Abigail's held back tears could no longer refrain from falling onto her forlorn face with spectacles now removed. She no longer felt strong and yearned for his comfort and support.

"Bethie and I are to leave for Savannah next week. We won't be coming back to New Hope for a longtime. Oh, Joseph… What am I going to do? I feel like I failed the child."

"It's not ya fault. It's mine… I'm the one done lost those papers."

Without hesitation or resistance from Abigail, he slowly put his arm around her shoulders and carefully pulled her to him. He rocked her gently for what seemed a lifetime, as she quietly wept onto his shoulder. Joseph stared off, his head felt numb as no words were said by either.

Joseph had physically changed over the past eight years. His once tall, awkward, and skinny body had matured into a graceful, broad, and muscular physique. Except for a few part-time hired hands, he did most of the hard, physical labor needed on the estate. He was a conscientious, hard-worker one could trust and rely on. Many of the other estates on the river or nearby farms offered him higher wages if he were to work for them. But he always refused their offers.

Although he was quite intelligent, as he solely ran the grounds of the estate himself, he hadn't much education. In her spare time, Miss Abigail taught Joseph to read, write, and as much as she could for that matter. His yearning for education was never ending and it pleased Abigail quite immensely to be able to help him.

At first, he was embarrassed to tell Miss Abigail of his ignorance but later became grateful for her time and patience. She wasn't surprised, most Negroes had little or no education. He felt proud when he went into town and signed invoices after reading them aloud to himself. The town's folk always wondering how a Negro man could be so educated.

Except for a small scar near his left eye, caused by the accident, his face still remained like a child's, gentle, smooth, and soft. He was quite handsome with gentleman like manners. He treated Abigail and all women he knew with much respect. And he absolutely adored Bethie.

But he had a secret.

One that lie in the far depths of his soul hidden. One he knew, should never be revealed. For all hell would certainly break loose, once again, at the Covington estate. Joseph was in love with Abigail. He had been from the day she came to the estate as Mary's assistant.

Joseph never spoke a word of it to anyone. He knew his place and respected Abigail far too much to ever cause a scandal. It would have ruined Miss Abigail's reputation regardless of what she may have felt or done about it. A Negro man could be lynched for even thinking of a white woman in this manner. It was entirely forbidden and he knew this. He thought of Miss Abigail as a lady, through and through, and never dared to even consider such an indecency.

Although he never made advances toward her, Abigail knew how Joseph felt for she too felt this forbidden desire. It would make her angry for thinking such things. For she believed herself to be a Christian woman.

As the years went by the harder it became. His eyes gave him away to her. They purposely tried to avoid one another except when business needed to be taken care of concerning the estate. The tender and affectionate manner in which he spoke to her often was much more than she could bear. Joseph always monitored the distance between the two, wanting to protect her reputation with his life.

She loved her sister very much and was relieved when she came to live at the estate. Along with Bethie, she would become a buffer or the wall between them. If Elizabeth knew, she neither appeared suspicious nor did she ever question either of them.

He rarely left the estate except for supplies or church on Sundays. Several of the more popular, young, Negro ladies sought desperately for his affections, all lovely and flirting shamelessly, but without success. They'd invite him to supper after church or to be so bold as to ask him for a carriage ride down by the river. He never became serious with any of them and took no wife as he began to approach midlife.

Abigail had been a school teacher prior to coming to the Covington estate. She came from a good Quaker family. Her sister warned her often that her child bearing days would soon be gone if she did not begin to seriously consider taking on a husband. She spoke often of her regrets of never being able to bear children.

Miss Abigail would try to convince herself and Elizabeth that she was much too dedicated to Bethie and running the estate to ever consider marriage. She knew the town folk thought of her as an unmarried spinster woman as she kept the truth buried deep within her soul. Abigail was a very proud woman and cared little of what people thought of her.

Joseph's mind again began to focus on Miss Abigail, as he continued to gently hold and rock her. Even against constant protest, only in his dreams had he dare to feel her so close. Trying to stay unnoticed, he lightly buried his face into her hair. The lovely smell of honeysuckles filled his head. How bold he had become this night, as he felt her warmth against his body. But still, he refused to subside.

It had all been so innocent, intending only to comfort Abigail during her most vulnerable moment of need. He would soon lose her and cared no longer of society's principles and rules made up by those who mattered nothing to him. Only God would judge, as he begged for restraint with mercy as he so desperately needed on this night.

Without further thought or hesitation, he discontinued the rocking motion and gently lifted her face toward his. He stared for a moment at the sadness that lingered in her tearful eyes. It became more than he could stand, as he slowly and gently kissed each of them wanting desperately to make the pain go away.

Again, he stared into her eyes for only a moment; they begged for her approval. *Will she be angry or reject my advances?* He could never bear it if she grew to hate him for this. But she said and did nothing except to stare back at him in disbelief; he had nearly taken her breath away with his actions.

He could not wait to know as he gently brought his lips onto hers. His mouth covered hers as she began to lose control of all learned principles. Abigail thought the kiss to be soft, gentle, and could feel his lips quiver from fear of his forbidden, now revealed, passion for her.

He brought his mouth only slightly from her own. His eyes never fully opened as his overwhelming desire for her took control. He again, placed his lips on Abigail's with a much stronger force. His arm slipped around her waist, as he gently pinned her against the bench and himself.

Abigail's body quickly flooded with passion, as she began to feel drunk from desire fueled by mere touch. The feeling was unbelievable, realizing it was one she had not felt before. He had total control of her as she let go, for a moment, without a fight.

She had several gentlemen callers in the past and had allowed them to kiss her on occasion. But she felt nothing like she felt this night with Joseph. There was a time she wished he would just kiss her so the wondering would end. They would realize there was nothing between them and go on being friends and work companions. But there was always that doubt it would not be the same as her past callers. She feared this and soon prayed the day would never come.

What is it about him? She was an educated white woman and he a Negro man, both from different worlds. *Is it simply the desire of something forbidden? I'm supposed to be a lady. But I don't feel like one right now... Am I losing my mind*, she wondered desperately.

Down deep she had always known the answer. She had refused to accept its simplicity. She loved him. Always had. And there would never be another, despite the opinions of others or the consequences.

His mouth felt good and warm, as he continued to hold her strongly in his arms. Their desire for each other was like that old river overflowing when a strong storm came. You could never stop it, only hope the damage could be repaired.

I can't do this... We can't do this! I've got to take control and stop this, thought Abigail arguing with herself. She was unable to make her body move to her demands. She was like a ragdoll in his arms, wanting and needing him desperately.

He was a normal man with normal desires and needs. He kept them neatly bottled up for years possessed with desire for a woman he could never have. He loved her, too. No other woman could compare.

For no reason other than desperation, the thought of Bethie entered her confused mind. *How could I think of myself at a time like this?* She felt sick with shame, as the past few minutes replayed rapidly through her mind. Immediately she began to regain control of her behavior. She abruptly pushed Joseph from against her, as she stood up hastily straightening up her hair and attire.

Frustrated and breathing heavily both stared at one another, overwhelmed. "Abby, I'm sorry..." blurted Joseph, begging for forgiveness. He stood, moving toward her again.

"Don't! Joseph, please... This should have never happened." Abigail turned from him. "I've never been so ashamed. Please go now."

Miss Abigail took the candle that sat lit upon the table and quickly fled up the staircase desiring to escape from Joseph's very presence. He stood watching as her shame overwhelmed him. He hated himself for ever touching her. He agonized over what he had done.

She quickly ran to her room shutting the door behind her, then flung herself onto her bed and wept in shame. *What is happening to me? This day will never be forgotten. It will be burned in my memory forever,* she imagined hopelessly.

Miss Abigail gathered her thoughts quickly as she remembered Bethie. She stood while trying so desperately to straighten her clothing. Her hair was a mess as she looked unwillingly into the mirror above her dresser. She quietly left her room, hoping not to wake Elizabeth. She descended down the hallway toward Bethie's room carrying the lit candle.

She quietly entered her room and placed the burning candle on the oak mantle mounted above the fireplace. The dim light showed the silhouette of her lovely face on the wall behind her bed. Her sweetness and pure innocence became more prevalent, as Miss Abigail patiently watched the sleeping child. How beautiful she was as Miss Abigail gently caressed her hair.

How could anyone hurt a child? It was beyond her comprehension, she agreed. Abigail gently kissed her cheek and pulled the covers up and over the child's shoulders. She began to retrieve the candle to leave when she heard a faint voice.

"Miss Abby… is that you?"

"Yes, dearest. It's me."

"I missed you. I'm glad you're home. I tried to wait up for you. But I guess I fell asleep."

"Well, I'm glad you did. It's quite late young lady and time for you to go back to sleep."

"Miss Abby… I have a confession to make."

"What is it, dearest?"

"I did something you told me never to do. I eavesdropped on Aunt Liz and Joseph's conversation today."

"Bethie!" exclaimed Miss Abigail, frustrated and shaking her head, exhausted.

"I know it was wrong. But you were wrong, too."

"What are you talking about?" replied Miss Abigail, guarded but concerned.

"I know you didn't go into the city today to shop for new clothes for me. And I also know there is some awful woman who is either coming to live with me—or has something to do with me! But what I don't understand is why you lied, Miss Abby. You've never lied to me before," Bethie rambled.

Miss Abigail shuddered in horror in finding out that Bethie's eavesdropping had to do with the day's events. Never did she want the child to find out about Emma Mae this way.

She swiftly went to Bethie's bedside and wrapped her arms around her, holding her tightly. She felt as though she'd never let her go for fear she would no longer be able to protect her.

"Bethie… it's true I didn't tell you the entire truth about today. But it was for a good reason. It's late and I do not want to get into the subject matter tonight. But I promise, when breakfast is over I will sit with you and explain everything."

"All I am asking you to do tonight is to forgive me and trust me, Bethie. Trust that I did what I thought was best for you. Can you do that?"

"Yes, Miss Abby. I trust you. I can wait till tomorrow. Can you stay until I fall asleep? I'm scared…"

"Yes, of course! I'll stay," answered Miss Abigail, as she lay next to the child in comfort. After all, she was scared too.

The sun shone brightly through Bethie's playroom and she had almost forgotten the worries of the past day. A lovely Blue Jay sang gaily outside her window; it filled the air with song. She played happily with her Miss Amy, as she gently placed the doll at the tiny table in which tea was about to be served. With delicate ease, she smoothed out the doll's dress, then retied her red, silk bow that was now slanting downward.

"A proper lady must always look her best, Miss Amy, especially at tea time."

Bethie, trying to be sophisticated, walked slowly around the small table holding onto both sides of her dress with chin up.

Pulling out her chair, she sat quite eloquently. "You never know who may come to visit. Perhaps even a gentleman caller!" With hand over her mouth, she giggled aloud from the silliness of her conversation with Miss Amy.

With her tiny pinkie extended outward, she carefully began to fill the little china cups with imaginary tea. "Would you care for one or two lumps?" Bethie hesitates for a moment as if the doll could really respond. "Then one lump it is, Miss Amy." From a small sugar bowl that sat between them, she began to scoop out imaginary sugar cubes.

"Thank you, Miss Amy. Why I don't know when I ever received such a lovelier compliment. Yes... I baked them myself you know, an old family recipe. I'm pleased that you are enjoying them. By all means, please, have another." Bethie was truly enjoying herself. She was content, Miss Abigail was home safe, and for now all was well.

Miss Abigail, who was trying to sit patiently as her sister paced back and forth in front of her, could no longer retain her patience. "Elizabeth, I know you are upset, but will you please keep your voice down. Will you sit down and listen to reason! For heaven sakes, isn't it bad enough that the child overheard you and Joseph bickering yesterday?"

"She isn't going to be living here much longer, and I wish to have her remaining days at the estate to be pleasant memories not one of constant arguments. Good Lord, things are stressful enough without you adding to them." Miss Abigail, quite frustrated, jumped up from the chair and closed the door to the sitting room.

"I am truly sorry, Abigail. I really don't blame you or Joseph. I know you've both done everything you could. And I don't want to make things worse than they already are. You know I love that child with all my heart."

"But it's hard not to be upset. I tell you, Abigail, if I wasn't a Christian lady, no tellin' what I could do to that woman. There's no doubt in my mind, I know she doesn't care for that child. She belongs here with us. No one could ever love her like we do. I'm just so afraid, Abigail."

Elizabeth's eyes began to fill with tears as she finally resolved to sitting. Abigail swiftly went to her side and put her arms around her sister. "Everything is going to be fine, Elizabeth. Don't cry, please. I need your strength now more than ever. The next few days are going to be difficult and I can't have you worrying."

"I'm a strong woman, sister—you know that. I'll take good care of Bethie. Nothing or no one will ever harm her. You have my word on that. Please don't worry."

"I know you will, Abigail. There was never a doubt in my mind of that. I guess I'm just feeling sorry for myself. These years in New Hope with you and Bethie have been some of the best years of my life. I'm getting old now, Abigail. Not only do I feel I'm losing Bethie, but the only sister that I'll ever have. I love you sister with all my heart and soul." Abigail smiled as she took her hanky from her sleeve and began to gently wipe the tears from Elizabeth's eyes.

"Look at you, Elizabeth. You're a mess!" Miss Abigail's remarks caused a smile to appear on Miss Elizabeth's face. "Elizabeth, how do you think I feel? I'm the one who has to leave Covington to live with someone I despise. In a place I've never been to. It's almost impossible to comprehend."

"But I must! What is done, is done. I can't change that. I want to do what is best for Bethie. She needs me, Elizabeth, and even more, I need her. Last night when I held that child until she fell asleep, I knew I had no choice. And to go on complaining and arguing isn't going to make a bit of difference."

"I have to abide by the law, Elizabeth. Or they could take Bethie away from us forever! Now I want you to keep your chin up and keep smiling. Do it for Bethie's sake as well as mine. I need you to do this for me right now, sister."

"Look on the bright side. The judge has given eight weeks every summer for Bethie to return to New Hope for a visit. We'll see each other again soon. In fact, Bethie will have grown so much by the time we come back next year, we'll be spending all our time in the city trying to clothe her." For Abigail's sake, Elizabeth forced another smile.

"I love you too, Elizabeth, and you keep that smile on your face! It's going to be hard enough explaining all of this to Bethie. She's going to be devastated when she hears that she has to leave Covington. The girl is so attached to you and Joseph… Well, I don't look forward to it."

"Abigail, promise me one thing… You're a wonderful human being. As far back as I can remember, all your life you've given so much of yourself with little in return. You must never feel guilty about the way things have turned out. Never worry about me or Covington. Joseph and I will take good care of her. I give you my word. You have done well for Bethie. God is pleased. Promise me."

"I promise, Elizabeth."

Miss Abigail entered the play area from the child's bedroom. She smiled lovingly as she observed Bethie while she played. By now, the sun had engulfed the room, along with the little girl's spirit, making the area feel warm, bright, and cheerful.

How she loved to stand back and just watch Bethie. She was so young and full of life. There was a definite newness about her that made everyone who came in contact with her feel young again. Bethie's imagination alone could capture even the narrowest of minds. Her long, brown ringlets of hair bounced to and fro, as she busily poured and sipped imaginary tea from a tiny, delicate china cup.

"Well, hello, Miss Sara Beth. If I had known that it was tea time, I most certainly would have brought my freshly baked blueberry muffins. Did you remember that we had an appointment today?"

added Miss Abigail, as she began to play along.

Wanting Miss Abigail to continue in play, she remarked, "Oh! Please forgive me. I must have forgotten our appointment. But Miss Amy and I are quite pleased that you have come during tea time. We enjoy having visitors. Please sit, while I pour you some tea. Thank you for offering to bring your delicious muffins, but I have baked some wonderful crumpets. Please help yourself," she giggled.

Bethie watched patiently while Miss Abigail pretended to drink her tea while continuing to act quite serious. "How are the crumpets? Do you like them?" Miss Abigail pretended to bite into an imaginary cake.

She took the lace napkin that lay next to her tiny plate and slowly dabbed both sides of her mouth making Bethie laugh aloud. "Yes, I must admit. They're absolutely divine. Don't you agree, Miss Amy?" replied Miss Abigail looking toward the doll who had now slumped entirely over, lying face down in her cup of tea. They both roared with laughter as Bethie got off her seat to hug Miss Abigail.

"You're the best, Miss Abby," exclaimed Bethie hugging her tightly.

"You are too, dearest, but unfortunately, it's time for Miss Amy to take her nap, while you and I have a long talk. OK?"

"OK, let me put Miss Amy in her bed and I'll be right back."

Abigail watched as the child picked up the doll and placed her gently in her wooden bed, making sure the blanket did not cover her face. Bethie leaned over and gently kissed its forehead. "Now you be a good girl and take your nap." She scrambled to her feet and skipped back to her little chair and sat again.

Miss Abigail took Bethie's hand. Her mood became quite serious. Bethie stared patiently as Abigail became nervous and forgot her preplanned speech.

"Bethie… I tell you what, let's take a picnic basket down by the river and sit awhile. It's such a beautiful day. Let's not spend it inside all day. I'm sure the river would be a more enjoyable place to talk. Don't you agree, Bethie?"

She was so excited she thought she would nearly burst. "Yippee! Can I go and tell Cook we're going on an outing?"

"Yes, Bethie. Run along and tell her to prepare us a basket."

"Right away, Miss Abby," she said, jumping up and down from joy.

The day was gorgeous. One too pretty to ruin, thought Miss Abigail, as she walked slowly alongside the river. The warm temperature was enough for a simple shawl and bonnet for her and a light cape and bonnet for the child.

Miss Abigail kept Bethie in constant view, as she skipped ahead of her picking daisies along the way. The river was always busy on Saturdays. The ferries and paddle boats drifted lazily by. Bethie waved to each one as they passed.

The water was full and high as the month had brought much rain. Luckily, the ground was dry where they walked, thought Miss Abigail.

The sweet smell of lilacs filled the spring air. Beautiful landmarks with quaint buildings lined the other side of the river making the sky line look almost romantic. Pretty, little buttercups as yellow as the sun grew in bunches alongside the clover and daisies.

How can I leave this place? Miss Abigail sadly pondered. She had been born and raised in Pennsylvania and knew no other home or could imagine one lovelier than New Hope.

"Miss Abby, how'bout this spot?" yelled Bethie, impressed and excited with her find.

From where she stood Miss Abigail looked over the area that Bethie had discovered. The grass was low and seemed wide enough for the two of them to sit. And there seemed to be more grass than rock and dirt. With much approval she responded, "Good find! I'll be right there."

Miss Abigail spread the cotton blanket over the area then neatly placed the braided picnic basket down upon it. She sat kneeling while thinking of how to begin, as Bethie searched for precious gems alongside the river bed.

"Miss Abby, why didn't Aunt Liz come with us? I asked her but all she said was that you needed to speak to me alone. Is it about that mysterious woman and your Philadelphia trip?" she questioned loudly.

Abigail recalled her sister's last remark before leaving the house. "You're stalling, Abigail. You must tell the child today! She leaves in less than a week. She'll need time to adjust." Just like often Elizabeth was right, agreed Abigail.

"Yes, I need to speak to you, Bethie. Please come and sit."

She skipped over to the blanket, flopping down hard on her tummy while propping her head up with her arms and hands.

"Please sit up straight, like a young lady," reprimanded, Miss Abigail. She shrugged, but obeyed, placing her hands on her lap.

"Bethie," she began, "you're a big girl now, why almost a lady. It is important that you try to understand and be very strong. What I am about to tell you will be as difficult for you to understand, as it is for me to explain. All I ask is that you try to let me finish before you get too upset. I promise I will answer all questions that you may have. Can you promise me that, OK?"

Bethie who was now quite curious answered, "OK."

"A long time ago, when we were talking about your parents, you asked me if you had any living relatives. Like an aunt or an uncle or possibly even a cousin. Do you remember, Bethie?"

"Yes, I remember, Miss Abby," recalled Bethie.

"I had told you to my knowledge I knew of none. Well, that wasn't true. I lied… and I apologize for that. But I did not lie intentionally."

"It all seemed too complicated at the time and I felt you were much too young to really understand. I know, Bethie, that I have been very protective over you all of your life. But you must know it's only because I love you so much. I never wanted to see you hurt or sad."

"But I now accept that you are growing up. It's time you know the truth so that you can learn to protect yourself when you get older and I am not always there."

"What do you mean, Miss Abby? We'll always be together you and I," she responded, trying not to become upset.

Miss Abigail smiled as she gently took the child's hands into her own. "Bethie, it's not that I wouldn't ever want to be with you. But you're growing up now. There will come a time when you will not want me with you every moment of your life. It's not because you wouldn't love me anymore. It's just part of growing up and becoming an independent, young lady."

Miss Abigail took a deep breath and began again. "You have an aunt. Her name is Emma Mae. She's a very powerful and wealthy woman. She owns a cotton-tobacco plantation in a city called Savannah in the state of Georgia."

"An aunt! I have an aunt? She lives in a con-fed-erate state. A rebel!" she added, dramatically, with eyes wide.

"Bethie! Please, let me finish."

"She is your father's only sister. I never spoke of her before because your father had forbidden me to. He made me promise that you would never know of her existence."

"Why_?" begged Bethie, confused.

"Well, your father never went into much detail with me, most likely out of shame. But your mother and I often spoke quite confidentially. We were very close. She loved your father so much."

"It broke her heart to hear some of the stories your father would tell her when in time of need. It would become at times, more than your mother could bear. He never knew this. She always wanted to be there for him. That was the kind of woman she was. So to ease her pain, she would confide in me. It worked both ways. Often, when I needed to, I would go to her."

"She had told me that your father and aunt were not close. She mistreated your father when he was a little boy in her care. He neither liked her, nor did he ever want her to know or be near any of his children."

"I know it must be very difficult to understand how a sister, or anyone for that matter, could hurt a child. But unfortunately, the world is not perfect and not everyone is loving. There are people who do evil things. Maybe because someone was bad to them when they were little. Or maybe instead of their body being sick, their mind is ill. I don't have all the answers, Bethie. I can only try to imagine."

"Anyway, after your parents had passed away, she found out about you. For years she has tried to obtain custody. She feels that because she is your only living relative, she is in the right."

"You won't let her, will you, Miss Abby?" pleaded Bethie, anxiously.

"Bethie, dearest, I'm not your mother. Aunt Liz and I are not even blood relatives. By law, there is only so much we can do. Along with your parent's lawyer, I have fought very hard these past years to keep her away."

"But I am so sorry to say, it was not enough. I went to a hearing yesterday in the city, concerning you. Do you know what a hearing is, Bethie?"

"Is it like a trial?"

"Kind of, I suppose."

"The judge in charge felt that it was in your best interest to go and live in Savannah so that you could have the opportunity of getting to know your Aunt Emma Mae. He thought it would be selfish to keep you from your only living aunt and cousin."

"Cousin! I have a cousin, too?" she questioned, overwhelmed.

"Yes, his name is William. He is two years older than you."

Bethie sat for a moment, forehead crinkled while staring downward trying to comprehend all that had been told her. "Leave Covington! Oh, Miss Abby, I don't want to go." Tears began to fill the child's eyes.

Miss Abigail swallowed hard and silently reminded herself not to cry for it would only make matters worse. She had to show Bethie that everything would be all right.

Abigail put her arms around Bethie and pulled her close. Don't cry, dearest... Everything is going to be fine, I promise."

"But what if she hurts me like she hurt Father?"

Immediately Miss Abigail turned Bethie around and looked deeply into her eyes. "You see here, Miss Sara Beth Covington! No one will ever hurt you. I will be there always to make sure of it. As God is my witness!"

"You're coming, too, Miss Abby?" replied Bethie, quite relieved.

"Of course! You didn't think I'd let you go away without me, did you?" she smiled.

Bethie returned the smiled, "No, Miss Abby. I knew you would never let anything happen to me."

She once again put her arms around Bethie and held her tightly. "Look on the bright side, Bethie. It won't be all that bad. You get to take a train ride. You've never done that before. And you have often reminded me of it."

"A train ride! Oh Boy!"

"There's more, too. You get to live near one of the most beautiful cities in our country. So I'm told... Do you know what they say, Bethie?"

"No, what do they say, Miss Abby?"

"They say your aunt is so rich that she has maids for every floor in that mansion."

"Oh my, Miss Abby, that house must be huge!"

"I'm sure it is."

"And just imagine... a cousin that is not much older than yourself."

"Too bad he's not a girl," she commented, with nose scrunched.

"Boys are not that bad. Who knows, you may become the best of friends. We always have to go into town for you to play with any of the local children. That's not very healthy, Bethie. You need a companion near your own age. You spend too much time around adults. You're a child. You need other children to play with."

"Can I take Miss Amy with us?"

"Absolutely!"

"But what about Covington? What about Aunt Liz and Joseph? Are they coming, too?"

"No, Bethie, they can't come. They have to stay here and take care of Covington. So that when you are old enough, it will be yours to run. But I promise we will come back every summer to visit them all. Agreed?"

"Yes, Miss Abby. Agreed!" answered Bethie, still a bit worried but excited and curious about her new, soon to be adventures.

For the next several days, at Miss Abigail's request, every adult at the estate tried eagerly to keep their spirits up for the child's sake. Miss Abigail refused to recall the events leading up to her and Joseph's encounter. She continued to keep busy by packing and making lists of instructions for Elizabeth.

As much as possible Joseph and Abigail kept conscientiously apart, as they tried not to bring attention to themselves. And because of the circumstances, their behavior blended normally and remained unnoticed. They were unable to look one another eye to eye, as every remark and request was of the utmost business like.

Finally the day came. It was early morning. Everyone hurried about eagerly making sure that both Bethie and Miss Abigail did not forget a thing. Their luggage was being loaded onto the carriage by Joseph, as Elizabeth nervously harped and lectured Miss Abigail.

"Now if you have any problems, whatsoever, sister, I want you to telegraph Mr. Holt immediately. He has assured me that I would be notified right away. If you are ill or Bethie becomes ill or Emma gives you any trouble or..."

"Elizabeth, please, stop! I'll never get to the train on time with you going on like this. Haven't we gone over all of this every day since the hearing? I love you immensely, Elizabeth, but frankly, you are getting on my nerves."

"I'm sorry, Abigail. I'm just so nervous about all of this. I am going to miss you so much."

"As will I, sister… As will I." Both sisters stopped to hold one another in comfort.

"Elizabeth, did you ask Abner to take us to Doylestown like I had requested?"

"No, I had intended to, but Joseph insisted on taking the both of you himself. I don't blame him. He is absolutely heartbroken to see you both go. That's all right, isn't it, Abigail?"

"That's fine, Elizabeth," she replied, trying to appear indifferent.

Bethie was already outside next to the carriage hugging and saying her goodbyes to the staff when Miss Abigail and Miss Elizabeth joined her. At least the day was a bright and sunny one, thought Miss Abigail not anticipating the inevitable.

She ran over to Miss Elizabeth and threw her arms around her chubby waist. "I'm going to miss you, Aunt Liz," replied Bethie sincerely.

Miss Elizabeth's eyes began to fill as she hugged Bethie tightly.

"Now Elizabeth, no tears. You promised," reprimanded Miss Abigail.

"I know, I know, but I am going to miss you too, dear. You and Abigail, both."

"Please don't cry, Aunt Liz. I'll be back next summer. I love you…"

"I love you, too, Miss Sara Beth."

Joseph helped Bethie into the carriage. Miss Abigail embraced her sister one more time, as they held each other for a few, long moments. "God be with you, my sister," she whispered lovingly. "And also with you, Elizabeth."

Miss Abigail's eyes looked downward, as Joseph gently escorted her into the carriage. Both continued to wave goodbye until they could no longer be seen.

Their destination was Doylestown, Pennsylvania where they would board a locomotive to begin their travels. They stopped only once at a lonely graveyard where Bethie's parents had been laid to rest. Bethie placed a bouquet of flowers arranged by Miss Elizabeth on both gravesites. Miss Abigail quoted a lovely prayer as Bethie stood with eyes closed and hands folded.

They arrived at the station on time; Bethie could hardly wait to get out of the carriage. She ran ahead ignoring Miss Abigail's warnings. Her anticipation of riding a locomotive for the first time had gotten the best of her.

Finally, as she turned the corner of the platform, there stood a humongous, steel, black monster. It hissed and whistled as mounds of steam rose high above her. Bethie stood still and stared in awe as she watched as though the locomotive was alive and breathing.

Miss Abigail's pace began to quicken from fear, as she quickly turned the corner of the platform where Bethie stood.

"Bethie! Young lady, I asked you not to run ahead! That is not like you to disobey me so."

"I'm sorry, Miss Abby, but I thought I'd surely burst if I had to wait another minute. Isn't she mag-nif-icent?"

"Yes, Bethie, she surely is quite a sight," agreed Miss Abigail looking with amazement at the size of the locomotive.

Bethie stayed with Joseph as Miss Abigail obtained the tickets. When she returned, Joseph removed their trunks and placed them next to the locomotive. He watched as they were loaded onto the train.

Miss Abigail and Bethie joined him as the conductor of the locomotive yelled out, "All aboard__!"

Miss Abigail leaned over to Bethie, "It's time to say goodbye to Joseph, dearest. Then I want you to go and stand next to the conductor while I go over a few last details with him."

Bethie nodded then slowly turned to face Joseph with tears forming in her sad eyes. "Joseph, I think I'm going to miss you most of all." His heart began to break as tears streamed down Bethie's little face. Regardless of who was about, he picked up the child and held her tightly.

She whispered in his ear, "I don't want to go, Joseph... Don't tell Miss Abby." He nodded sadly in agreement.

After a few moments of tender comfort, he gently placed her down then kneeled beside her. "Hush now, child, before ya go and make me cry too. We'll see each other very soon and I'll always be thinking of ya. I want ya to stay close to Miss Abigail and always do as ya told. Ya hear now? Promise me, child!"

"I promise, Joseph."

With eyes and head lowered, Bethie began to slowly walk away when she suddenly stopped to turn toward him again. "I love you, Joseph."

His heart was filled but empty at the same time as he responded back, "I love ya, too, Bethie girl. My heart is always with ya, child. No matter how far apart we are..."

Miss Abigail moved close to Joseph. And for the first time since their encounter, he and Abigail's eyes met. The pain and love they felt for one another was truly mutual- and cruel. Abigail could no longer hold back her emotions, as one lonely tear fell from her eye. Joseph's eyes, too, began to fill. Abigail stood frozen for a moment, as she realized, this was truly goodbye.

He took out a handkerchief from his pocket and gently pushed it into her hand. "I'm gonna miss ya, Miss Abigail... And I'm truly sorry for any pain I may have caused ya in the past. I hope ya can someday find it in your heart to forgive me... In my entire life, I have never met a woman like ya. And I truly believe, I never will again... Take care of yourself and the child."

Miss Abigail hesitated, trying to decide whether she should say the words she so desperately wanted to. "There is nothing to forgive, Joseph. I am sorry if I ever made you feel shame. You're a good, fine man. I hope and pray someday that you find a woman who is deserving of you. She will surely, be a lucky lady. Goodbye, Joseph."

Abigail turned away quickly, no longer able to stand the pain. She was helped onto the locomotive by the conductor, never looking back. She handed him their tickets, as he instructed his assistant to take them to their quarters.

Miss Abigail and Bethie were escorted to a private compartment located on the train. The gentleman lit a lamp that hung left to its private door, near an oak hat rack and pine storage closet.

The compartment was small and narrow, but suitable for the two of them, agreed Miss Abigail. Two long, finely, padded benches, facing each other, lined the room near the large window. To the right of the room were two bunks where they would sleep. He left the room, shutting the door behind himself. Abigail was grateful for the privacy.

She wearily removed her bonnet, hanging it on the rack. Bethie who was still quite excited blurted out, "Miss Abby, can I sleep on the top bunk?"

"Yes, Bethie, you may have the top bunk," responded Miss Abigail, finally sitting down, feeling numb.

She peered out the window only to become startled finding Joseph watching her from where he still stood. Their eyes locked, as the black locomotive let out two shrieking whistles and puffs of smoke. It began to move slowly as it passed where he stood. Their eyes revealed desperation, remaining locked until they were no longer in one another's view.

The journey to Savannah soon became a long and tiresome one. Their travels took them through many states and their countryside's. Miss Abigail and Bethie both hoped to arrive soon to their final destination. As like a child would behave, Bethie asked often if they would soon be there.

Miss Abigail spent much of her free time sitting next to the window reading a new book she had purchased for the journey called "Moby Dick". Bethie played with Miss Amy and her tea set on the floor of their compartment, in constant view of Miss Abigail.

From their window, one could view the beauty the south possessed. She was both lovely and elegant as a true southern bell would be. And unlike Atlanta, Savannah had been spared from complete annihilation. But along with her beauty was the unkind reminder of a war almost a decade old.

Every burned out building that once was someone's home, place of business, or a country landmark could surely tell a story, imagined Miss Abigail, remembering the war and its horrors.

A sad story that would begin with proud and brave souls who would rather die in tragedy and lose all in which they owned, than to admit that all men were indeed created equal. With it finally ending in defeat and utter destruction that would remind the south forever.

Emma Mae Calhoun

The train's pace began to slow, as the locomotive finally entered the city of Savannah. It was hard to appreciate her beauty the afternoon was dark, rainy, and downright dismal. Miss Abigail quickly helped Bethie to put on her coat and bonnet. "Now don't forget Bethie, this is a new and strange city. I am not familiar with the surroundings. So please, don't go wandering off. Stay right by my side until I figure out where we are going."

"Yes, Miss Abby. I will."

With Bethie in front of her, both headed down the slim corridor to the exit door of the train, the conductor's assistant following behind with their trunks. What a relief it was to be off the large locomotive, agreed Abigail, grateful to be on solid ground.

She held on tightly to Bethie's little hand swiftly looking about for shelter from the rain. "This way, ma'am," offered the conductor thoughtfully. He led the way with Miss Abigail and Bethie following quickly across a brick walkway leading to the station's pavilion. Though it did not have four walls, still there was a roof that would keep them dry for now. They quickly reached the pavilion, as the conductor's assistant placed their belongings near where they stood.

"You should stay dry here, ma'am. Is there anything more I can do for you?"

"No, I believe someone is to meet us here. We will wait until they arrive. Thank you for your kindness."

"My pleasure, ma'am. Hope you and the child enjoy your stay in Savannah. It surely is a lovely city. Good day to you both."

"Good day to you too, sir," responded Miss Abigail, trying to appear as though she was happy to be in Savannah.

They removed their bonnets while Miss Abigail tried to shake off the excess rain from them. She pulled out a handkerchief in attempt to wipe dry the child's face then her wet and foggy spectacles. Miss Abigail became a little worried as she wondered what to do next. *Bethie will catch a death of cold,* she imagined, wishing to remove the wet clothes from her.

Luckily, the rain had turned to a mild drizzle with the sun desperately trying to shine through. Thank God for small favors, thought Miss Abigail, hoping the sun would dry them. Next to their belongings was an old wooden bench, she instructed Bethie to sit while they waited.

Bethie sat as she began to curiously look about her surroundings. Although they were the only two people at the pavilion, despite the rain, there were many locals going about their daily business. It was midafternoon and the city streets were quite busy.

A carriage pulled by two beautiful black steeds pulled up alongside the pavilion. An old, white-haired, Negro man came down from the carriage and began to walk toward them. He was about medium height with a round, fat belly. He wore black pants and boots with a black vest to match. His straw hat moved side to side, as it was quite obvious that he walked pigeon toed.

He stood before Miss Abigail and quickly removed his hat. "Good afta-noon, ma'am! Y'all is waitin' ta head to the Calhoun plantation?"

"Yes… I am Miss Abigail Prescott and the child is Miss Sara Beth Covington."

"I'ze named Henry and it's a real pleasure ta make y'alls acquaintance. I'ze work for Miz Emma and is here ta fetch ya."

Henry paused as he looked down to examine the child. "Hello there, missy! Ain't no doubt—you is bout' as cute as a button."

Bethie blushed, "Thank you," smiling back up at him.

"Sorry I'ze bit late. The horses act a tad tempered in the rain. Silly old things, as big as day is, afraid of a little rain. Good Lord above, ain't never seen nothin' like it!" remarked Henry dramatically, followed by a few chuckles.

"That is quite all right, Henry. You're here now, and that is all that matters. Our belongings are next to the bench."

"Well then, come along ladies. I'ze best git ya in the carriage where it's dry and warm."

Bethie watched as Henry loaded their trunks onto the carriage. She leaned over to Miss Abigail and whispered, "I like him, Miss Abby. He's funny."

"I rather like him myself, too." Like a couple of school girls, they quietly giggled to one another.

Henry took it upon himself to become a Savannah tour guide, as the carriage began to leave the pavilion. He explained how they were currently positioned in the middle of the city and that the Calhoun plantation was situated directly outside of the city. Miss Abigail and Bethie soon became the curious tourists, despite the gloomy and rainy weather.

They looked about in every direction as the architectural beauty of the Victorian section captured their hearts. The lovely blocks of row houses with their columns and shutters, balconies, porches, and wrought iron gates were absolutely stunningly designed. Their towering azaleas and garlands of wisterias, together, were enough to take ones breath away. The gardens alone, magnificent and inspiring, were a sight to behold. They were filled with beautiful camellias and native shrubs.

Each cross section became a named square adding an air of wealth and refinement to the city. The scenery and grandeur could be compared to Europe, as it gave a similarity to the romance of Italy. Savannah was truly, an enchanted garden filled with architectural grace.

They passed by the business district and cobblestone water front. Bethie became amazed at how far the eye could see from the water level. To her, it was both massive and endless. The river in New Hope seemed insignificant in comparison.

The shipyard was filled with many merchant vessels; the vast majority owned by her aunt, explained Henry. How impressive thought Bethie, as she gasped in awe at their sizes. Never had she seen a place lovelier, admitted Miss Abigail.

As they began to leave the city their carriage traveled by an old confederate fort that had been badly burned. Along with many blocks thereafter were the scared remembrances of war long gone but still fresh in the memories of every true Georgian. Bethie questioned Miss Abigail about the massive destruction of burned out buildings that lay in near rubble all colored in black. It certainly seemed odd and out of place in a city as elegant and sophisticated as Savannah.

Miss Abigail explained to Bethie of Sherman's March and the destructive path created by him and his troops from Atlanta and continuing to the port of Savannah. Bethie now understood Joseph completely, as she recalled the stories he had once told. Stories of mass destruction with indignities, along with human suffering fueled by a war fought with passion by brother against brother. How quickly she would mature, agreed Miss Abigail sadly, and she knew it was only the beginning.

As the city slowly began to turn country both Miss Abigail and Bethie began to feel nervous. Although Bethie was told only what was absolutely necessary, both of their fears were that of the same. Miss Abigail put her arm around her as if to say, all would be fine. Mile after mile of pine, oak, and weeping willow trees lined their carriage on both sides, as they continued to travel on the dirt covered road.

After about an hour and a half from the time they had left the city, the entrance to the Calhoun plantation could be seen.

"We'ze here, ma'am!" yelled Henry, as the horses began their slow approach onto a long and straight stone entryway.

Reality quickly crept to mind. Miss Abigail could hardly theorize she was to actually live with this woman, as the beat of her heart immediately quickened.

"Now Bethie, remember what I told you. Mind your manners, and stay where I can see you. Do you understand?"

"Yes, Miss Abby. I understand."

"Remember, this is the south. Manners are everything. Don't forget to use the word ma'am at the end of every response. Understood, Bethie?"

"Ok, Miss Abby—ma'am," replied Bethie, anxiously trying to make light of it all. She could sense Miss Abigail's tension.

Miss Abigail, too nervous and upset, unfortunately did not find the humor in it.

The entrance was beautifully lined with shrubs individually, spaced perfectly. A few feet behind the shrubs, between them and on both sides, displayed a line of mature, elegant Weeping Willow trees. The drive was long as Bethie stretched her head out anxiously wanting to see the plantation.

The tree lined drive ended when the enormous mansion came into view. The building was massive in size causing Bethie to gasp. It was surely at least two or three times bigger than Covington, she estimated. As they came closer to the building, the drive opened to a large circular shape displaying a small pond in the middle filled with goldfish. Lily pads covered its surface.

The buggy pulled to the right coming to a complete halt in front of the main entrance. The mansion was magnificent and grand rising over three stories high, each floor with its own wraparound porch. Large, column pillars surrounded the building in every direction, each reaching high above the third level. Both the pillars and rails to the porches were painted bright white, as their architectural designs showed well even in the gloomy drizzle.

Beautiful gardens to the left and right of the mansion added color and absolute exquisiteness to the overall take of one's first impression. The building itself was painted an off-white, as she matched perfectly with the large, half moon, and three levels high, steps leading to the main entrance.

Miss Abigail, now leery and intimidated, held on tightly to

Bethie's little hand as they began to climb the stairs. The large, oak double-doors were painted white with two beautifully designed brass knockers hanging at eye level. Before she could knock, the door to the mansion was abruptly opened.

A woman about Miss Abigail's own age stood before them. Her hair was blonde and pulled back in a tight bun. She was tall, skinny, quite homely, and she wore a plain, neat dress. Because her expression was serious, her pointed nose became more prevalent.

"You must be Abigail Prescott."

"Yes… and this is Miss Sara Beth Covington."

"My name is Jane Sullivan. Mrs. Calhoun's private secretary." Both women shook hands.

The woman moved only her eyes as she peered down at Bethie. "Yes, Miss Sara, Mrs. Calhoun's niece. She has been looking forward to your arrival," replied the woman with no emotion. "I will be at your service if you need anything. Please do not hesitate to ask. If you follow me I would be happy to escort you both to your rooms."

They walked through the foyer into an enormous room, circular in fashion, with a staircase on both sides. As they headed toward it, Bethie looked straight up and could see far beyond the third floor. How little and insignificant she felt, as the building grew taller by the moment. Becoming a bit scared, she moved closer to Miss Abigail as her grip became even tighter. With Miss Jane leading the way, they followed closely behind her.

Abigail was not surprised when Jane continued up the third floor staircase, knowing the third floor was probably used for servants, leaving the second for Emma Mae and her son. Nevertheless, she said nothing accepting she had no rights in this mansion.

They finally reached the third floor, as Jane turned left and headed down a nearly darkened corridor. They were now facing the back of the building, as they passed a set of back stairs used mainly by the servants.

Miss Jane promptly stopped in front of the next door and opened it. "This will be your room, Sara Beth," exclaimed Jane in a matter of fact way. Bethie and Miss Abigail followed her inside.

Though the room was large, it was also quite plain. Not at all like a little girl's room would be, thought Bethie. Across the room were two long windows and a large fireplace between them. All the room consisted of was a pencil post bed, trestle table with lamp, a pine desk with a plank chair, and a cedar closet.

Although Miss Abigail could tell Bethie was a bit disappointed, she knew the room was clean, equipped with the essentials, and large enough for a separated play area.

"I'm afraid your room, Abigail, is located at the east wing of the mansion. This floor is rarely used except for this room and yours, I'm afraid the nearby ones are unattainable. I'd be happy to show you to your room now. If you'd like."

Bethie quietly gasped in horror at the thought of being all alone in an already uneasy situation. Miss Abigail could sense Bethie's fears and agreed, this arrangement would not do.

At first, Abigail was puzzled by the fact that her room was to be located clear across the other side of the mansion. There were so many rooms even in the nearby vicinity of Bethie's that were unoccupied and could be made livable, with little effort.

Emma Mae had plenty of time to make suitable accommodations for the two of them. Bethie who was only eight years old, most definitely needed an adult nearby for supervision and assistance. Not to mention the fact that the house was massive, and Bethie could easily get lost.

How could anyone be so insensitive? Could this be another attempt by Emma Mae to try and place distance between her and Bethie? Miss Abigail imagined accusingly. She soon came to the conclusion that their sleeping quarters had indeed been prearranged by her, as she began to feel annoyed and angry. Realizing Miss Jane was simply an employee of Emma's and only instructing what she was told to, Abigail tried to retain her emotions.

"I'm afraid that will be out of the question. I realize that I am simply a guest in this house. But I must insist that our rooms are either adjoining or next to one another," replied Miss Abigail quite stern to Jane.

"There is not much I can do about the situation today. It is quite late and none of the nearby rooms are suitable. Perhaps tomorrow I can speak to Mrs. Calhoun and try to arrange a more permanent arrangement."

Miss Abigail ignored Jane's snooty response, as she saw another door clear across the room that she had not noticed before. "Where does that door lead to?" she inquired, becoming curious.

Before Miss Jane could respond, Abigail swiftly opened it. The door lead to a small, adjoining, sitting room. It was occupied by a couple of hanging pictures, a Victorian sofa with two matching chairs, and a braided rug in the center.

"I'll take this room as my sleeping quarters," demanded Miss Abigail sternly. "But it's not-" Abigail interrupted Miss Jane. "I'll sleep with Miss Sara Beth tonight. And in the morning please have a few of the servants remove the current items in the room and replace them with a suitable bed for myself. I realize it is not much notice, but I will be more than happy to stay in Miss Sara Beth's room until the arrangement can be taken care of. Thank you."

Miss Abigail was unwilling to take no for an answer. Bethie was most impressed with Miss Abigail's stern demands, as she let out a sigh of relief. The whole idea of Miss Abigail's room being so far away had terrified her.

"Well, if you insist," said Miss Jane dumfounded and unable to think of quick enough argument against Abigail's demands.

"Indeed! I most definitely insist," replied Miss Abigail refusing to budge.

The tension was soon broken by Henry, as he entered the room with their belongings. Jane turned her attention from Miss Abigail, as she began to instruct him, "You may leave both of their trunks in this room, Henry. Also I would like you to start a fire and light the lamps in the room and hallway. It is starting to get dark."

"Yes, ma'am, Miz Jane," answered Henry promptly.

She again turned to face Miss Abigail. Her half smiling face gave away immediately that she was annoyed with Abigail, as she tried so desperately not to show it.

"Unfortunately, I'm afraid Mrs. Calhoun is a very busy woman and will not be able to meet with you both today. She has requested to see you both in the morning after breakfast. Mrs. Calhoun is pleased that you have both arrived safely and hopes that your stay here is a pleasant one."

"Your supper will be brought up to you for this evening as well as breakfast tomorrow morning. If you need anything else, please feel free to ask. You may use the back staircase that we passed earlier if you should need me this evening. It leads directly to the kitchen in which I can be easily located by one of the servants. Goodnight, Abigail. Miss Sara."

Both answered back with a sober, but relieved, "Goodnight."

They watched as she left the room leaving the door ajar. Abigail was grateful that her persistence had prevailed, as she began to relax and remove her bonnet and cape. Bethie watched Henry as he continued his chores at the fireplace.

Henry sensed their anxiety and tension, as he thought of a comforting word to say. "Don't give no mind ta Miz Jane. That juss her way, always has been. Uh huh, that's right, as long as I know her. Never known that woman ta be lookin' happy. No ma'am! Sometimes I think if that poor woman would smile, her face would juss crack in two from her never gone and done it!"

Bethie exploded with laughter, as she could hardly believe the words that came from Henry's mouth. Obviously, he was neither scared nor intimidated by Miss Jane.

"Bethie!" scolded Miss Abigail, trying not to laugh herself.

"I'ze not tryin' ta show disrespect ma'am. Juss wantin' y'all ta feel at home."

"That's quite all right, Henry. We appreciate that. Leaving our home in which we love dearly, for the both of us, has been very difficult. It's good to know we have a friend."

"That ya do ma'am! That ya do," responded Henry in a comforting tone.

Miss Abigail began to unpack their belongings, as Henry finished lighting the fire and lamps while he continued to converse with Bethie. She was curious, like most children, about her new surroundings. She had never seen or been on a plantation before. All she knew was what Joseph had told her.

Henry understood and tried to answer all of her questions. He was a good and patient man, agreed Miss Abigail. His witty demeanor seemed to comfort them both, and took the edge off.

Abigail gently laid their night clothes across the bed. Even as the drizzle turned into a heavy rain causing darkness sooner than usual, the room filled with brightness from the fire and lamps—and of course Henry.

"Well… I do believe y'all set now. If ya needin' anythin', ya best comin' ta me. I'ze take good care of ya both. Hopefully, tomorrow be a sunny day. Much better if ya gitten' ta see the plantation durin' the day. She be as pretty as can be. Hope ta show ya around a bit. Goodnight now, Miz Sara Beth."

"Goodnight, Henry. You can call me Bethie if you want. All of my friends do back home."

"Well surely, if ya like… cept for when Miz Emma's lookin'. I don't believe she'd take ta that. Goodnight now—Bethie." Miss Abigail accompanied Henry over to the door, while Bethie sat to brush Miss Amy's hair from the long trip.

"I meant what I says, Miz Abigail. I'ze there if ya need me. Ya best comin' ta me first. I think ya both real fine ladies. Surely hope ya can find happiness here. Miz Jane don't bother me none…"

Henry hesitates as he checks to see if Bethie is listening. He lowers his voice to a whisper and begins again, "But ya best take care when it comes ta Miss Emma. Between you and me, she a different breed all together. Uh huh… Ya best stay away from that one. Ya hearin' what I'ze sayin', Miz?" warned Henry.

"Yes… unfortunately, I do understand. We appreciate your help but most of all your friendship. Thank you."

"Ya quite welcome, ma'am. Goodnight now."

"Goodnight, Henry," smiled Miss Abigail sincerely, closing the door behind him.

Bethie tried hard to see the mansion's grounds from her bedroom window, but because of the rain and darkness she was unable to. She climbed on the windowsill and cupped her hands around her eyes with nose pressed against the glass for a possible better view.

Miss Abigail sat on the bed to watch Bethie for a moment.

"Bethie, come here please. I'd like to talk to you."

She scrambled off the windowsill. Abigail placed her arms around the child and pulled her close. "Hopefully tomorrow the sun will come out. Then you and I can take a little tour around the plantation. Would you like that?"

"Yes ma'am, I would."

"Is everything fine, Bethie?" she questioned.

"I'll be OK Miss Abby as long as you're with me." Abigail gave a little squeeze. "I like Henry. He makes me laugh. How about you? Do you like him, too?"

"Yes, very much. I think we've made our first friend here in Savannah," smiled Abigail, gratefully.

"I don't really care for Miss Jane. She looks so cross. I don't think she likes us."

"Now Bethie, you don't even know her. It's not fair that you decide not to like her before getting a chance to really know her. Don't you think?"

"We'll I guess… But still, I say she doesn't like me. And I don't think getting to know her will make any difference at all."

"Who wouldn't like you? They'd have to be funny in the head," teased Miss Abigail tickling Bethie on the bed. She giggled loudly, begging Miss Abigail to stop.

Although Abigail thought Emma Mae was rude for not seeing her only niece until tomorrow still, she was relieved for the extra day. It didn't seem to bother Bethie and would give them a chance to get settled in.

A small pine table and two chairs were brought to their room along with their supper that evening. Abigail told Bethie the table could also be used for their lessons and tea time with Miss Amy. They ate their supper alone then dressed for bed. After prayers were said, Miss Abigail read Bethie a story until the child fell asleep.

Abigail laid wide-eyed and worried and could not get comfortable in her new living arrangements. She absolutely loathed Emma Mae and wondered how she could ever possibly live in the same house with her. Miss Abigail knew, somehow, she must find a way. *What will tomorrow bring?* She wondered, once again praying for guidance.

Both woke early the next day and quickly dressed and ate their breakfast. Bethie sat on the windowsill with Abigail standing behind her. The sun shined brightly and a mild breeze swayed the weeping willows in the nearby fields. It was amazing what one could see from upon that window, agreed Bethie, as she viewed the entire grounds from where she sat.

Miss Abigail agreed that the plantation was absolutely beautiful. The gardens were magnificent with color. The grass was so green and sky bright blue that it only added to the loveliness of it all. Clusters of peach orchards could be seen west of the grounds.

Almost as far as one could see were fields of cotton already being attended to in this early morning. Various sizes of buildings were displayed throughout the land making Bethie curious as to what they were used for. Miss Abigail assured her that they would both find out soon enough.

"Look Miss Abby, horses!" blurted Bethie, excited.

Far west of their window they could see a pasture filled with beautiful horses eating and playing in the morning sun. Bethie loved horses and had often helped Joseph in feeding, washing, and brushing them, hoping he would take her riding. She was getting older now and would soon have proper instruction. Maybe even her own horse, she imagined excited.

They were interrupted by a knock at their door. Miss Abigail knew it was Jane coming to get them both. Unavoidably, the time had come for Bethie to meet her aunt. A rush of anxiety flooded Abigail as she quickly looked down at the child.

Bethie did not seem worried or upset; she was at least thankful for that. She was curious to meet her Aunt Emma but at the same time quite reserved for a child.

Miss Abigail opened the door calmly as she forced a smile. "Good morning, Abigail. Good morning, Miss Sara," greeted Miss Jane looking over toward Bethie. They both responded cordially. "Mrs. Calhoun has requested to see both of you this morning in her study. If you will follow me, I will show you the way."

"Bethie, it is time for you to meet your Aunt Emma," instructed Abigail, trying to remain calm.

"Yes, ma'am," replied Bethie with much maturity.

Abigail was very proud of her, especially over the past few weeks. It was astounding to her how mature and responsible the child had become.

Hand in hand, both followed behind as Miss Jane led the way. They back tracked the route in which Jane had taken them yesterday, once again finding themselves in the main corridor of the mansion. They began to head east on the first floor. She stopped before two double doors where plank chairs where positioned on both sides. Miss Jane asked them both to be seated, as she gently knocked twice then entered the room alone shutting the doors behind her.

They both said nothing to each other, as the moment drew nearer causing some panic within. Bethie's mind was plagued with many thoughts of her aunt. None really good. She even tried to answer each question in her little head, as one after another entered her mind unwilling to give her a break in thought. She hoped that her aunt would not expect her to express happy emotions. Bethie knew meeting her would make no difference.

Because of the love and trust she had for Miss Abigail her impression of her Aunt Emma, unfortunately, had already been formed. She believed her Miss Abby and had no doubts, whatsoever, what she had said to her was the truth. She told herself that she would be strong, but polite, and under no circumstances would she cry.

Bethie tried to think of something else, as she got up from the chair and began to look at the oil paintings that were displayed on the walls. Miss Abigail, unable to stay seated too, joined her.

"Who are the people in the pictures, Miss Abby?"

"I don't know, Bethie. I suppose they are your relatives, though I don't recognize any of them. Perhaps they are from your dead uncle's side." They studied the paintings on both sides of the walls. The diversion seemed to work as both became engrossed in them.

Miss Abigail's eyes fell upon one in particular. It was a portrait of a young lady, possibly in her late teens or early twenties, standing next to a little boy. He caught her attention more so than she. The two seemed quite odd together. While the girl stood confident almost grinning, the boy neither smiled nor showed any emotion.

His eyes were dull, lifeless, and appeared filled with fear. It was as though all hope and life within had been drained from them, thought Miss Abigail, as she studied the portrait even closer. She flinched in horror as she suddenly recognized him.

The young child's eyes captured her to only torture her heart, as tears began to form in her eyes. For he was indeed her one time employer, and most definitely her friend, Jon Covington, Bethie's father. She swiftly turned her back toward the painting wanting to shield it from Bethie.

Luckily, the door to Emma's study opened as Miss Jane instructed them to go inside. "Mrs. Calhoun will now see you."

Miss Abigail immediately straightened her appearance, whispering down to Bethie to remember her manners. It all seemed so formal thought Bethie, as she entered the room holding onto Miss Abby's hand. She felt several gentle squeezes as a sign of reassurance.

The room was quite large and decorated fancy in a business-like manner. The woodwork was exquisite. Except for the large fireplace, both sides of the walls had shelves filled with many books and several paintings and antiques. A large oak desk centered the room at the very far end. Though it was a sunny day, the room still appeared shadowed and dismal.

Centered in front of the desk with hands folded while slightly grinning, stood Emma Mae Calhoun watching the two enter the room. Miss Abigail stood tall and stiff looking directly at Emma Mae as both walked up to her. She gave an air of confidence and sophistication.

Emma Mae was now in full view as both began to examine one another. Bethie thought the woman to look dark and decrepit, as her attire, completely black, seemed to emphasize her impression. Her hair, which appeared grey, was pulled back so tightly in a bun that Bethie wondered if she were in pain from it.

Although the woman's physique was slim, her face was old and wrinkled as were her hands. Emma Mae's dismal appearance sent a spark of terror through Bethie's entire body. She swallowed hard to help fight back the fear.

Miss Abigail wanting to alleviate the formalities began, "Hello, Emma Mae," refusing to address her formally. Abigail felt they were both forced participants, simply two pawns, orchestrated by Emma through her money and power. But Emma Mae was amused, ignoring protocol. She truly believed she had won. The child was here—and she was now in control.

"Welcome, Abigail… I trust your travels to Savannah were a safe and pleasant one," she began, trying to be both civil and convincing.

"Yes, the transfer went well. Thank you." Abigail hesitated for a moment not knowing what else to say. "I'd like you to meet Miss Sara Beth. Sara, this is your Aunt Emma Mae." Miss Abigail let go of the child's hand and gently positioned Bethie in front of her.

Bethie slowly peered up to meet Emma's black eyes. "Good morning, ma'am," she said politely, refusing to be intimidated.

Emma Mae reached out her hand to shake Bethie's. The wrinkled hand felt cold and clammy, as Bethie wished the woman would, soon, let go.

"And good morning to you, too, Sara. So… finally after all this time, I get to meet my late brother's child." Emma Mae studied Bethie's face. "You don't look much like Jon," commented Emma as though Bethie was a specimen. "However, you are quite lovely."

"Thank you, ma'am," she forced, wanting to remain polite, despite Emma's remark.

"How old are you? Eight is it?"

"Yes, ma'am."

"It's a sin that eight years had to pass before I could meet my dead bother's only child. Simply a sin!" snapped Emma Mae. She deliberately terrified Bethie, catching her off guard by her quick change in tone. But still, she forced herself to remain calm, her face displayed no fear causing Emma to become annoyed. Miss Abigail's defenses were up as Emma Mae paid notice and soon backed down.

Emma, realizing that she had made a mistake, immediately calmed herself. "Well, this certainly is no time for ill feelings. I have always been a believer that the past, should stay in the past. And it's now high time to look upon the bright side of all of this," lied Emma Mae so easily.

"You're here now, Sara, and we're going to have plenty of time to get to know each other. I'm sure you must have been told that you also have a cousin. He is my only child. His name is William, my pride and joy. He will be returning tomorrow from boarding school. I'm confident the two of you will get along rather well."

"Furthermore," Emma Mae now looking at Miss Abigail too, "I do hope the two of you enjoy living here on the Calhoun plantation. I've instructed Jane to give you a full tour of the grounds this morning. Feel free to roam and enjoy its beauty whenever you like. This is now your home, too… Jane will go over the schedule with you. If you need anything, at any time, just let her know."

"I've been informed, Abigail, your quarters were not to your liking. Therefore, I have instructed Jane to correct the problem immediately. I do wish you both a pleasant stay and hope you do not become too home sick. Savannah is truly an enchanting city. I'm sure as time goes by, you both will agree as you find this to be true."

"Although I do eat most of my meals in private, I do expect Bethie to join me for supper every evening sharply at 6 p.m. in the main dining room. This period is strictly for family, and I wish not to offend, Abigail." Miss Abigail stared back at Emma Mae concerned with her demand but dumbfounded as to what to say. "I do not encourage lateness from William, and the same rules will apply to you."

"Yes, ma'am."

"Well then… I have business to attend to this morning. Jane will be waiting to accompany you both on the tour. Good day, Sara Beth, Abigail."

"Good day, ma'am," replied Bethie relieved that it was all over. Miss Abigail nodded, "Emma," then took Bethie's hand as they left the room closing the door behind them.

Emma Mae stood still as she watched them both leave. The child had finally arrived, as Emma felt a twinge of victory knowing a small battle had just been won. It's only the beginning, she thought, alone in her study grinning and pleased with herself.

They returned to their rooms to retrieve their bonnets. To Miss Abigail's surprise, the sitting room off Bethie's bedroom had already been converted while they had been with Emma Mae. The beds had been stripped and made with clean linen. The curtains in both rooms were pulled allowing the sun to engulf them. Even their breakfast dishes had been removed, and the table wiped clean and left neat with a bouquet of flowers in the middle.

Bethie found an entrance from Miss Abigail's new room onto the wraparound porch. Along with Miss Abigail's help, the two managed to pry open the swollen door. Abigail guessed it had been the first time it had ever been opened. What a waste of space, she thought, thinking of Emma Mae, her son, and a few servants as the only occupants of the mansion.

The sun felt warm on their faces, as their chins pointed upward with eyes shut absorbing its rays. The grounds of the plantation looked even more magnificent from where they stood, agreed Bethie, even more anxious than ever to go on the tour.

"So Bethie… tell me, dear, how was it meeting your Aunt Emma?" wondered Abigail concerned.

"She's OK, I guess… about what I expected, Miss Abby."

"Yes, I'd have to agree, Bethie, not a very pleasant woman is she?"

"No, she's not, Miss Abby," giggled Bethie with hand over her mouth.

"Do I really have to eat supper every night alone with her? Without you, Miss Abby?"

"Does she frighten you?"

Bethie, not wanting to worry Miss Abigail, replied, "No, she doesn't scare me."

"Well, she indeed caught us off guard with that demand, didn't she? The woman does seem to be very busy. And with any luck, won't be able to spend too much time with you. Remember your cousin is to return sometime tomorrow. So you won't be alone."

"I know she makes you feel uneasy, Bethie. I'll pray that changes as you and Emma get to know each another. I understand how living in a home that makes you feel uncomfortable would be quite difficult. But always remember, dearest, we are in this together. Thick or thin, right?"

Smiling, Bethie replied, "Yes, thick or thin, Miss Abby." She gave her a little squeeze and a kiss on the top of her head.

They met Miss Jane in the foyer as she had requested. She decided to give them a tour of the mansion before the grounds since they were already inside. Miss Abigail and Bethie found the staff to be quite pleasant, with the exception of Jane whom Miss Abigail did not trust or like from the moment they met.

An open carriage pulled by one black horse awaited them at the front of the main entrance. Bethie was pleased to find Henry to be their driver. The carriage pulled off the stone entryway onto a dirt path leading through a garden and around to the back of the mansion. They passed many buildings that had been abandoned since the end of the war and the abolishment of slavery.

A kitchen, smokehouse, and small slave cabins had been unused for many years. What was once the Overseer's house was now Henry and his family's. Next to the Overseer's house was a building in which candle making took place and beside it carpentry.

During their tour, they were introduced to all the members of the staff, both Negro and white. Most of the Negro staff seemed to be related to Henry in one way or another, as he pointed out his relatives as they continued along the trail.

The carriage took a path that led straight through the center of the cotton and tobacco fields. They were large and open as Bethie turned her head right to left trying to see where they ended. Many Negro workers stopped for a moment to say hello, as the carriage passed their way.

Miss Jane explained along with Mrs. Calhoun's shipping business, cotton and tobacco were sold for profit these days on the plantation. And that before the war, when Mr. Calhoun was alive, they had grown rice, pecans, and peanuts. Peaches and apples were also sold for profit. Once the Negroes became free, Emma Mae no longer felt them to be economical. Barely a quarter of the plantation was still in use.

The carriage began to head west, as the loud clinking sound of the cotton gin caught their attention coming from a large building centered in the middle of the fields. They passed the stables, barn, and a blacksmith's shop. Henry's son, who was the blacksmith, was shoeing a horse as they passed by. He stopped for a moment to wave to Bethie.

A small vegetable garden could be seen as they entered the peach orchards. The sweet smell of peaches entered Bethie's nostrils, as she soon began to feel hungry. From the pastures, beautiful horses gallop free in the warm sun. They frolicked to and fro, taking a moment every now and then to eat from the earth. The tour ended as the carriage entered onto the stone entryway from the west side of the mansion.

Miss Abigail made sure Bethie was dressed and ready on time for supper; though she did not look forward to the evening. Abigail reassured her, if needed, she would be in the kitchen close by. She walked Bethie up to the entrance of the main dining room but insisted she enter the room by herself. It was large, formal, and quite elegant as Bethie was seated by a servant.

Emma Mae who was already there and seated, greeted Bethie but never once said another word during the entire meal. Bethie kept to herself, feeling her Aunt's eyes on her constantly. This made it very difficult for her to maintain an appetite; she ate only what she could force down.

She was relieved when supper was over and given permission by Emma Mae to leave the table. But unhappy to find Miss Abby feeling under the weather. Miss Abigail who was still uneasy and unfamiliar with the mansion, asked Bethie to stay in her room that evening while she rested. *Perhaps it was something I ate,* wondered Abigail, light headed and nauseated.

Bethie awoke the next morning to find her feeling worse. "Would you like me to go and tell the cook to bring you up breakfast, Miss Abby?"

"No Bethie! Food, I'm afraid, would only make me feel worse. But perhaps a cup of tea with a bit of honey might help. I would really appreciate that, dearest. I hate to let you roam this place by yourself, but I don't think I can get out of bed yet." Miss Abigail gave another desperate attempt to lift her head from the pillow, only to find herself dizzy and weak causing her to lie back again.

"Do you remember how to get around?"

"Yes, I remember!" she blurted, excited in getting permission to go by herself.

After Bethie dressed, she went down to the kitchen to request a cup of tea for Miss Abby. The kitchen staff hovered over her, enjoying having a child in the house again. She ate her breakfast while being constantly doted upon by the cook and servants. She felt safe and appreciated the kind attention after meeting Miss Jane and her Aunt Emma.

As like yesterday, the day was bright and sunny. Bethie stood on the wraparound porch overlooking the plantation, enjoying its warmth. From where she stood, she could see Henry who was working in the cotton fields this early morning. He caught sight of her and both waved good morning to one another.

Even though Bethie felt obligated to take care of Miss Abigail, she wanted so to go outside and explore her new home. Abigail watched from her bedside contemplating whether to allow Bethie to go off on her own. She felt it to be unfair that the child should suffer indoors all day because of her illness. The day was warm, sunny, and much too lovely for a growing child to be kept inside.

"Bethie, come inside for a spell," requested Miss Abigail.

"How are you feeling, Miss Abby?"

"I'm afraid worse than yesterday, dearest. I must have some kind of stomach bug, I guess. My head is just spinning like a top… and I can't seem to keep anything down in that stomach of mine."

"I'm sure the sudden change of residence and traveling didn't help much. And I'm still not quite used to southern cooking yet… A lot of adjustments to be made, I suppose. But I'm confident in time, I'll get used to it all."

"Miss Jane said she would keep an eye on you today while you played outside."

"But I can't just leave you here all by yourself, Miss Abby! Someone needs to take care of you."

"Nonsense, Bethie! I'm sure I'll be better by tomorrow. I believe a day of rest will do the trick. Miss Jane insisted on sending for the doctor anyway. So don't you go worrying about your Miss Abby. I'll be fine, dearest. I don't want you stuck inside with a sick person all day. It's not healthy. It's too beautiful of a day to be wasted."

"You run along and play now. Wear your cape and bonnet. I can feel a little breeze in the morning air. Make sure you tell Miss Jane you're going outside before you leave the mansion."

"OK, I will, Miss Abby. I'll come and check on you often." She put on her cape and bonnet then gave Miss Abigail a gentle kiss on her forehead. She grabbed Miss Amy from her cradle, gently closing the door behind her and skipping excitedly down the hall.

Bethie took the back staircase that led to the kitchen in search of Miss Jane. Neither the cook nor servants knew where she was, although they told her to try the library located across from her Aunt Emma's study. Miss Jane had a desk in the library and often worked on the books there.

She remembered the location of Emma's study, as she left the kitchen with Miss Amy in hand. Before she could pass by the main staircase, she heard her Aunt Emma arguing with Miss Jane in the foyer.

Bethie did not want her aunt to notice her as she very gently and on her tippy-toes crossed the staircase. She knew she had been unnoticed and as quiet as a mouse when the pattern of their voices remained unchanged.

"Damn Negroes! Wanting more than they deserve. How dare they ask for more money!" shrieked Emma Mae, face beet red and nostrils flaring. "They're so ungrateful I tell you! Don't I give them a pick of any cabin on this plantation and free food along with their wages?"

"Yes ma'am, you certainly do," agreed a cowardly Miss Jane.

"They are disrespectful and ungrateful. I should rid every one of them off my land. Damn Lincoln… hope he rots in hell! Got what he deserved, he did."

"Yes ma'am, you're right…"

"Mrs. Calhoun… I don't want to seem a bit trifle or unsympathetic to your financial situation," shuddered Jane afraid of Emma when she got this way. "But you must know that Henry was offered higher wages from Basil Patterson. I overheard him talking to his son the other day about it. Because Basil's land is so large and in desperate need right now of cotton pickers, he offered to take his whole family too. With the price of cotton still down and it being his main source of income, he has to pick more now than ever to make ends meet."

"If we lose Henry, because they are all related, there is a great chance we will lose them all. Henry is your best worker, ma'am," pleaded Jane desperately.

"That is just like Basil going behind my back trying to steal my workers. Give'em what they want! Basil Patterson and his plantation can go to hell. You send him a letter from me, Jane. Let him know he may as well sell Patterson to me, because not one worker of mine will ever pick for him. You and he can be sure of that. You let him know I'm onto the bastard."

"Yes, ma'am! I'll take care of it right away," replied Jane relieved.

Though Jane's disposition was normally quite miserable, her heart wasn't as evil as Emma Mae's. She, like many others, was blinded by greed. Although Emma Mae did pay her well, throughout the years she had earned every penny. She basically did whatever Emma Mae requested, whether scrupulous or not.

Jane was both loyal and committed to Emma Mae. She was a smart woman who picked up on Abigail's immediate distrust in her. Jane was indeed loyal to Emma, always and first. But in her heart, she did not blame Abigail.

For whatever reason, she liked her and was glad she was aware of her relationship to Emma Mae. Slowly but surely, Emma's schemes, plots, and treacheries throughout the years were beginning to wear hard on her conscience.

After Bethie felt safe and out of view from her Aunt Emma and Miss Jane, she ignored their conversation and could barely make out their words. She was grateful for that and for the fact that her aunt looked dressed to leave the plantation for the day.

Bethie would be able to explore the grounds without worrying about running into her. She easily found Emma Mae's study and library on the other side of the hall. She decided to wait for Miss Jane and, once again, began to look at the portraits hung to help pass the time.

Searching for ones that she had not viewed yesterday, she came upon the one of her father as a boy. How sad the boy looked to her, thought Bethie, as she wondered if he had been ill.

"So... I see you have found the portrait of your father. When he was a young boy," commented Emma Mae in a matter of fact way. Bethie gasped in horror, as she became startled by Emma Mae's sudden appearance directly behind her.

"Excuse me, ma'am... I didn't know you were there," explained a frightened Bethie. She took a few steps back creating additional distance between them.

Emma Mae glared down at the child, grinning and delighted. Bethie was angry with herself for allowing her aunt to frighten her.

"It's a portrait of your father and me when we were both young. He was a handsome young man, wasn't he, Sara?"

Bethie swallowed hard trying to toughen herself, "Yes, ma'am."

"You know, we were very close in those days. I loved him very much. It breaks my heart to have never been able to say goodbye to him. He was the only brother that I ever had."

Emma paused for a few moments, remembering. Her facial expression turned bitter. "It wasn't until the Mexican war and he met that woman!"

Bethie knew immediately that she was referring to her mother. But still, she remained calm.

"My mother, ma'am?" pretended Bethie.

"Yes! Your mother, Sara. She ruined my brother. If it weren't for her, he'd still be alive today."

Tears began to fill Bethie's eyes as she gently started to shake. She squeezed her eyes tightly refusing to allow herself to cry.

"You know of course, your mother was a half-breed," added Emma Mae cruelly, refusing to stop.

"What do you mean, ma'am?" she questioned, confused and upset.

"Why, I don't believe it… Your dear, sweet Abigail never told you! Did she? Well child, let me offer you a bit of history concerning your family tree. I think you're old enough to know the truth."

"Many years ago, your mother's family settled west. During a Mexican rampage your mother's family was completely murdered except for your grandmother. She of course was ravaged then left for dead. It was a miracle she lived, at all. That was how your mother was conceived."

Bethie confused, shaken, and utterly horrified began to slowly walk backwards. "You're mean…. And awful! What a horrible thing to say! My mother and father were good people! And you know nothing about them!" Bethie turned and fled from Emma's near grasp, clinging desperately to Miss Amy.

"If you don't believe me, why don't you ask your dear Abigail," continued Emma Mae grinning, as she watched the child flee from her very sight.

She ran passed the main staircase straight to the foyer, as she desperately searched for an escape from the mansion and Emma Mae. She flung open the double doors to the front entrance and continued running without a notion of where she was running to.

Onto the path and through the gardens she ran, circling the mansion to the back. Though her eyes were both filled, she refused to allow tears to fall. She was disoriented and horrified as the past few minutes taunted her little mind.

Henry looked up from the field in which he was working to find Bethie running through the middle as fast as she could. He could tell she was upset and looked toward the mansion as if he knew. Her little doll bobbed about in her right hand.

"Where ya off ta, missy? Come back here now, ya hear!" yelled Henry concerned.

Bethie neither heard him nor showed any sign of slowing, as Henry nodded to the other workers he would go after her.

She stopped every now and then trying to catch her breath. Feeling as though she had not run far enough, she continued running. She climbed several hills, hoping they would blind the mansion from her view. But her boot caught a stone making her trip and tumble down the hill, causing her bonnet and Miss Amy to be thrown in separate directions.

Luckily the hill was grassy and protected her fall. She lay in the grass dirty and upset. Her long ringlets of hair were filled with blades of grass and leaves. After trying to wipe clean the dirt from her hands and elbows, she gave up and threw herself face down into the hill and wept. At least there would be no one to see her cry, she thought sadly.

"Miz Sara, Miz Sara Beth! Where's ya be, missy?" hollered Henry from afar, worried.

Bethie heard Henry calling her and abruptly sat up, wiping the tears from her face. "I'm over here, Henry."

He came over the hill to find Bethie sitting on the ground with legs straight out in front of her. He had gathered Miss Amy and her bonnet along the way.

He could see her dirty arms and face and realized she had fallen. "Is ya hurt?" he questioned, kneeling down beside her as he handed Bethie her belongings.

"I'm fine, Henry. I just had a little fall. Tripped over a rock or something."

"Why in Heaven's name were ya running like a wild horse? Somebody upset ya?"

"No, Henry! I was just playing and then I tripped and fell." He knew she did not want to talk about it.

"Best I take ya back ta the house."

"NO! I mean… not right now."

"What's wrong, child? Let me help ya…"

Bethie desperately needed someone to confide in. Unable to hold them back, tears began to fall onto her dirty face. She trusted Henry and decided it would be all right to cry in front of him. "My Aunt

Emma… she said terrible things to me, Henry. I don't know why she hates me so. I just got here. Why did she even want me to come? I don't understand," cried Bethie.

Henry put his arm around her little shoulder, sitting next to her. "Here now, child. Everythins' gonna be all right. I'ze gonna tell ya somethin' ya gotta keep ta yourself. Promise me!"

"I promise Henry," replied Bethie, curiously. She stopped crying to listen eagerly to what Henry had to say.

"Miz Emma… well, she a strange one—she is. Ain't much inside that woman. Some say she ain't got no heart, no indeed! I'ze gonna tell ya somethin' now missy, ya best not forget. Ya stay away from her. It don't matter none that she is ya aunt. Ya stay far away, ya hearin' me, child?"

"Yes sir," replied Bethie wide-eyed.

"None of it is ya doin', she always been this way. If ya need anythin' ya go to ya Miz Abigail or me. I'ze take good care of ya. I give ya my word, Miz Sara—I mean, Bethie," he smiled.

Henry convinced her that Emma Mae's attitude was not her fault and that she had always been a nasty woman, "not quite right, that one" as he put it, and she shouldn't take it personal.

She felt reassured and gave him a big hug. "Thank you, Henry. You're my best friend here!"

"Well I'ze be, what a fine compliment, missy. Thank ya," responded Henry, blushing.

"Now I best git back. Got work ta do. Ya come with me and I'ze show ya how good old southern cotton is picked."

"OK, Henry. But can I have a few minutes alone with Miss Amy first? I can walk back by myself."

"Well… guessin' it'll be all right. Ya hurry along then, hear?"

"I will," replied Bethie as she watched him return to his work.

She picked up Miss Amy and turned the doll around to face her. "I wish we were back in New Hope, Miss Amy. I miss Joseph and Aunt Liz terribly. I was so happy there and everybody was so nice to me. It seems so unfair that I had to leave. My new aunt is worse than I ever thought," she confessed, pushing back the tears.

"She hates me so, and says terrible things to me. I don't know why. She doesn't even know me… Well, Miss Amy, we at least have Miss Abby and Henry. That's more than some people have in a whole life time, I suppose."

After picking the grass from her hair and brushing off her and Miss Amy's clothes, Bethie got up to leave. Before she turned up the hill, her eyes caught a glimpse of a small island situated in a nearby lake.

She quickly ran to the top of the hill so she could get a better view. The island captivated her. She noticed it was completely surrounded by water. *A little island! What a great place to hide,* imagined Bethie. "She could never find me there. Nobody could!"

How secluded and uncharted it appeared to her. It wasn't too small, but on the other hand, it wasn't too big. *God must have made it for a child*, agreed Bethie, as she repositioned herself and tried to get a better view. "But how can I get across without getting wet?"

Bethie was determined to find a way and quickly made up her mind to investigate. She had completely forgotten her promise to Henry. This time she was careful to walk down the hill all the way to the edge of the water.

The island was magnificent, she thought. She began to walk the length looking for a way onto it. It was filled with trees and shrubs, wild flowers, and weeds giving it an exotic look.

To the far east of the island she noticed two large trees that had fallen from a storm onto the island itself. They caused a bridge between where she stood and the island. She hesitated awhile as she wondered what Miss Abby would say if she found out. But like on occasion, her curiosity had gotten the best of her. She was entirely captivated and transfixed by the find and felt compelled to explore her.

She climbed up onto one of the large trees that lay partially in the water and above its surface. Bethie thought it was such a coincidence how the trees had made a perfect bridge over to it, causing a child to become hypnotized and driven to wander to her. She slowly crossed and in no time at all was on the other side.

There was a path made by nature allowing Bethie to make her way through the trees and brush. She came upon a clearing completely surrounded and camouflaged from the world. How safe she felt, as she sat with knees pulled to her chin and arms holding tightly. "She's mine!" she swore, claiming the island for herself.

"You mustn't tell anyone about our find, Miss Amy. It must always be kept a secret! Promise me now… I promise too. I'll never tell anyone that she exists. Isn't she just perfectly, wonderful," blurted Bethie to the ragdoll.

"Henry! Oh no…"

Bethie quickly scrambled to her feet to leave. It wasn't as if she was purposely trying to disobey him. But her wonderful find had caused her to forget completely about the promise made to him. *He must be wondering where I am by now. I'm sure he's on his way to find me*, imagined Bethie, not wanting Henry to catch her on the island.

She was convinced that he would lecture her on the dangers, then forbid her to ever go to the island again. Perhaps he would even tell Miss Abigail. She was very ill and did not need additional worries, agreed Bethie. The secret existence of the island needed to be protected, as she quickly put on her bonnet and grabbed Miss Amy.

She began to leave the clearing, heading toward the edge of the trees looking for the path. Luckily her sense of direction was accurate, as her eyes caught sight of the entrance when a peculiar sound caused her to freeze where she walked. The sound was odd and unrecognizable; she wondered if she was being watched by someone or something.

Maybe it was just her over active imagination, she agreed, beginning to walk once more. Again, it was heard, as she began to back up toward the middle of the clearing. The sound of a twig breaking and brush being moved aside was quite evident. Something continued to move about and toward her; she began to become frightened.

"Who's there? Henry is that you?" she called aloud, trying to remain calm.

What if it is not someone, but something? Like a wild animal, wondered Bethie beginning to panic. Each time the sound was heard, she would reposition herself in the direction in which it came. She wanted to at least face whatever it was rather than being taken by surprise from the back. It was as though she were being made fun of, as the creature moved in all directions as it slowly taunted her.

She waited and watched, but still no one or nothing came beyond the brush into the clearing. Perhaps it was more frightened of her, hoped Bethie, annoyed and slowly losing her patience.

"Who are you? Come into the clearing and show your face! If you are trying to frighten me… well you haven't! Or are you simply a coward? Scared to face a little girl," snapped Bethie with feet slightly apart and hands now on her hips.

"How dare you call me a coward!" A young boy defended, as he promptly entered the clearing from behind a large tree.

"Who are you? And who gave you permission to be on my island!" he demanded angrily with a slight English accent. They stood facing one another, the boy with arms crossed against his chest and head turned sideways, and Bethie still standing with hands on hips, both glaring back at one another.

"My name is Miss Sara Beth Covington. My Aunt Emma owns the Calhoun plantation and this very land that you stand on! And… I didn't know this island was yours—or anyone's!" replied Bethie sarcastically. She stood staring back at him, wondering who he was and where he came from.

He wore a black velvet vest with matching knickers, blue stockings, and black shoes with silver buckles. The boy was taller than she with a slim physique. He was quite handsome with blonde hair falling about an inch passed his ears and eyes as blue as the sky above. He obviously was not a servant and must have come from a very wealthy family by the way he dressed, she imagined, curiously.

It suddenly dawned on her that he must be her Aunt Emma's son, her cousin, William. She remembered being told that he was to arrive today from England, and was probably the reason he was dressed as he was.

Pretending she was still unaware of who he was, she added, "And who are you?"

"My name is William. Son of Edmund Douglas and Emma Mae Calhoun. And owner of this here island that you are trespassing on!"

"Well, if I were told that this was your island, I would have never tres-passed in the first place! So if you'd kindly get out of my way, I'll just leave thank you!" she remarked with nose in the air as she pushed passed the boy.

"So you're Sara," knowing very well who she was from the start. Bethie stopped and turned to look at the boy again.

"My mother wrote to me about you… said you'd be here when I'd return. I've been away all winter at a private boarding school in London. I travel there every year on one of my mother's ships… spend most of my life there, actually."

"One day, I will own Mother's shipping business and this plantation. We're very rich you know."

"I'm very happy for you," remarked Bethie sarcastically and not at all impressed.

"I bet you've never been to London. You probably don't even know where it is, do you?"

"I may not have ever been to London, but I know where it is. I've had private study for several years now with my governess and caretaker, Miss Abby. And I'm no dummy! Miss Abby is one of the smartest teachers in the whole United States. Everybody knows London is in the country of England. And I also know that my… I guess our grandparents came from London. Now, it's time for me to leave your precious island. I told Henry I'd be back soon."

"Why do you think I'm here? Henry sent me to find you. Just like a girl to get lost."

"I'm not lost! Just wanted to see what was over here," defended Bethie annoyed. "Goodbye!"

"Wait!" yelled the boy, feeling as though he hadn't been very pleasant to his new cousin and hoping to start over with her.

Though William was disappointed that his only cousin turned out to be a girl, he longed for a playmate. The plantation was both large and lonely. Even though he was very close to his mother, he looked forward to the end of the summer when he could return to school and children of his own age.

"Since we are going to be living together, we might as well try to get along. After all, we are cousins. I'm sorry if I seemed a bit of a snob. Can we make a truce?" offered William sincerely, with a softer tone to his voice.

Bethie thought for a moment and decided that it would be nice to make a new friend. Especially because he was the only child on the plantation. "Truce!" she agreed, smiling.

William reached out his hand to shake Bethie's. In a gentleman fashion he began, "Hello, my name is William."

"And my name is Sara Beth… but my friends call me Bethie. You can call me Bethie, too, if you'd like. I'd rather prefer it," she replied very lady like.

"Nice to meet you, Bethie. Bethie… that's different. But I do like it. Yes, I think I like the name very much," smiled William. "I can tell you like my island. She's perfect isn't she, Bethie?"

"Oh Yes! When I first saw it from the hill, I wanted to come and explore right away."

"Nobody knows that I come here. I keep her a secret. But it can be both of ours if you promise never to breathe a word to anyone about her—not even to your Miss Abby! Promise?"

"Yes, I promise. Cross my heart, hope to die, stick a needle in my eye." She drew an imaginary X on her chest.

William suddenly spit in his hand then reached for Bethie's, "Let's shake on it!"

Bethie's nose crinkled up at the mere thought of him spitting in his hand and now wanting to touch hers. "Do I have to?"

"Yes, it's the only way I'll know you mean it. Don't be such a girl, Bethie!" Not wanting to seem squeamish, she eventually spit into her hand then shook his. The pact was made.

"Let me show you around. Come with me and I'll show you my

fort."

William led the way as he pushed aside a bush concealing a hidden path. "Now you stay behind me and keep a keen eye out for snakes."

"Snakes!" squealed Bethie, horrified at the mere thought. "Are they poisonous?"

"You never saw a snake before?" replied William in disbelief.

"No… I don't believe New Hope has any. That's where I'm from. At least none that I ever saw."

"Well we have them here," he boasted. "Fortunately, most can't hurt you. It's best you stay behind me. I know what the bad ones look and sound like." Bethie certainly couldn't argue with him, as she followed behind with eyes wide.

He led them up a hill hidden within the brush, centered in the middle of the island. When they reached the top, Bethie noticed how far she could see. The hill in which Henry and she had spoken on could be easily viewed.

"This is my lookout tower. We'll have to take turns guarding the island. If I stay and play too long, Miss Jane always sends someone. I can easily see if anyone is coming from here. It'll give us enough time to cross so we're not seen. Besides, I've made a lot of trails throughout the island. Short cuts you know." Bethie nodded, impressed with William's keenness.

From the right edge of the hill, he jumped to a level below. Bethie, not realizing where he had gone, quickly went over to the edge. She squatted to her knees, looking over the side for him.

"William, are you OK?"

"Yes, I'm fine. I do it all the time. It's how I get down here. Come on, Bethie!" He motioned her to follow him.

She was a bit concerned that the drop was too steep for her to jump. "It's too far, William. I'll break my legs."

"No you won't! Just turn around and crawl down. Use the stones in the wall to put your feet on. I'll be right here to help you. I promise you won't get hurt."

Bethie swallowed hard and leaned over even further to view the stones that were randomly lodged clear to the bottom.

"Don't be a scaredy-cat, Bethie. We don't have much time before they come looking for us. Come on!"

"I'm no scaredy-cat! I just need a little time, that's all," she replied defensively. She removed her bonnet from her head. "Here catch Miss Amy and my bonnet." William caught the doll as Bethie gently dropped it down to him with the bonnet following.

"Now don't let go. You don't have far. And try not to look down," warned William. She felt the edge of the first stone and began to place her weight on it. Finding it to be sturdy she continued, constantly pulling at her dress and cape. Slowly but surely, Bethie inched her way down. She soon felt William's hand on her foot trying to help her.

Bethie was about level to William's shoulders when her dress caught on a jagged rock. "William, my dress is caught! Help me!" pleaded Bethie, worried.

"Hold on! Don't move I'm coming." He began to climb moving closer to her, as he eventually pried the dress from the rock. Moving below her, he tried to gently aid Bethie down. Although his actions where purely honorable, the move caused both to awkwardly become entangled as they fell to the ground, Bethie landing nearly on top of him.

"Now look what you've done!" she snapped, dirtier than ever, with her bonnet now crushed from him landing directly upon it.

"I was only trying to help you, Bethie. Don't be so ungrateful. I should have left you hanging!"

"Well just look at me... I'm filthy and my bonnet is ruined. Miss Abby will be ever so angry."

"You were dirty when I found you! It looked like you were rolling in the grass or something."

"Well, I wouldn't boast about who looks dirty," responded Bethie defensively. "Look at you and that fancy outfit of yours." William took a moment to check himself and realized how dirty he had become.

"I think we're in big trouble, Bethie…" They each took a moment to look at one another seriously, then broke out in laugher. "Guess there's no use in worrying about it now. What's done, is done. Can't change that," he decided.

He stood to brushed his clothes off with his hands the best he could, then reached out to help Bethie to her feet. "Are you OK, Bethie?"

"I'm OK. But what are we going to tell them?"

William pondered a bit. "We'll tell them… that we were playing Ring Around the Rosie, then tripped and fell to the ground. Yes, that's right, it's why our clothes became so dirty."

"OK, but I don't like lying to Miss Abby. But if you think it will work, since she's sick and all," agreed Bethie deciding this excuse was as good as any other, certainly better than the truth.

"Well, we're already in trouble. I might as well show you what I brought you here to see. Come on! Come inside." He motioned her inside of a cave located in the wall of the hill. She was immediately intrigued and curious and followed closely behind him.

Because of the small opening the cave, shaped like a half circle, was larger inside than Bethie had expected. It was certainly large enough for the two of them to play in. The walls and ceiling were made from earth and stone. They could easily stand.

"What a wonderful fort, William!" she replied, extremely delighted.

"You're not disappointed anymore that I brought you?"

"No, it was worth seeing. But what do you do here?"

"Well, sometimes I just lay up on the hill and look up at the sky. Mostly when I'm up there, I pretend I'm a pirate on a ship watching for my next victim!" he added in a silly voice, making Bethie giggle.

"I even pretend that I drag my prisoners into the cave and throw them into the stockade."

"Where's the stockade?" she wondered looking about.

"Nowhere in particular. I just pretend I have one. I like to come here when it gets really hot, too. The cave stays as cool as a spring in summer.

Bethie saw a wooden box partially concealed at the other side of the cave. William tried to camouflage it by placing large rocks around the sides of the box. But Bethie could still make out what it was from where she stood.

"What's in the box?" she asked curiously.

"That's my secret box. Private belongings of mine and the cave."

She didn't want William to show her anything he didn't wish to and did not pry any further. But her curiosity was now stronger than ever. He thought a while and wondered whether or not he would show her. After deciding it was OK, since she had done the sacred handshake, "Come on, I'll show you."

With both hands, he removed each stone leaving them nearby. "Come on, Bethie. Help me lift it."

She went over to the other side of the box to help him. Together, they gently placed it in the middle of the cave where there was some light. William lifted the wooden lid exposing a variety of items inside. One, by one, he began to remove each item allowing Bethie to touch and examine each, as he explained their significance.

There were several books, an old cotton blanket that he spread over the floor of the cave so Bethie could sit, and a wooden sword.

"What's the sword for?" she asked, wondering.

"It's my pirate sword, silly! How can I be a pirate without a sword?"

"Oh, that's right, I forgot," replied Bethie embarrassed.

He also had some rope, pieces of wood, and a few pig iron nails.

"That's in case I need to make something."

Bethie shook her head in response. William finished showing her all the items, then gently placed each away as though it were truly worth something.

She handed him the sword to be put away in the box. He suddenly changed his mind, as he ran out of the cave carrying it in his right hand. Bethie stood at the entrance watching him curiously.

With the sword pointed straight and high above him in the air, he began to chant, "I, Sir William David Calhoun, claim this island for myself... and Miss Sara Beth Covington, Bethie. She will always belong to us and no others. We will defend and guard her with our lives, swearing never to reveal her existence," continued William, as he brought the sword down slashing the air around him from side to side. "Furthermore, trespassers will be dealt with no mercy!" Bethie giggled aloud from William's dramatic speech.

"Come forth Lady Sara and kneel before me," requested William looking over at her very seriously.

Bethie playing along did what he requested. She walked over to him, trying not to giggle, then knelt down in front of him. He laid the sword on her shoulder as he once again began to chant. "I dub you knight of the island. No one shall be higher than thee... except for myself. I'm, of course, king of the island!"

Bethie's smile suddenly disappeared, as she questioned him, "How come you're king and I'm only a knight?"

"Because I found the island before you did. Therefore, it's only fair I am king."

"But I thought you said the island was both of ours, equally?"

"OK, Bethie, don't make a fuss. We'll both be knights."

"Now it's my turn. You kneel before me so I can dub you," she demanded.

He did what she demanded and soon the ceremony was over. The two of them put all the items safely away then placed the wooden box back where it belonged. The stones where too heavy and awkward for Bethie, as she watched William put them each in their proper place.

"You can bring some of your own belongings to keep in the box, Bethie. Only each item has to be agreed upon. I don't want a lot of girlie things inside my box."

"OK, William. That seems fair enough. Thanks!"

"We better be getting back. We've stayed much too long. Mother will be beside herself," commented William, concerned.

Bethie's face quickly turned frightened, as she recalled the incident with her aunt that morning. William noticed immediately, "What's wrong, Bethie? Something scare you?"

"No… I'm just worried about Miss Abby. She looked so sick this morning. It's best we go now so I can check on her. Is there an easier way to get off the island without climbing?"

"Yes, we can walk along the hill until it gets small enough to climb over. Or we can walk until we get near the water then head toward the bridge. It's quicker, but we have to be careful not to be seen."

William tried desperately to fix and mold Bethie's bonnet back into shape, but really to no avail. When he had done the best he could, she sincerely thanked him and placed the mangled bonnet back onto her head.

"Miss Amy… Miss Amy where are you," she panicked, not remembering where she had laid her doll.

"Don't be silly, Bethie. Dolls can't talk. Besides, you put her in the corner of the cave. So we wouldn't step on her, remember?"

"Oh yes, I remember," she replied, promptly retrieving the doll, hugging her gratefully.

They eventually made their way to the logs with Bethie following close behind William, holding tightly onto Miss Amy. He gently helped her across and off the large trees that connected the island to the mainland.

Both had found a new friend in one another, as they began to plan tomorrow's adventures. Since William was two years older than Bethie, he already felt responsible to protect and guide her. And it felt good not to be the youngest anymore on the plantation.

They began walking up the hills leaving the island behind when Bethie turned to face her. "Look William! Isn't she lovely?"

"Yes, you can see the whole island from here. You know, Bethie, we ought to give her a name."

"Like what?"

"I don't know. Let's think about it. Can't be just any old name.

Has to be perfect! Just like her."

"Yes, William, I agree!"

"Race you down the hill," he challenged, already running.

"No fair! You started first," yelled Bethie giggling, running as fast as she could trying to catch up to him.

After reaching the bottom, both children fell to the ground giggling aloud. They lay in the cool grass staring up at the sky. "I'll tell you a secret, Bethie. If you promise to tell me one. This way, we'll know something about each other that no one else knows."

"OK, but you go first," she decided firmly.

Though she did trust William, she was a little apprehensive in sharing something so private with him. He leaned on his elbows and propped his head up to look at her.

"Well, alright. Let me think of one," he offered, pausing for a moment.

"OK. I have a secret I can tell you… My mother really isn't my mother."

"What do you mean?"

"Well I mean… she is my mother, except that she didn't give birth to me. My parents adopted me soon after they married in Philadelphia. That's when they hired Miss Jane. She's from Pennsylvania, too, and was initially hired as my governess."

"I heard one of the servants talking about it to another one day. At first, I was quite upset. Then after talking with mother, she convinced me that it didn't matter. In her heart, I was her son, whether by flesh or not!"

"Felt awful for the servant though… mother dismissed him right away. Had him run off the plantation. I didn't mean for him to get into trouble. Now that you know I'm adopted, do you think any less of me, Bethie?" William was somewhat apprehensive.

It all made sense she agreed, quite pleased with the news as she absent-mindedly replied, "I'm not surprised!"

"What do you mean by that? You take that back!" he snapped at her defensively.

She couldn't imagine him being born from her mean, old Aunt Emma. She was so stern and angry while he happy and forgiving. Adoption made a lot more sense to her. Bethie tried not to look so happy as she thought of what to say.

"I didn't mean anything by it, William. Honestly, I didn't. Just forget I said it."

"No! What do you mean you're not surprised? I demand to know right now, Bethie!"

He was quite upset as he jumped to a standing position placing both hands on his hips while glaring down at her. Bethie knew she had really hurt his feelings and must do something quick to alleviate the situation.

"Please don't make a fuss, William. I'm sorry if I hurt your feelings."

"Don't be so smug Sara Beth Covington. No feelings of mine are hurt. I'm a man. We don't bother with such nonsense," defended William with shoulders pulled back and nose in the air.

"It's…" began Bethie stumbling. It's just your mother seems so stern all the time, and you, happy and mostly always smiling. You don't seem very much alike, that's all."

He was relieved to find Bethie not trying to make fun but simply trying to compare him to his mother. William loved his mother but knew she could be a bit manipulating and stern at times.

"Oh! Is that all? Don't mind my mother," he replied, relieved. "She can be a bit stern, but she's really a wonderful lady. You know she gives a lot of money every year to an orphanage in Philadelphia. I guess it's the one they adopted me from."

"That's nice," Bethie added soberly, not convinced.

"What's wrong, Bethie? Don't you like my mother?"

"It's not that I don't like her, William. I don't think she likes me."

"That's silly, Bethie. Why wouldn't she like you? You're all she wrote about in her letters to me. Look, I'll have a talk with her. Ask her to be more pleasant around you."

"NO William!" she shrieked. "That'll make her even more angry with me."

"That's ridiculous, Bethie. Now you let me handle my mother."

A sly smile came upon his face as he sat beside her. "If I didn't know better, I'd think you were trying to get out of your end of the bargain."

"What do you mean?" she wondered, confused.

"Well you owe me a secret—and it better be a good one, too."

Bethie thought awhile, "You may be adopted, but at least you have a mother. My parents are both dead."

"Yes, I know, Bethie. That's not really a secret. My mother told me both took ill and died when you were a little baby. I'm very sorry for you. I don't remember my father. But I miss him just the same," he commented sadly.

"Well it's true my mother became ill when she was giving birth to me... but my father died of a broken heart. Least that's what I've been told. He loved my mother so much that his heart just broke in two when she died. Didn't feel much like going on anymore, I suppose."

"That's so sad, Bethie. I'm sorry for you," he replied again, sympathetically.

"Back home at Covington, that's where I lived. Sometimes I'd lay awake at nights for hours pretending that they were both alive. I'd pretend they just tucked me in after reading a long story to me. And they'd be very happy and very much in love all of the time."

"William... do you think it's possible a person can die of a broken heart?"

"I don't know, Bethie. But I suppose if you love someone that much. I guess it could happen. Seems kind of girlie to me. Can't imagine a man feeling like that." Bethie rolled her eyes at him as she lay in the tall grass contemplating.

They were suddenly interrupted. Even from a distance, both could hear Henry yelling for them. "Masser William... Miz Sara... Where is ya?"

"Come on, Bethie. It's Henry looking for us. Now you let me do the talkin'. I know how to handle Henry. I've known him longer than you." Bethie nodded without protest.

Both ran up the hill almost running into him.

"Where ya children been all this time? I'ze worried sick lookin' for ya's. What in God's good name have ya all been doin'? Look like ya been rollin' with the hogs," remarked Henry, frustrated by their filthy appearance.

"Been tellin' ya Miz Abigail a bit a nonsense bout' where is ya been playin'. Luckily ya momma been dealin' with cotton brokers all day ta notice ya run off, Masser William."

"We're sorry if we worried you, Henry. But I went looking for Bethie just like you told me to. But after I found her… playing with her doll, we just started playing Ring Around the Rose. We fell a few times. And that's why we're so dirty. Just forgot all about how late it was getting."

"Ya'll wazn't near that lake waz ya?" he questioned, suspiciously.

"No, sir! Not us. We know better," blurted William, lying.

"Fine then. Ya come back ta the house with me. The misses got some corn bread for ya both. Done gone and missed ya meal."

Both were relieved to see Henry finally calmed down. They skipped in front of him through the cotton fields, as he hummed an old slave song. Henry's wife, who was the mansion's main cook, was cutting vegetables on the back porch for supper. She gave them each some corn bread with sweet butter and a glass of milk. They thanked her kindly.

After finishing, Bethie took William to meet Miss Abby. She asked him to wait in her room while she checked to see if Miss Abigail was awake. Bethie tiptoed quietly to her bedside. Her eyes were closed, but she soon sensed Bethie in the room.

"Child, where have you been?" she questioned sternly.

Bethie was now in full view of Miss Abigail. She gasped at the sight of her dirty clothes.

"What in the world happened to your clothes? I sent word to Henry long ago to have you come in to eat. I haven't seen you. I haven't seen him. You're lucky I've been too ill to find you myself, young lady!"

"I'm sorry if I worried you, Miss Abby. But I met my new cousin, William, today. He's nice and we get along really fine too, Miss Abby. We started playing… and I got so dirty," pleaded Bethie, stretching the truth."

"Forgot all about how late it was. Please forgive me, Miss Abby. We just had such fun together," begged Bethie hoping to be forgiven.

"Well, I'm at least glad for that," she added, relieved to at least hear Bethie had a new friend.

She had hoped the two of them would like each other. They were close in age and could probably benefit from one another's company. But knowing Emma Mae, she did not have her hopes too high. Abigail prayed the boy would be nothing like her. Miss Abigail knew that William was adopted but also that Emma Mae had raised him from a baby. Chances were very strong, he had inherited some of her personality traits through the years.

"Would you like to meet him? He's in my room waiting," she said eagerly.

"Yes… I would be honored to meet the gentleman of the mansion," teased Miss Abigail. She easily gave into Bethie causing her to giggle.

She started to go and get William when she turned abruptly around, "Oh, I'm sorry, Miss Abby. How are you feeling?"

"Well, I still feel a bit under the weather but not as ill as this morning. I'm very weak, but I believe the rest is helping immensely."

"I'm happy you're better." Bethie gave her a quick kiss on the forehead before leaving the room to get William.

Abigail was not dressed properly or in the mood to meet anyone, but she made an exception in William's case. She watched him enter the room. Though he would not be expected to, she noticed how he looked nothing like Emma Mae. He was tall and handsome like a fine young man would be, thought Abigail impressed.

"This is William, Miss Abby."

"It is a pleasure to make your acquaintance, ma'am," replied William in mannerly fashion.

"It's a pleasure to meet you, too, William. Bethie's tells me that you both had a wonderful day. And I can tell it to be true by your clothes, too… But I'm happy to hear you both enjoyed each other's companionship. I can recover much easier knowing Bethie has someone near her age to keep her company. Thank you, William."

"You're welcome, ma'am," he replied politely.

"Now it's nearly supper, and I believe it would be wise if you both wash and change. Especially before Miss Emma sees the two of you," warned Miss Abigail.

"Can I show William some of my belongings I brought from Covington first, Miss Abby? It won't take long. I promise!"

"You know, Bethie, your promises are beginning to wear thin," she sighed. "But I suppose a few more minutes won't make a difference. Go ahead, run along, but don't dawdle, child!"

Bethie showed William several items from home, as they sat on the floor of her room. He didn't seem much interested in her tea set or any of Miss Amy's clothes, but they did finally agree on a few items to add to William's wooden box in the cave.

"Mother says she misses me terribly when I'm away at boarding school and may decide to keep me here in Savannah."

"That's wonderful, William," replied Bethie, very pleased. *Maybe living in Savannah won't be so bad after all,* she thought.

After she washed and dressed for supper, she spent some time talking to Miss Abigail about William. She was so excited to have a new friend near her own age. Bethie talked poor Miss Abby's ears off about the exploring they promised to do the next day. Never, of course, revealing the island in which she longed to return to.

She did not tell Miss Abigail about her unfortunate confrontation with Emma Mae earlier that morning. Bethie decided not to question Abigail of her mother's heritage, deciding it would make no difference to her. She may not have known her mother and father, but loved them just the same regardless of who or where they came from. Bethie was proud to be their daughter and a Covington.

William came to Bethie's room to escort her to supper. They skipped, talked, and giggled all the way into the main dining area in which Emma Mae had already been seated and waiting. Luckily they were at least on time, thought Bethie, wishing not to be scolded by her Aunt.

Emma Mae tried desperately to conceal her jealousy, as William pulled out Bethie's chair for her to be seated. He promptly went to his mother's side and kissed her cheek.

"Good evening, Mother."

"Good evening, Son, Sara... I see you've already met your cousin, Sara Beth. I was hoping I would have the honor of introducing the two of you. It must be quite a shock finding out after all these years of each other's existence. I was hoping I could make it a little easier on you both. But nevertheless, I see you have adjusted quite well without me."

William sat across from Bethie as his mother's eyes fell upon her. "Sara Beth..." Emma Mae took a deep breath as though it were torture to bring herself to say what she was about to. "I'm sorry if I startled you this morning. I hope I didn't upset you dear with my callus words. Sometimes, when I mean only the best, the words don't always come out right. Please forgive your Aunt Emma for her unruly behavior."

Bethie was stunned by her Aunt Emma's words as she stared dumbfounded. Not only physically, but her tone and voice where that of someone else's. Her demeanor was soft, gentle, and almost motherly, as Bethie continued to keep her guard up never for one moment falling for her almost convincing performance.

"I'm fine, ma'am. You didn't upset me. But thank you for asking," replied Bethie guarded, but polite. Emma Mae was sure she had not convinced her niece of her rehearsed apology but accepted that she was, indeed, a Covington and not easily deceived.

How bright she was for such a small child, thought Emma, as a twinge of fear sparked her soul for the first time. She agreed in her demented mind to be more careful of what she said to her in the future. Somehow she would control her jealousy and hatred toward her brother so she could slowly win the child's trust. I would die a thousand deaths before allowing my plans of one day owning Covington fail, swore Emma spitefully.

She changed the subject by turning her attentions to her son, "I've ordered the cook to prepare your favorite dishes."

"Thank you, Mother, that was very thoughtful."

"You can't imagine, Son, how pleased I am to finally have you home. It gets very lonely without you over the long winter months."

"I missed you too, Mother. I'm glad to be home… especially glad that Bethie, I mean, Sara Beth has come to live with us."

"Bethie… is that what you called Sara, William?"

"Yes, that's what they call her back home."

"Is that true, Sara? Do they really call you by that," belittled Emma Mae.

"Yes, ma'am. My friends do."

"I rather like the name. Don't you mother?" he questioned, eager for her approval.

It was apparent Emma Mae disapproved, but did not want to disagree with her son or further Bethie. "Very unusual, Sara… But I have always taken a liking to the unusual," lied Emma, easily.

Servants began to enter carrying many dishes filled with delicious foods. Their alluring aromas flooded the air, as Bethie and William's bellies ached from hunger. Placed before the two were fried chicken and ham, black eyed peas, greens, rice and gravy with biscuits and corn bread. They were all William's favorite foods.

Although Bethie was new to southern cooking she had quickly adjusted, as both children ate until their bellies were full and then some. A "Welcome Home" three layers high, chocolate cake was brought to the dining room at William's surprise. Unlike yesterday, Bethie ate quite easily and ignored her Aunt's presence. William made her feel safe and guarded. And she soon learned her aunt would say or do nothing malicious as long as her son was present.

Though it was difficult to imagine Emma Mae ever truly loving anyone, the feelings she had for her son would be the closest she'd ever come to caring for any being other than herself. She had raised him from an infant, promising that he would never be harmed or neglected by anyone—most importantly herself.

From day one, he had been given the best that money could buy. The best clothes, tutors, and schools were only a few on the list as he lacked for nothing. Luckily, his fortunate upbringing had never tarnished his soul. Unlike his mother, whose desire for more was never ending.

Although she loved him possessively and gave all that there was, she could never make him think in the same custom as she. He would always disapprove if she or anyone else around him would mistreat the staff. And it bothered Emma when her son preferred to play with the Negro boys over the rich, pompous ones. Finding them to be both boring and stuffy, not at all fun to be with, as he would explain time after time to a frustrated Emma Mae.

But through time she adjusted to his differences, convinced that it was only his immaturity that made them apart. She truly believed his wealthy, London boarding school would bring him around. But even so he remained fair, gentle, and caring, qualities Emma Mae lacked entirely.

Bethie could hardly wait for the following morning. She woke early to find William dressed and waiting for her. After breakfast they gathered Bethie's special treasures that were to be added to the box, and hid them under the porch directly outside the kitchen door.

Abigail had recovered but was still weak from her illness. She decided to remain in bed for an additional day. Emma Mae had given permission for her son and niece to ride two of the older, more settled, horses under the watchful aid of Henry's son. The two were to report to Miss Jane periodically throughout the day while Miss Abigail remained bedridden.

Miss Abigail did not object as long as Bethie stayed with William at all times. He was older and she felt him to be quite mature and responsible for his age. William knew the plantation well and would keep Bethie out of danger and from getting lost.

Dressed more appropriately than the day before, they headed to the stables in which Henry's son, Nathan, was preparing horses for both to ride. He had been the plantation's blacksmith for many years and knew horses better than any other in Savannah, boasted Henry proudly. It was a fine trade taught to him by the previous blacksmith when he worked as an apprentice slave at a very young age.

Each took their time getting to the barn as they frolicked and basted in the morning's warm sun. They giggled while playing leap frog, trying not to fall on each another. William was much more experienced at riding than Bethie and offered his know-how to her. She listened closely since she adored horses, but riding them most of all.

Their pace was slow at first with Nathan between them guiding each horse by hand while explaining in detail important instructions to Bethie. William, of course, adding his advice from time to time. Bethie, still polite, was becoming excited and impatient, feeling quite ready and willing to be let free. She neither feared the animal, which rose high above her, nor the chance to finally run with it.

She felt confident and in control when Nathan finally allowed them both to trot freely. How wonderful it felt to be free, agreed Bethie as she smiled immensely. Though the trot was slow, she could feel the cool air gently hitting her face causing her long brown ringlets to pull back from her head.

The horses trotted side by side with William occasionally looking over toward Bethie, as he watched protectively over her. Feeling more confident, their pace began to quicken as Nathan watched from afar. They rode between the cotton and tobacco fields stopping occasionally, as William and Bethie spoke to the workers. They were all so kind and the day so fine, agreed Bethie, wishing it would never end.

The two galloped toward Henry as he smiled joyfully to see

Bethie with a new friend near her own age.

"Well there, missy… I reckon someone's done takin' my place," he teased laughingly.

After a few hours, they returned the horses and helped Nathan to wash and brush them. Bethie and William searched for peaches that had fallen on the ground in the nearby orchard. After taking the first bite, they offered the remainder of the fruit to the horses. They watched from afar, as the horses galloped freely in the fields beyond the barn. William could see how much Bethie enjoyed them.

"We can go riding every day. If you'd like," he offered. She was thrilled.

"That would be wonderful, William! Thank you."

They ate their midday meal and checked in with Miss Jane who was quite busy and barely noticed them. They waved to Miss Abigail who felt well enough to sit in a rocker on the wraparound porch above them. She was happy to see them both getting along fine.

William took Bethie to a building which held the cotton gin. She had never seen one and was curious about how it operated. With hands over her ears from the loud noise, William yelled loudly over to her as he tried to explain how the contraption worked.

Henry's wife had given Bethie a basket to pick flowers from the gardens to be displayed in the main house. William wasn't interested in the chore but thought it would be a good deterrent, as they wandered toward the island. They secretly removed Bethie's items from underneath the porch and placed them on the bottom of the basket. They entered the gardens and quickly began to cover the items with a variety of flowers.

With the basket half filled, they skipped through the cotton fields taking turns chasing one another. The mansion was finally out of view, as the two ran directly up and down the hills stopping only when sight of the island came into view. Some of the flowers had fallen out of the basket, she tried to gather them from the ground.

"Don't worry about them now, Bethie! We'll collect them on the way back. Let's go! We won't have much time." William helped her to dump the basket, as they collected her items from the bottom and made their way toward the island.

They enjoyed the remainder of the day taking turns being captain of a pirate's ship using the hill above the cave as their lookout point. Bethie's items were added to the box. William pulled out some rope and pieces of wood and tried to make a rope ladder for her. It was obvious, a wonderful friendship filled with mutual trust and respect was forming. The two felt comfortable and happy in each other's company.

They played hide-and-go-seek then laid upon the grassy hill exchanging many stories both of the plantation and Covington. William could tell Bethie missed New Hope terribly, as he listened to her speak fondly of her home, Aunt Liz, and Joseph.

"I miss them both so much. I hope they don't forget me. Do you think they have, William?" she wondered sadly.

"Why would they?" He offered not knowing quite how to comfort her, but wanting to all the same.

"After all… I think you're quite splendid—for a girl that is!"

Affirmation

Several hot, but quite lovely, summers had passed in Savannah as Bethie, now ten years old, learned to adapt to the southern ways. But she and Miss Abigail missed Aunt Liz, Joseph, and Covington. Both were terribly homesick. Emma Mae with her deceitful and manipulative ways had managed to deter them from returning home the past summers, using one excuse after another.

Bethie truly believed it would not have been possible to survive in Savannah if it had not been for Miss Abigail and her best friend and companion, William. Luckily, Emma had permitted him to continue his studies in Savannah with her. The two had grown to be inseparable, closer to no other, causing Emma Mae's jealousy of her to become stronger every day. But her desire and greed for Covington and all Bethie's assets, still, were stronger than the love she had for even her son.

She learned to avoid her aunt, who because of her son's presence kept her dislike to an occasional nasty glare. But Emma did continue to try and manipulate Bethie's life whenever possible. But gratefully Emma Mae had become preoccupied with her finances caused by the fall of the banks, in which she had predicted earlier.

Most of her money had been well invested or kept in strong boxes hidden in the mansion's wall safes, prior to the disaster. She had become too preoccupied in Bethie's inherited wealth and discouraged by the fact she had no control over it.

Though she did not miss the cold, and sometimes harsh, winters of New Hope, Bethie longed for the feel of snowflakes gently falling upon her cheeks and tickling her nose. And the white blanket it left behind, covering as far as one could see.

The snow caused sleds to replace the carriage pulled by horses draped in bells. You could hear them jingle as the sleds passed one another in song, described Bethie to William who wished to visit Covington with her. Especially at Christmas, that particular time was the most difficult, she found Christmas without snow seeming quite odd and very much like an ordinary day.

Miss Abigail, who grew angrier by the day, had become discouraged at not being able to return to New Hope last summer, as promised by Judge Buchanan. She was determined to make Emma Mae understand there would be no excuses this spring.

She was concerned about her sister, whose health seemed to be deteriorating during the past several years. Although they wrote often to each other it was Mr. Holt, the Covington's attorney, who had informed Miss Abigail of her sister's ailing condition.

William pleaded with his increasingly possessive mother to allow him to accompany them back to Pennsylvania for a visit. But she refused, exclaiming that he was the man of the house and she needed him with her. He was a kind and obedient son who always tried to obey Emma. In his mind, he truly believed she was a good woman. He was twelve years old now, quite mature and eager to help his mother operate the plantation and shipping business.

As much as Bethie had grown to dislike her aunt, she never spoke harsh words about her to William. Bethie never told of the many incidents when Emma Mae would mistreat her. She felt in time, he would see the kind of woman that she really was and then decide for himself.

Despite her cruel and malicious behavior toward Bethie, she was his mother and she respected that. Bethie felt it wasn't her place, and soon her aunt's clever way of mistreating her when her son was not about would one day work against her.

She would never forget that her aunt took Miss Amy away. Though it was true, she did not actually catch her taking the doll she was quite convinced it had been Emma. Bethie had been constantly criticized by her aunt for carrying the doll where ever she'd go.

"You're much too old for dolls, Sara Beth! You look absolutely ridiculous carrying that dirty old thing around. You're a young lady—and in My home, you'll act as one," remarked her aunt one day, finding the two together.

Bethie started to hide Miss Amy in her cape before she'd leave the mansion. William never seemed to mind the doll. Bethie would often drag Miss Amy to the island with them. He never complained or teased so why should her aunt care, wondered Bethie upset and confused.

Finally, one afternoon when she had returned from her studies, her worse fear came true. She went to pick up the doll from her cradle, as she routinely did each day, only to find her missing. Miss Amy, of course, was gone and never to be found.

She believed a thorough search would be fruitless, but nevertheless for many days thereafter Bethie, William, and Miss Abigail searched the mansion from top to bottom. She was very upset for many weeks. William did his best to comfort her. He even searched the island from one end to the other, but to no avail.

Although she never joined the search, even Miss Jane felt sorry for the child knowing all too well it had been Emma who had taken the doll. Bethie never told anyone of her suspicions, without evidence she would have only gotten scolded for accusing. Miss Abigail suspected Emma from the beginning and eventually, as a last resort, confronted her but without success. She denied taking Miss Amy and blamed Bethie for irresponsibly misplacing the doll.

Miss Abigail offered to replace her, but Bethie knew it would not be the same. She thanked her but declined the thoughtful gesture. Bethie said a silent prayer to God to look over and protect her Miss Amy, where ever she may be. A special piece of her childhood had been wrongfully taken. From that day, she neither was given nor desired another doll.

"It's gonna be lonely all summer without you, Bethie," confessed William sadly.

"I'll miss you too, William. But I'll be back before you know it.

Just in time for our studies," reassured Bethie.

The two children lay staring up at the sky from the top of their lookout hill on the island.

"I promise to bring you something special back from New Hope. And I'll write often. I'll think of you every day. You won't forget me, will you?

"Of course not, silly," replied William.

"I'll miss playing here on the island terribly. Covington is near a river, but it doesn't have an island like this. Miss Abigail never allows me to go near it by myself. The water is usually pretty rough and scary."

William sat up abruptly, "Friendship Island!" he blurted loudly to her. She looked over at him confused. "That's what we can name her, 'Friendship Island'. It's a perfect name, isn't it Bethie? The name will always remind us of the first day we met and became best friends."

"Yes, it's a wonderful name for her, William," she agreed happily. "Let's go back and get some cloth and ink to make a flag. Then we can tie it to a stick and fly it here on the hill."

"Splendid idea!" William agreed, as both jumped up to hurry back to the mansion.

Meanwhile, Miss Abigail had gone into the city to meet with Mr. Holt. He had traveled from Philadelphia to accompany Miss Abigail and Bethie back to New Hope. He was aware of Emma Mae's constant excuses, and decided to accompany them himself in their return home.

For the past several years, he and Miss Abigail had kept in constant touch with each other. This had been his fourth visit to Savannah concerning Bethie. It gave him the opportunity to see Miss Abigail. He was sweet on her, and she was quite aware of it. Abigail always looked forward to Mr. Holt's visits. Thomas was a kind and caring man. He often visited Covington to check on Elizabeth and the estate for Miss Abigail. She was very concerned about her sister and was grateful to Mr. Holt.

They enjoyed a cup of tea together as he shared news from

Covington with Abigail. "So, how is everyone at the estate? Elizabeth… and of course Joseph how is he doing, she questioned unable to keep eye contact.

"Joseph seemed to be doing well, working as hard as usual. He misses you both terribly. Poor man, still thinks it's his fault you both were sent away… because of the lost will and all."

"Your sister can hardly wait to see you and Bethie, Abigail. She was quite pleased to hear that I would be joining the both of you in Savannah for the trip back. I don't believe she trusts Emma Mae for one minute. But I can't really blame her, can you?"

"No, Thomas. I can't blame my sister. I'm as anxious as she to return to Covington. It seems like a lifetime since I've been there. Darn that old Emma for keeping us from returning," she snapped. "I apologize, Thomas, but it has made me bitter."

"Well, that's mainly why I have come, Abigail. I'm here to make sure you and Bethie make it back to New Hope for the entire summer. I've got a court order from Judge Franklin. He's taken over Bethie's file since Judge Buchanan was removed."

"That's a sad story… happened only six months after you and Bethie left for Savannah. He got caught up in some scandalous mess, got him removed from the bench. I heard he's pleading his own case. Trying to keep from getting disbarred, I suppose. Though I can't say that I'm surprised."

"God works in mysterious ways," replied Miss Abigail. "What's the saying, 'we reap what we sow.' I wouldn't be at all surprised if it wasn't Emma's doing. She wasn't entirely pleased with Judge Buchanan's decision. Emma Mae is a vindictive, spiteful woman. I wouldn't put it passed her to be involved in some way."

"Your probably right, Abigail. She never did get what she really wanted. So tell me," he started, changing the subject. "How has it been living under the same roof with her?"

"Except for when it concerns Bethie, and because the mansion is quite large, we've been able to basically avoid one another. Thankfully, she's away on business quite a bit. When we do happen to meet, our conversations are awkwardly cordial and to the point."

"Now that I teach both Bethie and William, I must say, they keep me quite busy. William is a wonderful, young man. It's hard to believe he's Emma's son. He watches over Bethie like a brother. He's been so good for my Bethie, and I'm very grateful she has him. She absolutely adores the boy, follows him around like a little puppy."

"But what about you, Abigail, who do you have? That didn't seem to come out quite like I had wanted it to. I don't mean to intrude into your private affairs. But I'm only asking out of concern for you. We've known each other for many years now, Abigail, and I must tell you… I've grown to care very deeply for you," confessed Mr. Holt embarrassed, his cheeks turning red.

"Although I'm very dedicated to Miss Sara's wellbeing, it's because of you I come to Savannah so often." Abigail blushed and found it difficult to look into Thomas's eyes.

"Let me rephrase the question. I know you have Bethie to look after, and now William. But they're both getting old enough to care for themselves. So who cares for you, Abigail? Who do you talk to or go to when you need a friend? What I'm trying to say, Abigail, is that I have fallen in love with you. I'm asking you to marry me."

Even with prior knowledge of Thomas's feelings for her, Abigail had no idea they were this deep. His proposal of marriage was not expected and simply took her by surprise. She sat nervously staring back at him, not knowing what to say. Abigail could imagine hearing Elizabeth whispering in her ears. *Don't be a fool, sister! He's a kind and wonderful man. Say, yes!*

It was true he was kind, handsome, and a very successful lawyer, and in time probably capable of making her very happy. Still, she did not and could not love him, at least for now. She was condemned to loving only one man, a man she could never have. And Abigail knew it would take more than two years to forget him. She simply was not ready. She wondered if she would ever be. It would be unfair to Thomas, he would never understand why she could not return his affections, for she could never reveal the truth to him or anyone.

"Thomas, I don't know what to say," began Abigail embarrassed. "But I must say, you have caught me by surprise. I never expected you to propose marriage during tea." Both chuckled, helping to take away some of the tension.

"I must admit, it has been the letters from my sister and your visits that have kept me sane through these past two years. Though I am quite committed to Bethie, I do realize I'm also a woman. Even I need a friend from time to time. And I thank you Thomas for being that friend."

"You've been kind, generous, and very supportive throughout these trying years. I shall never forget your loyalty to Mr. and Mrs. Covington, Bethie, and myself. But unfortunately, I must decline your proposal. I could never leave Bethie here alone with Emma Mae. It's more than being her governess or caretaker of an estate. I raised that child from an infant and I love her as if she were my own."

"I would never expect you to leave Bethie, Abigail. I thought perhaps since her case is now with a new judge, one that I know personally is a good man, together we could fight for custody."

"I appreciate your kindness, Thomas. But I still don't believe we would win. And besides, Bethie has grown accustom to living here in Savannah. I don't think she would want to leave William. They've grown very close to one another and…"

"Abigail, are you sure these are not simply excuses for not marrying me. You can tell me… I can take it. Is there someone else, perhaps?" he interrupted.

"No! I mean, no there is no one else, Thomas," she replied defensively. She was annoyed that he could see right through her so easily. "I hope I have not insulted you, Thomas. You're a fine man. Any woman would be honored to be your wife. But I simply can't, not right now the way things are. I'm truly sorry… please forgive me."

"Please, don't apologize, Abigail. I'm the one who should be sorry for pressuring you. And also for questioning you about your private affairs, which are simply none of my business. Will you forgive me?"

"Yes, of course. I do hope we can remain friends."

"We will always be friends, Abigail. Because I refuse to give up on us that easily. One day you may change your mind."

"Perhaps, Thomas," she ended, blushing.

She returned to the plantation later that afternoon to find Emma Mae getting ready to leave for a late meeting in the city. "Good afternoon, Abigail… I trust all went well with your visit with Thomas Holt," pried Emma Mae eagerly.

"Yes, all went fine, Emma Mae. In fact, he will be accompanying Bethie and I back to Pennsylvania." Abigail, not wanting to have further conversation with Emma, moved quickly passed her toward the main entrance. But Emma Mae continued to question her.

"He certainly has traveled often to Savannah these past several years. Don't you agree, Abigail?"

What is she suggesting now, wondered Abigail frustrated, continuing to be detained by Emma. "He cares for Sara Beth and her wellbeing. That's why he comes Emma, nothing more."

"Well, I certainly agree. I hope you did not think I was implying anything more. I'm glad to hear you're aware that his visits are strictly on Sara's behalf. I wouldn't want you to get the wrong impression of him."

Miss Abigail, now annoyed, replied, "What exactly are you trying to say?"

"Well simply that it's obvious Thomas is quite handsome, wealthy, and very available. He is eligible, of course, for the right kind of woman. One that is on his level in society, that is. I'm happy to know your expectations are within reach, Abigail, and not dreaming about unrealistic possibilities."

She could feel the heat rise from her feet rushing up into her head, as she stood facing Emma Mae ready to explode. How obnoxiously pompous she was standing there with a stupid, smug look on her face. And to retaliate in anger would only add to Emma's satisfaction.

Abigail took a moment to calm down, "Emma, I don't want to appear rude but I simply must go and attend to my duties. Unfortunately I don't have all day to chat with you, and from the looks of it neither do you. I have much packing to do. We leave first thing tomorrow morning. So if you'll excuse me, good day." Abigail's response was not what Emma Mae had expected, causing the smug look to vanish from her wrinkled, old face.

Though leaving William behind had been very difficult, Bethie was thrilled and eager to finally return home. She could barely stay seated, as the black locomotive finally pulled into Doylestown.

How wonderful Pennsylvania looked to both of them, as they searched frantically for Joseph from their window. Unable to locate him, Miss Abigail quickly gathered what she could carry and hurried Bethie off the train. She shut her eyes for a moment and took a slow, deep breath. How sweet it was to be home at last, she agreed, thanking God above.

She was interrupted by a familiar voice, "Miss Abigail, Miss Abigail… Over here, ma'am," directed Abner standing next to a carriage.

"Where's Joseph, Miss Abby? Why hasn't he come?" questioned Bethie disappointed.

"I don't know, Bethie, but let's not hurt Abner's feelings. Perhaps Joseph was too busy today with his chores," she added, trying not to look too disappointed. She was relieved that Thomas had decided to depart the train in Philadelphia, allowing them to have a private home coming.

"But that's not like Joseph. You don't think he took ill… do you, Miss Abby?"

"No, I'm sure it's nothing like that. Now don't worry, Bethie. We'll find out soon enough."

"Hello, Miss Abigail, hello, Bethie. Good to see you! We're all so happy you both are finally home."

"Hello, Abner, very good to see you. We're very grateful to be home," she replied sincerely.

Abner began to place their bags into the carriage as Bethie and Abigail looked gratefully about. "How wonderful it is to be back home, Bethie," commented Miss Abigail.

"Everything is just like I remembered, Miss Abby. I can't wait to see Aunt Liz and Joseph. I hope Covington is the same."

"I'm sure it is, Bethie. I'm sure it is."

Though Miss Abigail was anxious to see her sister, Joseph seemed to occupy her mind even more. After all the years of longing for a man she could never have, her thoughts of him had only strengthened. She was angry with herself for having such impossible dreams. But it was no use the more she fought them, the more prevalent they became.

Perhaps he had left the estate after all, thought Abigail wondering why he had not come for them. There had been so many job offers in the past and with better wages offered. Maybe he had finally said yes to one. It would have been a decent sacrifice.

Joseph always did what was best for her and Bethie first, always placing himself last. But deep down, Abigail hoped it was not true. She lived for Bethie, but longed for a man she could never be with. And to imagine she would never see him again was too painful and immediately dismissed from her thoughts. If it were true, Bethie's little heart would certainly be broken, she agreed.

She then recalled their last several encounters. The sadness that lingered in his eyes, as he watched the train leave the station will always be an image never to be forgotten, agreed Abigail, wondering if he knew she too felt the pain. The feel of his mouth pressed against hers with bodies touching one another's was still fresh in her mind.

Why can't I let you go, her mind struggled. She tried desperately to push down inappropriate thoughts that seemed unwilling to subside. Abigail was thankful for the carriage ride, giving opportunity to hide these unwanted feelings for him. *You've possessed me too long and it's unfair. I long to be set free! You've sentenced me to love no other and I'm surely destined to live and die a very lonely old woman*, imagined Miss Abigail desperately.

They were now approaching New Hope as Abigail squeezed her eyes, pushing back the tears and began smoothing her coat and straightening her hat. She looked over at Bethie whose head was out the window becoming more excited the closer they came to the estate.

Abigail found it to be contagious, as both became more excited by the moment. How beautiful the countryside and river were, spring was everywhere, as they passed alongside bunches of yellow daffodils waving in the breeze and shining as brightly as the sun.

"I can't wait to give Aunt Liz and Joseph a big hug, Miss Abby." It would be comforting to have her sister's arms around her again, she agreed.

It had been too long since she lived under the same roof with adults who truly loved and trusted one another. For the first time in many days, she could let her guard down and relax with ease. To feel loved and safe were two emotions long overdue. Except for the occasional visits from Mr. Holt and Henry, Abigail had learned to trust no one at the plantation. She even became careful around William, although he was a good boy, he still was Emma's son.

The carriage began to make its way onto the cobblestone entryway, as they could see the faint image of Elizabeth waving in the distance. The estate was exactly how they had remembered her, the elegant stone building never looked so stunning. Bethie hoped her room would be as she had left it. Many of her belongings had been left behind and Aunt Liz had promised they would be untouched and waiting for her when she returned.

The carriage barely came to a stop when Bethie jumped to the ground, luckily landing on both feet. She ran into the opened arms of Aunt Liz anxiously waiting with tears streaming down her face.

"Aunt Liz! Aunt Liz, I'm home!" yelled Bethie, wrapping her little arms around Elizabeth's chubby neck as they held on tightly to each other.

"God Bless you, child. Praise the Lord for bringing you back to me!" cried Elizabeth happily. Miss Elizabeth would hug Bethie for a moment then stop to look at the child while trying to wipe the tears from her face then she'd begin hugging Bethie again.

From a distance, stood Miss Abigail watching the two embrace with tears in her eyes. She understood and respected their joyful moment together and did not interfere. Abigail stared at Elizabeth out of concern, she noticed how much her sister seemed to age in two years.

She had lost a few pounds, but now walked with a cane. Her face looked tired and worn, as Miss Abigail blamed herself for Elizabeth's ailing health. She had imagined from the beginning that her sister would never get over the two of them leaving and this day had unfortunately, proven her right.

Miss Elizabeth looked up to find her only sister smiling joyfully at her. "Abigail… my dear sister, I've missed you so!" cried Elizabeth reaching out to embrace her. Bethie joined the two as they huddled together hugging one another.

"Now sister, what did I tell you about all that crying," teased Abigail lovingly.

"I couldn't stop myself if I tried, Abigail. My heart lay broken for two long years waiting for you two to come home. Let's go inside and rejoice this blessed day!" All three walked inside hand in hand, crying, and laughing, each so very happy to be together once again.

They sat in the kitchen while Aunt Liz cut them each a piece of Bethie's favorite pie, while Miss Abigail poured tea and milk. Abigail immediately questioned her sister about her health. Mr. Holt's report had concerned her, but she never expected Elizabeth to look as bad as she did. Of course Elizabeth, never wanting her little sister to worry about her, denied the seriousness of her condition.

The two exchanged stories of New Hope and Savannah, as Abigail waited for the appropriate moment to ask about Joseph. Bethie had become too preoccupied at the moment and had forgotten her worries of him.

"May I be excused, ma'am? I'd like to go up to my room."

"Such manners we have brought home," teased Aunt Liz. "Yes, my dear; you may be excused."

Abigail waited until Bethie left the kitchen. "Elizabeth, I was surprised not to find Joseph at the station this afternoon. It's not like him to miss the opportunity to see Bethie right away, especially after being away all this time."

"Oh, Joseph! With all the excitement of you two coming home, I almost forgot. He had to attend to an emergency over at Emily's house. Her sister took to having her baby early this morning and they asked Joseph if he would go and bring the midwife. And you know Joseph, Abigail, always willing to help."

"He's a good man, been a loyal and dear friend. I'm going to miss him terribly when he leaves. He was so upset not being able to meet you and Bethie at the station. But I assured him that you two would understand. It was hard to convince him to go," rambled Elizabeth.

"Elizabeth!" interrupted Abigail exasperated, "Slow down please. What are you talking about? Did you say Joseph is leaving Covington? And who is Emily?"

"I'm sorry, Abigail, for going on so. Lost my head there for a moment. Almost forgot that you've been away so long… Emily is Joseph's fiancée; they're to be married in the fall. No ring yet. Just like Joseph dragging his feet to the end; women throwing themselves at him, shamefully. But she's the one that finally got him to commit. Bought himself a piece of land west of New Hope, says he wants to be a farmer."

"I never wrote you about her because I only found out about the courtship myself just recently. That's just like Joseph to keep something as big as this to himself. Always was so private about his affairs. But can you believe it, Abigail? Our Joseph, after all these years, finally tying the knot! Isn't it wonderful news?"

The news of Joseph's sudden marriage stunned Miss Abigail, nearly taking her breath away. She tried hard not to show her disappointment in front of her sister. But it was unexpected and caught her by surprise. She never really expected him to take her last words to him literally.

How could he, thought Abigail, as she felt her heart sink. How could it be so easy for him, and so difficult for her? *Perhaps he never did feel the same*, she wondered sadly.

She forced a smile, "Yes… it's wonderful news. I wish the best for them both. Of course Bethie will be upset to hear he's leaving."

Both sisters sat under a large oak tree while watching Bethie play in the sunshine. Miss Elizabeth beaming with joy, thanked the Lord for bringing the two most important people in her life home to her safely. Even her poor health, agreed Abigail, seemed to improve from the mere presence of Bethie.

Miss Abigail took her time while looking about, wondering how she could have ever left her lovely home and state. Even Bethie's overall personality seemed to be lifted by the return. The sometimes nervous and cautious child, traits developed only from the past two years, seemed to have disappeared.

"Joseph's back!" yelled Bethie excited while jumping about. She waved relentlessly as a wagon and the faint glimmer of a man and woman came into view. The horses came to a complete stop meeting Bethie at their side.

Joseph jumped from the wagon and swept the child from the ground twirling them both around. "Joseph, I'm home!" blurted Bethie overjoyed.

"Well, if it ain't my little Bethie girl! Hello child, it's so good ta see ya!" smiled Joseph still holding her. He placed her gently down, "Well, I'm guessin' not so little anymore. Let's take a look at ya."

Bethie turned and posed trying to impress Joseph with how much she had grown. "You're a fine young lady now. Guess I better start callin' ya Miss Sara," he laughed teasingly.

His attention left Bethie as he slowly looked up to meet Miss Abigail's eyes, no longer able to hold off the inevitable. And in that instant, she knew their long ago, secret passion and true love for one another, still remained. And that it had not been only in her dreams or flamed by her solely.

In fact, stronger than she could ever recall. Time and separation had only strengthened their desire for one another. He immediately became awkward and speechless, but Abigail couldn't help but feel, even for a moment, selfishly vindicated. He still loved her and she knew it.

Many would have called them sinners—or even cursed. But whether it was a gift from God, or perhaps their lack of ignorance, they knew more than the norm. They had the ability to see beyond.

Beyond ones flesh, its color, its clothes that it wore, and right through to the soul. The soul in which lies the truth of its makeup, every flaw, and all that was good.

And it was there, where they had fallen in love. A love not aroused by curiosity or because it was forbidden, but a love that was real, tender, and good. Regardless of all who despise it or found it to be repulsive. It was between them, it was a fact, and it was as strong as any two. Though in this world, still, it made no difference, they had finally come to terms with it. Unable to hide it, even before a stranger that he was betrothed to.

In her mind, she forgave him completely for that night in which she had never forgotten. No longer feeling shame or regret. And she forgave him for soon marrying a woman, whom she knew, he would never love. He, too, was condemned. She would not be alone in it.

Through her eyes they seemed to merge, as they locked frozen in time but silently in fear, not knowing what to say and even afraid to speak. Their faces becoming somber and serious, both very still. Abigail felt envious of a woman that she did not even know, and privately wished she were her. They had become two pathetic souls lost in a love forever condemned by others, at least in this world and time, and never to be spoken of.

They stared for what seemed much too long when Abigail forced herself to become aware of the woman in the wagon. But her eyes remained on him, unwilling to let go. He continued to hug Bethie, praying to go unnoticed. And for the first time in her life, Abigail stood up to society's opinion of such behavior. She neither cared if her sister, nor his bride to be, noticed or thought of their encounter as inappropriate. She felt selfish, deserving of it, and for even a moment, tired of sacrificing.

Joseph nervously removed his hat from his head, "Hello, Miss Abigail…" He swallowed hard. "Good ta see ya home."

"Thank you, Joseph… It's good to be home."

Bethie, unaware of the two, began to question him as she tugged at his shirt demanding his full attention. "Why didn't you meet us at the station, Joseph?" She was determine to get to the bottom of it, and unwilling to let him off so easily.

"I'm sorry, Bethie girl… I really wanted ta be there—"

"But it's I, you should be crossed with Bethie," added Emily cutting into Joseph's apology.

"I'll explain ta ya later, Bethie," he whispered, helping Emily down from the wagon.

"Miss Sara, Miss Abigail… I'd like ya ta meet Miss Emily, my fiancée." Joseph's eyes wandered while he spoke, unable to look at Abigail.

Emily was beautiful, petite, and well spoken. One of the most beautiful, black women Bethie had ever met. Her hands as well as her feet were small and delicate. She dressed very neatly and spoke intelligently. Her father was one of the first Negro doctors in country.

It was obvious she had been well educated, thought Abigail pleased, but unable to stop the jealousy. "How do you do, Emily? I'm very pleased to meet you."

"Like wise, I'm sure," responded Emily, totally aware of their attraction to one another but remaining cordial. "Joseph has spoken fondly of you both. So glad to finally meet you. Especially since we intend to marry as soon as possible," warned Emily, remaining polite and dignified.

Elizabeth placed her chubby arms around Emily, "Isn't she cute as a button, Abigail?"

"Yes… you're very lovely," answered Abigail, relieved her sister had stepped in. Elizabeth appeared oblivious to it all, believed Abigail relieved.

"Thank you, ma'am," responded Emily guarded, but confident.

It did not take long for Emily to win Bethie's permission and admiration, as the two spent many afternoons laughing and talking while helping Joseph with his chores. She came almost every day bringing him supper with a pie or cake she had baked that morning. Emily became quite open and friendly with Elizabeth, but only cordial and short to Abigail.

She knew Emily was very bright and understood the chemistry between her and Joseph from the day the two met. Abigail also suspected that it was also the reason she came so often. She didn't blame Emily, who stayed by his side as much as she could without appearing too unladylike.

It was quite easy to see that she loved him with all her heart, and was unwilling to take the chance of losing him. Emily had decided long ago that she would, indeed, have him despite his love for another. Joseph was a special man, in every way. And the odds were certainly in her favor, and she knew it, and in time she truly believed he'd forget what could *never be* and learn to love her.

Miss Abigail fought harder than she had ever in her life to forget and accept Joseph and his new, soon to be, life. She avoided the two of them both day and evening. It was important to Abigail, almost an obsession, to eventually prove to Emily that what was once between them, no longer existed.

She had spent much of her life not caring what others thought of her. *So why now, and why Emily? Does it really matter that this woman likes me*, Abigail pondered annoyed with herself. Perhaps it was she who needed to be convinced, thought Abigail confused and distracted with constant thoughts of him.

She refused to be alone with Joseph, day or night. He'd come into the room and she would leave just as quickly. They neither had conversation nor confrontation.

Joseph wanted desperately to explain or apologize or whatever she wanted him to do. He was confused with Abigail's behavior; it wasn't at all like her. What did she want from him? After all, it was her words that he should be married, recalled Joseph annoyed.

Her attitude toward him turned cold and direct, opposite from her kind and gentle demeanor. And she purposely portrayed this behavior in front of Emily, who was still unwilling to buy it. She had somehow lost herself, something even Emma Mae couldn't achieve—although she had tried often.

Abigail was worried Elizabeth and Bethie would question her behavior toward him. It was odd, she knew it, but she was unable to control her emotions when he was near, becoming overly defensive. *Perhaps I'm losing my mind*, she thought desperately. She did, however, try to become more cautious when they were all nearby.

It was late and Joseph had put in a hard day. He was hungry, hot, and tired, in no mood for Abigail's sudden and confusing anger toward him. He needed to go into town before the sun went down. Abigail who was sitting in the library looking over the estate's books, refused to lift her head as he came in after knocking.

"Excuse me, ma'am. I'm goin' into town. Are ya needin' anything," asked Joseph direct, but mannerly.

"No. I don't believe so. Good Day, Joseph," she answered coldly, unwilling to make eye contact.

Joseph had always been a very patient and gentle man with high regards and respect for women. He couldn't recall there ever being a time when he had raised his voice at any woman. But she had gotten under his skin and was driving him to frustration. He was fed up and had enough of her, undeserved, ill treatment toward him, as he immediately shut the door forcing the two to be alone.

Abigail became nervous, realizing he was upset. But she continued staring at the books, pretending not to notice. Over the long summer days, he had tried desperately to find moments when she was alone so they could talk. But she knew what he was trying to do, and always stayed one step ahead by avoiding him or by making excuses.

It had finally come to this, a force confrontation by Joseph himself. Very unlike his character, thought Abigail, knowing she had pushed him too far. She was actually almost relieved, just like Joseph, she had enough. It needed to end.

He stood in front of the desk for a moment watching her, as he tried to calm down before he spoke. He was a gentleman and did not wish to have harsh words with her.

"Abigail, please… I can't go on working like this. I'm sorry for anything I did ta make ya hate me so. If it's because of that night…"

"I don't know what you're talking about, Joseph," interrupted Abigail in a matter of fact tone, removing her spectacles. She continued looking away, unable to look into his eyes.

"I'm sorry if my behavior has led you to believe that I have ill feelings toward you. I'm a Christian woman, Joseph, we hate no one. As you can see, I've been very busy with the estate since I've come back. Perhaps I've been a bit short with you, if so, I apologize."

"And I would prefer," hesitated Abigail, unable to hold back. "Never to discuss that night, ever!" she snapped. The encounter had become a trigger, as she lost control. "Shouldn't your attentions be focused on your fiancée, rather than worrying about another woman?" She suddenly realized she had crossed the line, and there was no going back.

Joseph was stunned by Abigail's outburst. "It's Emily… ain't it? That's why you're so angry at me!" guessed Joseph believing Abigail was jealous. "If that don't beat all!"

"You couldn't wait till I was married, said so yourself. But I don't believe ya ever thought I'd do it. You guessed I'd be a hired hand takin' orders from ya for the rest of my sorry life before I'd take another woman. Keepin' just the right amount of distance, so I couldn't touch ya and make ya skin crawl! Like I'd done that night!" lectured Joseph angry and out of control.

His words cut deep like a knife, he had never spoken to her like that before. But she knew he was right and deserved every word. *Why did I ever bring Emily into the conversation?* Abigail struggled to remain calm, angry at herself. But it was too late, Joseph was on to her, as he stood grinning down at her making Abigail angrier by the minute.

"How dare you speak to me that way! That's absolutely ridiculous! It's about time you get something straight, Joseph. You work for me, nothing more. Is that understood?" snapped Abigail in defense.

"You look me in the eyes and tell me that, Abigail. And I'll leave and promise never ta speak of it again. I give you my word."

She was so mad and determined to make him go away, she immediately looked up to meet his eyes. But he was too clever for her. His mocking grin had been replaced with a serious, longing stare. He had trapped Abigail with his loving eyes, holding her captive, restricting her to speak only the truth.

But her anger soon broke his spell, "I want you to leave this room, Joseph. Get out!" She swiftly stood, desperate to get as far away from him as she could. His words left her stripped and vulnerable with no walls left to protect or hide behind, as she wished the moment could be over. Running from the room would not be quick or far enough, agreed Abigail trying to hold back the tears.

She quickly came around the desk as Joseph reached out and grabbed her, pulling Abigail to him and forcing her to look up. "You can't spend ya whole life running from ya feelins'. You think ya can just mother Bethie and ya won't be needin' anything else. But ya can't do it, Abigail. You're a woman, too, whether ya believin' or not. Even your Quaker upbringin' won't save ya from it."

Abigail tried to struggle free from his hold, but he was too strong. He knew she would never scream and bring attention to them as his grasp became stronger.

"Now you listen ta me, Miss Abigail Prescott! I love ya, always have, but in your world I'm nothin' but a Negro man, ain't nothin'__ gonna change that!" And with those words he pulled her body tightly up against his as she struggled, forcing his lips to come down hard onto hers. The kiss was long and passionate as she continued to try and pull away.

Only when he was finished and willing did he let her go as he stood watching her, adrenaline rushing. She was so appalled by his behavior that she immediately slapped him across the face. "How dare you, get out," lectured Abigail shaken and upset, trying desperately to keep her voice down.

The sting of her slap lingered, injuring his soul worse than any other human had ever done. He stood devastated by his behavior with tears in his eyes wishing he were dead. *What have I done*, thought Abigail, wishing this day had never come. She knew she had hurt him beyond repair and was unable to fix it.

"I'll be lookin' for someone ta take over my work tomorrow. I believe it's best for everyone. I'm sorry, ma'am... My behavior was unforgivable. I've never acted that way before. And I can't explain it..." His overwhelming sadness left Abigail speechless and afraid to say anything that could make it worse. He quietly left the room, gently shutting the door behind him.

Miss Abigail was so upset that she told her sister she was not feeling well and would not be joining them for supper. Concerned, Elizabeth reassured her that she would keep an eye on Bethie and check on her later. She was relieved her sister did not question her further as she hurried to her room.

She was so ashamed at her behavior toward Joseph. Between the tears and endless replay of the day's encounter, she prayed constantly. He was a decent man who only deserved the best. They had been friends for so long and the thought of losing his friendship was devastating to her. She searched her soul trying to find an answer as to how to make things right. But she knew it could never be the same again.

He did not return to Covington until late that evening. Miss Abigail felt guilty that he had missed supper and concerned because of his poor eye sight at night. She watched from her bedroom window until she could finally see the glimpse of a lantern, from a wagon, at the end of the cobblestone entryway. He was finally home safe and she thanked God.

Already in her night clothes, she sat in front of her mirror and began to take down her bun. She removed her spectacles from her face and brushed her long black hair. Abigail stopped for a moment to study herself. How different she looked with her hair down and spectacles off her face. She may have been beautiful, but in her mind a pathetic, spinster woman who was very lonely despite her Bethie. Joseph had been right; it would not be enough.

Miss Abigail checked on Bethie who was sleeping peacefully. She walked over to her sister's room and could hear her snoring from where she stood. Abigail quickly shut her door, hoping Elizabeth's snoring would not wake Bethie.

Dressed in her cape, she quietly made her way through the night carrying a covered dish. She headed toward a small house next to the barn. It was where Joseph lived.

She could see a dim light coming from his window. Abigail was relieved that he was still awake for she could not sleep this night without making things right between them again. Somehow she would make him believe that she was truly sorry. She desperately needed his forgiveness and would do whatever it would take.

Abigail stood before his door afraid to knock. She took a deep breath then finally began. It was abruptly opened as Joseph stood surprised at the door.

"Miss Abigail… Is there anythin' wrong? Is everybody alright? Bethie, Miss Elizabeth?" Regardless of the day's events, he was legitimately concerned. She had never come to his house that late.

He stood in the shadow of the lamp wearing no shoes or shirt, still wet from his bath in the river and obviously nearly ready for bed. Miss Abigail could not help but look at his naked chest, albeit embarrassed. She had neither seen a man without his shirt that close up, nor had Abigail ever been with a man.

His body was lean and masculine, very attractive to any eyes, agreed Abigail becoming even more flushed. She nervously answered, "I know it's late, Joseph. I won't stay but a minute. You missed supper and I thought you'd be hungry by now. I know you work so hard… and would probably be very hungry," she rambled nervously.

Joseph just stared in disbelief, stunned that Abigail had come to his home this late. He had never seen her hair down—and certainly not dressed for bed. She was much too proper. Again, it was so unlike her, thought Joseph astonished, overwhelmed by her beauty.

"I'll put it over on the table."

"Thank ya, ma'am," answer Joseph politely, not knowing what to do or how to act. She had nearly taken his breath away by her actions.

He could only watch as she entered, simply shocked by Abigail's presence. She walked around him slowly, straight to a little table where she placed the covered plate gently down. He continued to remain where he was simply frozen. Abigail lightly brushed by him as she tried to get between the door and his body.

Before leaving, she turned around and looked into his eyes with much sincerity, pain, and regret. "Joseph, I'm very sorry for my behavior. I don't know what's come over me. I guess it's just been the years of bitterness building up inside. Eating me alive, I suppose. It's been hard living with that woman. I miss New Hope so much; I'd give anything to stay…"

"But Bethie needs me. You mustn't ever blame yourself. Leaving Covington was more than just Bethie. Being near you… well it just wasn't right for either of us. I realize we can't change who we were born, that's just the way it is. I never meant to hurt you. I really do cherish our friendship. We've been friends for so long… I couldn't bear for you to hate me—"

"I could never hate you, Abigail," he interrupted.

"I hope you can forgive me. It would break Bethie's heart if you would go. She loves you so much. And… it would break my heart too." Abigail took a moment to pause, as she fought desperately to push back the tears.

"I really do wish the best for you, Joseph. Emily is a fine woman.

I know I can't give you what she can. I'd never wish you to end up like me, lonely and unable to love another. That's my hell. I wouldn't wish it on anyone..." He was overwhelmed by her.

"I've never loved a man like I've loved you. And I expect... I never will. I know it's hopeless. And I've tried so hard not to. But I can't seem to make it stop." Tears began to fall from her eyes as she meant every word spoken. He remained stunned and speechless, tears building up in his own eyes.

"You must know... in spite of what others may think, you and I are alike. Just two souls trying to do what's right. Servants to this world, trying desperately to survive against those who'd rather swallow us alive. Because to them, we are irrelevant. But in the end, we are really the same—you and I. Don't let the color of my skin tell you otherwise..."

She had never openly bared her soul to anyone, including herself. Abigail was relieved to finally say words that had been neatly hidden away for so long in the depths of her very being. She could now, finally be able to let him go. Abigail couldn't bear his sympathy. For him to feel pity for her would be the worst, she agreed, turning to leave and taking her eyes from his.

"Good bye, Joseph. I really do wish you the best..."

Suddenly, she could feel the powerful strength of his arm around her waist, as he quickly spun her around to face him. He brought his lips down on hers, as Abigail's arms fell around his neck. Joseph could feel her warm, wet tears as they fell upon his own face. He pulled her closer, wanting desperately to ease the sadness that filled them both. He paused only to look deeply into her eyes.

"There ain't nothin' irrelevant about you, ma'am. Lord help Savannah..."

"And us," she whispered to him.

He kissed her again, pulling her close, unwilling to take his mouth from hers or to allow Abigail to think and possibly protest. She would be his that night as the two filled with passion, unresolved and long overdue, kissed until their mouths were bruised. If for only the night, he lifted her from the floor and kicked closed the door shutting out the world as they knew it.

The Music Box

The rest of the summer had gone by quickly as late August was now approaching. It was time for Bethie to return to Savannah and begin her studies. Coming home to New Hope had done her a world of good, she was less nervous and more outgoing around others.

Though she loved Covington and would miss Aunt Liz and Joseph terribly, Bethie longed to see William again. They had written often, keeping each other up to date on their day to day adventures. She missed the island, plantation, and felt a certain obligation, unable to be defined, toward him. Returning to Georgia would not be as difficult as she had imagined.

Joseph had their bags outside ready to be loaded onto the wagon when he noticed an unfamiliar carriage coming down the entryway of the estate. When it came to a stop, a white man about his own age dressed in a suit came out of the carriage heading toward him.

"Good morning. My name is Mr. Alexander Gilmore, of Gilmore and Associates located in Philadelphia. I was sent by Mrs. Calhoun to escort Miss Abigail and Miss Sara Beth back to Savannah. I have a signed letter from Miss Emma Mae authorizing me to do so. You may announce my arrival to Miss Abigail. Please give her this note. I'll wait."

He handed Joseph the letter immediately, causing him to place down the bags where he stood. Although he looked familiar to him, he was not quite sure where he had seen this man before. Miss Abigail, Elizabeth, and Bethie were coming out of the estate as Joseph tried desperately to remember.

He did not like the looks of him and had a bad feeling from the moment the man came into view. "I was about ready ta take Miss

Abigail and Bethie to Doylestown myself, sir!" replied Joseph defensively.

"That won't be necessary. Looks like I made it just in time. You can put their bags in my carriage. My driver will assist you."

Joseph did not trust this man and refused to budge, "Joseph, we have a visitor?" questioned Miss Abigail, intervening. She immediately noticed Joseph becoming upset and worried.

The man took off his hat, "Hello, ma'am. My name is Alexander Gilmore. Miss Sara's aunt, Mrs. Calhoun, has requested me to accompany the two of you back to Georgia. She wanted to make sure you both had a safe return and hired me to escort the two of you personally. I have a written letter from her to give to you. Joseph reluctantly handed Miss Abigail the letter. He was looking forward to taking the two himself and was disappointed by this stranger's sudden intrusion.

Miss Abigail, not desiring to be escorted by a stranger all the way to Savannah, was also becoming annoyed as she read the letter to herself. "Well, I think that is quite noble of Emma Mae to be so concerned for us," responded Abigail sarcastically. "But Joseph will be accompanying us to the train station. We are in no need for an escort and can take care of ourselves just fine, thank you!"

"And I do not doubt that you are quite capable of returning on your own, ma'am," interrupted Mr. Gilmore. "However, I'm only doing what I've been instructed to. As you can verify, the letter was attached to a court order. You seem like a fine, proper lady and I'm sure you wouldn't want to go against the law. Now would you, ma'am?" He was unwilling to back down, probably out of fear of Emma.

"This court order, sir, was derived in Savannah. It has no jurisdiction in Pennsylvania. Are you aware of that, or did you think I would not be? I may not be a lawyer, but even I know the law… So, Emma Mae's worried we might decide not to return, is she! Had to hire your services, I see. What else do you do for her, Mr. Gilmore?"

"Would you like me ta escort this gentleman off the property, ma'am," snapped Joseph, moving closer to the stranger with clenched fists.

"No Joseph!" blurted Elizabeth, horrified.

"Joseph… will you put our bags in his carriage, please."
Abigail's eyes begged him to let the matter go as she turned and sneered at the man. "I don't wish to discuss this matter any further. However, we would appreciate it, Mr. Gilmore, if you would be so kind as to wait in the carriage so we can say goodbye to our loved ones in private. That is not asking too much, is it?"

"No, ma'am. I'll wait in the carriage," he replied, relieved that he did not have to confront Joseph.

Abigail waited until the man was gone before she spoke again. She turned and faced Joseph to find his disappointment and sadness more than she could bear. His heart was breaking. And hers, too.

An argumentative atmosphere was the last thought Miss Elizabeth wanted to remember, as she tried to change the subject by hugging and kissing Bethie goodbye. "I'm going to miss you, dear… The summer was just wonderful having you both home again," she added with tears in her eyes.

"Awe! Don't cry, Aunt Liz. We'll see each other next summer…" Bethie gave her another hug then turned her attention toward Joseph.

"Can I speak to you alone, Joseph?" she asked quite serious.

"Yes, child, of course ya can," he answered smiling, breaking the tension. The two walked away hand in hand until they reached the barn. He lifted Bethie up onto a platform so they could see eye to eye.

"What is it, Bethie girl?" he replied, concerned. He knew Bethie well. And he also knew how inquisitive she could be. He could only imagine what was on her mind.

"Joseph… I really like Emily a lot. I think she's really nice and really pretty too! But…"

"But what, child?"

"Please don't move away. I don't want you to go." She started to cry. Joseph embraced her again.

"You and Emily can get married then she can move here to Covington. And if you wait till the summer, I can come to your wedding. Maybe I can even be the flower girl. Don't you want me to, Joseph? You always said that I was your favorite little girl. Aren't I your favorite anymore?" she begged with tears streaming down.

Joseph heart was breaking a second time today. He did not want to hurt Bethie's feelings but could not help but chuckle at her well-thought-out plan for him and his future. She could be so unpredictable at times, causing him to laugh in astonishment.

"I'm sorry Bethie girl. Didn't mean to laugh at ya. Please forgive me… I know ya don't want me to go. It's killin' me too, child. More than you know… But whatever I do, I promise ya will always be my favorite little girl. Whenever ya need me or come back to Covington, I'll always be here for ya."

"You really promise, Joseph?"

"Promise, you child," convinced Joseph smiling. "Promise you…" He hugged her again, helping Bethie to feel more secure.

Both sisters were saying their last goodbyes, as Joseph helped Bethie into the carriage. He stood next to Elizabeth as he picked up Abigail's small hand bag wondering how he could let her leave him. His heart was breaking, a feeling he knew all too well. Abigail could sense his pain from where she stood, for their pain had become one.

She took her eyes from her sister's only to become lost in his. Abigail continued to remind herself not to cry, but her heart seemed to take control as the tears began to fall. Unable to control them, she looked over at her sister trying to convince her that the thought of leaving Covington again, had overwhelmed her immensely.

"Goodbye, Joseph. I will miss you… terribly. I wish you the very best. You deserve it." Although the words had been carefully rehearsed, she had to painfully force herself to say them. She had secretly hoped this day would never come.

"But I won't believe, we shall never see each other again. We've been friends for so long and my heart simply won't accept it."

Abigail took a moment as Joseph pushed a handkerchief into her hand.

"Please… keep it, ma'am," he insisted. She nodded, eyes downward.

She gently dabbed away her tears, as she looked up to find her sister crying too. Joseph stood speechless and lost knowing there was nothing he could say or do to make Abigail stay. His eyes filled with tears, as he wished he could take her in his arms one last time.

Abigail, ignoring her sister's presence, put her arms around him and gave him a long embrace. He was shocked by her actions. He fought the urge to reciprocate for fear that he would never be able to let her go, and all would be revealed. He longed to feel her lips against his own and to whisper in her ears the love that he felt so deeply for her. She finally let go, but before she pulled away she softly kissed him on his cheek.

No longer able to look into his eyes, she slowly reached out for the small bag that she kept by her side when she traveled. He watched as her gloved hand grasped the handle as it touch his own. Joseph was tired and angry with society's labels, rules, and the inability to control who he was born. He could not help himself as he quickly grabbed onto her arm in desperation, refusing to let go.

Abigail immediately became nervous and upset, her eyes begged him to let her go.

"Let her go, Joseph… I may be old, but I'm not blind," interrupted Elizabeth, sternly. She placed her hand on Joseph's shoulder. "Think about the child… She needs us. We're all she has, Joseph," she begged, softly.

They were both so taken by Elizabeth's words and prior knowledge of the two, they paused for a moment to stare at her. She neither scolded nor judged but only felt their situation to be hopeless, less important to the responsibility at hand.

Abigail was never more proud to have Elizabeth for a sister. She was wise, empathetic, and selfless in every way. Her love and understanding were never needed more than it was this day. She forced a smile through her tears as Joseph eventually smiled back, releasing his hold on her.

There were no more words said by the three as she slowly got into the carriage. The two stood silent and still, as they watched in the morning sun the two most important people in their lives leave them once again.

Abigail never looked back, but held Joseph's handkerchief tightly in her hand. But something was in it, other than her tears. She pushed it into the pocket of her coat. It wasn't until they were on the train to Savannah and Bethie was fast asleep did she retrieve the handkerchief.

In the shadow of a lantern, she gently open the cloth to find a woman's gold wedding band. She studied it closely, simply stunned. She could feel something had been engraved inside the ring. Placing her spectacles on, she moved closer to the light. Inside the ring read the word "ma'am", nearly taking her breath away.

Abigail swiftly unbuttoned the top of her nightgown and removed the chain which held a cross. She added the ring then replaced the chain back around her neck quickly closing the buttons, concealing the ring against her heart from the world as she knew it to be.

Still stunned, she let out a sigh falling back against the seat, "What have we done, Joseph…"

The return to Savannah was a quiet and somber one. Miss Abigail occupied her time by reading stories to Bethie. Everyday became a battle, as she fought the intimate memories of Joseph from her mind and heart. She lay awake at night reliving every word they said to one another, still able to feel his touch and warmth against her body. Only to finally, cry herself to sleep in bitter hopelessness. Bethie was a true comfort with her innocent, childlike behavior and unconditional love being a constant reminder of why she was.

To Bethie's delight, William and Henry met them both at the Savannah station. "Look, Miss Abby! It's William and Henry," blurted Bethie, joyfully running over to where they stood. She threw her arms around William who quickly became embarrassed hoping no one had noticed.

"William! I'm back!"

"Bethie, stop hugging me! Someone might see us," he remarked, embarrassed but excited to see her too.

"Well, hello there missy! Miz Abigail, ma'am," greeted Henry enthusiastically. "Been like an old southern funeral without ya two. Glad ta see ya home!" Bethie giggled, happy to see his sense of humor remained.

"Good to see you too, Henry," replied Miss Abigail, pleased and relieved that Mr. Gilmore had departed.

"Henry has to pick up some supplies before we head home, Miss Abigail. Can Bethie and I walk around some? I can watch over her. I know the city as well as anyone. You won't have to worry about us getting lost."

"Well, I suppose it would be all right. I need some supplies myself. I'll accompany Henry as long as you two promise not to wander too far."

"You have my word, ma'am," convinced William very maturely.

"Yippee!" responded Bethie, relieved to be off the locomotive and thrilled to be able to roam free with him.

From the station, the two headed east leading to the center of the city. The day was warm and bright, as the two hurried along trying to avoid running into people on the streets. The city was crowded and bustling.

William grabbed Bethie's hand concerned she'd get lost in the crowds. He pulled her to the side and away from the wagons and carriages. It was the first time the two had ever been allowed to roam on their own in the city. The feeling of freedom was wonderful, she agreed, holding tightly onto William's firm grip.

They walked passed elegant squares, each named differently. "Will you be able to remember how to get back to the station, William?" asked Bethie not certain of where she was.

"Don't worry. No one knows this city better than I do. I've lived here all my life. You can trust me. I won't let anything happen to you. Do you think Miss Abigail would have let us go if I didn't know how to get back?"

"I'm almost thirteen, quite old enough to take responsibility. Why I even helped mother to run Calhoun this summer when you were away. Even took one of her ships out to sea. Course Miss Jane came along too," bragged William, hoping to impress her.

"One day they'll be my ships and I'm going to travel the world, just like a real pirate. But I won't hurt anyone... or steal! Just travel about, seeing places I've never been to. You can come too, Bethie! We'll be pirates together. Yes, I believe it would be quite splendid to have you along!" he laughed. Bethie giggled along with him, happy to see that their short separation had not changed him in the least.

"Would you like to see mother's ships, Bethie?"

"Do you know how to get there?" she asked delighted.

"Follow me," directed William heading across the square in a different direction.

He moved quickly as she followed him through several small alleys situated between row houses with wrought iron fences draped with towering azaleas. Their gardens were stunning. Bethie's eyes caught one in particular; she stopped for a moment to look. The colors were bright and magnificent. It was filled with rose bushes, centered in the middle was a large, beautiful Magnolia tree.

"Bethie, what are you doing," hollered William, just now realizing she was not directly behind him. He ran back to where she stood.

"I just wanted to look at the garden. Isn't it beautiful? See all the roses? There must be hundreds of them! They're my favorite flower in the whole world. Aunt Liz and I planted many of them this summer."

"That's nice," he replied, becoming bored.

He began to climb over the fence, placing his feet between the iron bars. "Be careful, William!" warned Bethie, concerned about the intricate, sharp spokes displayed on top. When he was high enough, he swung his one leg over the top avoiding the spokes. When he was finally on the other side, he quickly ran over to the flowers picking the first one he could find, breaking off its thorns.

William carefully climbed back and handed Bethie the flower. "OK, now you have your rose. Can we please go now," he asked in a hurry, anxious to move on.

"Thank you, William. But isn't that stealing?"

"Girls," he shrugged, pulling Bethie along with him.

He led her to the waterfront. Both stood watching English merchant ships leaving the port laden with cotton bales. They walked to the edge of the cobblestone front. William pointed out his mother's ships to her.

"They're so big!" she gasped.

The ocean was so massive in comparison to any waters that she had ever seen. She imagined that England was at the other end. The sun seemed to reflect gold images off her blue, clear surface.

"Come on, Bethie! We don't have much time. Let's go!"

They headed toward a busy street lined with small shops and businesses. The trading post was busy as crowds filled the street. An auction was being held selling many items from Europe that had just recently arrived on ships.

The sweet and tantalizing smell of baked goods was in the air, as the two peeked in the window of a bakery. They walked over to watch a man making candles in the next shop. His door was left wide open allowing the mild breeze to cool the small, hot shop.

As they walked along taking in all that was around them, Bethie's eyes suddenly caught attention to the most beautiful music box. It sat at eye level on a dainty, white lace cloth in a picture window of a small shop for everyone to see. A lovely, elegantly dressed woman and gentleman, painted and sculptured on fine porcelain, held each other in dance.

Slowly the two turned as Bethie could hear the faint sounds of the most enchanting notes of music she had ever heard. A lovely waltz played romantically on the box, repeatedly, as it turned in motion.

William, noticing Bethie standing very still, silent, and in some sort of trance, walked over to investigate. He was anxious and curious to see what had captured his little cousin's heart and placed her in such awe.

He looked at the music box then at her and found Bethie's deep attraction to the box to be odd. To him, it was nothing more than a silly music box made for ladies and displayed in a window to purposely lure them. But he had never seen her so intrigued and did not wish to disturb her moment of wonderment.

"It's the most beautiful music box that I have ever seen. The music is so lovely," she added, still in awe.

By the looks of it, William could tell the box was probably quite expensive. He wished he had saved his money rather than spending it on gum drops and licorice for the two of them. But that probably still would not have been enough, he imagined, wanting so to please Bethie with this gift.

"I'll save my money up and buy the box for you some day, Bethie."

Her trance was broken by William's thoughtful gesture.

"That's very kind. But you don't have to spend your money on me. Thank you, William. Anyway… I'm sure it costs much more than we could ever save. But if we could buy it, I'd keep it in our special box on the island."

"Splendid," replied William, rolling his eyes. "That's all I need. Another girlie item in my pirate's box!" he whispered to himself sarcastically. "It's time to head back to the station, Bethie," he said, now bored with her newest attraction.

William suddenly recognized two young school girls that he knew, both around his own age. He tried to ignore their presence by quickly hurrying Bethie passed the shop, as he could hear them giggling to each other.

"Good day, William!" blurted loudly one of the girls trying to get his attention. He was frustrated with himself for not being able to sneak away sooner and unnoticed.

The two turned around as Bethie recognized them from their studies. She easily remembered their loud and flirty personalities, triggered by William whenever he was near. He, of course, had eventually become aware that they were sweet on him and wanted nothing to do with either of them. In fact, he found their behavior toward him down right obnoxious.

"Hello, Gwendolyn, Abilene," he replied, in a not so happy to see them tone. Bethie noticed him blushing and wondered if he found them to be pretty.

"Taking your little sister around are you?" questioned a nosey Gwendolyn.

"How many times do I have to tell you, Gwendolyn, she's not my little sister. She's my cousin from Pennsylvania. And if you don't mind, we're in a bit of a hurry." He was annoyed with their silly giggling.

"Got stuck watching her, huh," added Gwendolyn, trying to keep the conversation alive.

Bethie thought of them as two silly school girls shamefully trying to win William's affections whenever they thought possible. "I'm only several years younger than the two of you. And I certainly don't need anyone watching me. It's late, William! We better go," snapped Bethie dropping the rose as she began to quickly walk away. William secretly picked it up, hiding it in his jacket, trying to catch up to her.

Bethie's jealously of the girls had gotten the best of her, as she ignored him all the way back. He tried talking to her, but she refused by giving short yes and no responses to all of his questions. William was confused, as he finally gave up shrugging his shoulders as he led the way back to the station. Bethie directed her attention only to Miss Abigail and Henry, purposely ignoring him on the ride back to the plantation.

Henry unloaded their bags as Miss Abigail was greeted by Miss Jane at the main door. Though it was not her nature to smile or display joy of any kind, she seemed genuinely pleased to see them both. Bethie stood a short distance from the carriage, continuing to ignore William.

"Bethie, I'm sorry if those girls hurt your feelings. They're only silly. I wouldn't mind them too much." William's supportive words lightened Bethie's mood. She decided that she was no longer angry with him. She was pleased to find that even he found the two to be silly and uninteresting.

"They didn't bother me none," she assured him, blushing.

"Oh! I almost forgot… You dropped your flower on the way back to the station," he added, taking the mangled flower from his jacket and giving what was left of it to her.

She was pleased with William's thoughtfulness, knowing the subject of flowers seemed to just bore him. Her Aunt Emma frowned from her office window as she spied on the two.

"Thank you, William. I'll place it in one of my books so it will keep forever," she smiled brightly.

They went inside to greet Emma Mae. Bethie kept close to William's side until the inevitable, awkward, unwanted deed had been completed. Emma Mae, pretending to be happy with Bethie's return, forced a crooked smile as her jealousy of the child consumed her. Desperate and worried that her darkest fear had become reality. No longer able to control it. She could only watch as her son's closest love, which had been her, was replaced with the child named Sara.

April 14, 1878

It was almost three years since Bethie had returned to Covington. But most importantly, today was her thirteenth birthday. From William's suggestion, Emma had decided in giving Bethie a formal birthday party to be held outdoors. Not for the child's sake, but for her own, for she thought it was time that Bethie was introduced properly into society.

Emma Mae had travelled to London the past several summers on business accompanied by Miss Jane. She insisted on taking William, refusing to allow her son to remain on the plantation. He and Bethie did not want to be separated but he soon gave into Emma's demands.

Though Bethie and William were still children, Emma's growing jealousy of the girl had caused her to begin plotting and arranging her twisted plan of eventually taking Covington. It began with the desperate attempt to place distance between the two children, hoping to create a wedge.

She had convinced Miss Abigail that she was needed at Calhoun to manage her businesses while she was in Europe. Abigail was surprised by her request, although she believed it had been just a new, more creative excuse for them not to return to Pennsylvania.

Emma Mae, in her crazed, demented way felt more comfortable knowing the two remained on her property in which she felt a tighter control. She used Abigail's sister as a decoy, trying desperately to convince her that the summer visits to Savannah would be good for Miss Elizabeth's poor health.

Miss Abigail had eventually agreed. She too, secretly wished to avoid the estate. She was avoiding Joseph, no longer able to control her feelings toward him. Abigail had given herself to him and knew there would never be another. He held that power over her, and she was afraid. She went along with Emma Mae hoping not to trigger her curiosity, because neither of them rarely agreed on anything concerning Bethie.

Shortly after their last and only visit to New Hope, Miss Elizabeth wrote to say in a very short paragraph that Joseph had postponed his wedding to Emily, indefinitely. Never listing any reason, for they were both quite aware of why, only to say that he would continue to remain at Covington for the time being. Abigail felt entirely at fault, but her heart refused to regret. She had won, yet she still felt selfish but unremorseful.

Joseph had told Emily that he was simply not ready. All he could offer her was a sincere apology. But, yet again, he would feel the sting of a woman's scorn. However, this time he was ready, since it was expected and he felt it deserved. He took it like a man, a gentleman.

He could still recall her wrath as it was her words that would linger, bruising him more than the slap across his face. She was certainly furious, but her demeanor remained ladylike as she tried to regain calmness.

"Over some white woman?" Joseph could only stare back in disbelief. He neither confirmed her suspicions, nor would he deny them. Emily was a dignified lady and he would not insult her intelligence. But if necessary, he would take it to his grave to protect them all.

"Ain't never gonna happen... You're a fool, Joseph," she added calmly, but defeated. To this day, they avoided one another.

Though Bethie missed Joseph and New Hope, she looked forward to her Aunt Liz's visits and seemed not to mind too much. Miss Abigail was relieved that she did not protest and felt her only emotional defense against Joseph was simply to avoid him at all cost. He had become her Achilles heel. And he would have no other.

Although Bethie was disappointed that he had decided not to marry Emily, she was extremely delighted by the news. She believed her long talk with him before she left New Hope had been the reason. She was a child and knew no better, and all that mattered was that he would remain on the estate. And one day, they would be a family again.

At Miss Elizabeth's request, Mr. Holt had returned to Savannah to again accompany Miss Abigail and Bethie back to New Hope for the summer. Elizabeth's health had taken a turn for the worse, and she made Mr. Holt promise not to discuss her ailing condition with her sister. Miss Elizabeth understood how difficult Abigail's situation was and did not want to worry her further.

She was convinced that she was indeed near death and would not live past this year. Elizabeth wanted desperately for her family to return home once again, despite Abigail's resistance. Her illness would not allow her to travel and she wished to remain at Covington in case the inevitable came sooner than expected. Emma Mae, coincidently, had decided not to travel to London that summer after Mr. Holt sent a formal letter to her, acknowledging his intentions.

When he did arrive in Savannah, two days before Bethie's thirteenth birthday, Miss Abigail did meet with him to discuss business. He informed her, to his knowledge, Emma Mae had made several inquiries concerning the estate's financial standings. Miss Abigail, not trusting Emma, instructed him to keep an eye on the situation.

Abigail also asked Thomas to research Emma's past and supply her with all the information he could find. She felt something, more than usual, was not right and wanted any and all information he could gather. She felt it was in Bethie's best interest to know all that there was of this woman—and her past.

Abigail questioned him of her sister's health, but he remained vague through the entire conversation wanting to keep his promise to Miss Elizabeth. Abigail immediately sensed in his voice and facial expressions that her sister had become very ill. She did not continue to pry further but insisted on returning to Calhoun so she could begin preparing for their departure.

Bethie lay across the grassy hill sobbing, using her bent arm as a rest for her head. Her ignorance of puberty had left her feeling sad and hopeless with the thought of ultimate doom, surely near. Embarrassed by her condition, she felt too humiliated to even consult Miss Abigail, as the morning's hustle and bustle gave way to easily escaping to the only place she had ever felt safe.

How long would she be able to hide, she wondered, relieved only William was aware of the secret island. Their years of friendship and trust had remained solid and unspoiled, even despite Emma Mae. They had taken a vow of secrecy five years ago that continued to remain untarnished.

"Beth-ie! Bethie, are you here?" hollered William cupping his hands around his mouth, continuing to maneuver his way through the island. He came to the foot of the hill as she abruptly sat up quickly wiping away the tears from her face.

"William, I didn't hear you coming."

"What are you doing here, Bethie? Miss Abigail is having a fit looking for you. She's got nearly the entire staff trying to find you. Thank goodness for Henry. He came and told me you were missing. Thought I'd know where you were better than anyone else."

"People will soon be arriving and you're still not dressed. What's the matter with you anyway?" he questioned, irritated.

"Nothing. I just needed a little time to myself. Can't I come to the island without you always following me?" she snapped, annoyed that her privacy had been invaded.

"Well excuse me, ma'am! I thought this island was ours. I didn't know I had to get your permission to come on it. You know, Bethie, you're turning into a real bore these days!" lied William defensively, angry that she hurt his feelings.

He knew it was not like Bethie to ever be angry that he was with her. Though he had noticed a change in her behavior these past months, ever since he had returned from Europe the previous summer. She was so excited to see him, yet seemed to awkwardly distance herself a bit more. It had been nothing for them to take off their shoes and socks then wade in the lake. Or to play leap frog, one always falling on the other. But he was awkward, too. In truth, they were growing up.

In private, he had consulted with Miss Abigail. She explained that Bethie was simply turning into a young lady and probably didn't feel as comfortable with such activities anymore. He understood and soon accepted the reasoning and became more selective of the activities he would offer to do with her.

The closer William came to Bethie, the more she turned her face from him. She didn't want him to see that she had been crying. But it was obvious, her eyes were red and puffy.

"Bethie… are you crying," he asked, concerned and feeling guilty that he had become angry. He regretted his words to her.

On the outside Bethie was as lovely as a porcelain doll, but inside, she was as tough as pig iron. This had been one of the reasons William had grown so fond of her. He enjoyed her companionship as much as his male friends, even more.

They even liked Bethie. There was never a protest by any of them when she came along. Bethie was the only girl allowed when it came to group events. She was like one of the boys. He never had to worry about her crying all the time. Even when she'd fall or hurt herself she'd just pick herself up, wipe herself off, and then start up again. Usually mad at herself for being so careless in the first place.

"Is it my mother? Did she say something to upset you," questioned William, entirely aware that the two were not close to one another. How ironic it was, agreed Bethie, to be the first time ever her sadness had not been caused by Emma Mae.

"No William! It's not your mother. Everything is fine. I don't want to talk to you about it anyhow," she remarked becoming hysterical.

"You don't know anything do you? You're supposed to be my best friend, yet you can't even see before your own eyes that… Well, that I'm dying!" cried Bethie dramatically.

She ran from the hill leaving William standing dumbfounded while wondering what in the world he had done now. He shrugged his shoulders in frustration. "Dying? If that don't beat all! Girls! They don't make any sense. Why did God put them here anyway," he grumbled, stomping down the hill.

Bethie ran all the way back, through the cotton fields and past the servants setting up for her party. She hurried as fast as she could, worried she'd soon explode from overwhelming tears that could no longer be controlled. From the kitchen, she took the back stairs to her room ignoring Henry's wife as she called out to her. Down the dark corridor and to her room she ran hoping Miss Abigail would not be there waiting. She quickly opened the door to her room then flung herself on her bed and began to cry again.

A gentle hand brushed across the back of her head as Miss Abigail sat next to her patiently, deciding she would wait for Bethie to speak first.

"Miss Abby," cried Bethie, putting her arms around Abigail's waist tucking her head inward.

"What is it, dearest," asked Miss Abby trying to comfort her. "Something has been wrong all morning. You disappear, your new dress still sits on the trestle table, and guests are now starting to arrive for your party."

"Bethie, it's your birthday! One of the happiest days of the year for you. What could possibly be making you so blue?" she begged, wanting to get to the bottom of it.

"I'm dying, Miss Abby. I'm dying!" she blurted, with tears rolling down her swollen face.

"Bethie! What on earth makes you think you're dying," she responded, alarmed.

"Now calm down. Sit up and let's wipe those tears from your eyes. If you don't stop crying, your face is going to puff up like a blowfish." She helped Bethie to a sitting position and began to wipe her face.

"Hush now… Tell me what the problem is."

"It's embarrassing, Miss Abby. Even to tell you," confessed Bethie who had at least stopped crying.

"Bethie, I love you very much. There is not a thing in the world you can't tell me. It doesn't matter how terrible you may think it is. I'm here for you. Now come on, dearest. You've always been able to tell me anything."

"Well, the thing is… I'm bleeding, Miss Abby. A great deal, too! I'll surely die of it."

"Where!" she questioned frantically. "What do you mean you're blee…" Abigail froze, finally aware of what Bethie's problem was.

"Oh dearest, you're not dying. What is happening is that you're becoming a woman. This is my fault. I should have explained all of this before it happened. It's hard for me to accept that my little girl is growing up. I never wanted you to become so frightened. Please forgive me," she begged, hugging her tightly.

Abigail took her time to explain to Bethie what was happening to her body, ignoring the groups of people forming outside. Bethie soon understood and seemed to accept her non-fatal condition with much maturity. Miss Abigail helped her to wash up and do her hair.

She finally helped her into her new dress, then stood back in awe from the absolute beauty and loveliness Bethie portrayed in it. She had certainly grown, there was no question about it, agreed Abigail with tears in her eyes. No longer was she her little Bethie but a beautiful, mature, young lady.

Shy and blushing, Bethie slowly stepped outside embarrassed by the number of eyes that where upon her. The sun's brightness made her squint causing her vision to become blurred and making her feel even more inadequate. She felt as though she were an item on display for locals to view and judge.

Though there were a few children her own age, most were adults she did not know. By the way they were dressed and the manner in which they conducted themselves, Bethie assumed they were the rich and powerful Georgian aristocrats.

They resembled the individuals that on occasion would come for tea held in the parlor or in one of the gardens. In passing, she could hear them talking about politics, the state of the economy, or their favorite subject—their money. These were the type of people her aunt desired to be around. They were vain, shallow, and pompous, much like herself.

The silence was broken by William who started in with the birthday song leading everyone including her aunt to join in. It finally ended with a long, loud, clapping tribute. The event was quite formal for a little girl's birthday party.

The servants were neat and polished, dressed in their very best, serving glasses of champagne, lemonade, and tiny hors d'oeuvres to the guests. Even the grounds had been decorated so elegantly. Delicate lace cloths covered the individual tables. Placed in the middle of each was a bouquet of freshly picked flowers properly arranged. Colored lanterns made of thin dyed paper, hung from the nearby pine and willow trees.

William stood by his mother's side watching Bethie in total awe, as Emma Mae formally introduced her to the guests as though she were one of her finest ships. He had never seen her look so grown up or more beautiful from all the years he had known her. No other daughter or niece in the entire city of Savannah could hold a candle to her pure loveliness. Her beauty caused Emma to be the envy of all that day, as she gloated from the popularity of it all.

The pesky little girl who admired and followed William around like a puppy had disappeared. He felt a little sad to see his Bethie was finally growing up, yet happy as well to see her growing up. He felt awkward and confused.

Her long, dark brown ringlets lay softly against her delicate back pulled away from her lovely face with two bright ribbons. The lightly colored dress fell slightly below her shoulders with puffed sleeves. Her tiny waist tied with a matching ribbon, showed delicately while accenting the pleats that fell beneath it. She wore delicate, white gloves giving sophistication and maturity to her overall appearance.

Miss Abigail became preoccupied with the servants and arrangements checking to make sure everything was properly in its place. The party was a success even Mr. Holt, who did not care for Emma Mae, seemed to be enjoying himself. When all the guests had been met, William moved closer to her hoping she had forgiven him for something he was not even aware that he had done.

"Happy Birthday, Bethie. I hope you're enjoying yourself," began William sincerely. "Bethie…" he added, turning red and staring at the ground from embarrassment, "you're all grown up. You look like a real girl. I mean… that in the good way."

"Thank you, William," she replied blushing and smiling from ear to ear.

"Bethie, I mean Sara Beth. It's time to open your gifts," stumbled Miss Abigail trying to keep her promise to Emma that she would not use the name Bethie in front of the guests. She was eager to open her gifts and quickly tore through each wrapping.

She was grateful for the thoughtful gestures of people she did not even know, some of which were expensive and too elaborate for a thirteen year old. But her swift movements from gift to gift was not from greed or being spoiled, only from the anticipation of finding William's.

They had given each other birthday gifts all the years that they had known one another. It was always something given that had taken months to make, keeping its whereabouts and identity a secret until the day of the birthday. They kept their gifts to each other stored safe in the box on the island. But too many changes had occurred this day, agreed Bethie, as the last gift opened, sadly, was not from him.

Everyone moved from the gifts and to their tables, as the food was about to be served. Bethie tried to hide that her feelings were hurt. But she no longer had an appetite.

"Bethie," whispered William gently in her ear. "You didn't think I forgot, did you?"

"No, of course not," she lied, relieved he had not forgotten her.

"I want to give my present to you in private. Meet me in the library."

"OK," she whispered filled with anticipation.

"William… I'm sorry for my silly outburst at the lake today. I found, it seems… everything is fine. I hope you can forgive me."

"Well, I'm glad to hear you're not dying, after all," he teased, causing Bethie to blush from embarrassment.

With all the confusion going on brought about by the food, drink, and conversation, the two eventually slipped away unnoticed.

"What is it, William," demanded Bethie, unwilling to wait another minute.

"Hold your horses, Bethie. Let me shut the door first." He checked the corridor then shut the door quietly. It was all so mysterious, yet exciting she thought, bursting from anticipation.

From behind a chair, he pulled out an awkwardly wrapped gift.

"OK now, close your eyes," he instructed.

Bethie, giggling, closed her eyes while trying to open the gift. She allowed the paper to drop and began to feel its texture. It felt cool, smooth, and possibly fragile, she thought being very careful. "Can I open my eyes now?"

"OK, open your eyes!"

To her unbelievable surprise and utter delight, lay in her hands the exact music box that had once held her captive one summer day in the city, three years ago.

"Oh William!" she gasped, overjoyed. She stared in amazement, as she began to gently wind the box then placed it upon the desk to watch the lady and gentleman's romantic movements to the enchanting notes.

She kneeled on the floor to watch their poetic dance move in rhythm to the music. William remained silent, proud with himself to see Bethie never so pleased.

"I can't believe you remembered. However did you afford such an elegant gift?"

"I've been saving for years. I gave the store keeper some money to store it away until I could pay for the rest. He knows my mother all too well and was probably too scared to say no," he laughed.

"No one has ever given me a gift so wonderful. I'll keep it in the cave and cherish it forever. You've been so kind to me, William. I'll never forget our friendship," she promised sincerely.

"Bethie, we've been friends now for years. I've grown very fond of you. There's no other girl I trust or like more, and… and one day I plan to marry you."

"Marry me!" she blurted, thrown and shocked by his odd proposal. "You can't marry me! We're cousins. How inappropriate. Your mother would never allow it."

"Never mind my mother! You know as well as I that we're not blood related, Bethie. I can marry you as easily as marring one of those silly, giggling school girls that constantly throw themselves at me. They're all so silly, and I'll have nothing to do with any of them."

"The whole thing sounds so grown up and worrisome to me. And it hardly seems proper, William. I'm only thirteen. What do I know about such things? Besides, I can't imagine getting married anyway. I may stay single and free, like Miss Abby. Then, when I inherit Covington, we can both explore the world together! Like we said we'd do, remember? Wouldn't you rather do that?"

"You're such a child, Bethie! You don't understand anything. You will, one day when you're my age, and then I'm sure you'll change your mind."

"I'm no child, William Calhoun. You take that back or I'll split your lip!" Bethie was now insulted, gently placing down the music box to make a fist.

"Sara! Sara Beth! Answer me this instant!" yelled Emma Mae angry and frustrated to find the two of them missing together. They could easily hear her nasty voice clear across the mansion. They both became easily nervous from Emma's tone.

"You go and I'll clean up. Go quickly before she catches us in here," he demanded, motioning her toward the door.

"Bethie wait! One more thing," he quickly added, first checking whether his mother was coming down the corridor.

"What is it, William?"

Nervous but excited, he quickly bent over then suddenly smacked a quick, hard kiss dead center on her lips.

"Ouch!" she squealed. "What was that for," she demanded, feeling a bit violated and angry that he had not asked first her permission.

"For nothing. I never kissed a girl before and I wanted to see what it was like, that's all. Since I've decided to marry you, I certainly couldn't go around kissing other girls, now could I?"

Bethie pondered for a moment, but her head was spinning and she couldn't make heads or tails from any of it.

"Well… next time, you best ask first! Or I'll surely wallop you one, William Calhoun," she whispered in a reprimanding tone, as she began to make her way down the corridor toward the kitchen.

She was relieved to find the kitchen empty giving her the opportunity to quickly slip outside unnoticed. But it was all too good to be true as she soon felt Emma's presence behind her. Bethie abruptly turned to face her aunt while trying to hide the music box behind her back.

"Where have you been, young lady! Do you know how rude and unladylike it is to leave your guests at your own party? You ungrateful child. How dare you embarrass me!"

"Yes ma'am. I'm very sorry. I'll never do it again," begged Bethie terrified.

"What is that behind your back?"

"It's nothing, ma'am. Only a gift from William."

"Let me see. I demand to see it this instant," insisted a raging Emma Mae.

Bethie reluctantly produced the box in front of her as her aunt held out her hand. But she didn't trust Emma, past history told her not to.

"Let me have it, Sara Beth!"

"No! It's mine. I'll never give it to you!" she yelled defensively, as she began to run toward the door.

But Emma Mae was too close and was easily able to grab her shoulder and twist her around pulling the music box from Bethie's hands.

"Give it back!" she screamed, unable to be heard by the guests outside.

"How extravagant... So this is what my son is squandering my hard earned money on," remarked Emma Mae in a very jealous and bitter tone.

She led Bethie to believe that her intentions were to hand back the music box. Slowly, she pointed it toward her open hands only to drop it purposely in front of her, before Bethie could grasp onto it.

She was devastated as she watched the delicate porcelain dancers break in pieces before her, at Emma's sheer delight. But at the expense of her son who stood in the kitchen entrance witnessing the entire charade.

"Mother, how could you!" he swore, overwhelmed and upset by his mother's reprehensible behavior toward Bethie.

Her face quickly turned color and shape, as she suddenly became aware that her son had witnessed the travesty. She had finally been caught and was beside herself desperately searching for a way out.

"It was an accident, William. I'm old and these hands aren't as strong as they use to be," lied Emma, playing on her son's sympathy and love for her.

She took her eyes from him to glare down at Bethie, trying to force herself to be sympathetic. "It's so unfortunate, Sara Beth, that such a lovely and delicate gift could be so easily destroyed. Please forgive my clumsiness, I'll have one the servants clean up the mess right away."

"Meanwhile, I believe you have guests to attend to young lady. It was rude of you to leave them, and I hope in the future you'll show more maturity and act as a lady of your stature should." William was speechless, unable to imagine what he could possibly say or do to make Bethie feel better.

The special and dear gift that lay shattered had ultimately crushed her. She kneeled before the mess knowing the box was beyond repair. Eventually, she looked up at her aunt with cold, hard eyes refusing to cry or display any weakness. From the past years, she had truly pushed Bethie to such limits but none as cruel as this. She would never forget as she became filled with dislike and resentment toward this demented woman.

With no prior thought or control, words from the deepest part of her being spilled forth, "You're a liar!"

"Bethie, what are you saying?" blurted William in his mother's defense. He was confused, torn between the only mother that he had ever known and the little girl who was his dearest friend and companion.

He could not bear to imagine his mother as some kind of monster or that she had indeed committed this unspeakable crime intentionally. The mere thought made him feel guilty and dishonorable, not worthy of the Calhoun name. But Bethie, how could he doubt her? He knew her. She was not one of unjustified contempt toward others.

In silence, Bethie stood as she stared back at her aunt refusing to apologize or give in. Emma glared back with a half, twisted smile on her face, extremely delighted that her son had taken her side. Bethie's eyes moved toward his displaying utter betrayal and sadness. It made him feel shame, as he lowered his eyes and head to the floor. Calmly and like a lady, she turned and walked away from the two of them returning to her guests without even speaking another word.

"Bethie wait!" he yelled, going after her.

"Let her go, William," demanded Emma Mae. "She's obviously upset and needs to be alone. If she had remained with her guests, as she should have, none of this would have happened."

"Mother, why do you treat Bethie with such contempt? I don't understand. She told me that you didn't like her. Is that true? How could you not love your own niece? She's of your own flesh and blood. More than even myself!"

"Oh, William," laughed off Emma Mae as though he were being dramatic. "Of course I love Sara Beth. Well, she's like a daughter to me. But she's younger than you and needs more discipline. She has spent most of her life without proper guardianship, running around free to do and say whatever she felt pleased to. Why look at the way she just spoke to me!"

"But keeping her background and up bringing in mind, I won't punish her for it. I'm trying my hardest to raise and discipline her the best way I know how. I did good by you, didn't I, Son?"

"Yes, ma'am," answered William, confused. "May I go now?"

"Yes you may. But please don't worry about Sara! Let me take care of her. She isn't your responsibility, William. I've told you often, Son, it's about time you stop paying so much attention to her. It's beginning to look improper."

"Improper to who, Mother… to you?" defended William.

"I'll tell you what… To make it up to Sara, I'll send you into the city tomorrow with Henry to buy another music box for her. I'm sure they have others. If not, you can simply order another one. Since it was my clumsy mistake, I'll gladly pay for the box."

"You mean it, Mother? That would be wonderful! Thank you," he replied, relieved.

"Now run along and send Miss Jane to me. Please ask her to meet me in the Library. I need to speak with her right away."

"Yes ma'am," agreed William, happy to be finally able to go and find Bethie. He prayed she would forgive him.

Miss Jane quickly met Emma Mae in the library shutting the door behind her. Emma was pacing the floor with anticipation holding onto an opened telegram.

"Jane! Finally after all these years, I have them both where I want them."

"What are you talking about, ma'am?" she questioned, not really wanting to know.

"Abigail's sister, you fool! The old woman is finally near death. This telegram was just delivered from a hospital in Philadelphia."

"Abigail won't be pleased to find you've read her telegram."

"That was an accident. Simply thought it was for me," lied Emma grinning.

"We'll convince her to return to Philadelphia tonight on the 7:00. Because things are dire, I'm sure she'll agree. I couldn't imagine Abigail waiting until Monday to return to Pennsylvania, especially knowing that her sister is dying. Yes… I'm sure she'll want to get to her sister's bedside as soon as possible. The old windbag probably won't make it till then."

"She couldn't possibly take Bethie. How could she take care of the child and her sister at the same time? Yes… finally my day has come," laughed Emma maliciously.

"Mrs. Calhoun, I know you've been planning to separate them for a longtime. But I don't feel comfort—"

"I don't pay you to feel comfortable, Jane. You just do as I say! Or else you can find another employer, and it better be far away—if you know what I mean. Do I make myself clear?"

"Yes, ma'am… quite clear."

"Wonderful! Instruct Henry to take my son into Savannah tomorrow, first thing in the morning."

"Won't that be risky, ma'am?"

"Don't concern yourself with it. Just make sure you and Sara Beth are on that ship. You send me a telegram when you've arrived. I'm warning you, Jane… You better not let William and Bethie see one another in the city tomorrow. You have her packed first thing tomorrow morning as soon as Henry leaves. Do it while she's having breakfast. I'll tell her myself. I'll rather enjoy that. Now reseal this telegram and get Abigail in here."

Emma Mae gave the performance of her lifetime, as she soon convinced Abigail to travel to Philadelphia and to her dying sister's side. She promised Miss Abigail after she had made arrangements in the city, she would send Bethie to her. Abigail was too upset and worried about her sister; she could barely think straight.

The old woman had played on her most vulnerable moment, as she assured Bethie that she would soon be joining her. Bethie begged Miss Abigail to allow her to go with her. But understood she would not be returning to Covington but to a hospital where her sister lay dying. She felt mature enough to go with her and longed to be able to see her Aunt Liz. But she did not want to be a burden.

Miss Abigail, always trying to protect Bethie from life's miseries, did not wish for her to witness Elizabeth's possible death. She, emotionally drained and confused, unknowingly made a mistake in which she would forever regret.

Mr. Holt accompanied Miss Abigail as the two left Bethie's party and headed swiftly for the station. Bethie was worried about her Aunt Liz and the betrayal of her best friend. Unable to speak to him, she felt frightened, alone, and lost. She cordially said good evening to her guests, then retired early to her room. Only to lay awake troubled and unable to sleep, in constant fear of the following days without Miss Abigail to protect her from Emma.

The next day, too, had gone like clockwork. Bethie was confronted by Emma at breakfast that Miss Elizabeth had taken a turn for the worse and she had been left in Abigail's care, indefinitely. Emma lied through her teeth as she told the unprotected child she would be travelling on a ship to London that very day.

William and Henry had left early that morning hoping to surprise Bethie with a new music box by supper. She was alone, vulnerable, and became easy prey to Emma Mae's treachery and deceitfulness. Emma promised Bethie that she and her son would be joining her in a month and they would spend the summer in London together.

Miss Jane hurried the child onto the large shipping vessel in fear of running into the two in Savannah. Bethie neither believed nor trusted Emma Mae but was unable to disagree or retaliate.

She stood near the bow of the ship looking into the ocean praying that she would one day, again, see Miss Abigail and William. "How could you have left me, Miss Abby?" she cried, as the tears fell from her eyes. Not knowing whether she would ever see him again, Bethie wished she had forgiven him. "I do forgive you, William." With eyes closed and hands tightly clasped together, she said a silent prayer.

Miss Jane stood behind her desperately fighting any emotion that tried to surface. Never in Miss Jane's employment with Emma Mae had she felt such bitterness and resentment, as she whispered into the salty air.

"You've done it this time you old sea witch… Sitting in your elegant gardens gloating all the while." She peered down at Bethie with sincere empathy. "But the winds say you've won your last dirty deed. This small child before me will be the destruction of you yet. Then I will have my day, Emma—to gloat. Yes… my day!"

Boarding School

Although the music box was not exact, William was astatic in finding the store carried one similar. In fact, the woman's hair was dark brown rather than blonde like the original. He thought she resembled Bethie and was a perfect replacement. Even the tune that played was the same as the original. He was quite pleased with himself.

When they finally returned to the plantation he was so excited that he ran all the way up to her room yelling Bethie's name as he went along. He knew how much the gift had meant to her and was positive that she would soon forgive him from the day before.

While calling out her name, he knocked on their door several times before opening it unable to wait from anticipation. William slowly peeked in noticing immediately that something was wrong, as he pushed open the door wider. To his sudden shock and horror, the room had been completely vacated of Bethie's entire belongings. He began to panic, as he ran and flung open Miss Abigail's door to find it was also void of all her possessions as well.

Even Miss Abigail's bedroom furniture had been replaced by the old sitting room items that had once occupied its premises. Not a trace of the two could be found or that they had ever once occupied its space. The rooms had been stripped and cleaned of their very existence.

Shaken and upset he began to make his way through the darkened corridor and down the back staircase yelling, "Mother! Mother, where are you?"

Emma Mae was holding a private meeting in her study. Even with the door completely closed, she could still hear the muffled sounds of her son yelling for her in the background.

He darted through the kitchen and soon came upon the door, as he abruptly flung it open causing it to hit against its wall. Disconcerted and ignoring the well-dressed gentlemen seated around her desk, he stood frantic and accusing glaring across the room at his mother.

"Where is she, Mother? What have you done with Bethie? I demand to know this instant!" he screamed, filled with anger.

His disturbing, out of control behavior worried and embarrassed Emma. She immediately excused herself from the meeting, closing the doors behind her. Pretending as though she had not heard him, she responded, "What is it, William? Why are you so upset?"

"You heard exactly what I said, Mother. You may be old, but your hearing is sharp!"

Emma Mae was shocked by his attitude toward her. She had never heard him speak in such a tone and became nervous wondering if she would be able to lie her way out of this one. A diversion was all Emma could think of.

"How dare you talk to me in that tone of voice, young man! You interrupted a very important meeting and have embarrassed me immensely. That isn't like you, William. What in the world has come over you? Now you calm down and follow me into the library." He did as she requested as Emma swiftly closed the door behind them.

"Where is Bethie, Mother? What have you done with her?" he accused, still angry.

"Don't be silly, Son, I haven't done anything to Sara Beth. Abigail's sister took a turn for the worst last night, and Sara begged to go back to Pennsylvania this morning."

"What was I to do? She threw herself one tantrum. Well the way she was acting made it hard to believe she just turned thirteen. I couldn't stand all that hollering and whimpering, I finally just let her go. Unruly child, even I was unable to control her. Jane was kind enough to escort her back to New Hope, and that's the whole story, Son."

Emma Mae was so smooth and convincing; her performance was magnificent. But what she failed to consider was no one knew Bethie more than he, not even Miss Abigail anymore. And none of what Emma Mae said seemed familiar with Bethie's personality at all to him.

"She would never have left without saying goodbye. I don't believe you, Mother!" responded William, remaining unconvinced.

"Well, I've never been so hurt or disappointed in my entire life. My own son, calling me a liar." Emma pretended to look hurt, causing William to calm down. He hated to accuse his mother without solid proof but just could not bring himself to believe any of what she said.

"Why are all of their belongings gone? Isn't Bethie coming back?" he questioned, in a calmer but sad tone.

"I'm afraid, William, she won't be returning to Savannah. She requested, because of Abigail's sister's poor health, if she could remain in New Hope."

"Sara Beth wanted to be with Elizabeth during her last remaining days. What could I say, Son? I can be sympathetic too you know. She is very attached to those sisters. Well, I can't blame her, they raised her from an infant, as you are well aware of."

"Did she leave a note or give you a message for me?" he begged.

Emma became a bit nervous taking a moment to think, not expecting him to ask that question. "No… note, Son. She was in a hurry to leave, but… she did give me a message for you."

"What was it, Mother? Please tell me!" he begged, with much anticipation.

"Well, I believe she said to tell you… goodbye, and she wished you well. She thought saying goodbye in person would have been too difficult. Sara Beth asked that you don't worry or think about her too much. And that it was silly and unnecessary, and felt you should have more important subjects to concern yourself with."

"That's it? Did she say anything else?" questioned William disappointed.

"No, I believe that was all she said," lied Emma, pleased with herself.

"Well… she must have been quite upset about Miss Elizabeth. I understand how she could have left so sudden. Mother, I'm fifteen years old now, I believe old enough to travel abroad on my own. Please do not disagree… I would like to go to New Hope this summer."

Again, Emma Mae had not considered something. "I agree, Son, you are old enough, but I don't feel that would be appropriate. They all have their hands full with Elizabeth, and don't need additional worry."

"But I wouldn't be a worry, Mother. I could help out with the chores. I'm sure they would appreciate any help they could get."

"Well, I tell you what, Son… you write to Sara Beth, and if she and Abigail agree, then you have my permission.

"Thank you, Mother! Thank you so much. You've been very kind and understanding. I apologize for my behavior earlier."

"That's quite all right, Son. I understand you're concerned for your cousin. I'm also concerned for her wellbeing," lied Emma, grinning to herself. "And when you're finished writing the letter, give it to me. I will take care of it personally, you have my word, Son."

William hurried off to the island carrying fresh paper, ink, and the music box. He gently wrapped the gift in a cotton cloth then placed it safely away in their box. He laid on the hill as he wrote to Bethie about how sorry he was of Miss Elizabeth's condition. William hoped that she arrived safe and that her Aunt Liz would soon recover.

He apologized for his behavior in the kitchen. William also mentioned he had a surprise for her and would like to deliver it in person. After three and a half pages, he finally put down the ink pen and folded the pages together in order. *Bethie is sure to forgive me*, thought William, smiling up at the sky above him.

St. Anne on the Atlantic Ocean

After several days of feeling sorry for herself and worrying about Aunt Liz, Miss Abby, and William, Bethie decided to make the best of her travels to Europe. She had never been on a vessel as vast as the St. Anne and along with William, shared the dream of a fantastic voyage at sea.

Though it was disappointing not to have him there during her first sea adventure, the experience was much like he had described. She could recall many times when they would lay on the top of the hill dreaming of their future as pirates together.

By captain's orders she was made the ship's first mate, a highly bestowed honor never given to any girl ever before on his vessel, said Captain McNeal. Initially Miss Jane objected to Bethie's constant interest in the ship and its crew, believing it not to be a proper pastime for a young lady of her stature. But soon gave in, as she spent most of her days thereafter in bed, terribly ill from motion sickness.

The ocean did become rough at times, and they even went through a mild storm. But neither bothered Bethie, she rather enjoyed the intense drama of it all. She felt as one with the ocean and wished never to return to land.

Many times she had dreamt of becoming a pirate with William, travelling from one port to the next and how wonderful their life would be. The sea made her feel strong, without a care, and as though she were meant to be in its vastness.

The captain soon became used to Bethie's constant, inquisitive, interests of what everything was and used for upon his ship. He had taken her personally under his wing, as he taught her to respect the sea and all that was in it. "For there is nothing more mightier than her scorn," he would preach dramatically. She thought him to be a bit eccentric, but decided it was the reason she enjoyed his company so much.

The crew on board became somewhat rough at times, but it never seemed to bother Bethie. In fact, although years older, they reminded her of William's male school friends.

From the English Channel, the St. Anne arrived in a London harbor on a cool, crisp, Friday morning. It was the busiest day of the week for the nearby markets. The two waited near the dock as their bags were loaded upon a carriage.

It was difficult for Bethie to say her goodbyes to Captain McNeal and his crew, since they too would miss her. Bethie promised that she would one day, again, sail on their magnificent vessel.

During the long voyage, the Captain had grown very fond of the little girl. It did not take long for Bethie to feel she could trust him as she confided in him of her situation. He became concerned about her welfare and even offered to take her to Maine to live with his wife and sister until she reached legal age of her inheritance.

He promised that no one would ever know her whereabouts and she would always be safe. Captain McNeal was the only man, agreed Bethie, that she had ever known not to be afraid or intimidated by Emma Mae's relentless, unmerciful personality.

Over the years, revenge had become an art with her and from experience he knew her well. Bethie found him to be a brave and honorable man but could not allow the Captain to go against the law. He made her promise that if she ever needed him, she could find out when his ship was to return to London through the shipyard's clerk. Bethie hugged and thanked him, as she watched the Captain disappear in the early morning crowd.

Because of all the people, it was difficult for her to evaluate London. She could hardly see beyond the crowds, as the carriage moved slowly through the streets unable to convince the people to move out of the way more quickly. It was easy to see that London was quite larger than the city of Savannah, and Bethie believed she had never seen so many people at one time.

Along with adults, there were many poor children selling goods in the streets. Some of which were odd to her from never seeing them offered for sale in Savannah or New Hope. Flowers, birds, and apples were only a few of the items sold individually by vendors.

"Buy an apple for a penny for me sick wife, kind mate?" yelled a poor man selling apples, as he nearly walked in front of the moving carriage.

"Git outta me way old man!" snapped the driver. He cracked the whip down harder on his horses, causing them to move quicker and almost running the old man down. Bethie screamed in horror as the carriage barely missed him.

"Sorry, ma'am," said the driver.

"It's all right, Sara Beth. He didn't hit him," comforted Miss Jane the best she could.

"Driver! I insist you be more careful in the future. There's a child and a lady in this carriage. Have you no manners!"

"I'm sorry, Miss. The old bloke walked in front of me horses. That's the way it's done here. It won't happen again."

"See that it doesn't or I'll report you to the authorities!"

"Yes, ma'am," replied the driver as he scolded under his breath, "Bloody Americans!"

They were traveling down Oxford street as the driver directed the horses west, on Duke. The carriage turned onto a brick entryway of an estate, entirely gaited and quite large. Two stone statues guarded both sides of the entrance. The grounds appeared lovely and kept. The horses stopped in front of a large, elegant building architecturally designed with an air of sophistication.

A sign hung above the main entrance read, "Wharton School for Girls." The school obviously housed the most wealthy daughters of London and abroad. Bethie was confused but did not question where they were.

During the entire time at sea, Miss Jane had hardly spoken to her. She never talked about the abrupt manner in which they had left Savannah or what was really to happen to her once they arrived in London. Bethie never pried, she knew Miss Jane would reveal her true fate in due time. And that seemed to be enough for her, giving Bethie the opportunity to enjoy the voyage.

After reading the sign, Bethie began to understand why they had come and what was to become of her. Perhaps William will return to study in London also, she pondered, knowing all too well it was just wishful thinking.

Emma Mae's goal was to intentionally separate the two, and to place distance between her and Miss Abigail, leaving her vulnerable to Emma's unrelenting control. Because of Bethie's young age, Emma Mae believed it would be easier to accomplish. Not realizing the reality that Bethie, someday, would become a woman, a very strong one. Which should have been considered based on her, already, head strong personality.

Bethie was helped out of the carriage by the driver, never saying a word. She stood by the steps looking up at the tall building. Miss Jane knocked several times on the door. It was soon opened by a middle aged, dark haired, English woman appearing very serious.

"Hello, I'm Jane Sullivan from Savannah."

The woman thought some then realized who she was, "Yes… Mrs. Calhoun sent you. I'm Miss Catherine, head superintendent of this school. Please come in. I've been expecting you."

"This is the child Miss Sara Beth Covington," added Miss Jane, directing Bethie to the side of her. The woman slowly began to examine her from head to toe. Bethie could sense she found her to look inappropriate, but it didn't bother her. She was used to being around snobby, pompous individuals.

"All of the children have left for summer vacation. Other than a few servants, I'm the only staff member here at this time. This particular part of the campus house the dorms, and I currently live here with the girls. I do maintain strict supervision and expect the girls to behave as proper young ladies should."

"I believe the education taught is above all in Europe. We are rated one of the finest academic, private, girls' schools in the world. We are all very proud of our school and earned reputation. As I expect you to be, Sara Beth."

"Yes, ma'am," Bethie replied, finding the lady quite stuffy making her feel uncomfortable. She wished she were still at sea with

Captain McNeal and his crew.

"Please follow me… I will escort you personally to your room. I'll have one of the servants bring up your bags shortly." They climbed a long staircase to the second floor. Miss Catherine led them to a room occupied by two, twin oak beds.

The room itself was neat, clean, and quite lovely. The windows were large, allowing the sun's rays to fill it completely. Each bed displayed a colorful, embroidered bedspread with matching drapes. There were two separate cedar closets. A desk with fresh paper and ink sat between them. Two trestle tables positioned between a wall and bed held an elegant lamp on each. Even at the foot of each bed was a small chest for each girl's personal belongings.

"My office is positioned to your left as you come down the staircase. If you need anything, that is where you can find me. I hope you both enjoy London, this is a splendid time of the year."

"I'm confident, Sara Beth, you will grow to enjoy and respect Wharton, as all of our young ladies do." Miss Catherine closed the door behind her, giving them both privacy. Bethie went over to a bed and sat quietly. Not knowing what exactly to do next.

Miss Jane took the bed nearest to the window, as she sat staring out, wondering what to say. Bethie knew it was difficult for her, she neither blamed nor disliked Miss Jane. She had already decided many years ago, that Jane only did what her aunt instructed her to do. She, too, was a pawn.

Her awkward, inability to mother or comfort Bethie would become her most difficult task. Bethie found Jane to be weak, sad, and almost pathetic. She decided to help her out by breaking the silence herself.

"My aunt and William won't be joining us will they, Miss Jane?" she questioned, already knowing the answer.

Jane hesitated, feeling ashamed for her part in the deception. She was unable to face the child and continued to stare out the window.

"No… they won't be joining you, Sara. Once you're settled in, I've been instructed to return to Savannah. You will remain here at the school. This is where you will live and continue your studies, until… well until you've reached legal age." Bethie gasped.

"It's probably the finest girls' school in all of Europe. You'll have the best of everything here."

Miss Jane tried desperately to convince Bethie but mostly herself that it had all been for the best. But through the years, Emma Mae had worn her conscience to such a point that her nerves were becoming frazzled from guilt. Her mind told her that it was indeed Emma's doing, but her heart refused to allow herself to feel free of all responsibility. Believing she, too, was at fault for taking part in this inhumane, abandonment of this lovely little girl who never did anyone harm.

The worst was knowing the love Miss Abigail had for Bethie. Even if Emma wanted nothing more than to put her away for the time being, there was this good woman who loved and cared for her as a mother should.

Jane could no longer help but feel deep empathy for Bethie. She hated who she had become and no longer could stand the sight of herself, as she quickly went over to the child and knelt before her. "Listen to me, Sara Beth… You may not understand this now, but one day you will. Promise me you will keep what I'm about to say between the two of us. If Emma Mae found out, I don't even want to imagine what she would do to me—or you. Promise me, Bethie!"

Bethie was shocked by Miss Jane's desperate outburst and from never before calling her by that name. She had never seen her lose control before. Jane may not have had the ability to show joy or happiness, but she had always maintained total control. Never displaying emotion of any kind, always seeming cold and without feeling.

Her desperation caused Bethie to feel frightened. "Yes, I promise Miss Jane," she replied, hoping that it would calm her down.

"I've worked for your aunt for many years now. I believe no one knows that woman better than I. Like yours, my parents both died when I was very young. I was an only child with no relatives to turn to and soon was placed in an orphanage."

"Life in the orphanage taught me to be hard and unfeeling. Because there was no love, I never learned how to love properly. But it was shelter, and there was food. And with an empty belly, you soon become grateful." Unknown to her, Bethie was taken by Miss Jane's past. Her eyes revealed the pain as she continued to speak.

"They even educated me. I was one of the chosen few. When the rich came around at Christmas time, feeling a bit charitable, there I'd be. Clean, neat, and always well mannered. Believing they were my only hope, I learned to obey and respect them. My manners and behavior became impeccable. Even the head governess of the orphanage would say, "Choose Jane, she is our most well-mannered. Now there's a worthy investment! Never met a child more trustworthy and loyal."

"And that's how I became who I am today, Sara, trustworthy and loyal, regardless of principle or circumstances. You can't possibly understand, you were born into wealth. But this is how I learned to survive."

"You're wrong, Miss Jane," interrupted Bethie. "I do understand what it's like to be a child with no say over my own life. And the person in charge of it, doesn't seem to care for me. Is that sort of how it was?"

"Somewhat, Sara," smiled Miss Jane, something Bethie had never seen before. "But what makes you even luckier, than I was, is that you do have Miss Abigail. You may feel abandoned but be grateful that you are here."

"Emma Mae without even knowing has done you right by sending you here. She's a very bad woman, Sara, never forget it. Living here will keep you out of her grasp. When you're nearly eighteen you can return to New Hope and claim your inheritance. She'll have no hold on you then. You'll be finally free of her. But until then, thank the Lord she made the mistake of sending you here. Emma very rarely makes mistakes… it must be a sign of her old age."

"But what about William?" questioned Bethie concerned.

"Don't worry about William, Bethie. He's a whole different matter. Emma would never harm him. He's her pride and joy. If the woman has ever been capable of loving anyone, it would be him."

"But why does she hate me so, Miss Jane? I've tried so hard to be polite and stay out of her way. But she still hates me."

"You must always remember that it is not your fault. Emma Mae is a very troubled, malicious, greedy woman. There is something very wrong with her mind. I don't understand it either. She's never forgiven your father for running away from her. I've heard from others that she used to abuse him, much more severely than yourself."

"I'm sorry that you have to hear this, Sara. But I don't know why or what caused her to behave in that way toward him. She claims to have loved him but has never told me the entire truth. Although I really never wanted to know… But it must be something quite disturbing. Emma normally tells me everything, despite how inhumane or ghastly the act was. She's just mad, I suppose…"

"She's the type of person that you never cross. I've witnessed what she's done and can do. She's actually ruined lives completely and without any remorse. Some of whom—will never recover."

"I suppose that's why I do whatever she tells me. I'm not proud of the things I've done for Emma. But I'm a coward, afraid of her retaliation and afraid of being hungry. I know that feeling all too well and when one does, you never want to feel it again if you don't have to. Emma Mae is a very powerful, destructive woman. If you're able, you stay far away from her, Sara. Do you understand?"

"Yes, ma'am. I understand," answered Bethie, horrified by their conversation.

Hospital of the University of Pennsylvania, Philadelphia, PA

The morning's air was chilly with a mild breeze coming in from the west, as Miss Abigail sat still on a wooden bench that overlooked a Philadelphia park. She sat with her back facing the hospital hoping for a moment in which she could forget why she had come.

   With her hand in hers, Miss Elizabeth had died peacefully in the night. In the morning, she appeared as though she was in a deep, restful sleep, one of which was needed and well deserved. Abigail neither called for a doctor nor a nurse knowing quite well they would make no difference.

   She longed for the moment of privacy so she could tell her sister goodbye and how much she was loved, appreciated, and would be missed. Elizabeth was nearly 20 years older than Abigail, and often was more like a mother figure than a sister. It was a miracle that Abigail had survived birth, since her mother was in her late 30s. And like Bethie, her mother's life was taken during her birth. It was Elizabeth who, without hesitation, took charge and raised her. Still, Elizabeth was much too young to die, agreed Abigail.

   Abigail was entirely exhausted and unable to cry another tear when she felt a gentle hand on her shoulder. "I'm sorry, Abigail... Elizabeth was a fine woman. She'll be missed by many."

   Miss Abigail placed her hand on top of his, "Thank you, Thomas. She was rather fond of you, too."

   When he sat down next to her, it was easy to see how exhausted and worn she was. Her tired eyes were red and blotchy and her face pale.

   "Abigail, I'm worried about you. Let me take you back to your room so you can get some rest," he pleaded.

   "No, I can't do that, Thomas. I'm having Elizabeth's body prepared for burial today. We are returning to New Hope tomorrow morning. She's asked to be buried at Covington. She wanted to be near Bethie when she returns home..." The thought of her sister's passing and Bethie so far away made the tears once again fill her tattered, lost eyes.

   "Oh Thomas... I've committed a terrible injustice. For as long as I live, I will always regret it." She began to sob, covering her face with her hands, bringing her head toward her knees and nearly collapsing.

Mr. Holt became even more upset seeing her so devastated. He pulled his handkerchief from his pocket and gently pushed it into her hand. "Abigail, that's nonsense, you're a wonderful woman. You stayed by your sister's side, every moment. What could you have possibly done that's so wrong?"

Miss Abigail sat up to wipe her face trying to calm her shaken body. "I've deprived my sister and Bethie of being able to say goodbye to each other. What right did I have? Elizabeth died never being able to see her… one last time. I could sense her sadness. It was so overwhelming, Thomas. I'm solely to blame. How could I have been so insensitive? They mean everything to me."

"And here I sit alone with neither of them… I deserve to be alone. My whole life has become one great lie and mistake. Bethie's better off without me. I wouldn't blame her if she never forgave me," cried Abigail, overwhelmed.

"Stop it Abigail! That's not true. Bethie loves you very much, and always will. You've been a wonderful mother to her. Her personality is a reflection of you, Abigail. Don't be so hard on yourself. We're all only human. The decisions we make in life are not always the right ones. But we do the best we can…"

"But look what I've done, Thomas… I've left Bethie with that insane woman. I must be crazy myself. Why didn't you stop me? I've got to get back to her," she added, abruptly standing to leave.

Thomas immediately reached out, pulling her back to the bench. "Abigail, get a hold of yourself! If you don't start taking care of yourself, you're going to end up like Elizabeth. Then what good will you be for Bethie? Look at you! You're emotionally and physically exhausted…"

"Death is always difficult. At the time, you felt unable to take Bethie. You had no idea where you were even going other than this hospital. You were vulnerable, upset, and confused. If you want to blame anyone, blame me. I should have stayed in Savannah so I could keep an eye on Bethie."

"See Abigail, sometimes, we can all make the wrong choices. At the time, I felt you needed me more. But it is over and done with. I'll take you back to Covington then we'll leave as soon as we can for Savannah."

"No Thomas, please… I want you to stay in the city and keep trying to get word from Savannah. I keep sending telegrams but get no response from Emma Mae. I feel the worst has happened to my Bethie. Please, Thomas, I'm begging you to help me. I've never been so worried and desperate in my life. If she's hurt her, Thomas," added Abigail, terrified.

"Only if you promise to calm yourself. I care very much for you, Abigail. I can't stand to see you like this."

"Don't worry about me, Thomas. I'll be fine. I'll be able to sleep the entire trip back. Just find out about our little Bethie. She's become all of our responsibility, remember the vow that we made when her parents died. Along with Joseph, we are all she has. I know William cares for her too, but he's under Emma's rule. He won't be able to protect her."

"I have a longtime friend and associate in Savannah. I'll cable him immediately. Emma Mae is obviously avoiding you. Unfortunately, I believe your suspicions to be valid. Emma is up to something all right."

"I'll have him go directly to the plantation, personally. He's a good man. If anyone can get to the bottom of this, he can. As soon as I get word, I'll meet you in New Hope."

"Thank you, Thomas," ended Abigail, relieved.

The next morning, out of respect, Miss Abigail's carriage moved slowly behind Elizabeth's. Her body was carried in a black, elegant wagon pulled by a well-dressed driver. She had purchased a black, formal dress the day before in the city.

Abigail had already sent word to Joseph that Elizabeth had died and she would be returning the following day with her body. He was to contact her local acquaintances and friends, as the funeral would take place upon their arrival. She would waste no time. Abigail felt

Elizabeth would have wanted her to return to Savannah immediately.

It would be the first time in years that Abigail would see Joseph. She had even cabled the hospital before arriving, telling him to return to Covington and that he was not needed because she would soon be in Pennsylvania. There would be or could be, no more avoiding him as her mind could neither concerned itself nor worried of it. She was filled with much grief and constant worry, praying Bethie was safe.

The afternoon had become a blur as Elizabeth was laid to rest. From lack of food and sleep, Abigail barely recognized the people who had come to pay their respects. Though the funeral went quite well and Elizabeth would have been pleased.

Everything had been organized wonderfully by Joseph. From contacting the minister, family and friends, and even the lovely flowers. Joseph kept his distance, standing back and away from the group, never taking his eyes from Abigail.

Though he felt much sorrow for Elizabeth, he also felt guilty that he was unable to concentrate on anything but Abigail. She didn't even realize it was he who had arranged everything so perfectly or that he was even there. She was too distraught and detached from sorrow and exhaustion.

She accompanied Abner and his wife, as they thoughtfully returned her to the estate. Abigail turned their invitation for supper down but thanked them for their kindness. She watched as their wagon departed down the cobblestone entryway. Joseph came into focus, as he stood watching her with eyes filled with love and concern. And for the first time all day, she realized that he was there and how much she still loved him. In fact, more than ever…

"Joseph… Elizabeth is gone," whispered Abigail with tears streaming down her face. For a moment, he pushed his thoughts of her aside as he worried about Bethie. He had become disturbed to find Abigail without her. Joseph waited patiently, all day, for a moment when they would be alone so he could question her.

"Where's Bethie, Abigail? Where's the child?" he questioned, concerned by her distraught demeanor. Abigail took a moment to think about what was asked of her. She had become confused and disoriented, unable to think straight.

"I've left her, Joseph… Oh my, Lord… What have I done?" she remarked, horrified. Blackness began to fill her eyes as her legs started to give way, no longer able to balance herself. Joseph caught Abigail in time, as he quickly lifted her body and carried her into the estate.

She slept for days, tossing and turning with fever. Joseph gently took care of her, never leaving her side, as he began to worry for her life. He slept very little and sat in a chair seated next to her bed all night, so he could keep a watchful eye on her. Keeping her covered and bringing her soup, he wiped her head, neck, and arms with cool water. Only for a few minutes during the day would he leave her side, so he could feed the horses and other animals.

In the middle of the night he would be abruptly awakened by Abigail's delirious state of mind. She would thrash about calling out names, including his own, saying words that made no sense. After a couple of days, he felt her condition had not improved. He was out of his mind with worry and felt helpless, unable to help her.

When Abner arrived by the end of the week to take care of the horses, he asked him to go for the doctor. Abner's wife soon came, giving Joseph the break that he needed so desperately. They each took turns alternating shifts.

The doctor did all he could telling Joseph because of her lack of nourishment she had become worn and weak, easily accessible to the virus. It was now important to build her strength, only then could he say for certain if she would indeed survive the illness.

Miss Abigail slowly opened her eyes as she lay still, wondering where she was. She recognized her room at Covington then became confused as to why she was in New Hope. Soon, the memory of her lost sister came to mind and all of the details began to fall into place. The instant she realized Bethie was not with her, left behind with

Emma Mae, she abruptly sat up. It caused Joseph to become startled as he awoke from a dream.

"Abigail… thank God!" he gasped, relieved and happy to see her conscious. He put his arms around her waist and gently held her.

"Joseph… how long have I been ill?" she questioned, still confused.

"Almost three weeks now. Nearly thought I lost ya too! I'm sorry about Elizabeth, Abigail…"

"Thank you, Joseph. I know how much she meant to you, too… Three Weeks! Oh my Lord, Bethie. I've got to get to her, Joseph. She needs me," blurted Miss Abigail, trying to get out of bed only to have him stop her.

"Now ya just settle down here, woman! Ya ain't goin' nowhere. Don't you realize… I almost lost ya. Now God has givin' ya another chance, and I'm gonna see to it that you respect it. You'll be no good ta Bethie if your dead! Now git back in bed and lay still. I'll go and get ya some real food. Stay put now, Abigail! I mean it," he demanded sternly.

Abigail did not argue or fuss, she knew he was right, as the room began to spin making her head ache from pain. She laid back, allowing him to cover her. He gently bent over to kiss her cheek, but she turned her face intentionally causing his lips to fall upon her own.

The kiss was soft, gentle, and unexpected, making Joseph blush from Abigail's unheard of forwardness. "I'm… gonna get that food now," he stumbled, grinning but embarrassed at the same time. Before he left her room, he hesitated but turned to face her. "I love ya, Abby—always will. There never be anyone else…"

"I know, Joseph. I, too, my love…"

With his help, Abigail soon recovered and was determined to return to Savannah immediately. Joseph begged to return with her so they could both bring Bethie back together. But she soon convinced him that he was needed at Covington, more than ever, now that Elizabeth was gone.

She promised to write as soon as she arrived to let him know that Bethie was safe. Abigail also promised she would, again, try to convince Emma Mae in letting her return to New Hope where she belonged. Abigail pleaded with him to let Abner take her to the station, wanting desperately to say their last goodbyes in private. They were both still so desperately in love, and Abigail worried that it must be obvious. No longer able to be contained, and perhaps putting them all in danger.

Before she could reach Doylestown, her carriage was intercepted by Mr. Holt's. He frantically ran over to her appearing upset and distraught.

"Thomas, what is it?" shouted Abigail from her window.

He opened the door abruptly and sat across from her, trying to catch his breath. "Abigail, I have some bad news," began Thomas nervously.

"What is it? Is it Bethie? Is she hurt?" questioned Miss Abigail, frantically.

"No, no, not that I'm aware of. But… but Emma Mae has sent her to London. To a girls boarding school. She waited until we left. But I believe it was certainly planned."

"I received a trunk with your belongings a few days ago. Along with the trunk was a letter from a judge in Savannah who authorized her transfer. I would have come sooner. But I needed to take care of a few important matters concerning Bethie. I'm truly sorry, Abigail," he ended, extremely disturbed.

"That horrid woman going behind my back like this! Poor Bethie, she must be terrified! It's my fault for allowing myself to ever trust her. How could I have been so stupid?" she blamed herself, devastated by the news. "Do you know for certain that Bethie is safe, Thomas?"

"I'm not certain, Abigail. There wasn't enough time to wire London. But I have the address of the school and the letter noted that Miss Jane had escorted Bethie, personally. Emma isn't about to place

Bethie's life in danger. Not until she figures out a way to take her inheritance."

"If Bethie has been hurt, in any way… I'll kill Emma with my bare hands! I promise Thomas, I'll do it!" she snapped, out of control.

"Calm down, Abigail! There's no time for this," he interrupted.

"I must go to London immediately. Abner, please take me to Philadelphia!" ordered Miss Abigail over Thomas's shoulders.

"Wait! Come with me in my carriage. I have to return to Philadelphia anyway. I've already purchased a ticket for you on a vessel stopping in New York, then traveling directly to London."

"I was able to get Judge Franklin to place a violation against Emma Mae for breaching court orders. By law, she was unable to send Bethie without first getting your permission. Emma knows the law and she went against it intentionally. Her behavior was quite blatant. The court did appoint you as Bethie's legal guardian, and no judge in Savannah can change that. But unfortunately, he was unable to lift the order given by the judge in Savannah."

"He claims not to have known that Emma Mae was not her legal guardian. She led him to believe that Bethie had been abandoned to her. He refuses to lift the order, says the boarding school is the very finest in Europe and in her best interest."

"Regardless of the violation, Emma is insisting on paying for this expensive charade. She may be relentless but also clever. She knows if she takes financial responsibility, not too much can be said about it. One good thing has come from all of this, Emma Mae has lost all rights over her. Because she has violated the original order, Bethie never has to return to the plantation."

"Forgive me, Lord… But damn that Woman!" she snapped, with clenched fists. "She continues to manipulate our lives. Sending Bethie to London, a whole other country in which she's never been to. She's determined to tear her apart and all who love her. Why doesn't she just let us be? She has all the money she could ever possibly spend in a lifetime. Can anyone really be that greedy? Why doesn't she just leave the child alone," ended Abigail, exhausted.

"I don't believe it's about money anymore, Abigail. There's more to it, I'm sure. And I'm working hard on getting to the bottom of this mess created by Emma. I won't give up on having Bethie returned to New Hope. I'll continue to do all that I can. Now that Bethie is out of Emma's control, it should be easier," promised Mr. Holt.

"Is she, Thomas? Is she really out of Emma's control?" questioned Miss Abigail sadly, not convinced. "William must be devastated. I'm sure he's had no part in this. Poor Bethie, hold on child, I'll be there soon…"

Miss Jane stayed with Bethie as long as she could, ignoring two of Emma's telegrams but becoming worried by the third, threatening one. Jane tried to convince her that she was better off in London and away from Emma Mae's controlling and harmful behavior.

Bethie became witness to a different side of her, as the two became close, sparked by the simple humane inability to dislike this wonderful child. Bethie thanked Miss Jane for her honesty and wished her the very best, as she was left in the hands of Miss Catherine.

The days thereafter became long and lonely, Bethie spent most of her time in her room writing letters to William and Miss Abigail. During the few nicer, more sunnier, days she would walk the grounds of the school enjoying the lovely gardens that surrounded it.

On occasion Miss Catherine would insist on Bethie accompanying her to the theater, something that was new but exciting to her. Miss Catherine was strict and overly proper, as the two said very little to one another. Bethie felt awkward and uncomfortable in her presence.

One foggy London morning, as Bethie sat staring out the window feeling sorry for herself, came an unexpected knock at her door. She had already eaten breakfast, completed her chores, and couldn't imagine why she was being summoned. "Come in," she replied, a bit curious.

The door slowly opened as the bright and beautiful image of Miss Abigail stood before her with eyes filled with tears and begging for forgiveness.

Bethie cried out in joy as she ran and threw her arms around Abigail's waist. "Miss Abby, you've come! I prayed you would," cried Bethie with tears of joy.

"Please forgive me, child, for ever leaving you with her. I promise… I'll never leave you again—so help me God!"

Guilty Before Innocent

Bethie was never more grateful, in her entire young life, as she was that foggy London morning. The mere sight of Miss Abigail brought color to her face and life back into her spirit. The once inquisitive, adventurous child had returned to life now brighter than ever before. There was nothing to forgive, only a time to be thankful to God for all that he gave and made possible.

It was true he took Elizabeth, but he also brought them back to each other. It was a time for healing. Only once, had Miss Abigail held Bethie as she cried tears of sorrow for her Aunt Liz. They believed Elizabeth would not have wanted them to be sad. She would be much happier, proud, and relieved to find them both together standing tall, and fighting back.

With the aid of Mr. Holt, Miss Abigail had come to London quite prepared. Her unavoidable, unpleasant experiences with Emma Mae had awakened her maturity and intelligence to a higher level. All naivety from her personality had been washed away. Never again would she be made the fool of anyone's attempted, gluttonous gains or twisted schemes.

She walked into the boarding school stern, confident, and with a court order giving her total custody of Bethie. Although the child had to remain in school, she did not have to continue her lodgings on the premises. Abigail made it quite clear she would be taking Bethie immediately. She had no interest or patience to even care to listen to Miss Catherine's objections. Like the others, she was aware Catherine was working for Emma Mae and had no real interest in what was best for the child.

She was direct with the superintendent and told her if she had any reservations to take it up with the proper London authorities. Abigail felt certain Emma would soon be receiving the news, and it pleased her to know she would no longer be able to manipulate or control the situation.

Since the death of her sister and Emma's betrayal, something had come over her. She was still the same Miss Abigail but much stronger and persistent. The violation against Emma Mae had lifted her self-esteem and hopes tremendously. She had become renewed.

Even if they could not immediately return to New Hope, the confirmed knowledge of Emma's lost control over Bethie was a sign from Heaven. A sign that gave truth, that good will always prevail over evil. Though London was new to them both, what a relief it was to be so far from Savannah. Miss Jane had verified Bethie's fears of her aunt and she wanted nothing more to do with her.

She missed William terribly, and it was difficult not to think of him. A day wouldn't go by, without Bethie wondering how he was and if he thought of her too. Though she could no longer do anything for him, Miss Abigail understood Bethie's concerns. She knew how close their friendship had developed and she, too, had grown fond of the young man.

Harboring little confidence herself, Abigail tried to convince Bethie that he was strong and smart. And because he was older, he would soon be able to break away from Emma's control. Perhaps he would even, one day, come to London for a visit.

Although Bethie had not yet received any correspondence from him, Miss Abigail encouraged her to continue to write with the hopes that she would soon get word. Bethie wrote him every day with Miss Abigail accompanying her to the nearest posting box so not a day would be delayed.

Abigail rented a townhome only a block from the school. This way Bethie could walk and they would never be too far apart during the day. The house was small but adequate and quite lovely, as the two settled in quickly.

Miss Abigail wrote Joseph she was with Bethie and they were

both safe. She left him in complete control of the estate with Mr. Holt to operate all of the other properties, businesses, and assets. Bethie added a message of her own, describing London, and the boarding school with hopes of soon returning to Covington so they could be a family once again.

She missed Joseph terribly, but felt confident that one day they would all be together again. Mr. Holt continued to work persistently in getting the judge to allow Bethie to return to the states permanently but with constant blockage and resistance from Emma Mae.

The end of the summer came quickly and Bethie was about to begin her studies feeling reluctant but excited. Miss Abigail walked her to the entrance of the school and promised to be waiting at the end of the day. Bethie insisted she go in by herself and that it was necessary she make the new adjustment on her own. Abigail, though somewhat leery, respected her mature decision and did not protest.

From the gate of the estate to the front of the main entrance was filled with girls around her age up to late teens. Some talked among themselves while others stood with their parents. A few of the girls that lived in the dorms exchanged tearful last goodbyes with them while others anticipated the new year and what it would bring. Bethie joined the crowd of girls who were beginning to enter the building leaving Miss Abigail standing in the background watching with concerned eyes.

It was difficult for her since she had privately tutored Bethie and even taught at the same Savannah school in which she and William had attended, never being too far away from her. But she was aware of Wharton's wonderful reputation as a fine academic school, and Bethie was growing up needing more independence and friends.

She was still naive thought Abigail, worried about the wealthy, snobbish, young ladies she would probably encounter. Other than Emma Mae and her acquaintances, she was not used to children of her own age acting in such a way.

Bethie was nervous and shy as she continued to move along with the crowd, unaware of where she should go and do. She knew none of the girls and hoped to make friends soon. Miss Catherine and the other teachers met them in the large hall or dining room as the crowd immediately became quiet and still.

She began with the introduction of herself and the other staff members to those who were new and welcomed the others back for another year. The school and her own rules were clearly defined as she maintained a strict and serious demeanor the entire time. Each girl's name was called out alphabetically. Finally, the girls were given to an instructor who directed them to a classroom down the hall.

The group moved quietly pass Miss Catherine, no one daring to speak a word. It was obvious they were intimidated as they moved by her like little tin soldiers. "Move along, ladies… Choose a desk and be seated quietly. I'll be in shortly to begin our studies," instructed Miss Kate, the school's English teacher.

She left them for a moment as the girls began to fill the desks. Bethie chose one that was situated in the middle of the classroom, not wanting to be too close to the teacher or at the back in case she could not hear her clearly.

But before she could sit, she was approached by a girl about thirteen or fourteen blocking the entrance of the seat.

"I believe that is my desk you're about to sit in, Bethie… Isn't that what I heard your mother call you outside, a short while ago? What kind of name is Bethie?" remarked the girl in a snotty, sarcastic tone, as the other girls in the class laughed aloud causing her to become embarrassed and red in the face.

She was an English girl whom Bethie believed was probably quite wealthy and spoiled by her attitude. The girl was thin but stood taller, more awkward than Bethie. She had long blonde hair that had been arranged in one long braid with a large yellow bow matching her hair centered in the middle of her back. Because her skin was so fair and her hair so yellow, Bethie, unable to help herself, thought she resembled a big banana.

The girl's attitude had angered her, but it was the first day of school and she wished not to cause a scene. She decided to give up the desk to avoid an argument. "You may have your silly desk, and my name is Sara, Sara Beth. Only my friends may call me Bethie."

She walked away without saying another word leaving the girl dumbfounded as the class became quiet. The girl was not accustomed to being spoken to in such a manner. She wondered who this new girl was and felt certain Bethie couldn't possibly know who she was.

Bethie found an empty desk two rows behind to the left of the room. Again, the girl followed her as she stopped in front of it glaring down at her.

"This, I'm afraid, is also my desk. I insist you remove yourself from it this very instant!" commanded the girl trying to cause Bethie additional embarrassment.

The girl was angry and insulted that she had been retaliated upon and was determined to punish Bethie. She was used to her victims whimpering from embarrassment and becoming skirmish, as they moved swiftly away trying to hide in the background.

Unfortunately, Bethie had met her first unlikable peer. She knew the girl was simply toying with her and decided to put a quick end to it before the teacher came back.

"How could this possibly be your desk when you insisted that the other one was? Is your memory so short that you have already forgotten the other?" questioned Bethie sarcastically, causing the class to laugh abruptly in her behalf.

She became so furious and frustrated with Bethie's quick, bold, and witty response that her face appeared as though it would burst from redness.

"Apparently, you are new and are not aware of who I am. My name is Margaret Wharton," she began, pointing her nose upward. "My grandfather is the founder of this very school you are so fortunately attending. And I am not accustomed to having anyone speak—"

"How lucky for you. Lovely to meet you," interrupted Bethie unimpressed.

"Yes, we're all very pleased to know of your family tree, Margaret. But if you do not mind, I would prefer it, if you would now take a seat so that I can begin class." Miss Kate added, coming into the room as the girls roared in laughter. "That will be quite enough, ladies! Take one book and pass the others back and let us get started."

The rest of the day went swiftly, even with Margaret's occasional glare or whispers to her friends. Bethie seemed to enjoy her new school. There were a variety of subjects taught and to choose from. Although she had always found Miss Abigail to be very intelligent, the teachers at the school seemed more knowledgeable about current events and their methods used quite interesting.

At the end of the school day, she was leaving the main building to meet Miss Abigail when a girl around her own age approached her. She was about Bethie's height and weight but with red hair and freckles. Bethie thought she had about the reddest hair she had ever seen.

Though her hair was pulled back in a tight braid, because of her wild bangs, Bethie could tell her hair was naturally very curly and that a braid was probably the only way to control it. The girl was not homely or beautiful, but her looks fell about cute.

"Don't pay no mind to Margaret. She always bullies the new girls. But I must declare, you have certainly left some first impression. Why you've become quite popular and only- your first day here at Wharton! Most of the girls are glad you're here, in fact, they've told me to tell you so myself. Welcome!" she added, confident and smiling. The girl was most definitely not from London, her southern accent was quite prominent.

"What do you mean, popular?" questioned Bethie, guarded.

"Margaret is not used to being outwitted. Why most of the girls are plain afraid of her. They simply back away with heads down and tails between their legs," giggled the girl making Bethie smile.

"You're the first, I've witnessed, to ever stand up to her. You're a real hero to the other girls. Mind you, I'm not afraid of her. But I normally just prefer to keep my distance. And finally too! That Margaret is so rude and obnoxious, nothing a good spankin' wouldn't cure!"

"Oh! Where are my manners?" she replied, feeling embarrassed she had waited so long to introduce herself. She extended her arm outward and shook Bethie's hand vigorously. "My name is Georgia Lee. Georgia Lee Work. Originally from Atlanta, Georgia, but my family has a home in Savannah where we've lived on and off."

"Our plantation in Atlanta was completely burned from the war. Since the plantation was rebuilt, we've just kept both, going back and forth whenever we feel fit to. And I can tell by the sound of your voice that you're not from around these parts either. You're also from the states, am I right?" rambled, Georgia Lee.

"Yes," Bethie answered, getting cut off.

"Wait! Don't tell me where you're from, let me guess. You don't sound like no southerner… so you must be from the north! You're a Yankee, ain't ya? Please don't take offense. I meant it in the highest regard," she giggled.

"We're all one big happy country now, united as one. And thank the Lord for that. Course my papi is still in a tizzy about losing everything. I don't think he'll ever get over that dog gone war. Personally, the stories and constant reminiscing has gotten to be such a bore. A war that you and I wasn't even born yet, all their complaining and all. Why, I look forward to coming back to London every year!" continued Georgia Lee, as Bethie wondered if she would ever pause for air.

"All right now, let me see… you're from the state of… Delaware! Yes, Delaware, that's my guess. Are you from Delaware, Sara Beth?"

"No, actually I'm from New Hope, Pennsylvania," replied Bethie.

"I don't believe I know where New Hope is… or have ever heard of it for that matter," Georgia Lee responded, perplexed.

"It's not too far from Philadelphia."

"Have you lived there all your life?" Georgia Lee continued.

"No… the last five years I've live with my aunt… in Savannah."

"Well! I'll be a cat's meow," exaggerated an excited Georgia as her voice became louder. "If that don't beat all… Two sisters of Georgia standing right next to one another in London of all places! How terribly wonderful!" she blurted, completely delighted by the news.

"I've been coming to this school for three years now, praying for a sister from the south. Tell me now, who's your aunt? Maybe I've heard of her," she questioned eagerly, unable to hold back.

"Her name is Emma Mae Calhoun," responded Bethie, reluctantly.

"Miss Emma Mae is your aunt?" replied Georgia Lee slowly, astonished by the new found information. "Well I know who she is… Who doesn't? Most everyone in Georgia knows your Aunt Emma Mae. She's only the most wealthiest lady in Georgia! Nearly owns all the shipyards from Charleston to Savannah. And has the largest plantation in the country."

"My papi is just green with envy! My mother and Miss Emma are very good friends. Have been for many years now. How lucky you are to come from such a fine family like the Calhouns."

"My name is Sara Beth Covington! I'm a Covington, not a Calhoun!" snapped Bethie, defensively.

Georgia Lee knew she had touched on a sensitive topic. She wanted Bethie to like her and thought desperately of how to make it up to her.

"I'm ashamed to admit, I've never met any members of the Covington family. But I'm certain, after meeting you, your family must be fine people. I would be proud to have known them, Sara Beth."

"Thank you, Georgia Lee. They were really fine words you just said. I'm sorry for becoming so upset. I do hope we'll become friends," replied Bethie sincerely.

Georgia Lee was both relieved and grateful she had said the right words. She was aware, much too often, the wrong ones seem to come out of her mouth as though she were unable to control them.

"I hope we will too, Sara Beth. It would mean the world to me."

"Bethie…" called Miss Abigail from a distance, near the gate entrance. She was pleased to see Bethie had made a friend already.

"Well, I have to go now. Goodbye."

"Goodbye, Sara, see you tomorrow!"

Bethie nodded and smiled. She began to walk away then stopped and turned toward Georgia again, "You can call me Bethie. I'd like that."

"I'd like that too, very much. Goodbye, Bethie," smiled Georgia Lee brightly.

As the school year progressed, Bethie and Georgia Lee became best of friends. Bethie found her new friend to be a bit loud and talkative at times, but thoughtful and devoted to their friendship. After writing her parents and getting permission, she would often come for supper at the townhome or stay for the weekend. Georgia Lee's parents would send her by ship to London after each summer vacation in Atlanta or Savannah, always chaperoned, but never by them.

She confided in Bethie that she was not very close to either parent. They always seemed to be too busy or preoccupied, but she loved them just the same. It didn't seem to bother her that much, and throughout the years she had developed a mature adjustment to their relationship.

Georgia Lee and her roommate never seemed to get along. She complained almost daily to Bethie about her annoying habits. Bethie felt sad for her being so far away from any family and having to live in the dorm. She remembered what it was like and could easily understand Georgia's loneliness when it came time for them to part. An idea came to mind, as she began to fill in the details.

After first getting Miss Abigail's permission, Bethie told Georgia Lee to write her parents about living with them. She would at least be happier and Miss Abby was a terrific guardian. Abigail was fond of Georgia, even with her sometimes loud personality and did not object in the least.

She thought it would be good not only for Georgia Lee but for Bethie too, since she had no brothers or sisters. But mostly, with the hope of filling the void and sadness caused by the abrupt separation of her and William. She questioned Miss Abigail constantly of why he did not respond to her letters. Knowing Emma Mae's behavior, Abigail could only imagine but decided not to speculate and told her in time he would.

Georgia Lee was ecstatic by the invitation and soon convinced her parents she would be much happier living with Bethie and Miss Abigail. The adults never met formally, but wrote to each other on behalf of the girls. They shared the same bedroom and giggled and laughed about anything silly they could conjure up.

Other than the days with William, Miss Abigail had never seen Bethie happier. The two shared each other's clothes and shoes, deciding each weekend how they would wear their hair the following school week. They talked Miss Abigail into doing their hair, trying all the latest styles. All three found London to be quite the fashionable place to live. Late at night, the girls would share their most intimate secrets swearing never to tell a soul.

Every Saturday, Miss Abigail and the girls searched for an unexplored site of London that had not yet been conquered by the three. The House of Parliament and Buckingham Palace with its 600 room occupancy were only a couple of the magnificent architectural buildings viewed on their all day tours. The abbeys and churches were among the most elegant of all, decided Bethie, looking up at a lion and a unicorn gracing the pediment of the church of St. Martin-in-the-Fields.

The three had so much fun together, talking and giggling as they went from place to place. Miss Abigail felt so young and so free and except for missing Joseph, had finally found peace. They were far from Emma Mae and having the time of their life.

London was a busy and wondrous city, filled with intricately designed buildings and beautiful gardens, wonderful operas, theaters, artists, and mouthwatering foods prepared by the finest chefs in all of Europe. The girls even looked forward to school every day, as they walked each morning side by side with Miss Abigail leading the way.

They were a world away from America, almost becoming oblivious to her. London was not home but a temporary place of refuge, creating a certain detachment and alleviating them from responsibility to all current events that occurred there, whether good or bad. Even with the sorrowful news of President Garfield's assassination, the next four years of their lives in England would always be remembered fondly.

"Come on Bethie, fess up, you're dying for me to tell you what news mother sends of William!" pressured Georgia Lee, as the two lay across their twin oak beds.

Bethie had her nose in a book while Georgia Lee read a letter from her parents. "I'll do no such thing, Georgia Lee. I see that imaginative mind of yours is working feverishly again! I refuse to humor you by giving into any idle gossip concerning my cousin. He's a grown man and what he does is none of my business!" she scolded pretending not to care.

"Goodness Gracious! We've been best friends now for four years. And we've told each other all our secrets, Course... you've never really admitted that you're in love with your own cousin. But, I declare, he has been the only boy you've ever mentioned or given a second thought to!" teased Georgia Lee relentlessly, making her feel uncomfortable. Bethie didn't appreciate her accusations as she tossed her pillow at Georgia's head.

"Ouch! What was that for? I was only teasing, Bethie. I'm aware you and William are not blood related. There is nothing wrong with having feelings for him. You're just still angry that he never responded to any of your letters. It was so long ago, Bethie... It's about time you forgive and forget. And besides, that's just like a boy, not writing back. Most hate writing letters to girls and—"

"Hush now, Georgia Lee Work! You're making my head ache. It makes no difference to me now. I'm seventeen years old. We were children then… I no longer harbor any ill feelings toward William David Calhoun. That was so long ago. I hardly even remember," lied Bethie trying to convince Georgia Lee.

"Now you go on and hush, Bethie! You forget who you're talking to? You might have convinced yourself, but never me. Remember, I was the one who stayed awake all night with you while you cried over him. Well, I'm gonna tell you anyway. After all, he is family. Aren't you even the least bit interested?" probed Georgia Lee, continuing to be persistent and unwilling to subside. She waited for a response from Bethie who continued to ignore her question. She shrugged her shoulders and began again.

"Mother says, he studying to become a lawyer. According to her, he's quite the apprentice. Studies with an elite law firm right there in Savannah. He's become the most handsomest and richest catch in the whole state of Georgia. Mother says, every girl in Savannah has her eyes on him. But he hasn't taken to courting anyone yet. I wonder why… What do you think, Bethie?" pushed Georgia, grinning.

"Maybe he's waiting for his little Bethie to come home," she laughed teasingly, not realizing she had gone too far this time.

"Now you stop it, Georgia Lee! I've had enough of your silly gossip and opinions. Either change the subject or go to bed!" she snapped, annoyed with her friend.

Georgia Lee's feelings were hurt, but like on occasion her mouth had gotten the best of her. "I'm sorry, Bethie. I really didn't mean any harm," begged Georgia sincerely.

"That's your problem, Georgia Lee. You never really mean anything. So why can't you be more careful about what you say before you say it?" reprimanded Bethie.

After a few minutes of silence, she knew Georgia was upset from her harsh words and decided to let her off the hook. "I'm sorry for losing my temper, Georgia Lee. Talking about William is not easy for me. I would prefer, in the future, if you wouldn't talk about him."

"Well I know I can be a bit much at times… But always know that I love you like a sister, Bethie. Course since I don't have one, I could only imagine," she giggled, causing Bethie to smile.

"Oh Georgia, for as long as I live, I'll never meet another quite like you. You're one of a kind. I'm sure going to miss you this summer!" she giggled shaking her head.

"Bethie, you're so lucky and you don't even know it. You're only about the most beautiful young woman in London. Popular with all the girls, even nasty Margaret Wharton tries to be your friend. Every young gentleman in England stares and asks about you. They all follow you around like a bunch of sick pups. You're the envy of every girl in London—including me!"

"I'm only saying this for your own good, Bethie… Please don't take offense. If I were as pretty and popular as you, I wouldn't waste my heart on someone who thinks of me as nothing more than a silly child. He's hurt you so much over these years, never having the common decency to even write one letter back. I don't even know the man personally and yet he makes me so angry. I just don't want to see you sad any longer, Bethie."

"First of all… you are very pretty Georgia Lee. And second, I appreciate your concern, but don't worry about me. I'm just not ready for men yet. None of the ones I've met in London interest me, and what's the hurry anyway."

"You know what your problem is? You're just plain boy crazy! That's all you ever talk about these days—boys, boys, boys! And as far as William is concerned, it's true I don't think of him as much as I used to. Except, of course, when my best friend constantly brings him up!" she teased loudly.

Miss Abigail and Bethie escorted Georgia to the London shipyard. Bethie and Georgia Lee said their sad goodbyes to one another, promising that the summer would go fast and they would soon be together again. Every year Georgia Lee begged Bethie to come with her to Georgia. But each year she declined, using the excuse that Miss Abigail would become too terribly lonely without her.

She couldn't bear to take the chance of running into William in Savannah, and most definitely Emma Mae. It would be too embarrassing for her after all the unrequited letters she wrote him. Bethie was convinced he had forgotten her and moved on with his life.

She fought desperately to rid herself of the bitter feeling of resentment toward him, trying to make herself believe they had only been children when they knew each other. But it was still quite painful for her. By the time the carriage returned to their townhome it had started to rain heavily. They ran to the front entrance where Miss Abigail was greeted by a carrier with a telegram addressed to her attention.

After changing their wet clothes, both sat in front of the fireplace where it was warm and cozy. Bethie wondered who had sent the telegram and waited patiently while Abigail read its contents. Her face began to change from curious to frighten as she continued to read on with nervous eyes.

"What is it, Miss Abby? What's happened?" questioned Bethie, becoming worried by her facial expressions.

"No! I can't believe it… It can't be!" gasped Miss Abigail in horror, slowly lowering herself into the rocker. "It's Joseph, he's in trouble…"

"What kind of trouble?" questioned Bethie concerned.

"He's been arrested and placed in jail. They're accusing him of killing a man. It's all so unbelievable… Joseph couldn't hurt anyone. This doesn't make any sense to me. It must be a mistake."

"Is the telegram from Joseph?" continued Bethie, trying to make sense of it all.

"No, it's from Mr. Holt. He says he got to Joseph just in time. The town was in such an uproar. They wanted to hang him without even giving him a fair trial. Thomas would never make up such horror. So this all must be true. Somehow I have to help him… But I don't know how."

"Please, I'd like to read the letter myself, Miss Abby," Bethie pleaded, as Abigail handed it to her.

What she spoke was true. He was being held in a Philadelphia jail, and Mr. Holt was doing everything he could to help him. It had been a longtime since Bethie had seen Miss Abigail so distraught. The alarming news caused her to go in shock, as she sat staring into space, her face both pale and horrified.

Bethie was also very upset and wanted desperately to help him. "We should leave immediately for Philadelphia!" she blurted, not knowing what else to do. "He probably feels alone and scared. He needs us."

"I can't go to him, Bethie… I don't believe it would be in Joseph's best interest. God knows, I want to," continued Miss Abigail desperately.

"I don't understand, Miss Abby. Why wouldn't you want to go and help him? He's family," questioned Bethie confused and upset.

"Believe me, dearest, it's not that I don't want to go and help him. That is all I've thought of these last few minutes after reading this disturbing letter. It would be so easy for me to get on a ship and return home with you. Being so far away makes it feel even more hopeless. I need to be near him to know everything will be fine."

"But it's not about what I need that's important right now. The thought of returning to New Hope has been on my mind every year, about this same time, in fact.

"Why haven't we gone home during the summers?" interrupted Bethie, demanding to know. "Every year I ask, but you always make excuses. Emma Mae can no longer prevent us from returning. We have all summer to visit as long as we return to London before my studies begin."

"It's you Miss Abby… isn't it? I believe you are the one who does not want to go home," accused Bethie, becoming even more upset.

"I have always loved you like a real mother. But I'm seventeen now, New Hope is my home and you have avoided taking me back for four years now. If anything happens to Joseph... I don't know what I'd do. You and he are the only family I have in the whole world, and I will do anything I can to help him."

"If we don't at least try, frankly, I don't know if I could ever forgive you. Don't you understand, they could find him guilty. Do you know what they do to a Negro accused of killing a white man? They will certainly hang him. Maybe even before he's tried. Don't you care about what happens to him? Now I demand to know why we cannot return to New Hope! I'm not a child anymore, Miss Abby. I know you're keeping something from me. What is it?" she demanded upset, with eyes filled.

Her words were more than Abigail could take as she broke down in tears. Bethie had never spoken so harshly to her before, but it was not the reason she wept aloud. Feeling guilty, she tried to comfort her. "I'm sorry, Miss Abby... I guess I just lost my head. I'm so worried about Joseph."

"No need to apologize. You are right, Bethie," she replied, lifting her head as Bethie handed her a handkerchief.

"Because of the circumstances, I feel I have no other choice but to tell you something that I have never spoken of to anyone. You must understand that it has nothing to do with your age but has always been something very private and personal to us. To have confessed to anyone, could have caused much anger to many who believe differently. What I'm about to confess is to be kept in complete confidence. I know I can trust you. I only pray you can understand."

"You can trust me," she promised, intrigued with curiosity. Miss Abigail paused for a moment to wipe the remaining tears from her face. She was terrified by what she was about to say to Bethie. Would she be angry or think less of her? She tried to imagine, wondering how she would ever cope with Bethie's disapproval of their behavior.

"It's not New Hope I'm avoiding… it's Joseph."

"Why would you avoid Joseph? He's the most wonderful man I've ever known. He's the only father figure I've ever known! Are you angry with something he's done? Don't you care for him anymore?"

"No, on the contrary… I love him, Bethie…"

"I love him, too, Miss Abby. But it still doesn't explain why we can't go home and try to help."

"You're not listening to me, Bethie." She paused for a brief moment to take a deep breath while Bethie waited patiently for a response. Abigail slowly exhaled and began again, "What I meant to say… is that I'm in love with him. Like a wife would love a husband. Secretly, we have loved each other for many years."

"That's the big secret?" Bethie replied, disappointed. "That's no secret to me. I've known for years. I might have been a child, but I wasn't blind." Abigail could not believe her ears, as she remembered her own sister's words. She was flabbergasted as she stared at Bethie in disbelief. The knowledge of her knowing of their love for each other all those years continued to replay in her mind.

But part of her was not surprised. Bethie had always been so bright and aware of her surroundings. It would be just like her to have known and never to say anything, understanding even as a small child the havoc it could have caused. What a special young lady she was, she agreed, proud and honored to have raised her.

"How did you know about us?" questioned Miss Abigail, astonished.

"It was obvious by the way you two looked at each other. And after walking into the barn and finding Joseph kissing you so romantically, I knew for sure then."

Abigail blushed from embarrassment. "You've kept this to yourself, all these years?" questioned Miss Abigail, still surprised by it all.

"I love you both and didn't want to see either of you get in trouble."

"Thank you, Bethie, for your love and understanding. We are so lucky to have you." Miss Abigail put her arms around her as they gave each other a long hug.

"Aunt Liz always said you two were asking for a heap of trouble!" added Bethie.

"What! Elizabeth… my sister. You talked about this with my sister?" questioned Abigail stunned.

"Yes, we talked about it occasionally. It made her really nervous. But I used to tell her not to worry and that everything would turn out."

"She used to say you both were touched in the head. It made me laugh hysterically. But then she would say it was no laughing matter. And we would all be tarred and feathered then run out of town if other folks got wind. But I told her that I wasn't afraid and I didn't care what people thought. I really miss Aunt Liz. She was the best…"

"Yes, she was, Bethie," agreed Miss Abigail smiling, quite amazed by it all.

"There's something else you should know, Bethie…"

"More?" she gulped, intrigued.

"Yes. There's more… You should know that Joseph and I were secretly married by his pastor… He would not be with me, in that way, until I agreed."

"Lord have mercy!" exclaimed Bethie, astonished. There was a moment of silence, as Miss Abigail studied Bethie's face wondering what she thought. Bethie was simply speechless, trying to contemplate all that had been told to her.

"It won't be long now when I am of age to receive my inheritance. When we finally return to New Hope for good, Covington will be mine. I never want you or Joseph to ever leave. You two are my family. And I will always, I give you my word, accept the two of you. If I have to build a wall around the estate to keep nosey people from our business, I will Miss Abby. On my land, in my home, will be our business—not the towns."

"But until then, I want you to use as much Covington money as it takes to help Joseph. Along with Mr. Holt, he is to have the best lawyers money can buy. A dozen, if that's what it takes."

"Thank you, dearest… You're a wonderful young lady. Joseph and I will never forget your generosity and love you've given us all these years."

"I don't expect you to entirely understand. I know you're mature enough to imagine the trouble that would occur if people found out about us. But that is not what I'm concerned about. It's Joseph. I won't place his fate in further turmoil. If a small, bright child can see so easily, then I am convinced so could others."

"Trying to help him from a distance is the best I can do for him. You see, Bethie, I love Joseph very much. For years now I've tried to fight these feelings, but it's simply useless. What I feel for him has, at times, made me feel shame and even sacrilegious."

"But then one day, I realized that those feelings were only formed from what I had learned from society. The way we've been raised and taught by our elders. But we are all only human, made from flesh and blood. And humans make mistakes, sometimes devastating ones. So what if judging people by the color of their skin is wrong? Except for societies treatment toward others, what proof is there that what we feel for one another isn't beautiful? Isn't right?"

"I began to believe the only sin committed was the sin of judging another by the color of their skin. But I'm only one among many who strongly believe differently. People who would go on believing until the day they die all men are not created equal. Despite whether God himself appeared and spoke of its injustice."

"It isn't enough to free someone or document that all are equal. You have to truly believe before it can ever become a part of our past. I finally resolved myself to accepting that I will never love another and only God can judge. And when we die, let him judge us. If we were wrong, let him punish us appropriately."

"Because of my love for him, I decided when I came to London that it was for the best. This way I could keep a distance between us and you from Emma Mae. I could never forgive myself if anything happened to him because of our relationship. And because he is a Negro man, his life will always be in more danger than mine could ever be."

"People would point their fingers at him. Judging me as though I was a naive, unmarried, white lady that had been taken advantage of by this big Negro man. And maybe even judge you—or worse, take you from me. I would never let that happen. If I appear to be a coward, then so be it. For me, it's not about being a martyr but only about loving this man. Loving the two of you so much that I would protect your lives with my own. If I had to, there would be no hesitation," ended Miss Abigail strongly.

"I may never understand what it feels like to be in love with a man whose skin color is different from my own. But I do know what it is like to love a man that I will never have. I may be young. But I already know what it is like to have my heart broken. And still, spend years thinking of no other. No matter how hard I try to forget. The image of his face, the sound of his voice, is burned in my mind forever." Miss Abigail listened closely as Bethie sadly confessed her inner most feelings.

"Sometimes I feel that I'm being punished. Cursed by him, never to be freed. At least, you have been loved back. I can't imagine a worse pain than being so easily forgotten. Ignored and tossed aside as though I were nothing more than a silly, annoying child from his past. I'll never forgive him for forgetting me. Or for making me feel this way…" Miss Abigail gently laid Bethie's head on her shoulder as she quietly wept.

"You're so young Bethie to have your heart broken. I wish there was something I could do to help you feel better."

"Just understanding and being with me helps, Miss Abby."

"I pray you will find it in your heart, one day, to forgive William. You were only children then. Who knows what lies Emma Mae might have told him. But no matter what she may have said, she can never take away the childhood memories that you two shared and will always remember and cherish."

"Do you think he remembers?"

"Yes, Bethie... I have no doubts, he remembers."

Calhoun Plantation, Savannah, Georgia

Captain McNeal stood nervously in front of the main entrance of the Calhoun mansion. Over, and over again, in his mind, he rehearsed what excuse he would give if Emma Mae should approach him. Though she was co-owner of his ship, the day of their business transaction would always be the worst remembered. At the time, he desperately needed her because of financial reasons, losing the St. Anne had been inevitable.

Emma offered a solution that soon caused him to regret for the rest of his life. He was indeed aware of who she was, but had little hope that he could ever recover without her funds. He ignored the warnings from friends and business associates. And knew, he would be unable to cope with the loss of his livelihood. At the time, he felt he had no other choice. Even over the years when his finances became brighter, she refused to buy him out. He disliked the woman immensely and did all he could to avoid her.

But the vision of young Bethie flashed into mind. He could still see her beautiful, sad face pleading for his help. She had left a message at the shipyard in London. And when he had arrived, went immediately to see her.

She begged him to take word to William pleading that it was not for her sake, but for a dear friend who was imprisoned in a Philadelphia jail while others decided his fate. Her selflessness was her most endearing charm, agreed Captain McNeal, who had over the years become fond of her as though she were the daughter that he never had.

Never once had he come to London without joining her and Miss Abigail for supper. From that deceitful day in which she had boarded his ship, they had kept in contact with each other. He gave her his word that he would help and she could rely on him. The Captain was a man of his word and both thanked him from the bottom of their heart.

Bethie maturely put her feelings aside to help her friend Joseph. As he for her, she would have done anything to save his life. She remembered William as a bright, strong young man. And was sure, along with the Calhoun reputation, he could indeed help Joseph. Because he had never written back to her all those years, she wasn't even sure he would concern himself to help her—let alone a strange Negro man. But she felt compelled to at least try.

Miss Jane, to her surprise, opened the door to find the Captain standing anxiously. Out of respect, he quickly removed his cap. "Captain McNeal… hello, what a surprise. Is Mrs. Calhoun expecting you?" asked Jane, unaware that they were to meet today.

"No, ma'am… Actually I've come to see her son, William." He responded swiftly, trying to keep his voice down, not wanting to arouse any further attention.

Miss Jane immediately sensed that this was about Bethie and came outside pulling the door slightly closed behind her. "I'm afraid William isn't here right now. Is there something I can help you with?"

The Captain hesitated but then began again, "I have a letter addressed to him from… from Miss Sara Beth, ma'am." She told me if I was unable to speak with him, you would know what to do."

"How is Sara? Is she well?" questioned Miss Jane, genuinely concerned.

The Captain gave a little chuckle, "You'd hardly recognize her now, ma'am. She's grown up so much. A real fine lady, and a beautiful one at that."

"But is she happy, Captain?"

"Yes ma'am. I believe she is. Miss Abigail has taken real good care of her."

"I'm pleased to hear that. Tell her… tell them both, I wish them the very best."

"Yes, ma'am. I'll make sure I tell them."

Miss Jane motioned the Captain a few feet away from the door, so they could not be heard. "I don't believe it would be wise to give me the letter. I couldn't promise that it would be delivered. Do you understand?"

"Yes, I understand," replied the Captain, knowing Emma Mae all too well.

"William studies and works with a reputable law firm right here in Savannah. The firm is Emerson and Associates, located at 112 Lafayette Street. If you go now, you'll find him in one of their offices."

"Thank you, ma'am," replied the Captain. He hurried off to leave, not wanting to place Miss Jane in any further danger.

Jane flinched by the sudden, startling sound of Emma Mae beckoning for her immediate attention. She made her way back into the mansion as swiftly as possible.

Because of her old age, most of the major responsibilities of the plantation and shipping business were now being taken care of by William.

Emma spent most of her days ordering poor Miss Jane around. "Jane! Who was at the door? Was there someone at the door," yelled Emma Mae from the parlor.

Jane entered the room with a fresh pitcher of Lemonade. "No ma'am. No one was at the door. Just left to get you something fresh and cool to drink," lied Miss Jane, unable to keep her eyes on Emma.

"Are you sure there was no one at the door? I distinctly heard an unfamiliar voice," continued Emma not believing her.

"No ma'am. There was no one at the door!" replied Jane sharply, looking into Emma's cold black eyes, refusing to cave.

The Captain soon found the law firm as he stood in the building's foyer arguing and insisting that he see William immediately. From two rooms away and because his door had been left ajar, William could easily hear two voices bickering. When he heard his name mentioned, he became curious and came out to investigate.

"Can I help you?" questioned William, entering the foyer.

"This man insists on seeing you immediately, sir. He has no appointment and refuses to schedule one. I told him you were a very busy—"

"That will be all, Luther," interrupted William, annoyed with his rambling, pampas attitude.

"I can take it from here. You can go now."

"My name is Captain McNeal."

"Yes, I'm aware of who you are. My mother is part owner of your ship. What can I do for you?"

"I'm not here on behalf of my ship. I've come from London with a letter addressed to you. I promised to hand deliver it myself."

William thought a moment, but could not imagine who the letter was from. He wondered if there was a problem at the London shipyard concerning their vessels.

"The letter is from Miss Sara Beth Covington."

William was immediately stunned from not hearing the name spoken for so many years. Except during the private moments of his dreams could he hear her name spoken repeatedly, but never in reality. His eyes became large as he stood surprised and in shock. He was speechless, unprepared for the sudden impact of emotions brought forth by this man's visit. All hope had been dismissed, never did he imagine she would ever contact him.

The Captain thought his reaction was most peculiar, until it dawned on him that William was the young man Bethie had spoken so fondly of during the long voyage to London many years ago. It was quite obvious, he was in love with her. Or, at the very least, the memories of their childhood days together.

"Did you say the letter was from Miss Sara Beth Covington? Bethie…"

"Yes, she needs your help and has asked me to deliver this letter immediately."

"Please… come into my office. We'll have more privacy there.

It's this way," directed William swiftly, still quite stunned and feeling lightheaded and confused.

"Mr. Calhoun, you have a meeting with Miss Ruth in a few minutes," replied Luther interrupting the two before they could enter William's office.

"Cancel it! Something has come up. Clear the rest of my day."

"But Mr. Calhoun…" shrieked Luther. William closed the door quickly, cutting him off, refusing to acknowledge his last comment.

He offered the Captain a chair and some tea as he tried to calm himself, not wanting him to see that he had upset him. William slowly sat behind his desk, unable to refrain from asking about her any longer.

"How is she? Is she ill?" he questioned, demanding that he be told immediately.

"Miss Sara and Miss Abigail are doing well. Please, read the letter," urged the Captain as he handed it to him.

****

Dear William,

For not the sake of my own, but the fate of my good and dear friend Joseph, I plead for your help. He is in a prison accused of murdering a white man in Philadelphia, Pennsylvania. If you cable Mr. Holt, you will be able to receive further information regarding his plight.

I am convinced he is innocent. But fear because he is Negro, for his life. I've been informed you are an attorney in a prestigious firm. And along with the Calhoun reputation could possibly help my dear friend.

I beg you to help him. He and Miss Abigail are all the family I truly have left. I will pay you whatever you ask. The money means nothing to me. I trust that you will find it in your heart to help save this man's life.

Respectfully Yours,
Bethie

****

Forgetting the Captain sat waiting William reread the letter carefully, as though in fear of missing any important words she may have written. It had been so long since he had contact with his Bethie, and the letter was the closest he could feel being next to her.

"What is Bethie doing in London?" he questioned, confused and overwhelmed by it all.

"Don't you know, sir?"

"No what, Captain?"

"Your mother sent Bethie to live in a boarding school in London, four years ago."

The hair on the back of his neck stood erect, as the vein that ran vertically near his temple pumped and pulsed as though it would soon burst. His face became hot and flushed as the anger built inside him like a volcano about to erupt.

The Captain knew immediately he had said the wrong words, "You didn't know… I'm sorry to have to be the one to tell you." He tried to comfort him with his words.

"For years my mother has played on my trust, making me into her little fool. You'd think by now I would have learned. There is nothing more shameful than sitting in front of you as a grown man confessing this." Embarrassed, William lowered his angry head as the Captain leaned in trying to display sincere empathy.

"It wasn't too long ago that your mother made me the fool when she refused my offer to buy back the St. Anne. Even the best of us, Son, have fallen before her." Captain McNeal's words seem to inspire a spark of strength, as William vowed to do all that he could for Bethie and her friend Joseph.

He abruptly stood from his chair and said firmly, "Consider the St. Anne yours, Captain."

He was so surprised by William's offer, he hardly knew what to say. The words "thank you" seemed not to be enough, he agreed gratefully.

"Give Miss Abigail and Miss Sara Beth my regards. Please tell Bethie I will do all that is in my power to help Joseph. And when it is all over, I wish to come to London and give them the good news myself."

"When will you be in Philadelphia, Captain?"

"In about two months, I believe."

"Good. I shall see you then. But now I must go and prepare to leave for Philadelphia, immediately. I can't begin to tell you what your visit here today has meant to me."

"I believe I already know," replied the Captain as he shook his hand goodbye.

William entered the mansion in a wild frenzy, his voice loud and eyes filled with anger. He ordered a servant to pack a trunk and demanded to know where his mother was.

"Mother!" he screamed loudly and out of control. He made it to the parlor as she was abruptly awakened by his alarming screams for her.

"Mother! Damn it, Mother!"

"What is it, Son? Please calm down and close the door."

Miss Jane abruptly stood while slowly backing out of the room. She knew exactly what fueled his anger and wanted no part of it. This was Emma's doing and felt she deserved all that came with it.

"I'll do no such thing, Mother. What I have to say to you I hope everyone in this God forsaken house hears! Darn you for making me your fool again. But I guess I'm deserving forever believing a word you say. Why do I continue to trust you? So that you can tear my heart apart with your treacherous lies!"

"What is wrong with you, William? Please, stop speaking to me with those words and calm down!" demanded Emma Mae, becoming frightened by her son's behavior. Never had she seen such anger in his eyes, and apparently aimed toward her.

"What did you think, Mother? I'd never find out about Bethie? Why do you assume everyone is beneath you, too stupid to ever figure out your twisted schemes? How could you do that to her? How could you send your only niece alone and away from all who love her? What a terrible and cruel thing to do to a child… to me and Bethie, both. What kind of monster are you? My God, Mother, she's of your own flesh and blood—even more than I!" he accused, with crazed eyes.

"Son, it isn't true… Who told you?" pleaded Emma Mae desperately.

"Don't even start… It is of no relevance who told me. You've been caught. It's over. I now understand why Bethie never returned any of my letters. All this time I'm sending them to Pennsylvania, and you never stopped me. What were you doing, Mother, laughing at my ignorance behind my back?"

"No, Son, I would never do such a thing. Please let me explain."

"Never! I'm leaving for Philadelphia immediately. Bethie's friend and caretaker of her estate has been wrongly accused of murder. I intend to do everything in my power to help him. Now you listen here, Mother. If I find you had anything to do with Joseph's imprisonment. Or if he is found guilty and hangs. I swear to you… I will never lay eyes on you again," he promised with much contempt.

"No, Son… Please don't speak to me this way," begged a pathetic Emma Mae.

"You use every bought lawyer and judge you own in Georgia and Pennsylvania and you get him freed. For once in your life, you use your power for good. You owe Bethie. Or my God, Mother… I'll never step foot on this plantation ever again!"

William quickly left her sight, unable to bear another moment with his mother. He ignored her cries as she begged him to forgive her. Pleading what was done had been for their own good. But he refused to listen as he moved swiftly out of the house, grabbing his trunk and tossing it onto the back of the wagon.

Henry was by William's side ready and waiting to help him in any way he could. He was aware of what had happened, not surprised but angry just the same. It was difficult not to have heard William's accusing voice directed at his mother. He cracked the whip hard and jerked the reins swiftly down on the horses, moving as fast as possible to the Savannah station.

"Jane! Jane, get the hell in here!" screamed Emma, still tormented by the words spoken by her son and the thought of possibly never seeing him again. She was never more terrified in her life. "Yes, Mrs. Calhoun," she answered as if unaware of all that had gone on.

"Get my lawyer here, tonight! I don't care how you do it. But you better damn well get him here!" demanded Emma Mae with a vengeance. "When I find out who told my son, they'll wish they had never been born," swore Emma, under her seething breath.

"Move it, you fool!" commanded Emma, as Jane promptly left the parlor. She closed the door behind her and took a moment to slowly inhale as a small, crooked grin appeared on Jane's face.

Finally, after all these years, Emma's lies and devious plots were coming undone unraveling before her very eyes. And it never felt more pleasurable than to be a simple staff member, also a victim of Emma's, able to bear witness to her own well deserved, self-destruction.

The Stranger

William immediately visited Joseph at the jail, even before he had made lodgings or visited Thomas Holt. He wanted him to know that he would do everything in his power to help him, and that the women had sent him.

"I know who ya are, Son," responded Joseph gratefully. "Bethie girl spoke often of ya. Your friendship—and your kindness. She is very fond of you. And I can tell… you of her." He smiled causing William to blush.

"Yes, sir. I am," responded William respectfully.

"Thank ya for being here." Both shook hands vigorously.

"Bethie spoke often about you. Missed you terribly. I know how much you mean to her. I looked forward to meeting you. So sorry under these circumstances… But I'll do everything in my power to help you. I give you my word," assured William sincerely.

"I believe you, Son… Can't thank ya enough. But when this is over, bring them both back to New Hope. Where they belong…"

"I'll do everything I can, sir… They mean a lot to me, as well." Both shook hands again. "Let's get started…" began William, filled with encouragement and conviction.

Within weeks after William joined Thomas Holt, in behalf of Joseph's defense, an entire fleet of the most powerful attorneys from Atlanta, Savannah, and the Philadelphia area joined their crusade of justice.

William was quite aware that they had been sent and paid by his mother. But it made no difference to him, he believed Joseph's story and was grateful for all the help he and Mr. Holt could get. He reassured Joseph that combined, they were indeed the most powerful team ever assembled. Joseph was grateful, he was certain it had been Emma Mae behind his troubles and was confused as to why she would help him so relentlessly.

The trial lasted for three long weeks in the August heat, which did not help control tempers. Twice, William was warned by the judge that he was out of order and needed to calm himself or his sleeping quarters, too, would be the county jail alongside Joseph. He was the youngest in the group and was counselled periodically. But he was a fine, young lawyer with strong convictions.

William believed, except for Mr. Holt, most of them played on the wrong side of the law most of their practice. Nevertheless, they were the best and could teach him better than any law school could.

Alexander Gilmore had been the man murdered in the old lumber mill outside Philadelphia. It was late evening when they presumed he had been killed. His assailant shot him once in the heart, ending his life instantly. William and Thomas concluded it to have been a paid hit, certainly an accomplished marksman. There was no evidence found at the scene of the crime and it had apparently occurred very quickly and smoothly, all too professional.

To no surprise to either lawyers, there was a significant connection between the man and Emma Mae Calhoun. William had a bad feeling the moment he read Bethie's letter and felt the pain of his mother's betrayal, that somehow she would be connected. Emma had permanently changed him and whatever she did from that point on would neither shock nor surprise him.

Mr. Gilmore had been instructed and paid by Emma Mae over seven years ago to accompany Miss Abigail and Bethie back to Savannah. When he approached Joseph at the estate, he knew he had seen this man before but at the time could not remember where. He spent many days thereafter driven and determined to remember, until finally recalling it had been along the canal and river.

Joseph knew immediately why he had been startled by the man when approached and introduced. The time he had first seen Mr. Gilmore was shortly after the tragic deaths of Mr. and Mrs.

Covington. He was still recovering from his accident but had no doubt this was the man he saw walking along the river outside Covington, seeming as though he was looking for something along the riverbed.

Because he was a stranger, he found his behavior to be peculiar. Joseph was preoccupied and paid little attention because of all the tragedies that had recently occurred. Yet, he still remembered this man.

He thought the timing in which he had first seen Mr. Gilmore and the fact he worked for Emma Mae Calhoun was all too much of a coincidence. He strongly believed the man was sent by her to try and recover the lost will. Knowing this lost document held the key that could forever break the ties between Bethie and Emma Mae, he felt he had no other choice but to investigate.

These papers had become a constant reminder of his failure and last remembrances of his good friend and employer, Jon Covington. But he was finally given the opportunity to make amends. The thought of bringing Bethie and Miss Abigail home and to fulfill Mr. Covington's last request of him, could not be ignored.

He remembered the gentleman's name and where he had said he was from. Joseph had Abner watch over the estate while he left swiftly in search of this man in the Philadelphia area. When he finally found him, though the man denied searching for the lost will, he did admit that he was in New Hope during that particular time. But that he simply had been interested in land along the river as an investment, and for no other reason.

Even after offering the man money, he continued to deny what Joseph suspected was the truth. Greed was always a powerful bargaining tool, agreed Joseph, as he told the man he would stay in Philadelphia for two nights in case he changed his mind. Just as he predicted, a note was hand delivered the very next day for him to meet Mr. Gilmore at an old lumber mill outside Philadelphia that evening.

By the time he found the mill, in the black of night, there was a swarm of officers inside and out of the old building. He knew there had been trouble and headed back to his room. The next morning he was arrested for Gilmore's murder. The case was based mainly on circumstantial evidence, being, the two had been seen by many arguing the day before.

And if his troubles were not grim enough, the following day, a bizarre twist took hold. An apparent witness to the crime came forward claiming it had been Joseph she recognized as the man she seen shoot Mr. Gilmore.

The lawyers, including Emma's, worked feverishly trying to find evidence that could exonerate Joseph of the crime. Though no one wanted to learn the truth more than William, he still loved his mother despite whether it could link her to the murder. He knew he could never fully forgive her unless he could prove to himself she had nothing to do with this man's death or the intentional, manipulation of Bethie's life and loved ones.

It was not unusual to find her lawyers constantly reminding him and Mr. Holt to focus on the issue of why Joseph could not possibly have done it, rather than who really killed Mr. Gilmore. Using the reasoning of time being of the utmost importance. But William agreed, this was no time to dwell on his own feelings but to try and save Joseph's life.

Though they had all worked very hard, it was William who made the major difference in the deciding vote toward Joseph's freedom. He spoke clearly, intelligently, and became very convincing on his behalf. William became the key to Joseph's freedom.

The defense based its case around Joseph's poor eye sight and the witness's old age. Because it was dark and the fact that Joseph was legally blind in one eye, it would have been impossible for him to have even been able to see the man from the distance he apparently was seen by the lady. Let alone make such a devastating, accurate shot. A reenactment of the events leading up to the shooting, according to the old woman's deposition, made all the difference.

From his words and actions, William soon convinced the jury of

Joseph's innocence. Although the answer to his mother's true involvement had never been revealed this was about the proudest day of his life, as he witnessed the tears of joy and utter gratefulness in Joseph's eyes.

William and Thomas Holt became good friends and colleagues over those weeks. Though he was older, Mr. Holt no longer saw him as a child but a fine, inspiring, young lawyer. He even offered him a permanent position with his firm with a possible partnership after the first three years.

William was humbled and honored, but declined appreciatively for the time being with the notion of reconsidering his offer in the future. Thomas advised him not to worry too much about his mother's involvement. He had too much going for him to allow Emma's shaded affairs to consume his every thought.

The trial was over, Joseph was back at Covington, and most likely the truth would remain hidden forever. William was desperate and compelled to find the good in his mother. This was the same woman who raised and cared for him. It was impossible to imagine there was not any good in her. He could hardly bear the thought of it.

Still believing in innocent before guilty, he sent a telegram to his mother thanking her for sending help in Joseph's defense. He informed her that he would be traveling to London to see Bethie and Miss Abigail and would not be returning to Savannah directly. Another letter was sent by Mr. Holt to London bringing the two the wonderful news of Joseph's release.

Thomas wrote that it had been William who really saved his life, and how wonderful it was to have worked with him. He noted that William would be coming to London on the St. Anne and would soon be joining them for a visit. And that he longed to see them both.

When the St. Anne finally came into port, the Captain could tell by William's expressions that all had gone well with the trial. He was pleased with his success and knew Bethie and Miss Abigail would be relieved and thankful to God for the wonderful news. He insisted that William travel on his ship to London and would not take no for an answer. The Captain knew the two were in love, and he wanted to bear witness to their happy reunion himself.

On the morning of the departure, William stood speaking to Mr. Holt as his trunk was lifted aboard by one of the Captain's men.

"I do hope they both enjoy the package. I know how much Bethie still loves sweets, it's hard to believe how the years have gone by. Bethie nearly eighteen, and you an inspiring young lawyer. I am getting old," added Mr. Holt shaking his head.

"Maybe a little older, but nonetheless wiser," complimented William smiling.

"I miss them both and wish I were going with you. But it's so busy at the firm, always is after you win one," chuckled Thomas. "Please send my love. And try to convince Bethie it won't be long until she can return to Pennsylvania for good."

"I will, Thomas. Thank you for all your help. Since I've known Bethie, you've been a very loyal friend to them. I'm glad you're on their side."

"Goodbye, sir," ended William sincerely.

"God be with you and the Captain," added Mr. Holt, becoming interrupted by an abrupt yell from the far distance.

"I'm looking for a Mr. William Calhoun, Mr. William Calhoun!" hollered the young boy looking about.

"Over here, young man," yelled Thomas.

"I have a telegram for Mr. William Calhoun from Savannah, Georgia."

"I'm William Calhoun," he replied curiously.

"Please sign here, sir," he instructed, handing the letter to him.

He took a minute to read the contents as a grim expression fell upon his face.

"What is it, William?" Thomas questioned, concerned.

"It's from Mother's doctor... He claims she has suffered apoplexia—a stroke."

"I'm sorry to hear that, William. I know you love your mother. What will you do now?"

"I don't know… I guess I have no other choice but to return to Georgia."

"Please, don't mind my prying. But is it serious? Will she pull through?"

"I don't know how serious it is. He doesn't say. But I suppose all strokes are serious. Aren't they?"

"Yes. I believe they are. But… forgive me if I seem a bit insensitive. You don't suppose this is another one of your mother's schemes to keep you from travelling to London. Do you William?"

"I'm not certain. But I have to give her the benefit of the doubt. I don't think I could forgive myself if she were to die without seeing her one last time. All I would ever remember were the last horrid words I said to her."

"I know my mother has committed many wrong doings in her long life. But she's still my mother the only one I've ever known. She really believes what she does is for the best. I still can't believe they've all been intentionally directed to cause pain without even a remorseful thought. Perhaps I'm a fool… But nevertheless, I've left the plantation in Henry's hands and I could imagine he needs me."

"But if I don't go to London with the Captain, I may lose Bethie's friendship forever. I couldn't bear it after finally making contact with her after all these years. But I suppose that's the chance I'll have to take. I feel, either way—I lose. All I can say is that this better not be another of mother's twisted ploys to keep us apart… She better well be ill!"

Miss Abigail, Georgia Lee, and Bethie stood waiting at the harbor searching for a mere glimpse of the St. Anne. Bethie never looked more lovelier and grown up. She wore her most complimented dress and her face glowed with excitement.

"How is my hair, Miss Abby? I wasn't sure if I should wear it this way. But it was always William's favorite. Does it make me look too young? What do you think, Georgia Lee?"

The two could not help but giggle aloud at Bethie's nervousness caused by the reunion of her long, lost friend and companion. Never had she been so excited to see a man. It was obvious no matter how hard she tried to hide it. Though she tried to convince the two it was only because she missed her cousin's friendship, both knew her feelings went deeper.

"You are and look simply beautiful, Bethie. Please don't worry yourself so. Forgive us for laughing, but we've never seen you in such a tizzy before," commented Miss Abigail lovingly.

"Look! It's the St. Anne!" blurted Georgia Lee pointing.

They moved closer as they watched with much anticipation as the crew and passengers left her. Bethie's eyes roamed the massive vessel with hopes of seeing him first, trying hard not to appear too excited. But when almost all had departed, she began to worry. Finally, they could see the image of Captain McNeil as Miss Abigail waved eagerly to him.

As he began to approach where they stood, an overwhelming sinking feeling began to flood Bethie's body. All the excitement from the anticipation of seeing William, and the bright color from her cheeks, had all but left her lovely face. She tried to hide it, but it was impossible.

"Welcome, Captain! It's so wonderful to see you again! The news of Joseph's release was God sent. How can we ever repay you?" begged Miss Abigail sincerely.

"Perhaps one of your home cooked meals will call us even," he chuckled aloud. "Hello Miss Abigail, ladies," he added, removing his cap.

"Bethie... I'm sorry to be the one to tell you that your cousin could not make the trip. Your aunt took ill. He felt he had no other choice but to return to Savannah. William wanted me to tell you how very disappointed he was not to be able to visit. I can tell you, honestly, it was a difficult decision for him. He sends his love to the both of you with hopes you will allow him to visit at a later time."

Her disappointment was quite evident. But she did not want to appear selfish after all the Captain had done for her. She forced a warm smile and a gentle hug for her friend.

"Although it is unfortunate he was unable to make the trip, I'm very grateful to both of you for helping Joseph. As well as, Mr. Holt. We will be forever in your debt. Please thank him for me when you return to Savannah. Let him know, for his sake, I hope his mother recovers soon. I know how much she means to him."

"But I would prefer if he would not make the trip to London on my behalf. My studies are almost completed here. And I look forward to returning to Pennsylvania, immediately. Thank you, Captain."

His heart went out to her. But he could not think of anything he could possibly add that would make her feel better. Her heart, yet again, was broken. Perhaps this time unable to be mended, she imagined sadly.

"Please join us, Captain, for supper," insisted Miss Abigail trying to brighten the moment. They could all sense Bethie's sadness and thought it best to move on.

"I would love to, ma'am," he quickly agreed, delighted.

Bethie asked if she could return later, feeling as though she needed some time to herself and wanting to take a short walk. Miss Abigail understood and did not protest as she gave her shoulders a little squeeze, "Are you ok, Bethie?"

"Yes, Miss Abby. I'll be fine, really! Go ahead. I'll be along soon. I believe the fresh air would do me good right now."

"All right, dearest. See you shortly," ended Miss Abigail, concerned about leaving her by herself.

"Would you like me to walk with you, Bethie?" offered Georgia Lee, wanting to comfort her best friend.

"No, Georgia Lee. I'd rather like to be by myself. You understand, don't you?"

"Yes, I understand. Bethie… I'm sorry he was unable to come this time."

"It's really all right, Georgia Lee. What is important is that Joseph is free and I really do thank God for that. Don't worry about me, I'm fine! It isn't unusual to want to have some time alone. Please don't be offended. Now run along before the carriage leaves without you," teased Bethie, as she waved goodbye to them all.

She was relieved when she could no longer see their carriage. The tears had been building up inside and she had no idea how much longer she could hold them back. Bethie walked vigorously through the crowded streets, trying to find a place in which she could find some privacy.

To her, it felt all eyes were upon her as they laughed and pointed for being so foolish. To think he could really care in the same manner as she. Bethie walked onto a bridge overlooking the mouth of the Thames. With her back to the world, she leaned up against the iron bars as she finally allowed the tears to fall freely.

It always made her feel better when she could cry, and today would be no exception. A sharp, fall breeze came up from the water causing her to be chilled as she pulled her cape tighter. From the inside of her coat, she tugged out a book in which she had kept since childhood that had become very dear to her.

The book had been one of her father's handed down to her. She was told it was his favorite and that he would have wanted her to have it. Bethie must have read the old novel a dozen times, feeling a little closer to him each time. And she soon understood why the book had become her father's favorite, for it had become hers too. Each time she read its pages, became a new experience.

She thumbed through the book until she came to the pages that kept and held the shrunken, dried rose that had been given to her so long ago. It was all she had left of the childhood friendship that had engulfed and captured her heart, unable to be forgotten. Not a day went by that she did not recall, except for Emma Mae, what would become some of the most wonderful memories of her lifetime.

The flower was held in her hand for a moment so she could remember one last time how it had been obtained. The enchanted loveliness of the squares of Savannah, gardens, and wrap-around porches immediately came into mind. With her eyes closed she could still smell the sweet and tantalizing aroma of peaches grown in the large, open orchards on the plantation.

Bethie recalled how she and William would eat them right from their branches allowing the juices to run down their cheeks, as they laughed and chased one another through the cotton fields. She could still see the elegant horses that roamed the pastures for all to admire as their grace and beauty held you in awe.

She laughed aloud to herself as she remembered Henry and his humorous antics and carefree personality. The long winters when they would spend hours studying with Miss Abigail who tried desperately to keep the class's attention. But it never seemed to bore the two. They were happy where ever they were as long as they were together.

She recalled how the subject of Geography had always been their favorite. They would dream of the day when the two would be old enough to travel abroad together and become pirates of the sea. How young and silly they were, agreed Bethie blushing.

But from all the memories of Savannah she could ever recall, none would ever be so prominent as the memory of their own special place, "Friendship Island." She wondered if he still went to her. But now that they were adults, why would he? She assumed that his maturity had probably led him to forget such trivial, childhood play.

But she also agreed, it would not matter how old she would become, she could never forget the island and what it had meant to her. It represented a safe haven in which a child could find freedom. And the ability to dream and create any and all adventures that the mind could conjure. She truly missed Savannah, the island, and her long ago best friend, William.

When finally convinced of what had to be done and when she felt ready, she closed her fist tightly around the dried flower then extended her hand over the water. Bethie watched with tears in her eyes, as she opened her hand to find the flower had been reduced to mere dust, as the river breeze picked up the pieces and carried them off across the water.

The moment became the start of a new chapter and beginning, in which, she felt was desperately needed. She was determined to never again dwell or recall long ago promises that were made by two children who knew no better. It was time to move on and she would soon come of age when her studies would be completed and would be free to return home, to Covington, where she belonged.

Even with London's elegance, bustling streets, and the absence of Emma Mae, she could never be thought of as home. Or Savannah, as fond of her as Bethie had become, would never be home, as well. She longed to see the river, which carried the ferries, boats, and barges sometimes pulled by mules along the canal strip. And the strong and handsome face of her friend Joseph, who had almost given his life for her. Truly, the only father figure she had ever known.

The sophisticated beauty of the stone estate with its rolling hills, creeks filled with tiny falls, and the sometimes mighty river that sat next to her. New Hope, Pennsylvania was her home; no other state or town could ever take its place.

This day had changed her. The sadness from disappointment had caused her to grow up some. She came to realize that it was more painful to live in the past than to start fresh, unaware of what lie ahead. Some of the teenage, carefree spirit had been washed away and no longer would she be so trusting, naïve—or so hopelessly love-struck by impossibilities.

It was true she was young, intelligent, beautiful, about to receive her inheritance, and should be looking forward to an exciting future. Now all that remained was the difficult task of convincing herself of all of that.

After a few minutes of staring into the waters that lay beneath her, finally able to clear her mind of all thoughts, she decided she felt better and was ready to return home. Bethie turned swiftly to leave the bridge. To her sudden shock and surprise, she had stepped too far into the street causing a quadricycle that was nearly upon her to swerve and hit the other side. The driver lost control as he and the odd looking bicycle landed on their side.

"Oh dear Lord!" shrieked Bethie, horrified that she had indeed been responsible for the accident. She rushed over to the site to find the man slowly beginning to sit up. "Are you all right, sir?" she questioned, upset.

"Yes, I believe so... I don't feel as though there are any broken bones," replied the man after checking himself thoroughly.

"Thank God! Please forgive my absentmindedness," pleaded Bethie distraught. "When I stepped out into the street, I didn't even see or hear you. I'm sorry. This hasn't been a very good day for me. I guess I was in deep thought at the time and—" rambled Bethie, apologetic and embarrassed.

"Please, it's all right! I really am fine. Look..." said the man standing, "not a bruise, cut, tear, or even a scratch. Maybe a little dirty, but that can always be fixed," he smiled, causing Bethie to relax some.

"How is your riding machine? Is it broken?" she questioned, trying to look over the complicated device. He lifted the bicycle from the ground then kneeled beside a pedal, as he began to manually turn it with his hand.

"No, on the contrary, all seems quite well... would you like to see for yourself? I'd be happy to give you a test ride?" offered the gentleman teasingly.

"Oh my! That won't be necessary. I'll take your word for it," answered Bethie embarrassed and frightened by the contraption. Although bicycles were very popular in London, she had never been on one and felt intimidated by them.

"I don't believe we've been formally introduced. My name is James... James C. Burton. Originally from New York City. And I can tell by your accent that you also are not from around these parts either, are you miss?"

"You're from New York? How wonderful!" she replied, delighted to have met someone from the United States and especially the north.

"My name is Sara Beth Covington," she continued shyly, glancing up into his eyes and becoming a bit enthralled by how handsome he was. "But my friends call me Bethie." He was tall, well-built, and extremely handsome and charming. His dark brown hair and eyes only added to his overall good looks.

"I'm from New Hope, Pennsylvania. A small town not too far from Philadelphia," added Bethie, allowing him to shake her hand. But instead, he turned it gently and softly kissed the top then replied, "Very happy to make your acquaintance, Miss Sara. If you don't mind, I prefer to call you Sara. It suits you much better."

She became hypnotized by his quick, romantic moves, unable to speak, and becoming even more embarrassed as their eyes locked.

Other than William, it had been a long time since Bethie found a young man attractive. As Georgia Lee had once commented, she was admired and sought after by many of the men that knew of her in London. Although she became friends with some of them, she never took any seriously or had any romantic feelings. Even her simple walks to and from school would cause men to turn their heads, and shamefully, even the married ones. But it wasn't their fault, she had grown into an alluring, beautiful lady.

"Actually, I happen to know where New Hope is. In fact, I've even been there," remarked James smiling, as he continued gazing down at her romantically. "When I was a little boy, my father traded goods. Our ship would travel from New York to Philadelphia. Then from Philadelphia, we would travel the ferry tracks toward New Hope. We would continue west to some of the mills alongside the river."

"What a wonderful coincidence it has been to meet you," Bethie responded, breaking away from his stare.

"Please excuse my excitement. But it's simply delightful to meet someone from the states. Especially from the north! I believe you are the first that I have met in the last four years from those parts. I must be honest and tell you, Mr. Burton, it has been such a dreadful day. But after meeting you, though I wish under better circumstances, has been truly enlightening." She was blushing, unable to continue looking up into his handsome, brown eyes.

"Well, I don't know when I've ever received such a generous compliment, and please… you must call me James."

"Oh my… I feel foolish. I really don't normally go on like that. It's just that before I nearly ran into you, I was longing for home. London is so far away. Sometimes I get homesick."

"Please, don't be embarrassed. I think it's lovely to have made your acquaintance, too. And I must confess, I would do it all the same for only to have met you. I'm not trying to cause your cheeks to become any redder than they already are. But I must also admit, by far… you are the loveliest lady I've met in London. Or the states," confessed James flirtingly, but appearing quite serious.

Feeling flushed, Bethie felt entirely overcome by his charm and decided it was time she said her goodbyes.

"Well… again, I'm pleased you and your machine are fine. And it has been very good to have met you. But it's getting late and I really must be getting along. Good day, Mr. Burton—I mean… James," ended Bethie smiling, as she awkwardly began to walk away.

He was not about to let her leave that easily and quickly began to follow her, pushing along the bicycle by hand. "Wait! May I call on you, Miss Sara?" he begged, worried she might decline his request.

Bethie hesitated then turned around and replied, "Well, I suppose that would be fine."

"Can I give you a ride home? Please don't be afraid. I really am a good driver. As long as lovely, young ladies don't walk in front of me," he laughed, causing Bethie to giggle too.

"Thank you, James. But I don't believe it would be appropriate for a lady to accept a ride from a complete stranger. After all, we just met. What would people think? Perhaps we shall see each other again. Good day, Mr. Burton," she ended, smiling but stern as she again turned to leave.

Bethie walked swiftly from the bridge making her way through the crowds wondering if he would follow her again. But she dare not look behind her, for fear that he would indeed know she found him attractive. Curiosity had gotten the best of her for he had left a lasting impression on such a dreadful, disappointing day.

She admitted that he was quite handsome and that she would not mind seeing him again. Bethie suddenly wondered how they would ever meet again. London was so large and they never discussed where she lived.

Without hesitation, she turned around with hopes that he had continued to follow her. But to her disappointment, he was nowhere to be found. She looked up and down the streets but could not see him or his contraption anywhere. Perhaps he was only displaying curtesy, wondered Bethie, thinking that he may not have found her all that lovely. She shrugged her shoulders as though it did not really matter and began to signal for a carriage.

"Can I give you a lift, ma'am?" offered James, cutting between her and the carriage that had stopped directly in front. "That won't be necessary, driver. She'll be riding with me." The driver of the carriage nodded then continued on.

"I wish you would not have done that," replied Bethie, trying to act as though she were annoyed.

"Well, I was just being the concerned friend. Rather hoped you would allow me to accompany you home—over a complete stranger on a carriage! After all, this is not the first time we've met, Miss Sara Beth Covington," he added cleverly.

"Please forgive me if I've assumed incorrectly. But you don't seem to be the type of woman that worries too much of what others may think of her. You strike me as more of the adventurous, strong willed, confident with herself, but always very much a lady, type. Please, feel free to correct me if I've judged you wrongly, Miss Sara."

"Well that may all be quite so," replied Bethie, flustered by his persistence and charm, "But it is not the—"

"No! It can't be," he interrupted. "You're not afraid to ride on my quadricycle, are you? Forgive me for not realizing. You've never been on one, have you?" questioned James, pretending not to have known.

Bethie did not appreciate his pity, as though she were actually afraid to ride the silly machine. She became insulted and refused to allow him to think that she was nothing more than a frightened, little, school girl.

"It may be true that I have never ridden on such a thing… But your machine Mr. Burton, I assure you, neither frightens nor intimidates me in the least. I simply don't find it to be proper to ride upon a contraption, such as this, with a man I barely know."

"Furthermore, I don't believe making your way around the block and back, only to find me again, makes our knowing each other anymore stronger or humorous," she ended sternly.

"However… I don't intend for you to consider even the remote possibility that I would be afraid of such a silly device. Therefore, I've decided to accept your offer and allow you to take me home. Holding you entirely responsible for my wellbeing. Now, all I need is for you to explain how to get on it," requested Bethie, trying to figure out where she would sit.

James was shocked, but overly delighted, he had finally won her over and was quite proud of himself. "Allow me, ma'am," he offered, helping her onto a small seat between the two larger wheels located at the front of the bike.

He showed Bethie where to place her feet and explained how to hold on so she would be safe. She was very nervous but refused to show it, as he slowly started to pedal forward. After a few bumps and turns her confidence became stronger and she again opened her eyes. He was a good driver and could control the bike with much ease. James was relieved to find Bethie starting to relax for he knew she had been very nervous about the whole ordeal.

Both began to talk more freely about themselves as the speed of the bike became faster causing Bethie to enjoy the ride even more. The cool, brisk air felt good against her face as the quick movements of their pace caused her tummy to be tickled. What a wonderful machine, agreed Bethie, pleased she had taken him up on his offer. It had been a long time since she had enjoyed such an exciting adventure. Perhaps since her childhood days with William, she thought, feeling much more confident.

They turned onto the street in which her townhome was located. She was disappointed that the ride had to end so quickly as James brought the bicycle to a slow halt. He helped Bethie off the seat as they laughed unaware of the nosey neighbors watching from their windows and porches. Realizing they had brought attention to themselves only increased their uncontrollable laughter. Bethie's hair around her face had become loose and wild from the ride and her cheeks rosy from the chilly air.

When they finally calmed down from all the laughter, James parked the bicycle up against the fence and the two sat on the steps of the porch. "I can't remember the last time I've had such a wonderful time, James," she whispered smiling, as she tried to keep their conversation private.

He had met many ladies in his life but none as lovely as Bethie. Her beauty was captivating, he agreed, as he tried desperately not to stare at her. But again, she caught him staring making her blush and him embarrassed.

"Forgive me for staring. I'm not trying to make you feel uncomfortable with me, but… you are so lovely. It's difficult to not want to."

"Thank you… But you must stop all of these compliments or I really shall become embarrassed every time we are together. My poor face, I'm afraid, will become permanently red," she replied grinning.

"Well, I certainly do not want that to be the case. And, I am very pleased to hear that you are considering seeing me again. Perhaps? I want more than anything for us to become the best of friends and spend much time together. I'll do my best to make you, always feel, very comfortable when you are with me."

"And with that, I believe it's time for me to go. I don't want to over stay my welcome. Goodbye, Miss Sara. May I call on you again?" asked James hoping he had impressed her.

"Yes, I believe I would enjoy that." The two became interrupted by Miss Abigail coming out of the front door.

"Bethie, I'm glad to see you are home. We were becoming worried. The Captain was about to call on the constable," she added, cautiously looking over James. Seeing Bethie with a strange, young man had given a jolt to her being.

Other than William, she hadn't yet shown much interest in them. Even with the young men she had met, who tried desperately to win her affections, none of the encounters amounted to anything romantically. Bethie had grown to be a young lady with high standards and principles. Unlike Georgia Lee, her studies took much precedence over boys.

"I really do wish you wouldn't worry about me so much... I'd like you to meet a young man I met today. I'd like to introduce Mr. James C. Burton. Originally from New York City! James, this is Miss Abby, my legal guardian."

"Hello, ma'am. It is my pleasure to make your acquaintance," responded James, offering his hand to Miss Abigail. "I must take full responsibility for Miss Sara being late. It has been a long time since I've met anyone from the states. I suppose I nearly talked her poor ears off... Please accept my humble apology."

Miss Abigail could tell he had made quite an impression on Bethie, which made her very interested in getting to know this stranger even further.

"Very nice to meet you, too," replied Miss Abigail, unsure of what to make of him.

"James gave me a ride home today on his... What is the name of your machine again?"

"It's called a quadricycle."

"Yes, a quad-ricycle. It was absolutely wonderful, Miss Abby! You really must try it," she insisted, delighted.

"Oh my Heavens! Bethie you rode upon that?" questioned Miss Abigail, mortified. "It looks absolutely dangerous. I don't believe a young lady, such as yourself, should take such risks. No offense, Mr. Burton. But accepting a ride from a complete stranger? Bethie, how could you?"

"Oh, Miss Abby! James was quite responsible and very much a gentleman. Please don't be angry… It was the most fun I've had in ages!"

"Well, I thank God you're home safe and I don't suppose any harm has been done. Supper is nearly on the table. It's time to go in, Bethie. Please, come and join us, Mr. Burton. It has been a long time since we've met someone in London from the states. And from the north, no less… What a remarkable coincidence," added Miss Abigail suspiciously.

"Well, I really should be going," replied James, feeling as though he had not made a good first impression on Miss Abigail.

"Please," she interrupted, "I won't take no for an answer."

"Well then… I would be delighted to join you all for supper. Thank you, ma'am."

Miss Abigail's persistence made Bethie feel awkward and embarrassed. She knew Miss Abby wasn't pleased she had accepted a ride with a complete stranger. And of course, on his bicycle made matters only worse. But she did find James very handsome and he made her laugh. Something she needed more than anything right now, agreed Bethie, as she showed him the way in.

She thought Georgia Lee's eyes were about to pop out as she stood before him, wide-eyed, red in the face, and grinning with delight. Miss Abigail introduced him to the Captain who immediately joined her with a list of suspicious questions.

"He's absolutely gorgeous, Bethie!" whispered Georgia Lee unable to keep her voice low enough.

"Georgia Lee, please!" she whispered, shrugging her shoulders, as a grinning James watched from the corner of his eyes.

They all sat down to supper but the questions continued coming from both sides of the table. As soon as he would finish answering the Captain's, there would be an immediate one followed by Miss Abigail. Bethie prayed they would run out of questions soon, totally humiliated by their interrogation.

But James was wonderful. He answered each and every one with calm, intelligence, and gentlemanly manners. He neither protested, nor became intimidated by the two of them. This impressed Bethie even more as she listened to his clever responses, always smiling, and every now and then giving her a quick, romantic glance.

"I'm in London on an academic scholarship. I study at Cambridge and reside at a gentlemen's boarding house.

"How impressive," responded Miss Abigail soberly, "Cambridge is one of the finest colleges in the world."

"Yes, I've been very fortunate. I thank God every day."

"A doctor! How marvelous! Don't you think so, Bethie?" gasped Georgia Lee in awe over the handsome James.

"As wonderful as it may seem, Miss Georgia Lee, it has been a very long and hard road. I normally have very little time to myself. If I'm not buried in my studies, I'm working at a local hospital. It was actually a fluke to meet Miss Sara today. But a very pleasant one," added James smiling, glancing over to her.

"This has been one of the few and rare times that I have had free."

"Yes, like I had mentioned earlier- a real coincidence, Mr. Burton or is it Dr. Burton?" questioned Miss Abigail interrupting.

"Please, call me James. Mister or doctor seems so formal when you are among friends- or in this case, new friends I hope."

After the meal, James cordially excused himself from the table. He thanked Miss Abigail for the lovely supper then said his goodbyes to everyone. He had an exam to study for that evening and could no longer delay. Bethie offered to walk him outside, closing the door behind her, as the three continued to watch them from the foyer.

"I'm truly sorry, James… Please forgive Miss Abby and the Captain's constant questioning. They really are good people," she begged, embarrassed by them. "I really don't know what has gotten into the two. Their behavior was quite odd. And Georgia Lee, I'm afraid, is normally that way."

"Please don't fret, Miss Sara, I thought they were all quite charming. There is no doubt, you are loved very much. Miss Abigail was only being concerned. Who could really blame her? I only wish I could have made a better impression on her. But between a complete stranger accompanying you home and my quadricycle, I believe were more than she could handle in one day." His smile was gentle causing Bethie to relax a bit.

"Yes, I suppose you are right. But I did have a wonderful time today. Thank you, James."

Unexpectedly, he took her hand into his own and became quite serious as he gazed deeply into her eyes. "May I see you again, Miss Sara?"

"Yes, I would like that very much. Thank you," responded Bethie blushing.

"There is a musical and literary program at the college pavilion tomorrow evening. Can you join me?"

"But what about your studies?" she questioned, concerned.

"After tomorrow's examine, I'll need something to look forward to. And I can't imagine anything I'd rather look forward to more, than seeing you again." She again became spellbound by his romantic words and gestures.

"Well, I suppose that would be fine, James."

After a brief pause, he gently released her hand and left Bethie standing on the porch watching as he collected his bicycle.

"Please, bring along Miss Georgia Lee. I'll introduce her to some of my friends. They're really good old chaps, good manners and all. Well, at least most of the time," he chuckled. "I'll make sure they stay in order. This time we will travel by carriage, hopefully that will please Miss Abigail. Until tomorrow night... good evening, Miss Sara Beth Covington."

Bethie went inside to find all three still standing in the foyer where she had left them.

"I do hope none of your ears became too strained," she remarked sarcastically.

"Well… I believe it's time for me to return to my ship." The Captain commented, helping to break the tension.

She gave him a hug and thanked him again for all of his help. "Bethie, I know it is none of my business, but I've grown very fond of you over the years. You know I care for you, like a daughter. I only want to say, be careful… be leery of those you meet by chance. I can tell you rather like Mr. Burton and there's nothing wrong with that. But be a little cautious. Don't rush into anything you may regret later."

"I appreciate your concern, Captain. But we are simply just friends. We've only just met. But you all have me walking down the aisle with him!" she giggled aloud.

"Please… everyone, stop worrying. I'm almost eighteen. Have some faith in me," she ended exhausted.

After the Captain had left, Bethie knew it would be Miss Abigail's turn to give advice.

"So tell me, Bethie… what did you think of James?" she pried, pretending not to know.

"I thought he was charming," answered Bethie nonchalantly.

"Yes, perhaps a bit too charming," added Miss Abigail seriously concerned.

"Oh, Bethie," started Georgia Lee, grinning and swooning, "he is so handsome. Are you in love?"

"Georgia Lee! For someone who claims to be so knowledgeable about men, you can be such a child at times!"

Return to Savannah

"It's been six months, Mother, your doctor says you've completely recovered. You should at least be attempting to try and walk with a cane. It's important that you begin to work your legs. Why don't I help you out of that chair and we'll work together with the cane," insisted William frustrated.

"Nonsense, Son! I don't care what my doctor says. I know these legs and they're not ready. What does he know? I barely have the strength to sit up in this godforsaken chair, let alone try and walk!" snapped Emma Mae.

William shook his head out of frustration then walked over to the window as he tried to relieve some tension.

"The plantation and shipping business are both running quite smoothly. There is no reason on earth why I cannot travel to London. Miss Jane is here to take care of you. And you have an entire staff of lawyers to help with the business when I'm away."

"But you can't go, Son... What if something should happen to me?" pleaded Emma, playing on his sympathy.

"It's not going to work this time, Mother. I'm leaving and that's all there is to it!" he replied, angry. "Now I'm sorry for getting cross with you, but you make me crazy sometimes. I've been by your side now for six solid months while you've been recovering. You're the strongest, most independent woman I have ever known. Your success proves it! No way am I going to believe that you need me to stay and hold your hand any longer."

"What about your law studies?" questioned a desperate Emma Mae.

"My studies will be here when I return," he responded sternly, unwilling to give in to her demands.

"Then what about Elizabeth?"

"What about her, Mother?" he replied sarcastically.

"You can't just leave her behind! A girl like that doesn't wait around forever. What about your engagement?"

William could feel his blood pressure rise from his mother's last comment as he slowly exploded.

"You're unbelievable, Mother!" he began, overwhelmed by her imaginative mind.

"What engagement? I have never proposed to her. Or have I ever even considered it! How can you question something so untrue—so personal? As though it is fact! Just because you say it is truth, doesn't make it so. I refuse to discuss my relationships with you. I ask that you please respect my feelings and stay out of my personal life!"

"I'm sorry, William," she replied, backing down, "I only assumed the two of you were becoming very close."

"I think Elizabeth is a fine lady—albeit, a bit pushy at times. That is all, Mother. Please do not make anything more of it. It's true I enjoy her company from time to time. But it doesn't mean I want to marry her, any time soon! The only ones bringing up marriage is the two of you. Shouldn't I have a say? I wouldn't be surprised if you both haven't plotted about it behind my back when I'm not around."

"I only want what's best for you, Son—and so does Elizabeth."

"And I am grateful that you care… But don't you think I'm old enough to figure out what is best for me?"

"I have an idea… Why don't you bring her along with you to London? I'm sure Abigail and Sara Beth wouldn't mind. It's just the two of them. They probably have several guest rooms available," rambled Emma Mae excitedly.

With eyes rolled upward and hands thrown above his head, he plopped down into the sofa positioned next to his mother's chair.

"You're never going to give up, Mother, are you? You're determined to run my life—even as an adult! I'm not on your payroll and I don't care about Elizabeth's money or prestigious, family name.

And your money makes no difference to me either. Don't you understand, I came back to take care of you because I love you. But you may as well accept that you will never control me. With or without your blessing—or money, I will go to London to see Bethie."

"Why can't you finally be honest with me?"

"I don't know what you are implying, William?" lied Emma Mae.

"This isn't about you needing me or marrying Elizabeth. It's all about Bethie. It always has been, hasn't it? After all these years, you still continue to try to keep us apart?"

"Why do you hate her so?" he questioned, demanding to know the truth.

"That is utterly ridiculous, Son! I love her. She's my brother's only child. Why would I not love her?"

"I don't know, Mother. Why don't you tell me."

"There is nothing to tell… Sending her away… I believed at the time was for the best."

"What gave you the right to manipulate and permanently scar our lives," he accused angrily, now standing, unable to remain seated.

"What gave me the right? What gave me the right!" yelled Emma Mae losing her temper with him. "I'll tell you, young man, what gave me the right. The fact that I am your mother is what gave me the right! I felt the two of you were becoming much too close. You were too young to be so attached to anyone but me. It made me feel uncomfortable and was totally inappropriate—and quite disgusting, I might add!"

Feeling depleted, William took a moment to relax. He did not want his mother to become any more upset than she already was. Never had he realized how jealous she could get. They were two innocent children who found within themselves, common interests, trust, and the ability to make one another laugh and love life to its fullest.

But all his mother could do was turn their friendship into something perverted, he thought disgusted. She made him sick to his stomach, as he thought how very pathetic and wrong she was. He imagined perhaps because he was her only child and heir could this be the reasoning behind her twisted, jealous, interpretation of the two? But despite her bizarre opinions she still was his mother, the only one he knew, and would continue to love and stand by her as long as he could.

"I apologize for getting you so upset. I didn't want that to happen… but you are going to have to allow me to live my own life, Mother. Your opinion of us as children is simply untrue and doesn't change anything."

"I know you care about me, and I truly appreciate having a mother that loves me. But the truth is I am an adult capable of making my own decisions. And if at times they are wrong, then at least, I will learn from them. Isn't that what life is all about, learning from your mistakes? Making one stronger and perhaps a better person?"

Emma Mae, realizing that she would not win this battle, began to cave. "I'm sorry, Son, if it seems that I put my nose in places where it should not be. But if it is true, it's simply because I love you. You're my only child and my entire life… Please forgive me," she added, hoping to win her son's pity, while desperately trying to think of another diversion.

"I may, at one time, have been a strong woman able to take on anything. But since my illness, I feel quite vulnerable and need you by my side now more than ever. At least for the time being… Won't you please try to understand?"

After a few moments of silence between the two, Emma Mae thought of a brilliant idea, one of course, to her advantage. But she wondered if she could convince her son of it.

"William… Sara Beth's studies are almost complete and soon she'll be of legal age for her inheritance. I assume she and Abigail intend to return to New Hope. Perhaps together, we can convince her to visit Savannah before going home to Pennsylvania," suggested Emma Mae slyly.

"Mother, why on earth would Bethie want to return to Savannah," questioned William flabbergasted. "Especially after the way you've treated her."

"She is my niece and I would like to make amends with her before I die. I'm old, Son, and I don't believe there are many years left in me. Before I die, there is nothing more I'd rather do than to gain her forgiveness." Lying had become an art with her, as she appeared so convincingly.

"Even if she did decide to visit, there is no guarantee she would ever forgive what you have done to her."

"I'm aware of that. But I would like to die knowing that I at least tried to make things right between us."

Other than a last desperate attempt to keep him from London, William did not know what to make of his mother's suggestion.

"I'll give a masquerade ball in honor of her eighteenth birthday!" offered Emma Mae, delighted with herself. "I will write her myself and plead for her merciful forgiveness. She'll have much to celebrate after successfully completing her studies and finally coming into Covington. Being able to return home, should be a strong enough reason for her to want to celebrate."

"And whose fault is that, Mother?" accused William.

He shrugged his shoulders in disbelief, "I still can't imagine how you'll ever get her here. With everything that's happened, she'll probably never step foot in Georgia as long as she lives. And who could really blame her? I think the suggestion is quite admirable, but she doesn't even want to see me. I've already received word that she would rather me not come for a visit."

"You see, Son! She doesn't even want to be bothered by you. Why can't you just let her be? There are too many years between you both. She is not the same little girl you once knew. Why set yourself up for a terrible disappointment. She has her own life now, and so do you. Both separate and very apart from one another," preached Emma Mae.

"Even so, it makes no difference to me, Mother. Please give it up!

I will still go to London, despite the fact that she does not want to see me. If necessary, I will plead on her doorsteps for her forgiveness. Even if she continues to refuse to see me, I would at least know that I truly tried," he ended, exhausted by his mother's relentless behavior.

Again, he sat silently next to his mother in thought. "I'll give you two months!" he somberly agreed. "If you can convince Bethie to return to Savannah for a visit, within that time, I will stay. But I promise you this. If she refuses, I will go to Europe immediately without ever discussing another word with you. Do you understand, Mother?"

"Yes, Son. I understand perfectly," answered Emma Mae, again thrilled with herself.

It had been a longtime since William was on the island, as he sat on the hill remembering his childhood days. As an adult, how small it all looked from his point of view now. Once, it seemed to both of them far too large to cover in a day's expedition. But now, from where he sat, it did not take much for the eye to see all in which she held in one simple glance.

His muscular, broad shoulders and long legs, now, took up most of the area where the two would lay for hours together staring up toward the heavens. They would dream and make promises to one another of their future as pirates of the sea. One for one, trustworthy and loyal to each other first, and always and forever together.

He recalled how they had looked as children and wondered if she would recognize him today. His once, short blonde hair was now long and pulled back. And the once, freckled covered face was replaced each morning with stubble.

And Bethie, with her long, dark brown ringlets bouncing off her delicate shoulders. Her little button nose with those large, beautiful, brown, doe-eyes that would easily captivate then melt any heart.

Would he know her from a simple glance in a group of many? He thought for only a moment, and confidently agreed, that he would indeed know his Bethie if she were even among hundreds in a crowd. As would his to her, Bethie's eyes would always give her away.

The image of them had been permanently sketched in his mind from the day he hid behind the large tree on the island. Simply to catch a glimpse of the curious intruder that had wandered upon her. That is how he knew so much about his friend. Her eyes revealed all that was within her. Revealing to him when she was happy, sad, and even frightened.

He carefully held the music box that had been gently wrapped and placed in the box, so long ago. He began to wind the knob as he watched the dancers perform before him. Perhaps Bethie would resemble the beautiful lady dancer, wondered William, as he tried to imagine how she would appear as an adult.

The gift still made him smile knowing how much joy the original had given to a little girl. Whose nose became pressed up against the glass of a small shop, one hot day in the city. Though now it wasn't worth much, but at one time, every penny that he had saved. He had promised himself, one day he would finally present the gift to her.

Feeling hopeless and ashamed, he wondered if perhaps his mother was right. He was confused, frustrated, and incapable of loving another. And what was he in love with? He tried to imagine with much despair. Was it the memory of a long ago friendship that would hold dear in his heart forever?

For years he had buried himself in his studies, ignoring the flirtations of many lovely ladies. And when he was finally questioned by his peers, he had taken a few always honest and up front explaining that his heart belonged to another. Never would he reveal her name to anyone, including himself. This time on the island would be the first in which he would face the truth, unable to go on lying to himself wishing desperately to be whole.

Was he destined to love no other and live a life of complete and utter loneliness? It was so long ago, and they were only two young children who played and told secrets to one another. So why did she continue to fill his thoughts and dreams?

He had hoped, perhaps, the older he would become the less he would be reminded of Bethie and their adventures on the plantation. Nevertheless this was not so, in fact, the complete opposite. Over the years, the memories of her became stronger every day despite his relentless attempts to ignore them.

Seeing her again, had never become as necessary as it was right now. It would be the healing instrument to his freedom—and long term sanity. He was a man with needs and responsibilities, infatuated with his past, fighting against his own heart and refusing to spend any more precious time dreaming about a girl that he knew long ago.

A little girl that had captured his heart and stolen his sole. He decided she must have bewitched him and wanted what was his back, to put away or diminish the memories of their past would not be so unkind. The years of separation and not knowing what had happened to her, had been enough and more than anyone deserved.

With his body filled with emotions about to erupt, he clenched his fist above his head and yelled in anger, "Why do you plague my mind? Let me be!" From the top of the hill, his screams of despair echoed beyond the island and through the cotton fields. To him, it was certain, seeing her again would be his only chance to truly be set free.

London, England, 1883

"Can you believe the nerve of that wretched woman?" scorned Abigail angrily as she paced about. "To even imagine Bethie considering such an insane request. She actually believes she can just wipe away the years of abuse and betrayal by simply writing a few words of apology. The woman is mad I tell you!" she yelled out of control.

"Please, Miss Abigail! Calm down… The entire city of London can hear you," begged Georgia Lee nervously.

"I'm sorry, Georgia Lee… I don't mean to take this out on you. But I'm just so angry I could spit!" added Miss Abigail, frustrated by it all. "I prayed we'd seen the last of that old woman. I honestly believed that part of our life was finally behind us."

"Perhaps," offered Georgia Lee, hesitating, "she truly is sorry for how she treated Bethie."

"Nonsense!" snapped Abigail, angrier than ever. "The woman hasn't a kind bone in her pathetic body. In all my years, I've never met such an empty, conniving—greedy person. This is just another one of her twisted ploys to try and manipulate Bethie. I'm sure of it. She knows quite well Bethie is about to turn eighteen and come into her inheritance. The woman can't stand it and I'll put nothing passed her. She'll do anything to take what is rightfully Bethie's."

"I have this terrible feeling at the pit of my stomach. I'm so afraid, Georgia Lee," remarked Abigail, retreating into the Victorian chair. Fear and desperation filled her face as she hopelessly stared off into space wondering what to do.

Georgia Lee started to become worried, "What are you afraid of, Miss Abigail? She rejected Miss Emma's invitation, immediately. I've never seen her so angry and overwhelmed with dislike for anyone. I can tell you, she didn't believe one word of Miss Emma's apology. Even after James and I begged her to visit Savannah she continued to strongly object. You'd think I asked her to walk a pirate's plank or something. She nearly bit my head off!"

"I do declare… this Miss Emma Mae must be some horrid woman to make both of you so upset," remarked Georgia Lee worried, as she tried to imagine. "I've never seen either of you so upset before, and frankly, you both are scaring me to death. So I think it's only sensible that we put the letter behind us and go on with our lives. Bethie is a smart woman. You don't need to worry about her so. She has made it quite clear she has no intentions of visiting Savannah, now—or ever!"

The London fog had set in so thick that Bethie could barely see James directly in front of her. He held on tightly to her hand but it was still not enough to relax her. Even against Bethie's wishes,

James had insisted they walk to the park. The weather was damp, cold, with poor visibility. But he had convinced her that he needed to speak with her privately, away from Abigail and Georgia Lee's wondering ears.

Although the past six months had strengthened their friendship, he had become entirely too possessive at times making her feel uncomfortable. He was handsome and charming, this was true, but she was still unable to give her heart to anyone. Perhaps in time, she had told him during the last rejected proposal of marriage. He had promised space would be given, only to continue being more demanding and impatient.

Miss Abigail did not make matters any easier. Over the months of getting to know him, though he tried harder than deserved, she never did take to James. It was a feeling she had, Miss Abigail would say, making Bethie more confused than ever as to what she meant. Abigail found him to be arrogant and too smooth, never really trusting James from the day they had first met.

She even questioned why he would want her to return to Savannah. Since he had no family or friends there, she found this to be quite odd. But he and Georgia Lee begged Bethie to accept Emma Mae's invitation. Miss Abigail was sure he was aware of William, Georgia Lee had teased often about him to Bethie when James was around. Bethie, of course, denying any leftover feelings and becoming embarrassed. But Georgia Lee never meant any harm, she truly loved Bethie and it was only her nature to act incorrigible at times.

Miss Abigail could not understand why James would encourage Bethie to go and be near the only other man she had ever really given a serious thought to. But Bethie would accuse her of an over imaginative mind and that she worried too much. She would say as though it were rehearsed, "There is nothing between William and me, Miss Abby—and there never will be!"

"We probably wouldn't even recognize each other today if we passed in the street. It was a very long time ago and we were two children. Please stop making anything more of it. James is too mature and intelligent to concern himself with insignificant jealousies of my childhood past. He's just trying to be supportive. That's all!"

Then Miss Abigail would say James was demanding and pushed too quickly for her affections, not allowing her to have enough time to think clearly. Abigail warned her constantly to be cautious and to examine all requests made by him. Even his age, which was five years older than Bethie, bothered Miss Abigail who felt he was much more experienced than she and could easily take advantage.

She wondered if some of Miss Abby's accusations had been correct, as she abruptly stood from the park bench frustrated. "James, hadn't I explained myself thoroughly, not so long ago?" His relentless pursuit of marriage was beginning to annoy her. "I'm simply not ready, you have to give me more time than a few weeks. Perhaps when your studies are complete and you return to New York."

"You're stalling, Sara Beth. What is it? Another man, perhaps," he accused.

Bethie laughed out of amazement as she shook her head at him. "James, how can you even make that accusation? You know I see only you. We see each other almost daily. If there was another, don't you think you would have run into each other by now?" she questioned sarcastically, but smiling.

"You don't have to be near someone to love them, Sara!" remarked James soberly. She knew what he was implying but refused to acknowledge his comment.

"James, I've grown very fond of you over these past six months, but-" she hesitated.

"But what, Sara… You don't love me, do you?"

"I need more time… I feel as though I still don't know you very well. Won't you please try to understand?" Although he was disheartened, he realized there would be no convincing her today.

"Perhaps we should head back," she began, trying to break the tension between them. "I don't want to worry Miss Abigail needlessly. I do wish they would catch that killer soon. The thought of him free and about just sends chills down my spine."

"You needn't worry. I would never let anything happen to you, my love." He gently wrapped his arms around her making Bethie feel safe, as she smiled up at him. "Thank you, James."

"And besides, you're not the type he prays on," he added nonchalantly. "The women he desires are far beneath you. So don't worry your pretty little head about it."

She always hated when he spoke to her as though she were a naïve, helpless child. "What do you mean, I'm not his type?" she questioned, pulling away from him.

"You know what I mean, Sara Beth."

"No, I'm afraid I don't. Enlighten me, James," she demanded, becoming defensive.

"Well, all right… ladies of the evening, type. Need I go on?"

"No, James. You've said enough. I want to go home, now!" she snapped, turning quickly to leave.

"What's wrong, Sara? What did I do?"

"Never mind, James. Let's just go!"

"No!" he argued, grabbing her arm. "Pardon me, but I've offended you and I'd like to know why."

"You really don't know, do you?" she questioned, examining his blank expression. "Those poor, sad women were literally ripped apart and you speak of them as though they were worthless. As though their deaths mean nothing. There's a monster out there slicing women apart. Have you no heart?"

"I'm sorry, Sara Beth. I didn't mean to appear so insensitive. Please forgive me…"

"I don't want to talk about it any longer. Please, just take me home, James." Never had she been so angry with him. His pompous attitude had been enough.

"Wait! Before we return, there is more I need to say. I promise it won't take long. Sara, you must know that I love you. Even if you don't feel the same, I'm sure in time you would learn to love me. I'm willing to have you any way I can," he insisted.

"I'm sorry James… but the answer is still no. I can't marry a man that I don't love. Perhaps, it would be best if we part and give one another time-"

"No! I mean… please don't ask that of me," he interrupted desperately. "I'll wait. I'll wait for as long as you need me to. As long as it takes."

The walk home was a brisk and silent one. Bethie was relieved when they had finally reached the front door of the townhome. As like times before, she felt James was disappointed but knew there was not much she could say or do. She wanted to love him, to love anyone, and hated not being able to feel what he wanted her to. But the more she tried to force the feeling, the further away she drifted from him.

To her unexpected surprise, but delight, stood Captain McNeal in the foyer. She did not recall that they were expecting him or that his ship was due to dock in the London harbor. But nevertheless, Bethie was pleased to see her good friend.

"Captain McNeal! It's so good to see you," greeted Bethie happily. "We didn't expect you for three weeks. But I'm so glad you've come sooner."

The Captain was all smiles as he welcomed Bethie in his arms giving her a gentle squeeze.

"Bethie, you get more beautiful each time I see you," replied the Captain sincerely.

"Thank you, Captain," responded Bethie blushing, as she glanced over to Georgia Lee who was smiling from ear to ear.

"You remember my friend, James," she asked.

"Of course… Hello, Dr. Burton. I've heard you've been keeping our Bethie quite occupied." The two shook hands as the captain returned his attention again toward her. Georgia Lee, unable to refrain herself, let out several giggles as Bethie wondered what was wrong with her.

"Shhh!" reprimanded Miss Abigail.

"What's going on? Something has happened. Someone please tell me," begged Bethie confused but curious.

The Captain felt it was he who should explain as he cleared his throat and began, "I've returned to London sooner than expected because of you, Bethie."

"Because of me… Why?" she wondered.

"I was hired to bring you something special. All the way from America, in fact," he said quite seriously.

"Something for me? What is it? Where is it?" she questioned, excited with anticipation. She could tell that it must be something wonderful because of their grinning faces.

"It's in the parlor," answered Miss Abigail smiling.

"Oh, Bethie! I just can't stand it. If you don't go and see right now, I think I'll just burst!" remarked Georgia.

"Is it from Joseph? Mr. Holt? Perhaps a welcome home present? Tell me, Captain, Miss Abigail?" demanded Bethie. "A gift from you, James?" turning to him.

"No. I'm afraid not from me," he replied, jealous.

"Go and see for yourself, young lady," instructed the Captain, positioning her toward the door.

Bethie hurried out of the foyer and to the parlor as she threw open the door anxious to see what had been delivered. The entire splendor of it all needed a few moments to register. She stood in awe, totally amazed at the sight that was before her. With mouth open and eyes wide from the shock, she stood frozen trying to see all that there was. Never had her eyes looked upon a more beautiful sight.

The entire room, from top to bottom, including the floor, furniture, windowsills, and piano had been covered with beautiful roses ranging in a variety of colors. Ever since her childhood, when Aunt Liz was alive, roses had been her favorite flower.

She slowly walked in picking up the first pot, gently feeling the velvety texture between her fingers. She closed her eyes and buried her nose in the soft, silken pedals so she could fully inhale the wonderful, alluring aroma.

How sweet the room smelled, as Bethie easily agreed, she had never received a gift lovelier than this. Without a second thought, she knew who had sent her the flowers. Only he would have known the tremendous impact such a gift as this would bring. She took her time to examine and hold each arrangement that filled the room.

Bethie slowly made her way to the sitting room in which everyone had gathered. She looked only at the Captain not knowing what to say. "This is also for you," he said, handing her a box. "I believe there may be a note inside."

"Thank you… I'd like to open this in private. Please excuse me," she added as she swiftly went up the stairs to her bedroom and closed the door behind her.

"What's this all about?" demanded James, becoming annoyed with all the mystery.

She sat on her bed staring at the box, wanting to savor all that had happened. *Another gift from William*, she anxiously imagined, as she began to slowly open it. Her hands gently trembled, as she tried to remove the paper that had been wrapped around the object for protection. Beads of perspiration formed on her forehead as her heart beat rapidly. *Is this a dream? Could it be possible… after all this time he wondered of me too?* She cautiously dared to imagine.

The remainder of the paper fell onto the bed, as the gift at last was revealed for her to behold. The last tug of the paper had caused her finger to press against the winding mechanism, activating the box. It played the identical notes that mesmerized a little girl so long ago. The elegant dancers moved in rhythm while holding one another closely, as they gazed longingly into each other's eyes.

After a few minutes her eyes became blurry, as the tears filled them causing her vision to become distorted. The tears became too much for them to hold as they fell onto her cheeks. With both hands gently wrapped around the music box, she brought the smooth, porcelain dancers up against her face. She closed her eyes and could still feel the tears continuing to fall, as she whispered, "You do remember…"

She dried her eyes then pulled out the letter buried at the bottom of the box.

> My dearest Bethie,
> I pray that you are well and
> are pleased with the gifts that I
> have sent. Nothing would make me
> happier than to see you once again.
> Won't you Please come to Savannah?
> Yours Truly,
> William

Bethie returned to the sitting room to find the group becoming silent as she entered. She was nervous but completely sure of what she had to do. "I have an announcement to make that concerns you all. After further- and much consideration… I've decided," she hesitated. "I've decided before returning to New Hope, to visit Savannah."

"How marvelously splendid!" burst Georgia Lee, overly pleased. "You are all welcomed to stay with us. Mother and Father will insist," she rambled, delighted. "Just imagine, Bethie, a ball in your honor… How wonderfully exciting!" she gasped.

"Yes, how wonderful," added James, confused by Bethie's change of heart but pleased nevertheless. Miss Abigail did not say a word but excused herself from the room. The Captain could sense she was upset and followed behind. He found her standing in the parlor overwhelmed by all the flowers.

"What shall we do with all of them?" she commented, looking about the room in a daze.

"I suppose that is Bethie's concern now. Miss Abigail… I can feel something is wrong and it is not what to do with all of these roses, is it?"

"Perhaps, after she has enjoyed them and before we leave

London, she could give them to one of the poor ladies who sell flowers in the square." She continued to ignore the Captain's question.

"Abigail… Bethie needs to return to Savannah, and you know this. Neither one of them will ever truly be happy unless they see each other again. I mean no disrespect, ma'am. But it's high time the people around them stop trying to keep them apart. They are two, intelligent, young adults who are quite capable of making their own decisions. Forgive me if I have over stepped my boundary," added Captain McNeal, hoping Abigail would not be offended. "You must have faith in her."

"Yes… I suppose you're right, Captain. But it's not William, I fear."

Savannah, Spring of 1883

How little everything had changed, thought Bethie, as the carriage began to leave the city. The voyage to America had been a long and tiresome one, but well appreciated. It gave her time to think and calm her over flowing emotions that seemed to change with the wind.

During the voyage, old memories of Emma Mae's betrayal came back to haunt her. She again found herself standing in the place she had once stood staring deep into the ocean, lost and sad from neglect and abandonment. Had she made the right decision? She constantly questioned. Would returning to Savannah only add to her painful accounts of time long ago?

The lovely city was exactly the same as she had remembered. At times, London could be compared to Savannah with all its sophistication and beauty. But London had become a safe haven, far and away from her aunt's malicious deeds.

She no longer felt the security that another country had given her, as Bethie soon recognized the beginning of Calhoun's many acres of land. The horses bore at the fork as Bethie gave a sigh of relief. She reopened her eyes, breathed easier, and wished they would move faster far away from Emma Mae's reach.

The Work plantation was smaller, compared to Calhoun, but just as lovely. The two mansions were separated by miles and gratefully too, agreed Bethie, no longer able to see Emma's land. Georgia Lee's parents were in Atlanta but had left an entire staff of servants awaiting their arrival. Bethie roomed with Georgia Lee, while Miss Abigail was given a large guest room. There was a small guest house situated between a gazebo and the mansion in which James was offered as his quarters.

They had arrived the day before the ball giving Bethie ample time to unpack, relax, and collect her thoughts. Though William had been sent word that they would be attending the party, they would not be staying at the Calhoun plantation. Bethie made the Captain promise not to mention Georgia Lee's family plantation to him. She wanted some time to be able to unwind before confronting him. He understood and had done as she wished.

The next morning everyone at the mansion was buzzing about. The servants were preparing their baths, laying out the gowns, and helping with their hair. Georgia Lee was beside herself with excitement and anticipation of the coming event. Her mother had written how extravagant Emma's parties had always been and tonight would be no exception.

She felt honored to be the guest of honor's best friend and delighted to be attending. Miss Abigail spent most of her time worrying about Bethie. She made her promise if Emma Mae tried anything, they would leave on the next locomotive heading north. Abigail was anxious to return to Covington and wished the whole ordeal would soon be over. Bethie knew she longed to see Joseph, for she missed him terribly too.

James was dressed handsomely in a long, brown topcoat with a satin insert at the lapel. He wore a brown top hat of brushed beaver. His hair was neatly combed and his boots shone brightly. Both Abigail and Georgia Lee wore beautiful, full length, formal gowns made of taffeta and silk.

All three ladies had purchased new dresses for the ball while still in London. Both, Miss Abigail and Georgia Lee, wore their hair up with bonnets that matched their gowns.

"You ladies look absolutely lovely this evening!" remarked James as he helped them into an awaiting carriage. "Where is Sara Beth?" he questioned.

"I suppose I'm running a bit late..." she apologized, coming toward the carriage from the mansion. His eyes quickly left the ladies and immediately became fixated by the beautiful sight standing before him. Never had he seen her look lovelier, he easily agreed, or any woman for that matter.

"Miss Sara," he exclaimed in awe. "Never have you looked more beautiful. You're absolutely a vision to behold. I'll be the envy of every man at the ball!" he added bragging and feeling quite good about himself.

She wore a formal gown of white satin and lace that bustled in the back and hung gently off her slender shoulders with puffed satin sleeves. Her hair was styled away from her face, accenting her large, brown eyes but left long in the back in French curls.

Instead of a bonnet, in her hair was a delicate, diamond tiara that had once belonged to her mother. Around her neck was a string of fine pearls with matching earrings. In one of her long, white gloved hands, she held a masquerade mask colored white and lined in tiny pearls.

If not in the presence of Miss Abigail and Georgia Lee, he would have taken her in his arms and kissed her where she stood. But unfortunately for him that seemed hardly ever to be the case. He couldn't wait to have Bethie's approval in marriage and to be finally done with the two of them.

But until the time came, he would have to put up with Georgia Lee's silly personality and Miss Abigail's constant hovering and watchful eye over Bethie. Abigail's continuing dislike for him made the wait seem even longer and harder, he agreed, wishing they were alone and could make the two of them disappear.

Instead, he took her hand and gently kissed it. "It's an honor to be with such an exquisite, lovely lady."

"Thank you, kind sir," blushed Bethie teasingly.

James helped her into the carriage as it slowly began its way in the direction of the Calhoun plantation.

"Bethie, you'll be the most beautiful woman at the ball," replied Georgia Lee sincerely to her friend.

"You look absolutely stunning, Georgia Lee."

"Do you really think so, Bethie?"

"Yes, most definitely," she insisted, smiling to her friend.

Miss Abigail leaned over and whispered in her ear, "Are you all right, dearest?" she asked concerned.

"Yes, Miss Abby. A bit nervous, but I'm glad that I came."

"Promise me that whatever happens, you won't be too disappointed if things don't turn out as you may have hoped."

"The truth is… I've done much growing up this past year. I try to see things now for what they truly are. I have little expectations of a reunion based on memories of a time long ago. Visiting Savannah has become the last page in an ending chapter of my past."

"Don't you see? I had to come so that I could be set free to start a new and happy life in New Hope."

"Yes, I understand why you had to come. And I stand by your decision. Always know, that I love you very much."

"And I love you… Mother," ended Bethie sincerely.

Miss Abigail was completely caught off guard. Never expecting to hear that word, especially on this night when Bethie's thoughts were elsewhere. Nevertheless, it took her breath away as she forced back the tears and joyfully smiled back at her. She would not make this night about her. It was Bethie's night as Miss Abigail gave her hand a comforting squeeze.

They were escorted down from their carriage by a formally, dressed servant in front of the main entrance of the Calhoun mansion. After looking about, she agreed all seemed the same as old memories of Emma Mae sent a nervous chill throughout her body causing her to gently tremble. The circular drive was lined with elegant carriages and the grounds lit with many delicate, colored lanterns displayed in various places.

William's eyes roamed the floor of the crowded ball room, filled with Georgian aristocrats, trying to get a glimpse of Bethie as Elizabeth desperately fought for his attention. Though it had been so long ago, he was certain he would recognize her. The masks made it more difficult to see each lady's face, as he waited until they took them away for a moment giving him the opportunity to check. He decided that she must not have arrived yet and worried if she had possibly changed her mind.

Bethie entered the large foyer and in no time met eye to eye with Emma Mae who sat in a crowd of her socialite friends. The two met halfway, as Miss Jane pushed the chair the old woman sat in with Miss Abigail following behind Bethie.

"Hello, Sara Beth... Abigail," she began cordially.

"Emma," replied Miss Abigail short.

"I'm so pleased you accepted my invitation to come to Savannah. You've grown to be lovelier than I had ever imagined," she added, trying to hide her disappointment and jealousy. Miss Jane nodded and smiled back at them both, extremely delighted.

"You can't imagine what this means to William and me," commented Emma Mae, trying to be sincere as she reached out to her niece.

How very old and frail she had become, thought Bethie, refusing to embrace her aunt and taking a small step back. As she sat in her chair looking wrinkled, frail, and very small, Bethie knew one thing had certainly changed. She no longer had to be concerned with pretending not to be frightened or intimidated by this dreadful woman. Perhaps it had been because she was a child. Nevertheless, she would never have that power over her again.

"Hello, Miss Emma," replied Bethie, refusing to call her aunt but continuing to remain cordial. "Hello, Miss Jane," she added smiling back at her. Unlike her Aunt Emma, Jane had changed very little over the past five years.

Her face became serious again as she looked into Emma Mae's black eyes. "I see that you are well, and thank you for your thoughtful gesture. I hope you were not too inconvenienced. But truly... you really shouldn't have," continued Bethie somberly. "I must confess, William is who I came to see before returning to New Hope. So if you'll excuse me-"

"I believe he is with his Elizabeth. In the ballroom," interrupted Emma. "They have been seeing each other for some time now. He plans to propose to her very soon. She is a fine, young lady from a very prominent family," bragged Emma deliberately.

"I'm sure she is... and how very lucky for him—and you," replied Bethie sarcastically.

"But certainly, before you go and see my son, you must allow me to introduce you to my guests. After all, this party is given in your honor," she insisted sternly and annoyed. Miss Abigail could see her pompous attitude was still with her.

"Perhaps later, Emma," interrupted Abigail, both swiftly leaving her, as Emma's mouth hung wide in astonishment and disbelief.

They entered the crowded ballroom as the lovely sound of music filled the air. How elegant it all was, agreed Bethie, looking at the people all dressed so formally most of them she did not know. There were chandeliers hanging from the high ceiling and walls covered with beautiful pictures. Servants carrying trays of champagne and hors d'oeuvres could be seen everywhere. Bethie held her mask up to her face with the hopes of seeing him first.

The lingering wait had become too overwhelming as he excused himself from Elizabeth's side and began to make his way through the crowds. "William!" snapped Elizabeth annoyed, while he continued on ignoring her demands as though he was unable to hear her.

He had always been the kindest of gentlemen but tonight his mind and spirit became controlled by a relentless force even he could not explain. William neither cared that she had become offended by his behavior nor the men who found him rude, as he made his way toward every dark haired lady whose face was concealed. Even his conversation with those who stopped him along the way became short and to the point, for he seemed not to be able to help himself.

Every potential young lady, soon, became a disappointment. Other than to apologize for his intrusion, he neither asked for their name nor gave a second glance. The ladies becoming annoyed only when discovering it was someone, other than themselves, he searched for. For William, all it took was a simple glance into their eyes to know immediately that she was not the one as he continued on with his weary search.

Feeling frustrated, his eyes again began to search the dance floor from where he stood. When all seemed hopeless, his eyes caught sight of a beautiful lady dressed in a white gown next to the entrance of the ballroom. She had apparently just arrived and had barely made her way into the room when a crowd of young men formed around her. He could not see her entire face, because of the mask, but was compelled by her beauty as he without further thought moved closer to her.

Who is this lovely lady? He tried to imagine, forgetting his former expedition, trying desperately to get a glimpse of her face. The nearer he came to where she stood, the more intrigued he became. Then suddenly he stopped in the middle of the dance floor, unaware of the dancers who stared and found his behavior to be odd. "Bethie…" he whispered. Both overwhelmed and stunned, knowing only she could hold such beauty that could cause men in a room to encircle her.

Before he could swiftly make his way toward her again, he heard a familiar voice from the past calling out his name. "Hello, William… My goodness, you have certainly become quite the handsome young man. Tell me, how are you?" asked Miss Abigail. She was so pleased to see him. He immediately recognized the voice.

"Miss Abigail, so good of you to come!" he replied smiling,

turning toward her. "I missed you both terribly through the years. Since you went away, I've never had a lovelier teacher or governess. I must confess… I was never quite the same after the two of you left. The happy, spirited young boy seemed to have left with you both. Never to return, I'm afraid," he confessed truthfully, as they embraced.

"If I could have taken you with us, I would have. I'm so very sorry, William," responded Miss Abigail sincerely.

"I know you would have. But I survived and we are now together again. I can't recall when I've been happier." He leaned over and kissed Abigail gently on her cheek then whispered, "Is she the young lady in the white gown?"

"Yes, go to her William. Don't worry about me. I know exactly how important this reunion is to both of you. Go now," she insisted. He hugged and thanked her again, as he quickly made his way to Bethie.

He cut in front of the gentlemen who were all standing around her as they fought for her attention. Bethie shyly peered down keeping the mask to her face. She was becoming overwhelmed and wished James would find her soon to make them all go away.

"May I have the honor of this dance, Miss?" asked William, pretending not to know her. It was not necessary for Bethie to see his face. She immediately recognized his voice. She became nervous and gently began to tremble. Although she wished it, there was nowhere to hide. She slowly peered up into his eyes keeping the mask against her face.

How tall and very handsome he had become, she thought, wondering how her dreams could have been so accurate. But she was not surprised. "I'm afraid you'll have to wait in line, sir!" snapped one of the gentlemen not knowing who he was.

William became annoyed by their presence and angrily sneered over to them, "Go away—all of you," he calmly but sternly suggested. Realizing it was he, the group shrugged their shoulders and soon dissembled without another word.

Immediately, his attention went back to Bethie who continued to keep her face covered. "About that dance," he asked again, starting to become irritated with the mask. Except in his dreams, it had been so long since he had seen her face and to know only a simple mask kept him from this seemed more than he could bear.

"Do you always behave so uncivilized when you desire a lady to dance with you?" she questioned. Becoming annoyed in the manner in which he had made them go away, but pleased nevertheless.

"Only when the lady is one that I have waited, patiently, for many years to dance with," answered William. He took the mask from her hand, unable to go another minute without seeing her entire face.

"Please, let me hold…" he started, only to become frozen by her beauty. He had never forgotten how lovely she was as a child but never had he imagined how truly beautiful she would become as a woman.

Time seemed to stop and the room and all who occupied its premises disappeared, as they stared deeply into one another's eyes. All became quiet, still, and irrelevant except for the two of them. To only the blind, could they continue to deny the truth. An incredible force took hold unwilling to relent or release them from the hypnotic trance they had fell into. They passionately examined each other's face wanting desperately to see all that they had become.

To him, she most definitely was more beautiful than any porcelain doll or lady that he had ever laid eyes upon. Her large, brown, almost exotic eyes seemed to place a spell on him, one he wished he'd never be released from. He could hardly believe it was her, standing right before him. It had been so long.

Hoping not to offend, he was unable to refrain from touching her face. How soft and lovely was her skin, as his fingers brushed against her mouth. He smiled as he gently touched her hair, remembering the long brown ringlets he teasingly pulled so often as a young boy.

He noticed how tall and full her figure had become, trying hard not to stare. It was amazing to him, as though he had almost expected to see the young girl he once knew. "Bethie…" he whispered in awe.

"Is it really you? You're all grown up," he added, astonished, filled with joy, and very much in love.

Never before had she felt so confused. It had taken her months to accept how foolish she had been. Constantly dreaming about a man she knew only as a boy. Could she have been wrong? Was it possible dreams could become reality? Or was this a dream? She questioned herself, becoming detached, feeling light headed and no longer able to judge what was real.

He was everything she had imagined. Handsome, strong, and able to cause her emotions to run wild, making her unable to move or speak. The feeling of lost control made her uncomfortable and even annoyed, as she fought desperately to regain herself. For her, this was new and caused mixed feelings of both excitement and fear.

She recalled his eyes as blue as the oceans they would one day sail. And even they, had become more brilliant in color. His blonde hair had been grown long and pulled back giving him a gallant, princely appearance. But what pleased her most of all was when she looked deep into his eyes, she could still see the young boy she had once known.

Without further thought, he was indeed her childhood friend— and love. Forcing her lips to move she whispered back, "Hello, William." With much happiness, both beamed, both obviously overwhelmingly in love.

Their private world became intruded upon, as James with Georgia Lee tagging behind abruptly approached them. "Bethie! I've been looking all over for you. How in the world did we become separated?" demanded James. He was annoyed and now jealous by the way the two looked at one another as he glared at William.

It had been Georgia Lee's doing. She had made it her mission to keep James occupied, as much as possible. So that her best friend could reunite with the only man, she believed, Bethie would ever truly love. But with all her good intentions and because of his possessive, demanding personality, he soon became irritated and angry. He was determined to find what he believed was his, refusing to be distracted or detained a minute longer.

From where she stood, Miss Abigail could sense trouble as she swiftly hurried to Bethie's side. She immediately interrupted his questioning, "William, I'd like you to meet Bethie's friends, Georgia Lee Work and James Burton."

With his eyes still fixated on Bethie, he replied, "Hello, very good to meet you both."

He then wrapped his arm around Bethie's waist, as she nervously accepted his hand. They left the three and began to waltz onto the dance floor. By now, James had become overwhelmed with jealousy and rage, as he began to approach the dancing couple.

To Georgia Lee's utter delight, Miss Abigail quickly moved in front of him, "I believe you promised me a dance," she remarked, pretending as though all was well.

From a slight hand gesture to the orchestra's conductor, William requested the enchanting melody that had lingered in her mind for many years and now played inside the box of the dancing lovers. "Tales from the Vienna Woods" by Johann Strauss never sounded more beautiful. How appropriate and thoughtful he was, she decided, taken by William's charm.

He held her tightly, unwilling to let go or to allow her to be taken by another, as they continued to gaze deeply into each other's eyes. Both moved perfectly together, resembling a couple that had practiced and were made for one another. Always maintaining a firm but gentle hold, he expertly whirled her around taking complete control. Bethie closed her eyes and imagined that they had become the porcelain dancer's, as the sensation of their poetic movements made her slightly dizzy.

Without Bethie noticing, he had waltzed her from the ballroom out onto the balcony overlooking the lush gardens. The music could barely be heard, as she abruptly found herself face to face with him alone and far from the other guests. He continued to keep his arm around her waist, as the expression on his face became serious making Bethie nervous wishing she could run and hide.

"You are so beautiful, Bethie… Even in a hundred years, I'd know you anywhere. Do you believe in destiny?" All she seemed able to feel was confused, overwhelmed, and afraid to answer or even move.

He slowly leaned over and gently placed his lips onto hers. A thousand emotions seem to flood her body. She soon concluded the kiss to feel nothing like the abrupt, unauthorized, and unappreciated one he had given her so long ago.

With his mouth still on hers, she trembled beneath him afraid of the overwhelming, intense passion that they felt. But not wanting him to ever pull away. Never had they felt such emotions with another, as his body slowly moved closer to her own. She could feel every part of him against her as both of his arms became tightened, devouring any will she may have had left.

Between the passion and surrender, thoughts of the past still haunted her mind. They taunted and teased making cruel fun, laughing relentlessly and unwilling to subside. Bethie had never completely healed or forgotten the horrid moments she had fell victim to, at this very place. Although childhood memories of William had always been her fondest, she still could not forget the abandonment of all whom she had known—including him.

Once again, the angry and bitter resentment shot through her like a hot flame causing her to become defensive. She pushed him away with all the force she could muster. "How dare you," she cried, moving away and placing a comfortable distance between the two. "Who do you think you are?"

"What's wrong, my Bethie?" questioned William confused and upset.

"I'm not your Bethie! And I never will be!" she snapped angrily. "Who do you think you are? Do you honestly believe because you are a Calhoun that you can take whatever you please? Whenever you desire to? Perhaps it has been the style in which you have grown accustomed to, but not with me—not ever!"

Angry and distraught, Bethie began to panic looking in all

directions for somewhere she could flee to. Because of her state of mind, it was impossible to return to the ballroom. She wanted desperately to be alone and far from him. She thought of the gardens leading to the front entrance where the carriage had been. She began to run as he caught her by the arm, refraining her from movement.

"Let me go, William, this instant!" she demanded, as the tears began to fall from her eyes.

"No! Not until you explain why you are so angry with me. You're not a child anymore, Sara Beth Covington. You can't just run and hide every time you feel angry. I won't allow you to put me through that any longer. It's time you act as a woman and give me the courtesy of an explanation," he demanded, becoming furious with her.

She twisted away and fled down the steps into the gardens with William following behind. Emma Mae, leaning on her cane, stood grinning at the top of the balcony. She watched Bethie's rejection of her son unfold, making her extremely pleased and relieved.

Although the tears began to blind her, the gardens had been lit for the evening making a path in which to run. William soon caught up to her as he grabbed her around the waist, spinning her quickly around making her feel faint and nauseated from the high anxiety that the night had brought.

"Please let me go, William," she begged exhausted, as she let her head drop, unable to hold it up and not wanting to look into his eyes. With her hands she pushed against his chest trying to free herself as she trembled and shook.

"Stop it, Bethie! I'll let you go if you promise to calm down and talk to me sensibly."

"It's no use, William," she cried. "Don't you understand? You treat me as though there has been no time between us. Your mother sends me away as though I were a disease needing to be gotten rid of. And for years I wrote, praying for even one response from you. Something to give me hope… telling me that you, of all people, really cared about me. I'm not the same girl you once knew, stop living in a dream. It'll only make things worse."

William could hardly believe his ears. What she said made no immediate sense to him. "That's not true," he begged, desperately trying to convince her of his honesty. "I wrote every day. Sometimes even more. It was you that I never received letters from," he insisted, confused.

"I don't know what happened. But I beg you to forget the past and forgive me for whatever pain I may have caused you. It's time to face the truth, Bethie. We are destined to be together. And I know you feel the same. I see it in your eyes. They've always given you away. Did you think I'd forgotten?"

"That's not true," she pleaded, lying.

"Look at me, Bethie!" demanded William shaking her. "Look me in the eyes and tell me you do not love me. Then I will believe you and let go."

She tried desperately to make the words come out, but could not. "Your mother would never allow us to be together. She'd surely kill us first."

"I don't give a damn about what my mother thinks!" he snapped. "I've loved you since we were children. Not a day has gone by that I haven't wondered how or where you were. It took a lifetime to get you back and I'll never let you go!" insisted William passionately.

Desperate, confused, and unable to think of anything else, she smacked him across the face causing her hand to sting and William to release her. "How dare you! After all these years, think that you can decide what's to become of me. I'm leaving Monday for New Hope and wish never to see you or your mother again! I only wish I never came," she ended, turning quickly as she fled from the gardens. William stood stunned and heartbroken as he watched her carriage leave the plantation.

The events following their long awaited encounter played over and over again in his mind, as he stood on the balcony overlooking the gardens. Never had he imagined their reunion to end in such utter resentment or had he ever felt so lonely and sad.

The more he thought of what Bethie accused him of, the more convinced he became that it had been his mother behind the lost letters. He had never known Bethie to lie as his heart sank to his feet. Feeling once again, the utter betrayal of his mother's deceit. But unlike others, this would mark a time in which he would never forget, despite the outcome.

He found her retiring to her bedroom, relaxed and content that the evening had gone as she had hoped and anticipated. If it were not for the music that played in the ballroom, their voices could have been heard for miles. His anger had been driven to a level in which she had never witnessed and for the first time in her miserable life, made her tremble in fear. She eventually gave in to his demands and confessed that it was indeed she who had taken the letters and hidden them in the safe of her library wall.

"I'm going away tonight, Mother. And when I return it will be only to collect my things. I'm leaving Savannah. I don't care about this plantation or your dreadful money. I wish never to see you again," he ended in a slow, bitter tone. Never had he felt such dislike toward her.

Emma Mae's world began to crumble about her as the mansion echoed her screams, "William!"

He left quickly from her bedside without even another glance, as he made his way to the library ignoring all that he passed along the way. Closing the door, he went over to the fireplace and picked up the black iron poker that sat to the side of it. He flung the painting that hung over it to the floor and with all his strength pried open the safe.

As the door eventually gave way, to his sudden shock, came the towering heap of letters from a time long ago tumbling to floor beneath it. He took the pillow sack that he had stripped from his mother's bed and filled the bag entirely with the many letters that lay beneath him.

In a feverish pace, he rode his horse to the edge of the waters. He carried a lantern for sight while making his way onto the island.

After building a fire, he sat before the pile rummaging through the contents in total disbelief of just how many there were. Amazed, he wondered why his mother would have kept them. As though they were some kind of distorted, twisted trophy.

He separated the letters that had been written to him from a little girl, many years ago. With tears in his eyes, "Mother, how could you be so cruel?" he whispered in despair.

Moment of Truth

"Whatever shall I do without you, Bethie?" confessed Georgia Lee sadly. With tears in her eyes, she embraced her friend lovingly.

"You'll be fine, Georgia Lee... It will be good for you to spend some time with your parents now that your studies are over. You've been away from home for a long time now. Perhaps you'll be able to work out your differences."

"I envy you," smiled Bethie.

"Envy me? Why would you envy me?"

"Because you have something I shall never have. You have parents who are alive and love you very much. I would give anything to remember even a moment of time with my mother and father. Always cherish them, Georgia Lee. Life is much too short and unpredictable."

"Bethie... you have known me for a long time now. You know I'm not one to keep quiet when I really believe in something so strongly. You've been the sister that I never had. I say these words only out of love for you... Please don't disagree with me. You don't even have to say a word. My carriage is outside waiting and we don't have much time. Let's not argue. I only ask that you listen."

"What is it?"

"When our driver came into the ballroom and explained that you had left early, Miss Abby and I knew something terrible had happened. You may have thought I was sleeping, Bethie. But I heard you sobbing in the middle of the night. It nearly broke my heart but also made me angry! You're the kindest, prettiest girl I know. But also the most stubborn!" she added sternly.

"Now I don't know what happened. And I know you don't want

to talk about it. I'm not trying to pry. But I saw the way the two of you looked at each other last night. You're both in love with one another. It's useless to deny it. We've known each other much too long for that—and Miss Abby knows too! I understand and sympathize about the horrors that old woman put you through as a child. But you're not a child any longer. Let go and stop dwelling on the past."

"You tell me of how lucky I am. Well, you're lucky too. And I envy you also. To have a man as wonderful and handsome as he is. It was so obvious the man could see no other last night. Learn to forgive him, Bethie. If you don't… you'll grow to be a very lonely, bitter, old woman. You're not blood related. There is nothing for either of you to be ashamed of!" convinced Georgia Lee.

"It is not for Emma Mae to decide! But nevertheless I fear her. Stay far from her reach. You don't love James… You never did, or could you." Bethie sat staring at her friend sadly, not saying a word, as she listened with an open mind.

"Now I have to go. Mother and Father are waiting in Atlanta. Let's say our goodbyes here. I don't think I could bear this again at the carriage. Promise me you'll never forget me!" cried Georgia Lee embracing her friend one last time.

"Georgia Lee Work. You're so dramatic… But I do love you. For as long as I live, I could never forget you! Stop talking as though we'll never see each another again," Bethie teased smiling.

"Now remember, you promised to come to New Hope next spring. We'll have lots of fun. You'll see! There's the New Hope Playhouse… remember how we loved to go to the theater in London?"

"Yes, I remember," smiled Georgia Lee.

"We'll take in every play and dine along the river every evening!"

"How marvelously splendid, Bethie!" she blurted excited. Promise you'll think about what I've said?" questioned Georgia Lee seriously.

"I promise… goodbye my friend," Bethie ended, giving her one last hug.

Bethie watched from the window as her friend was helped into the opened carriage then swiftly departed from the estate. She felt her heart sink now that her best friend was gone. The events from the last evening only added to her sadness. And the morning seemed not to improve when Miss Abby gave her the news of her good friend Henry, who had been their protector and advocate often in the past, had passed away over the winter.

"There is someone to see you, ma'am," announced a servant to Miss Abigail.

"Thank you," she replied, curious as to who might be calling this early in the morning. She walked into the foyer to find an anxious Miss Jane waiting by the door.

"Hello, Abigail. Forgive my early morning intrusion," she begged.

"Not at all. Would you like a cup of tea?"

"Thank you, but no. I really can't stay but a minute." She fidgeted in the pocket of her dress and pulled out a letter that was neatly folded and addressed to Bethie, quickly handing it to her.

"Please give this letter to Bethie. If… if Emma Mae knew I was here… I don't know what she would do to me," confessed Miss Jane worried.

"Say no more, Jane. I will give Bethie the letter immediately. You know Bethie told me what you did for her in London. I don't know how to thank you. You must know we don't blame you for what happened in the past. Just Emma—and her devious ways."

"But she'll have her judgement day when she meets our maker. Why don't you come with us to New Hope? We could use your expertise. You don't have to stay with that woman any longer. There is plenty of room at Covington. These are not only my words, but Bethie's, too."

"Thank you, Abigail. I will consider your generous, undeserved offer. Please tell Bethie I said thank you." Jane's eyes filled, overwhelmed by the offer. Embarrassed, she turned to leave when

Abigail gently reached out and touched her arm.

"You really are brave, Jane… Don't allow her to make you feel any differently—any longer."

"Thank you, Abigail. Your words mean more than I can say. I'm humbled by them," she smiled as she left the mansion promptly.

Bethie lay across her bed as the memories of the night before ran relentlessly through her mind, stopping only by the sudden knock at her door. "Come in," she said sitting up, trying to appear as though she was fine.

"Hello, dearest… haven't decided in coming downstairs yet, I see. James was worried about you. He came over first thing this morning looking for you. He told me that he was going into the city this morning to purchase two tickets for the circus tonight. That should cheer you up a little, don't you suppose?"

"That was very kind of him. But I don't think I feel much like a circus tonight. I feel somewhat under the weather. Perhaps you could go in my place?" suggested Bethie.

"My Bethie… turning down a circus? How utterly unlike you, dearest," teased Miss Abigail trying to get her to laugh.

The phrase "My Bethie" triggered her to remember the last evening when William had used the same words. She began to wish never to be referred to again as anyone's or with those words. They made her feel as though she was still thought of as a child when she felt very much like a woman, especially in William's arms.

Miss Abigail could see how sad and forlorn she had become and wished there was something she could do. "Bethie, I know you told me that you did not want to talk about it this morning. But you look so sad is there anything I can do?" pleaded Miss Abigail concerned.

"No, Miss Abby. This time I'm afraid you can't fix what ails me. I just need some time then I'm sure I'll be all right. I'm looking forward to going home to Covington tomorrow. I only wish it were today. I've never wanted to leave a city so quickly before. But tomorrow will come soon enough I suppose."

"Well, if you need me, I'm here. Oh, I almost forgot. I have a letter for you from Miss Jane. She brought it herself this morning. I asked her to stay but she was very anxious and said she couldn't. Poor woman… I urged her to leave Emma Mae and come with us to Pennsylvania."

Bethie took the letter and opened it and began to read. Her forehead became wrinkled with a bewildered expression appearing on her face.

"What is it?" question Abigail anxiously.

"I don't know… She wants me to come to Calhoun immediately."

"Absolutely not, Bethie!" insisted Miss Abigail sternly. "You never have to take another step on that old heathens land ever again!"

"Wait Miss Abby! I'm not to meet with Emma Mae or even to go inside the mansion. She wants me to wait silently in the west gardens. Something about seeing and hearing something of great importance to me and my future. Very mysterious, isn't it?"

"You're not considering it, are you?" questioned Miss Abigail alarmed.

"Yes, I'm going now. I trust Miss Jane. She wouldn't harm me intentionally. And I'm not concerned about running into William. I don't believe this has anything to do with him. Please ask the gardener to saddle up a horse!" she demanded sternly, refusing to give into Miss Abigail's wishes.

"Bethie… rumors flooded the ballroom last night. Rumors that William and Emma Mae have said their last words to each other. I believe he has left Savannah vowing never to return. This is more of a reason not to go. Bethie, please! With Henry and William gone, who'll protect you? There is not much Miss Jane can do, not against that woman," begged Abigail panicking.

"I do not wish to discuss it any longer. I'm going, and that is final!" Bethie was firm and determined becoming annoyed with her. She sprung to her feet making her way swiftly outside and to the barn. Miss Abigail joined her outside as her horse was finally prepared for riding.

She rode briskly over to where Miss Abigail stood upset,

watching from a distance. Bethie reached out her hand in comfort, "Please don't worry or follow. I have to do this myself. If I'm not back in a couple of hours, send James. He should be back by then."

"Be careful, Bethie," warned Abigail, as she watched her gallop quickly away.

Bethie was an excellent rider, and in no time had reached the Calhoun plantation. She dismounted and was tying the horse when she began to hear familiar voices in the background coming from the gardens. After listening more carefully, she was certain that one of the voices heard was that of James. An overwhelming flood of anxiety filled her body as she began to tremble.

"Oh… please no, James," she whispered, praying frantically that her thoughts were untrue.

She nervously began to approach the path to the gardens feeling compelled to follow the voices. Bethie stopped only before the clearing, praying that she would not be seen. Between the trees, azaleas, and wisteria, she could easily see the silhouette figures of James and Emma Mae as her worst nightmare began to unfold.

"I didn't take you from that poor, wretched life you maintained for nothin' in return. I've been paying for your education for years now, and you owe me!" scorned Emma Mae angrily.

"I was young and foolish then. Things have changed, Emma Mae. And your threats don't scare me. I don't care about your money. I'm in love with Sara Beth."

Emma Mae cocked her head backwards and laughed loudly. "You silly fool! Do you think I wouldn't tell Sara Beth the truth about you?" The smile left her wrinkled mouth as she became quite serious. "If you cross me, or even consider it, I'll tell her so quickly your head will spin!" she threatened.

"I know her well… She'd never forget it. And you know it! Are you willing to lose everything we've worked so long and hard for, including your beloved, Sara Beth? We are so close. I can taste it. All you have to do is convince her to marry you. Hell, you can even have the wedding here. Only then will my William give up on her and come home to Calhoun. Where he should be!"

James began to pace, frustrated, "I'm doing the best I can, Emma! She's a stubborn woman—and that damn Abigail keeps getting in my way. I know she doesn't trust me and fills her head constantly," insisted James.

"I told you to watch out for that one! She's a smart woman and I'm not surprised that she is on to you. So it makes it even more imperative that you convince her today to marry you."

"I'll do the best I can. But you keep that son of yours out of the way!" he snapped.

Bethie had heard enough as she began to slowly back up. Panic and the awful feeling of betrayal filled her mind and belly. She quickly spun around and ran with all her might to her horse, as they fled undetected from the plantation and from Emma's reach.

She ran straight to her room shutting the door behind her as she flung herself on the bed and wept. Miss Abigail did not wait to knock, going immediately to her side and taking her in her arms. "Oh Miss Abby! Why am I constantly being made the fool? Am I really that naive and gullible?" she cried hysterically.

"What has happened, Bethie? Tell me now," demanded Miss Abigail upset.

"It's James… He's not who he says he is… All this time he's been working for Emma Mae. I heard them myself talking in her gardens. It's all been lies!" cried Bethie devastated.

"I knew it!" screeched Abigail consumed with anger. "Let me handle him," she insisted, hearing the sound of a horse coming closer. She immediately went to the window to see, but found it was not James.

"It's William, Bethie."

She jumped up from the bed. "Oh please, Miss Abby! Make him go away. I can't see him right now, please!" begged Bethie. Miss Abigail, wanting to protect her from any further pain and embarrassment, left her room promptly. Bethie stood against her closed door panicking as she prayed for him to go away.

William had already entered the house, unwelcomed, against the servants' protests and in a feverish state. He had already made his way to the staircase when Abigail blocked him half way up. "Out of my way, Miss Abigail. I mean no disrespect. But I must see Bethie now!" he demanded.

"She does not want to see you. She told me so herself. Please, let her be! You're only making things worse," insisted Abigail.

"I don't care that she does not want to see me. I need to show her something very important. Now please let me pass!"

"William, listen to me," started Abigail becoming angry and quite determined as she lowered her voice. "I know Bethie loves you. But she can't be pushed… Give her some time and then I'm certain she'll come around," promised Miss Abigail desperately trying to convince him.

"You believe she is in love with me," questioned William beaming, as he calmed down wanting desperately to hear the words again.

"Yes, I do. But so much has happened. You must let her come to you. If you don't, I'm warning you, William… You'll push her away forever!"

"But what if she doesn't come to me? I won't take that chance! What I need to show her could make all the difference in the world. I know you are leaving tomorrow. I'll go now. But I will be back this evening. Talk to her, Miss Abigail. I beg of you. If you care anything for us."

"We belong together! I've never been more sure of anything in my life. And as long as I am alive… nothing will stop me from making her see how much I truly love her. I promise you, Miss Abby… I shall never betray or mistreat Bethie. I will give her the world and always protect her, with my life if necessary!" swore William with much conviction.

"I believe you, Son. I'll do all that I can," she replied with a gentle smile.

She believed William was sincere, but it wasn't what filled her mind with fear. Emma Mae would destroy them all before giving into their wishes. Simply running to Pennsylvania, she feared, would not be far enough.

After returning to Bethie's room to check on her, she was surprised to find her quite calm and together. "Thank you for sending him away… I'm fine now, Miss Abby. It was the sudden shock of it all that had me so upset. I'm angrier with myself for becoming so easily made a fool of."

"But you have always been right. We learn from our mistakes. And I shall never again be so easily deceived. I don't know how I can ever repay Miss Jane. She knew I would have to see for myself. Still, it is so hard to believe just how far a person will go for the love of money. So very hard," she ended wearily.

The dust kicked high around them making mounds of clouds as William galloped swiftly up the long entryway of the Calhoun plantation. After years of missing Bethie, only to find her exile was by the hands of his mother was more than he could bear. He continued to feel the devastating pain of betrayal, unlike any he had ever experienced in his life.

Along with the betrayal and shame, he could never blame Bethie for choosing never to see him again. Despite the love she may have felt. He sadly wondered if he would be a constant reminder of her past afflictions. This, too, was something he could not bear. Perhaps Miss Abby had been right and he only selfish, allowing her to be set free could be the only decent tribute his family could ever give her.

He quietly made his way up to his room, hoping to avoid Emma Mae, as he began to gather some of his belongings. The offer in Philadelphia would be taken seriously and the distance from Savannah and his mother would prove healthy. He prayed, that in time, Bethie would learn to forgive and forget. Only then, would they have a chance of a happy life together.

William moved to a window to gaze one last time over the land where he had been raised. Knowing in his heart, he would never again roam the fields of cotton or eat from the orchards that bore the sweet peaches. The extravagant gardens would remain always in his heart. He would remember them for their incredible ability to bring such happiness and joy to a young, little girl who asked nothing in return but to stand within its beauty.

As he reminisced of the times that had been good, his thoughts became interrupted by a man pushing his mother's chair cautiously from a garden entrance. He moved quickly to another window as he immediately recognized him as James, the stranger from New York who sought after his Bethie's affections. The interruption had caused him to forget why he had come, as he quickly made his way down the back entrance of the mansion.

As he followed slowly far behind James's horse, he began to realize that he too had become a greedy pawn in his mother's twisted web of deceit directed toward Bethie and all she would inherit. How could anyone be so wicked and desire money as though it gave life itself, he thought, deciding that there indeed was no limit to how far she would go.

He had always been a kind and forgiving man, respectful of all life. But in his mind he rehearsed and imagined how he could easily kill this man, without regret or sorrow. He had taken part in the pain and anguish of the only woman he would ever love and somehow he would pay. He begged God for restraint.

She waited calmly and patiently inside the gazebo as Miss Abigail begged her not to put herself through any more additional grief. "I know your intentions are good. But you cannot fight every battle that I have—or do I want you to!"

"This will give me great pleasure. And I'll have no one do it for me," remarked Bethie in a cool tone, quite focused. Miss Abigail was overwrought with worry in never seeing her in such a state of mind. She knew James would not give up so easily, as she too prayed for help.

Bethie watched in a deep-seated daze as James entered the grounds. He caught sight of the two, as he began to walk toward the gazebo smiling with great confidence in finding her waiting. His arrogance had become abundant, as he boastingly imagined she stood anxiously anticipating his return.

"There is still time—" begged Miss Abigail panicking only to have Bethie cut her off.

"Please, go now!" she insisted, fixated on the vision of her imposter coming toward her.

In passing and without speaking a single word, Miss Abigail stopped only to scowl up at him with much disgust as he continued walking, confused by her undesirable greeting. James decided that he was fed up and unwilling to tolerate this woman any longer. It was imperative that he convince Bethie to marry him today.

"My darling… I'm so happy to see you up and about," he began in a cheery voice, carrying a bouquet of flowers hidden behind his back. "I worried last night when I heard you were feeling under the weather and had left so abruptly. I do wish you had told me. I would have left with you."

The closer he came, the more she began to feel nauseated. But she wasn't through with him yet and allowed him to embrace and kiss her on the cheek. The mere sight of James touching her, made William growl under his breath. He again begged for restraint trying hard not to reveal his whereabouts, as he stood silently hidden among the trees watching the two of them from a distance. Bethie thought she would become sick, loathing the feeling of his body close and touching her own.

"Is that what you think…? I need someone to take care of me? Perhaps my assets too," questioned Bethie in a matter-of-fact tone. She was without expression making James uncomfortable and bewildered.

"Well… I have always believed such things should be left to the husband. Don't you agree, Sara? Oh, these are for my lady," he added, offering the arrangement to her.

Unable to control herself any longer, she responded in a sarcastic tone, "How lovely and so very thoughtful of you."

Because of her sarcasm, he was now certain something was

indeed wrong and became quickly frustrated. "What is wrong, Sara Beth? And what is wrong with Abigail? I know she doesn't care for me. But do I have to put up with her undeserved, unkind behavior toward me?"

"Really, Sara... Please tell me you'll marry me. And I'll take you from this constant reminder of unhappy memories. I cannot wait any longer. Or will I take no for an answer! Please, Sara Beth. Tell me you'll have me," he demanded, deciding not to allow her to stall a day longer.

"Such lovely roses... They resemble the ones my aunt grows in her gardens." she responded slyly, ignoring his proposal.

"What? Sara, what does that have to do with anything? You're avoiding the question!" he insisted becoming a bit heated.

"How do you know I have unhappy memories of Savannah," questioned Bethie, trapping him. With all his charming and clever moves even he could make mistakes, as he began to sweat nervously under the hot, Savannah sun.

"I don't know, Sara... Perhaps it was Georgia Lee who told me— out of concern for you. Nevertheless, it is irrelevant!" he lied, knowing she would never believe that Abigail would ever have confided in him.

"Enough!" she screamed, unable to listen to another lie. "For your sake, I am afraid it is very relevant, James. Your charade is over. I'll never believe another word you say!"

"What are you talking about, Sara? Why are you so angry with me? I demand to know this instant! Enough of these silly games," he demanded becoming annoyed with her.

"I saw you, James... I heard you and Emma Mae in the gardens this morning." He immediately became aware that he had been caught and that it was useless to try to lie his way out. Bethie was too bright and he could never convince her of anything other than the truth.

"It was a long time ago, Sara Beth. I was foolish," he pleaded frantically. "You must believe that I've changed. The money means nothing to me. Say you'll forgive me... Marry me. I promise to make it all up to you. I love you," he begged, coming closer to her as Bethie nervously moved away.

"Don't touch me or I'll scream! I want you to leave, now. I never want to see you again, James. Please go," she insisted, beginning to move swiftly from the gazebo, as he caught her by the arm ripping the sleeve of her dress.

"I don't think so! You belong to me—and you will be my wife!" he yelled with crazed eyes glaring down at her.

Bethie's body trembled in fear as she cried, "I'd rather die than become your wife. I'll never marry you. Never!"

She could feel the strong grip of another hand wrap tightly around her arm as she was forcefully pulled away from James's hold. To his utter surprise and before he could react, William's fist landed sharply across his face causing him to be thrown from the gazebo to the ground below. From the wooden platform, William lunged on top of him causing the two to roll feverishly in the grass, throwing punches whenever the opportunity seemed upon them.

For a short time, James lay flat giving William the opportunity to try to stand. He regained ground, only to be thrown face down into the dirt as James grabbed his feet yanking him backwards. He straddled William as both hands went around his neck, trying savagely to squeeze the life from him.

"Stop it, James! You'll kill him," screamed Bethie distraught and frantic, as Miss Abigail came running from the mansion with two of the groundskeepers.

From the dirt, William tore desperately at James's grip as his face began to turn blue. With every ounce of strength his body could muster, William clenched his fists sending two hard blows to James's head. Immediately, he released his grip falling hard to the ground. William straddled him as he began to hit him repeatedly with both fits across his face causing James to begin losing consciousness.

"Stop it! Stop it, William!" cried Bethie, unable to take another minute of their abuse to one another. She was overwhelmed and upset as she ran from the gazebo. Seeing James's horse, she quickly mounted her and sped off in the distance.

"William! Stop or you'll surely kill him!" He was beyond reason or compromise as he continued to pound every breath out of him. "If he dies, you'll be convicted of murder. Your dreams of ever being with Bethie will die with him!" screamed Abigail frantically trying to convince him.

Her words made him stop as he wearily climbed off James who lay bloody and dazed. In an angry rage he turned around and grabbed a fistful of James's shirt as he abruptly yanked his head high and level with his own. "You get out of Savannah right now! If you ever come near Bethie again… let there be no doubt in your greedy mind—I will surely kill you!" He let his head drop as James lay spinning and woozy.

William staggered as he struggled to pull to his feet wiping the blood from his mouth. He spun around looking in all directions as he began to panic, "Where's Bethie?"

"She took off on James's horse. Please go after her before she gets herself hurt," insisted Miss Abigail worried. "Don't worry about him," she commented, glaring down at James, repulsed by the very sight of him. "We'll take care of him. Go quickly and find her!"

He swiftly leaped onto his horse as they dashed away from the mansion. Following the dirt road leading away, he could still make out the dusty trail caused by her horse.

Bethie came upon the fork not knowing what direction to turn as she slowed down contemplating what to do next. She was afraid, upset, and unable to think straight. To the left would lead her into the city and to the right the Calhoun plantation. She wanted to stay far away from Emma Mae, but had no money with her and knew no one in the city.

She suddenly heard the sound of a horse's hooves coming in her direction, as she turned quickly around to see who it was. From a far distance, she could see the figure of a man heading toward her as panic ran through her, "Oh no, James..." With a firm grip on the reins, she cracked down hard against its neck causing the steed to take like a bolt of lightning.

The island immediately came into mind, as she left the dirt road heading straight onto Emma's land. Since childhood the island had been kept a secret, told to no one, not even Georgia Lee. It was the only place she could think of where to hide from him.

William could now see her as his pace quickened. Keeping Calhoun to the far right, she continued to maintain a straight path. She decided only after seeing the water's edge would she cut right toward the island. This would reassure her of remaining undetected by Emma or any of her servants. William began to gain ground as he realized that her horse was beginning to get out of control. He increased his speed trying desperately to catch up.

He finally reached the side of her horse as he yelled frantically, "Bethie slow down or she'll kill you!"

She immediately breathed easier finding it was William who was following her, not James.

"Help me, William! I can't control her!" she begged terrified. Keeping in pace with her horse, he positioned himself as close to them as possible. Maintaining control of his horse with his right hand, he reached out with his left trying to grab hold of her horse's reins, but was unsuccessful.

As the lake came into view, he became determined to try to save her as quickly as possible. Moving in even closer he wrapped his arm as far as he could around her waist pulling Bethie closer to him. "Let go of the reins, Bethie, now!"

She did as he commanded, as he quickly pulled her from the saddle holding onto her with one arm. Her horse continued to gallop away as he worked to bring his horse to a halt. The awkward distribution of weight caused it to become uncomfortable and wild as it bucked high in the air causing the two to be thrown from the saddle.

Fortunately, the horse had slowed before doing so as the two rolled in separate directions near the bank of the water. Bethie lay dazed, bruised, but conscious. After deciding that nothing was broken and she could walk, she pulled herself to a standing position looking about the area for William. He lay still with eyes closed and barely appearing to be breathing.

"Oh my Lord!" she cried, running over to him as she knelt down beside him. "William! William! Can you hear me?" cried Bethie, unable to wake him as she frantically shook his shoulders. She quickly ran to the edge of the water to wet her handkerchief. As she ran back, she suddenly stopped. With hands on her hips she frowned down at William who was now leaning on one arm grinning up at her.

"William David Calhoun, how could you? I thought you were really hurt. You terrified me!" she snapped.

"What can I say? I must have just come to. Forgive me, Bethie," he responded teasingly.

She shrugged her shoulders and walked over to him again kneeling by his side. "Your face is bleeding. Let me help you," she insisted as he lay flat gazing up into her eyes. She fought to ignore his staring and began to wipe his face gently.

"You didn't—" began Bethie nervously.

"Kill him?" interrupted William finishing her sentence. "No, I didn't kill him, Bethie. But I gave him a headache he won't soon forget!" he laughed.

"Thank God!" she sighed, relieved.

"Who are you thanking God for? James or me?" questioned William trying to force Bethie to reveal her true feelings for him.

"I thank God that you two silly fools didn't kill each other," she remarked in a matter-of-fact tone.

"Well, you took off so suddenly. I could only imagine that you didn't even care what happened to me," he accused teasingly.

"If you recall... when I left you had indeed obtained the advantage. From where I stood, James appeared quite unconscious."

"So it's true! You do care for me after all," shouted William grinning. Although it was true, Bethie tried hard not to smile at his arrogant assumption.

"Tell me William," started Bethie intentionally changing the subject, "however was it possible that you showed up with such perfect timing?"

"Well, I must confess… I could see and hear the two of you from the tree I was hiding behind. Quite perfectly too, I might add."

"Oh William!" she snapped annoyed. "Some things never change, do they? Once a spy, always a spy," she accused, throwing the cloth down at him, recalling how they had first met.

She carefully examined his face with the gentle touch of her hand as William longed to hold her. But he knew how fragile she had become and did not want to frighten her away with his advances.

Her hand brushed slightly against his face, "It's not too deep. You'll be all right," she reassured. As her hand came down his cheek, with a sudden turn of his head he kissed it softly. Caught off guard, Bethie jerked her hand back blushing and feeling a flood of emotions run through her.

"Stop it!" she demanded, annoyed. "I've had enough of you men for one day!" Her angry comment made him laugh aloud. He tried not to reach for her, as she moved away placing distance between the two. The truth was that he made her feel overwhelming emotions every time he touched her causing Bethie to feel anxious, nervous, and a loss of control. The dizzy, head spinning affect could only be best compared to, agreed Bethie, when she was a young girl twirling about freely in a bed of daisies.

He again, sat propped up on one arm as he grinned over to her. "I apologize for making you so nervous, Bethie."

"How dare you imply such nonsense," she snapped. "Don't know what you are talking about," she lied, unable to look into his eyes. "I'm not afraid of you—or any man!"

His smile widened, "Then why do you move away from me?"

Bethie searched her mind for another subject to talk about when she noticed how dark the sky was becoming. "I think it's going to rain. Don't you?" William took a long, deep breath, as he sat up deciding Bethie wasn't about to answer his question. He looked up at the sky and became concerned.

"It doesn't look good. We better take shelter in the cave," he insisted, as he stood to retrieve his horse.

"It's been so long since I've been on the island. I do miss her. But can I trust that you'll be a gentleman?" she teased, looking over at him.

"I'm always a gentleman. And unlike the imposter James, have never forced myself on any woman—including the one I love." She blushed, looking away from him. "I assure you that you are quite safe with me," he insisted.

"How very charming you've become, William. Tell me... How many women have you told those words to?"

"Oh... hundreds, I suppose," he laughed, following behind her with his horse.

Rain began to fall slowly as William urged, "Get on the horse, Bethie, we'll get there faster."

"No, I'd rather walk, thank you. How I've missed the warm, summer rains of Savannah," she confessed, as she began to twirl and dance in the rain with hands reaching outward. With eyes closed and head toward the heavens, she paused to allow the gentle drops to fall on her face cooling her body from the hot, afternoon sun.

He watched his Bethie closely and couldn't help but smile and feel very pleased to see how happy she was. He was so thankful to be with her again, as he could easily see past the beautiful woman like features to find the child inside still existed.

When they finally reached the site at which they would cross over, Bethie sat in the saddle as William waded them across the lake. "I have a surprise for you waiting in the cave," he teased, remembering how impatient she would become when he kept secrets from her.

"What is it, William? Tell me now!" she insisted, as he helped her slowly down from the horse. He could feel her body brush against his own as his yearning for her spiraled. She, too, felt an overwhelming desire for him. They paused to gaze longingly into one another's eyes. But still, he resisted the temptation to embrace her in his arms as he soberly suggested, "I better find a safe place for the horse."

Bethie who was quite relaxed by now and taken by the moment, felt a little disappointed that he had not tried to kiss her. She felt safe. He always made her feel safe. "I'll race you to the cave!" she shouted. "Wait!" he responded, as she ignored his plea running ahead of him.

He chased her teasingly toward their destination as he soon advanced ahead, undetected and in hiding, only to jump from behind a tree startling her. "William! You frightened me. You horrid beast!" she screamed laughingly.

Bethie ran ahead of him as he caught her around the waist and began spinning the two of them around as they laughed aloud together. After placing her down she turned around to face him feeling dizzy and trying to catch her breath. After calming down some, she looked up to find him staring again.

He slowly bent down as though to kiss her. After closing her eyes and deciding that she would allow him to, he mockingly changed his mind as he spun away leaving her embarrassed. He knelt beside a bed of wild roses cautiously picking the prettiest one he could find, trying not to be pricked by its thorns. She graciously accepted his gift smiling.

"Thank you, sir," she replied, suddenly pushing him off balance and continuing the race.

The opening of the cave was upon her as she quickly went inside. Trying to catch her breath, she was excited about being on the island again. She slowly began looking about taking everything in. William's fire from the night before still burned as she noticed the blankets that lay on the ground making up his bed.

Inquisitive of its contents, she walked over to what appeared to be a large pile of papers. To Bethie's utter shock and surprise were the long, lost letters of two childhood friends.

She slowly kneeled before them and began to weed through the large, endless pile of letters not knowing which to choose from. She was in awe. Picking up one that had been addressed to her, she opened it quickly and began to read. She was overwhelmed with joy and renewed trust as her eyes filled. William entered the cave silently, not wanting to disturb her moment of truth.

Unable to refrain himself any longer from her, he walked up behind Bethie. He knelt down against her body, wrapping his arms firmly but gently around her waist. She shut her eyes and leaned into him, wanting desperately to submit into his arms.

He began to gently kiss the back of her head then the length of her neck. She neither objected nor was afraid as her heart beat rapidly with his. "I love you, Bethie… I've loved you for a lifetime," he sighed passionately, unable to ponder straight, feeling drunken by her touch. "And I you, my love" she whispered wishing that he would not stop.

He pulled her around as their faces touched until he met her mouth. Kneeling on their knees, they kissed passionately until they began to lose control, not wanting to stop or be let free. He became overwhelmed with desire and began to feel nervous realizing there would be no protest from her. She had all but surrendered to him.

After several futile attempts, he forced himself to pull away as she looked up at him confused and disappointed. Their bodies overflowed with passion as each heart beat rapid and loud.

Bethie whispered, "What's wrong, William… Don't you want me?" she asked sadly.

He smiled at her, pulling her to him, "You're so beautiful. You can't imagine how much I want you. But… not like this. If we don't stop now, Bethie… I don't think I'll be able to," he confessed, wanting her desperately.

"I don't want to take advantage of your vulnerability. Or be blamed for seducing you. As long as I live, I shall never love another. I want you to marry me, Bethie. Tell me you'll be my wife. Say it, Bethie. Promise you'll have me," he begged.

She looked longingly into his eyes, "I could never marry another. You've had my heart, long before this day. Yes, I'll be your wife, William." Her promise made him sigh in relief, as he pulled her back into his arms. They held each other tightly.

New Hope

Reality and sleep seemed to blend into one, as he awoke smiling remembering all that had happened. He reached out to hold her, wanting to feel her heart against his own. To touch the softness of her flesh, inhale the fragrance of her hair, and to kiss her mouth again.

Instant panic set in as he sat abruptly with eyes wide and frantic in finding himself alone in the cave. Had it all been a dream? He wondered this, terrified that it might have only been his imagination playing a cruel, distorted trick on him.

"Bethie! Bethie where are you?" he yelled desperately, as he jumped to his feet trying to put on his boots and walk at the same time. Coming out of the darkened cave he squinted in pain from the bright, morning sun and the bruises acquired from the day before. He looked in all directions for even a clue, "Bethie!" he called as loud as he could.

"I'm here William! Up on the hill," she replied loudly. He felt relieved and thanked God that it had not been a dream, or had she left from disappointment. After washing up in the lake, he quickly hoisted himself up and over the side of the hill where he found her sitting in the middle of a pile of opened letters.

"Good Morning," she smiled blushing. Reaching over the pile he gently lifted her, as some of the letters fell from her lap to the ground. With arms around her waist, he kissed her softly and slowly. "When I woke up and found you gone, I panicked. I thought perhaps it had all been a dream. Or maybe you had left in regret," he confessed, as they gazed into each other's eyes.

She softly caressed his face, "But it was a dream. A dream that came true. I can't believe we are together again."

Embracing her tightly he closed his eyes and buried his face in her hair. "I love you, Bethie. I've never been happier in my life than I am right now, here with you."

"And I love you," she sighed, wishing the moment could last forever.

"William, these letters," she began, pulling him to the ground where they lay. "I've already read each letter that you ever wrote to me. It was amazing as though I was given the opportunity to fill in the blanks of time in which we were apart. I'll always cherish them. Thank you."

"I felt the same when I began to read your letters. That is why it was so important that I bring you here. It was the only way I knew how to make you believe in me again."

"I'm sorry I ever doubted you…" He kissed her again.

"I love this hill. Do you remember when we were children? We would lay atop it for hours dreaming of being pirates together one day."

"Yes, I've never forgotten," he confessed laughingly.

"This spot used to make me feel so safe and secure. I remember thinking I could see the whole world from up here. But now, it doesn't seem so big. I suppose I must have grown," she smiled.

"Look what I found buried in the box!" teased Bethie, as she began to pull something up from underneath the pile of letters.

"The sword!" exclaimed William delighted. He hadn't seen the old thing for such a long time and was pleased she had found it. She offered him the sword, "Thank you, fair maiden."

He began to perform for her as he stood in a proper fencing stance, pretending as though he was protecting her honor from a treacherous villain. "You dare come between me and the woman I love! On guard you silly fool!" She laughed hysterically as he began to move about cutting back and forth, in and out, slashing the air at virtually nothing. With a final imaginary blow to the heart he held his sword high up into the sky in victory.

"From this day forth, may no man, woman, or beast try to come between me and the woman I love. She who sits before me as the lady Sara Beth. Known to family and friends, of course, as Bethie," he added humorously.

Bringing down his arm he dropped the sword by his side, and knelt down in front of her becoming quite serious, while he gently took her hand in his. "For you are my love, my life, and every breath that I now take. And I will always be faithful and never shall I harm you. I will protect you with my life. And if I had to… would die for you. These words I vow to you this day, forever more. For you have eternally enchanted, every part of my being."

Never had Bethie been quoted such words of devotion so romantically, her eyes filled with tears as he kissed her again. "We'll get married in the city today, Bethie. I believe it would be wise," he suggested, forcing himself to pull away from her tempting arms.

"No William! Please, not in Savannah," she begged. "Take me home…"

"Well, if it means that much to you."

"It does," she insisted, relieved.

"Then I insist we leave today for Pennsylvania. I'll take you back to Miss Abigail. Then I must go back to the plantation to collect my things. I promise I won't be long."

"Take me with you, William," she pleaded.

"No Bethie! I don't want you near my mother. I can't trust her. Her jealousy of you is completely out of control."

"Please let me go with you. I don't want us to separate. I can't explain… Only that it frightens me to be apart from you while we're still in Savannah. I promise I'll stay near the horse while you go inside. It makes no sense to take me to Miss Abby only to travel right back here. We'll save time and I promise not to come inside. I'll be safe, William. I'm no longer afraid of your mother," rambled Bethie.

"Fine. You've convinced me. But you're not to leave my horse. Is that understood?"

"Yes. I promise," she smiled relieved.

Excited but apprehensive in what lie ahead, they left the island with the understanding that it most likely was the last time they would ever journey upon her again. Unable to leave them behind, Bethie had convinced William to allow her to take the letters. The childhood memories of time long ago would remain in the box, camouflaged in a cave for another young explorer to discover.

So his mother would not know that they had been on the island, they travelled back in the same direction in which they had come. When they finally reached the fork leading to Calhoun and the city, William hesitated for a moment, a voice deep within tried desperately to caution him. But he shrugged his shoulders as he continued onto Calhoun, deciding paranoia must be setting in.

He entered onto the long path to the plantation slowly, stopping about midway. "Are you sure I can't take you to the Work plantation, Bethie?" he offered again, becoming worried for her safety.

"I'll be all right, William." Leery and unsure, he continued, increasing the trot praying it would all be over soon.

The horse came to a complete halt in front of the main entrance of the Calhoun mansion as William quickly dismounted. Taking her hand, he looked deep into her eyes with much concern. "Don't forget, Bethie. You're not to get off this horse. If you sense any trouble, leave immediately for the Work plantation. Do you understand?"

"Yes, I understand," lied Bethie, knowing she could never leave him here.

"Remember… I love you." They were his last words as he entered the mansion hoping that he would make it to his room undetected, unaware that he had not closed the double doors tightly.

He swiftly began to climb the main staircase leading to his bedroom, only to be abruptly stopped.

"How dare you enter my home after you've been with that harlot!"

Angry with himself that he was unsuccessful in avoiding his mother he replied, "Your overwhelming words of affection for your own niece is quite touching. You needn't worry, Mother. I'm only here to collect my things."

Realizing that he felt no shame or regret she began to panic, "Wait, Son!" Her desperate plea was ignored as he continued to his room.

What am I going to do now? Struggled Emma Mae, terrified with the thought of losing the only child she would ever have. "Think woman. Think!" she blurted aloud, trying to come up with a working plan before he came down. She did not want to resort to the only alternative that would certainly stop him. But Emma believed there to be no other way.

Emma Mae forced herself to face that he was in love with Bethie and would never forgive her as long as the two remained together. She had buried the truth for many years, not because of her son's sake but her own. Though, in her twisted way, she did love him. It would never be greater than her money or status in the community. As ignorant and blind as she truly was Emma really believed that she was respected, a trait that could only be obtained through wealth and power.

With the help of her cane, she slowly made her way to the double doors. Upon closing them, she gave a quick glance across her front entrance as a wide, malicious grin fell upon her wrinkled, old face. All was so perfect as though it had been planned in her favor, she gloated.

Instead of closing them like she had originally intended, keeping in the shadow of the doors, she began to widen them even more so. How appropriate it would be, she contemplated, to have the earth shattering information about to be revealed heard by that one too. In a demented mood, she was quite pleased with herself as she waited patiently for him.

Seeing the door opened wider, Bethie wondered if it were he. "William… is that you?" she questioned, curious as to what was happening. Against his wishes, she felt compelled to see for herself as she came down from the horse. Bethie cautiously climbed the stairs to the mansion.

It did not take but a few hurried minutes for him to return to the foyer, only to find his mother waiting calmly. She smiled in a way that he recognized from the past when she was about to expose information that would make an impact. This made him worried as he quickly began to go around her, wanting to make sure Bethie was safe.

"I'm sorry William for what I said earlier," she began quickly, trying to stall him. "I beg you to let me explain."

"I can't imagine anything you could say, Mother, that would make me feel any different. Or am I interested," he snapped, standing with his back to her.

"Even criminals before a judge are given the opportunity to defend themselves. I can't take back the pain that I may have caused Sara Beth, but if you hear me out you will understand why I did all that I am accused of."

Bethie could barely make out the voices as she moved closer to the doors. She positioned herself against a door not wanting to be seen, recognizing the voices as William and his mother. Listening to them argue, only confirmed her previous fears that it had been a mistake for them to return to the plantation.

"I refuse to hear any more of your lies. I've had enough. I'm going away with Bethie and there is not a thing you can do to stop us. Nothing you could say would ever make a difference."

She panicked as he began again to leave, only bluntness would stop him now. "Sara Beth is your cousin. Have you no decency?"

"She is not blood related and you know it. Goodbye Mother!"

"That's not true, William! The two of you share the same blood."

"You lie!" he screamed, whipping around to face her. Bethie's heart seem to stop, caused by the words Emma spoke.

"I know you think of me as a liar, a manipulator. But if you've ever believed anything in your life, believe this! You are a true Calhoun. I gave birth to you. I met your father in Philadelphia. He had been there on business. We became lovers… Unexpectedly, I became pregnant with you."

"You may never understand why we kept it a secret from you. But I wanted to save your father and myself from the humiliation of bearing a child out of wedlock—a bastard. And at my age, I would have been the brunt of every joke. I was so old to be with child, chances were slim that you would even survive."

In utter shock, William and Bethie stood frozen unwilling to believe what was being said.

"I stayed in doors for months, hidden from the community, until you were finally born. You were healthy and strong. We mutually agreed to be married and take you back to Savannah as our adopted son."

In a crazed frenzy, William began to laugh, "Do you think I'm that stupid to believe a word of this nonsense?"

"I can prove it!" she insisted, pulling a folded birth certificate out of the pocket of her shawl. Emma Mae attempted to hand it over to him, but he refused to accept it. She tossed the note before him, "Pick it up, William. I know you refuse to even acknowledge this information. But what if you're wrong. You have no choice."

He took a long moment as he contemplated what to do. Odds were high that it was, indeed, another one of his mother's twisted lies. But what if she spoke the truth? Could it be true that he and Bethie were blood related, first cousins? The idea of such a horrible discovery caused panic as he shook slightly from the thought. One thing was certain, he had to see for himself. She had been unable to tell the truth in the past and he hopefully prayed, this time was no exception.

He reached down to pick up the note as Emma began to relax some. She had again, caused irreversible havoc and was delighted with her distorted success. When he began to read, terror filled his face as he trembled uncontrollably.

"You've lied to me all these years," he slowly cried, horrified and confused.

Bethie's head started to swell, as she slowly began backing up from the mansion, almost tripping on the steps. Feeling dizzy and nauseous, she held onto her stomach trying not to become sick. She fled frantically from the plantation, in such horror and shame that she did not notice Miss Abby in the passing. Bethie galloped frantically toward the Work plantation.

Leaving the main entrance wide open, she ran up to Georgia Lee's bedroom closing and locking the door behind her. With her mind numb and confused she went over to the small, pine desk that sat between the two beds, up against the wall. She pulled open the top drawer that held the confederate silver and pewter dagger that had once belonged to Georgia's father.

There were times when she privately harbored ill feelings toward her father for taking his life and abandoning her. Though deep down she still believed life was a gift from God and should always be respected, it seemed easier to understand him now. She neither could undo her feelings for William, nor could there ever be another. This was certain. She desperately tried to keep control as her mind fought against her will.

Unaware of her surroundings, no longer able to make sense or logic, she ran the tip of her fingers along the sharp edge of the blade. Since the war, how sharp it had remained, agreed Bethie amazed. She watched as the tiny drops of blood fell from her hand in a slow drip. Devastated in shame, believing all was hopeless, she studied the knife in awe.

William studied the birth document as though it could change into something else if read long enough. "How could a mother tell her own son that he was adopted? Just so you could save your own apparent reputation! How could you lie to me for all those years?"

"What kind of monster are you!" he screamed, as he fell into a chair dazed and in utter despair. The devastation of finding out the truth after all these years, but mainly the threat of losing Bethie was more than he could stand. He knew for certain, as the day turned into night, he could never live without her.

The thought of Bethie caused him to suddenly jump, as he rushed over throwing open the large double doors only to find she was nowhere to be found. "Son, don't leave! It's no use. Can't you see that it's hopeless to dwell on what can never be?" Her words cut deep, as he hopelessly sat once again.

"How can you be so cruel? You think because I now know that you are my real mother it somehow changes what has happened? As long as I live, I will never forget what you have done. Never! I'm ashamed of the Calhoun name. It represents all that I loathe."

"And I promise you this... even after all that I now know, I will still leave and you will never see me again. You may have hurt the two of us beyond repair, but you have lost me forever!" The anger and animosity felt toward her made his nostril's flare and his face turn red.

"Everything I did was for you!" begged Emma Mae desperately, as her world began to cave around her.

"Everything you do is for yourself! Your pompous greed is beyond any I have ever witnessed. Anything that you did that appears good has always had a material gain attached to it."

"That is not true, William. I gave you life and everything that there was. Most men would die to possess the riches that you have— and will inherit."

"You still don't get it, Mother, do you? You may have given me life, but you stripped me of knowing my own identity. You can't buy respect... You can't use your money to undo the damages that you've created so maliciously and intentionally. But most of all, Mother, you can't buy me. You don't know me do you? If you truly did, you would have known that..."

"Where will you go? You can't go back to her. It's not right! Stay with me, William. I promise to make it up to you," begged Emma Mae desperately.

"No!" he shouted, moving away from her cold reach.

"Don't listen to her, William," yelled an angry Miss Abigail as she entered the mansion unexpected.

"Get out of my home. You're not welcomed!" screamed Emma Mae furiously.

"William, listen to me… For years I've had Thomas Holt delve into her past in fear of what she would do to Bethie. I've always known she disliked her. Even when we first came to this house, I felt her animosity. I became compelled to find out, to find the truth about her."

"What is it, Miss Abby?" he questioned anxiously.

"Don't listen to her, Son. She lies!"

"It may be true that you are her real son. That I do not question or do I care to. But, it is also true that she shares no blood with Bethie. She never was and never will be a true Covington."

"Are you sure, Miss Abby?" he questioned, overjoyed by the news as Emma Mae gasped in horror.

"As sure as the sun shines this day," she replied smiling. "Did she also tell you that your father left everything to you, at the age of 21? Or did she forget to mention that tidbit of information? Thomas read his will. It's all yours, William."

"Emma Mae was adopted very early in their marriage. That is why there was such an age difference between her and Jon. Her sickening jealousy was why she hated Bethie so. She couldn't stand not being a true Covington and decided if she couldn't be it by blood, she would take what she believed was hers. Go on William, ask her to deny it."

"If you're capable of telling the truth, then tell me now. Is this true, Mother?" With all her might, she tried desperately to lie but could not. His eyes begged for the truth and for the first time in her pitiful life, she was unable to place her selfish needs first. She looked toward the floor, preferring it over actually confessing the words.

"That's all I needed to know. You're pathetic, Mother."

He walked over to Miss Abigail, "Bethie, where is she?"

"I suppose she has returned. In coming, I passed her on the way. She looked so odd and didn't even recognize me. I fear something terrible, go quickly, William." He dashed away as fast as he could in destination of the Work plantation.

Exploding in a frenzy with all the strength left in her withered, frail body Emma began to move toward Miss Abigail. "I'll kill you for coming between my son and me!" screamed Emma Mae furiously and completely out of control, as she lifted her cane high in the air to strike Abigail.

But Miss Abigail was sharp and much swifter than she, as Abigail quickly moved to the side avoiding Emma's blow. Before she could raise the cane against her again, Abigail was able to yank it away throwing it far beyond her reach causing Emma to fall against the chair. Trying to catch her breath she desperately pulled herself up from the floor and into the chair. Abigail watched, finding her behavior revolting.

"It's over Emma… You'll never hurt either of them ever again," began Abigail in a calm but stern voice unafraid of Emma Mae. "Your hell begins with the knowledge of knowing you alone created this situation. You have desecrated every known decency this world had to offer you. You deserve to be alone."

"But I'm not here to judge you. A higher being awaits that repulsive task. Your son was right. How very pathetic you are. You had everything. But that still wasn't enough, was it? Even the money, the businesses, but most of all your own son couldn't break through the malicious greed that lines your soul."

"Don't look so surprised, Emma Mae. I know you. I've always known you. I made it a point after I realized just how destructive you really are. Take away the money, control, and all that's left of you is simply, bitter resentment."

"Enough! Get the hell out of my home. I won't listen to another word. Jane! Jane!" screamed Emma Mae distraught and enraged.

Miss Jane, who had been in the library during the entire charade, had heard everything. She ignored Emma's demanding cries for her as she walked slowly up to her room, closing the door behind her. All of what she had predicted so many years ago was coming true. Believing Emma deserving of all that was said to her, she was not about to come to her aid despite the cost.

"You killed Jon's parents. Didn't you? Go on Emma, no one is here but the two of us. And there is no evidence for a conviction. You made sure of that many years ago." With the relentless pursuit by Miss Abigail, and no longer able to control her thoughts, Emma Mae began to reminisce about the events leading up to their deaths.

"You didn't mean to walk in on them. You didn't even know they were in there. Did you? You couldn't stand the two of them so happy, so in love, when you were so angry. And to make matters worse, walking into that barn finding them making love—how sickening they made you feel."

"It made you remember. Didn't it? It made you remember the dirty, little girl. Who was told to get out as she waited so patiently, sometimes for hours, sometimes even in the cold. Waiting for your mother to get finished with all those men so she could tell you to come in again. It was how she supported you. Wasn't it?" pushed Miss Abigail. Emma Mae shook relentlessly in agonizing horror, as she faced the truth for the first time in her life.

"You were so angry to see them like that. They made you sick to your stomach. You wanted to punish them so you locked the barn doors so they couldn't get out. But they didn't notice at first. Because they were too busy with themselves, right Emma?"

"They deserved everything that they got!" snapped Emma Mae fiercely, unremorseful.

"It was hot that day. Didn't rain for weeks. It didn't take long for the barn to burn. You probably stood back as they begged for mercy for you to let them out. But you didn't, did you… It was the first time you experienced the taste of sweet revenge, and it made you feel good."

"It did," confessed Emma crazed. "I was in control. I now had the power. I knew everything that was theirs was now mine. And no one would ever take it from me!" she swore in a vengeance, falling into Miss Abigail's trap of confession.

"It ate you up inside not being born a true Covington. So you did what you thought was the next best thing—you stole it. And then there was Jon… You were so jealous. Even though they had saved you from the streets, legally adopting you as their own, and did everything they could to make you believe that you were truly their own was still not enough!"

"Jon never had a chance, did he?"

"Say what you will. But I know they made a difference. I was first. They didn't need to have him. We were fine until he came," replied Emma Mae feeling sorry for herself.

"For the love of God, Emma Mae, they never even told him you were adopted!" she screamed, becoming enraged. "They made no difference! The only difference you saw was created in that distorted, twisted mind of yours."

"I couldn't believe the horrors that you inflicted on him. They were so inconceivable. But I knew Mary was incapable of lying so they had to be true. Because of your own childhood abuse, you took it out on him. No matter who got hurt, destroyed, and even—your own birth son! Now I understand why you had their wing boarded. It was your private hell in which you could abuse Jon. No need to worry about intruders or objections, right Emma!"

"Pain… Pain! Why don't you see the pain he put me through," she snapped, lifting up the sleeve of her dress and exposing a three inch scar caused by Jon. That was a gift from my dearly, departed, pathetic brother. Whom you seem to admire so fondly," blurted Emma sarcastically. "He was a sniveling coward, taking his life for that half breed!"

"He should have killed you when he had the chance!" replied Abigail with conviction.

"It was you who had Mr. Gilmore shot. Wasn't it, Emma Mae? You had paid him to find the last will. But out of greed, he was about to sell the truth to Joseph. But you couldn't let that happen. So you sent an innocent man to jail. You knew he was Negro and would probably hang, but you didn't care. Like all the times before, you worried only of your own precious hide despite the consequences! I could kill you for hurting Joseph."

"What do you care about some Negro," scoffed Emma Mae,

studying Abigail's face. It finally dawned on her as she cocked her head back, laughing hysterically. "You're in love with that Negro... It's true, isn't it? Giving up Thomas Holt, for a Negro! Always knew you were a crazy fool!"

Peering down at Emma Mae in discuss, "You couldn't tie his shoes," replied Abigail with much contempt.

"They were insignificant!" screamed Emma Mae, disappointed that she could not intimidate Abigail.

"Who do you think you are, Emma Mae? Judge and jury over all you unfortunately come in contact with? Insignificant! I'll tell you what is insignificant—it's you! If anything has happened to Bethie, I'll be back to finish off what Jon should have done a long time ago! Lord have mercy on me..." And with that last threat, Miss Abigail left the Calhoun plantation in a fury.

Late that evening, after Emma had sent away the entire staff including Miss Jane, she sat for hours in a darkened room staring into a blazing fire. A dark shadow appeared behind her, bruised and battered filled with hatred and anger. He hated the wrinkled, old woman that sat before him and could easily have wrapped his hands around her neck, ending her life right where she sat.

But there was a much stronger hate that awaited his attention, as he resisted the temptation, leaving that pleasure for another time perhaps. Without turning around or even making sure that it was he that stood behind her, she said, "You know what to do... I only wish I were strong enough to do it myself. I envy you for taking this pleasure from me."

"Tell me something, old woman... I know I could never allow another to be with my Sara, but you—your own son."

"My son is already dead... Question me no further and do as you're told!" The shadow swiftly disappeared as Emma's last evil plot began to take its course.

Like a snake in the grass, he stood hidden deep within the forest waiting patiently for the perfect hour to strike. And when he felt all was still and had been laid to rest for the night, he made his way cautiously up to the mansion of the Work plantation. Like the expert he was, skillfully the dry wood was planted alongside of the front of the building. He moved about in the dark quietly and undetected.

Carefully the wood was soaked with the solution using every drop. Randomly, he set the wood ablaze from one side to the other. He stood back grinning and pleased, as he watched the lovely, Georgian architecture become ablaze. It soon became fully engulfed by the vicious fire that continued unnoticed by all. He waited through the early hours of the morning, feeling quite confident that there had been no survivors before finally leaving the scene of the crime.

Even after the night's iniquity, the morning came as the warm, bright sun shined brightly on all God's creatures, including the evil ones. Emma Mae instructed Miss Jane to pack their bags for a sudden business trip that could not wait. She thought it peculiar after all that had happened and Emma's poor health, but did what she was told. Emma Mae refused to divulge the whereabouts of the journey causing Miss Jane to become suspicious.

But nevertheless the two began the route toward the city to board an early train. Unaware of the happenings that had occurred as she slept the night before, Miss Jane's eyes became widened after seeing a tall, endless stream of smoke towering above the forest when they reached the fork.

"Something is on fire! Should we see if we can help?" shrieked Miss Jane upset.

Grinning and with much calm, Emma replied, "Yes… it seems as though you are correct, Jane. Looks like the Work plantation. What a pity," smiled Emma pleased, "but it's no concern of ours. Continue driver!" directed Emma Mae sternly as horror and panic filled Miss Jane's very being, making her quiver in fear.

It did not take her long to figure out that it was Emma Mae's doing. And that she was the culprit responsible for the destruction of the beautiful mansion, but most important life. In shock and unable to move or speak a voice deep within prayed, *Forgive me, Bethie*.

During their long travels north, Miss Jane never again questioned where they were headed and had become quite incoherent. She was an intelligent woman and knew completely where the train would lead them.

Jane recalled how relentless Emma Mae had been as she lied conning her way onto the board of The House of Philadelphia, orphanage for children, finally obtaining the majority stock. It had been documented, in the case of Bethie's death all assets would be transferred to the home. The very thought made Jane's skin crawl as she dreadfully questioned, *how could she have won? Is there no God?*

Their travels became delayed several times, as Emma Mae's health began to deteriorate. But her greedy, relentless drive toward what she believed was hers would not be abandoned. She would neither return nor delay one day longer as the two continued on, despite her serious condition.

"At last!" blurted Emma Mae, not caring who was about as the carriage began to leave Doylestown, finally entering the small town of New Hope. She had waited a lifetime for this moment believing in her twisted mind that she was deserving of it all, despite how it had been obtained.

Though her health was poor and she should not have taken the risk of travelling so far, she refused to give up. The relentless, greedy dream of standing on land that once belonged to Jon, claiming her now as her own, was too much of a thrill. Emma Mae felt no remorse, sadness, and most definitely no regret. Her soul had been stripped many years ago as a small child, irreversible damage had been done causing her to be unable to feel such emotions.

Her thoughts were interrupted as the carriage came to a sudden halt. "What is it? Why has he stopped? Go and see for yourself, Jane!" demanded Emma Mae becoming impatient.

Jane returned shortly and replied, "There is a wedding ahead of us and the street is filled with carriages. He can't get around them, so you'll have to be patient. I could make out the bride and groom coming out of the church. So I imagine it will all be over quite shortly," insisted Miss Jane, praying Emma Mae would not make a scene knowing how impatient she could become.

"I've waited forever for this day. A few more minutes won't make a difference. Help me out. I could use some fresh air and it's been a long time since I've seen a wedding. Finding her cold touch repulsive, Miss Jane swallowed her disgust for the old lady as she helped her down from the carriage. With the aid of Miss Jane on one side and her cane on the other, she insisted on moving closer so she could see the wedding.

Although she had been feeling under the weather the past several days, never had Emma been more ecstatic than this day as she grinned to herself not at all angry that she had been detained.

She watched as the bride and groom exchanged hugs and thanks to the guests lined outside, always keeping their backs to her. Unaware of why or what had caused it, a twinge of panic seemed to strike at her. She let go of Jane's arm, compelled in moving closer as the newlywed figures began to take on a familiar resemblance.

"It must be this hot sun. I'm losing my mind," she mumbled quietly to herself.

But as convinced as she was that her imagination was playing tricks on her, curiosity continued to plague her mind as she moved even closer. And it was at that very moment when the bride and groom turned and faced the carriages, when utter shock and hysteria flooded her like a wave crashing hard and quick against the rocks. "No… It can't be," screamed Emma Mae, whose cries became lost in the crowd's cheers of joy.

Her face turned white, frozen in place, as she began to feel her heart explode causing her legs to buckle beneath her. When she began to fall toward the ground, Miss Jane ran to her side as the sudden recognition of the bride and groom caused her to stop and stare.

"Thank you Lord," she said as the tears streamed down her face from happiness, something uncharacteristic.

"Help me, Jane," whispered a pale, pathetic Emma desperately clinging to life as she tried to reach up her hand for her. But as relieved and happy as she was Miss Jane was unable to reach down in aid, as the old woman's arm fell to the side of her twisted, dead body.

Two years later…

William and Joseph helped the ladies down from the carriage. Bethie kissed William softly as they gazed longingly into one another's eyes. She handed the young baby into his loving, protective arms as he motioned her on with much confidence.

Joseph stood by his side smiling, as Abigail gently took Bethie's arm and the two walked side by side entering the private grounds in which their loved ones had been laid to rest.

Abigail handed her a bouquet of roses that she laid on the sweet grave of her Aunt Liz. Bethie smiled, remembering the loving lady that in a very short time had brought so much happiness into her life. "They were always her favorite," smiled Bethie looking up at Miss Abigail who tearfully returned the smile.

She walked over to the sites positioned side by side one another and knelt down before them. Bethie ran her fingers across the words inscribed on their headstone. She closed her eyes and said a silent prayer, never feeling closer to her parents. And before the two left the plots, with tears in her eyes, she was handed two roses that she laid gently one on each grave.

As their carriage began to descend further toward the horizon, the wind began to kick and show her fury as though to make a point. The thistle and brush that once lay peacefully giving respect to all that were placed there, began to dance relentlessly. And it was at this very moment that the legend claims, at both grave sites in which a rose was placed, a most wondrous phenomena occurred.